MEDIUM DEAD

Chris Dolley

Book View Café

MEDIUM DEAD

Published by Book View Café

Book View Café Publishing Cooperative
P.O. Box 1624
Cedar Crest, NM 87008-1624

www.bookviewcafe.com

ISBN 13: 978-1-61138-403-1

Cover art: © Abdul Qaiyoom - Fotolia.com
　　　　　© micoud78 - Fotolia.com
Cover design by Chris Dolley

First printing, July 2014
First digital edition, June 2011

An early version of the first two chapters of this book was published in 2010 by Book View Café in the anthology, *Dragon Lords and Warrior Women,* under the title, 'Headless Over Heels.'

MEDIUM DEAD

Chris Dolley

Books by Chris Dolley

Resonance

Shift

French Fried

What Ho, Automata

An Unsafe Pair of Hands

Magical Crimes

International Kittens of Mystery

How Possession Can Help You Lose Weight

Chapter One

There's only one thing worse than being able to see the dead and that's having to listen to them. They're so whiney. *Why me? I'm too young to die! Why didn't I go to the doctor earlier?*

When Brenda saw her first ghost she thought she was going crazy. The final destination in a year-long descent into hell that had seen her marriage, her career, her home of six years – all disappear in the messiest of messy divorces.

Other wives got alimony, Brenda got dead people. And to make matters worse, her lying, cheating ex-husband hadn't been one of them.

Now, four years on, she did her best to ignore them, busying herself with whatever task she could find while waiting for them to leave. That was one good thing about the dead – they never stayed for long. They drifted in, complained, then faded.

Except this one. She'd been in Brenda's kitchen since before breakfast. Just standing there by the fridge door, a translucent mouse of a woman – mid-fifties, pinched features, short brown hair and wearing what looked like an ankle-length dressing gown. She'd watched in silence as Brenda ate her solitary breakfast and watched a recording of her favorite daytime soap – the so-bad-it-was-addictive, *The Rich, The Spoiled, and the Surgically Enhanced*.

And all through that the ghost hadn't said a word. Even when Celeste, who last week had become a lesbian, discovered that Geraldine, her new partner, was actually her father – who'd had to have a sex change ten years earlier when he'd been forced into the witness protection program following his wife's murder by the albino Mafia. Or was that the Albanian Mafia? It was difficult to tell in the excitement. Celeste was screaming so loud, and Brenda's coffee had gone down the wrong way.

But the ghost hadn't reacted at all. Not to Celeste, or the choking Brenda. She'd just hung there, impassive and staring.

And exuding an odor that Brenda euphemistically named, 'freshly dug.' That was another thing about ghosts – the slightly musty, slightly sweet smell they sometimes brought with them. Brenda had to keep a can of air freshener handy at all times.

"Well?" snapped Brenda, gathering up her cup and bowl from the table. "Are you going to say something, or are you just going to stand there all day?"

The ghost said nothing. She didn't even flicker. Her empty black eyes followed Brenda from the table to the sink.

Then, as Brenda was stacking the washing up, the woman spoke.

"He's coming for *you* next."

Brenda swung round in surprise. "Who...."

But the woman had gone. No wisp of fading ectoplasm, no shimmering patch of air. Nothing.

Until Brenda turned to face the sink again and almost jumped across the room.

The ghost was in her sink. Well, half in her sink. The woman was standing there as though the sink didn't exist – her feet presumably on the floor while her torso rose out of Brenda's washing up.

"He's going to kill you like he killed me." Gone were the ghost's empty eyes and impassive face. She spat the words out. "He's been watching you for weeks."

"Who?"

The ghost turned her head to one side. "I can hear him coming." The corners of her mouth curled up in a hint of a smile. A far from pleasant one. Her face swung back to challenge Brenda.

"Run! Get out while you can."

There was no warmth in the warning. Just hostility.

Brenda folded her arms. "I'm not going anywhere until you tell–"

"You're not listening!" The ghost stabbed an ethereal hand at the back door. "This is your last chance. Open that door and run!"

Brenda stayed where she was, arms folded and determined not to say another word. She'd experienced enough ghostly histrionics over the past four years. Some spirits were angry and confused. Others were just plain angry. And the more you responded, the crazier they became.

A look of contempt settled over the woman's face. "Don't say I didn't warn you."

And with that, she vanished.

Brenda let out a deep breath and rolled her eyes. What was it with ghosts? Had all the friendly, well-adjusted ones found the bright white light and passed over?

She looked down at her crockery in the sink. Was that ectoplasm on her breakfast bowl? Calcium deposits were bad enough, but ectoplasm...

That's when the front doorbell rang.

Brenda froze. She glanced towards the living room, then back at the sink. Coincidence? She wasn't expecting anyone. No one called on a Saturday. No one called most days.

The doorbell rang again.

Okay, thought Brenda, I'm thirty-one and far too old to be spooked by a spook. It'll probably be Jehovah's Witnesses.

She stepped into her living room, cast a quick glance around to make sure it was presentable and walked towards the door. Then hesitated.

"Who is it?" she asked, standing a good two yards back from the door.

"Brian Murphy. I'm sorry to disturb you, but my car's broken down outside your house."

Brian Murphy? The name didn't ring any bells, but he didn't sound threatening. He sounded middle-aged, educated – not the kind of person who'd pull a knife and come crashing through the door the moment she slipped the chain.

But that warning...

"Hello? Are you still there?" asked the man outside.

Brenda bit her lip. This was stupid. It was nine o'clock in the morning. Broad daylight in a crime-free suburban neighborhood. She wasn't in any danger. This was the Midwest, not New York or London. Her neighbors were probably out in their driveways washing their cars, or playing with their kids. No one would try anything in front of so many witnesses.

She stepped forward and opened the door a crack, letting the chain pull taut across the gap. A middle-aged man peered in, business suit, clean shaven, slightly built. And nervous. It wasn't hot outside, but three beads of sweat glistened on his forehead.

"My car's there," he said, standing back to point at a black BMW parked across the entrance to Brenda's drive. "Can I ... would it be all right to use your phone?"

He smiled – a quick nervous smile – then looked away.

Brenda's internal threat status rose from guarded to elevated. *He wants to get inside your home. Why doesn't he use his cell?*

She swallowed, her mouth suddenly feeling dry. "I'll call the local garage for you. I've got them on speed dial."

"No!"

He couldn't disguise the panic in his voice. Though he tried.

"It's not a garage I need to call. It's uh my office. I'm late for an important meeting. My job depends on it."

Brenda looked at him hard. She wanted him to be telling the truth. She didn't want a fuss. She wanted a nice, simple, conflict-free life. And he might be telling the truth. Important meeting, career on the line, car breaks down on the way. Who wouldn't panic?

But...

"Don't you have a cell phone?"

He closed his eyes and exhaled deeply. "You must think I'm a total idiot. I'm usually so organized but ... it's this meeting. It's really knocked me sideways. I forgot to charge the battery last night. The thing's dead. Along with my career and my marriage if I don't sort something out."

He looked at her pleadingly. Brenda wavered. He didn't look creepy. He looked frightened and nervous – which could be explained if this meeting was as important as he said it was.

But...

He could be spinning her a line. You heard about it all the time. Serial killers and their ploys. *My car's broken down. I've lost my dog. My child's hurt. Please, can you help?*

And once you slipped the chain or got in their car, that was it. No way back. They'd whack you from behind or drug you. And the next thing you knew you were face down on some cold floor being raped or murdered.

She was not slipping that chain.

"You can borrow my cell," said Brenda, keeping her voice bright and confident. "I'll fetch it."

She'd barely turned away from the door when she heard the click of a gun.

"One more step and I'll blow his head off."

A second man's voice. Young, threatening, and hitting all Brenda's alarm buttons. She swung round. The older man's face had been pushed down and squashed against the doorjamb. A gun pressed against his ear. The second man – tall, early twenties, black greasy hair – glared at her through wild eyes.

"Open the door, or I'll spread his brains all over your carpet."

Brenda couldn't move. Her gut told her to run. Let him inside and he'd do whatever he wanted. Her only chance was to run and duck and hope she could make it out the back before he smashed his way in. But his eyes told her he'd shoot her in the back before she made it to the kitchen.

Time stretched. The only sound the slow tick of the wall clock. Nothing from outside. No shouts, no voices, no children playing. Where were her neighbors when she needed them?

"I'm counting to three," he said. "One...."

Brenda still couldn't move, still listening for that one sound – a slowing car, a shout, a passing savior.

"Two."

She rushed to the door, hands trembling, fingers turning to thumbs as she struggled to slip the chain off the latch. The door swung open, knocking her backwards. Two men bundled through. The older man was shoved towards the center of the room, off balance and falling. He hit the floor and rolled, banging into the edge of the sofa.

The younger man closed the door and locked it. "Anyone else in the house?"

She wanted to say 'not yet.' She wanted to say her husband was on his way home. With his brothers. All Navy SEALS.

But he ran at her and the words vanished. There was so much anger in his face. She shrank back against the wall – trapped. His left hand thudded into her sternum, pinning her there.

"I said, is anyone else here!"

His breath stank. She could barely think. "No!" she gasped. "No one."

"You live alone?"

"Yes."

He pushed himself off her, smiling as he did so. Every part of her body was shaking. Why hadn't she listened to the dead woman? She'd been warned!

The gunman hurried to the windows and drew all the curtains. He switched on the room lights and ripped the phone out of the wall.

"Give me your cells. Now! Both of you!"

Brian fumbled in his pockets. The gunman stood over him, beckoning impatiently with his fingers, before snatching the cell from Brian's trembling hand.

"Mine's in the kitchen," said Brenda.

He grabbed her by the arm and pulled her from the wall. "Show me. And you," he turned and pointed the gun at Brian. "Don't move an inch. I only need *one* hostage."

Brian didn't say a word. Or move. He just sat there, on the floor, looking like a helpless animal caught in a spotlight.

Brenda was pushed towards the kitchen. She tried to walk calmly. She tried not to look at the rack of knives by the draining board. She tried to focus everything on collecting her phone and handing it over with the minimum of eye contact. But her brain was in a spin, screaming at her to *do* something, screaming at her – no! She had to wait. *There's no time to wait! He'll tie you up in a minute and you'll be helpless. But fight back and he'll kill you! Do as he says and you'll get through this. Make him realize you're a person, do all those things that hostages are supposed to do. Wait him out!*

She grabbed the cell with shaking fingers and handed it to him, keeping her eyes down and fixed on the phone. She didn't dare look at him. One misread look and anything could happen.

He reached forward to take the phone, his left hand enclosing both the phone and the tips of her fingers. And there it stayed. His hand in contact with hers. Gently squeezing.

"That's a good girl. We're going to get along fine. I can tell."

Brenda swallowed hard, her imagination on fire. She had to get out of this room. She was trapped in a corner. He was between her and both doors.

"Shouldn't you be locking the back door and closing the blinds?" she said.

"You like it in the dark, do you?"

Shit! Shit! Shit! She closed her eyes, squeezed them shut. She could feel him inching closer, his stinking breath warm against the top of her head. His other hand brushed against her shoulder, sliding down and across...

Crash! The sound came from the living room. Breaking glass. The gunman turned, already moving towards the sound. He yanked Brenda along behind him, his fingers digging into her arm.

"It wasn't me," said Brian, rising from the spot where they'd left him. "It just fell down. I haven't moved."

Brenda believed him. There was a dead woman standing by the far wall, a few yards from an empty space where a mirror had been. A different dead woman – not the one from earlier – and were those bruises on her face? And her clothes – they were ripped and ... was that blood?

She looked so sad and tearful, rippling against the far wall – opaque, transparent, half here, half there. Had she managed to dislodge the mirror from the wall? All the ghosts Brenda had seen passed straight through matter.

The gunman let go of Brenda's arm and turned on Brian.

"I told you *not* to fucking move!" He pointed the gun straight at Brian's head. "Where do you want it? In the head? The chest? The leg?"

The gun zigzagged in his hands, pointing at Brian's head, his chest, his thighs.

"You can die quick or slow. It's up to you."

"He didn't *do* anything!" shouted Brenda. "The screw holding the mirror's been loose for ages. I meant to get someone in to repair it!"

He ignored her, the gun dancing in his hands. He was enjoying himself, smiling, tormenting, his eyes locked on

Brian's terrified face.

"What would he be doing over there?" shouted Brenda. "If he wanted to escape he'd have gone for the door!"

A second passed. Then another. Brian just stood there, eyes tight closed and face screwed up in silent acceptance. The ghost by the wall started to cry.

"No!" she wailed.

The gunman relaxed. It was like a switch had been thrown. One second he was about to kill, the next he lowered his gun, turned to Brenda and smiled.

"Not your lucky day is it? First me, then the mirror."

His smile tightened, then vanished. He started to move towards her. "Do you know the difference between me and a mirror?"

She shook her head, backing away at the same time. One wrong word, one mistaken glance and she could set him off.

"You get seven years bad luck for a mirror. But with me ... you get time off for good behavior. If you know what I mean."

Brenda nearly threw up. The way he said it, the way he smiled, so smug, so ... eugh!

"Now move! Both of you! Over there where I can see you."

He herded them into the lounge area of the open plan living room, the section in the far corner by the television. "Sit down!"

Brenda took the near armchair so she could keep an eye on the dead woman who still hadn't moved from her place by the wall. Brian perched on the far edge of the L-shaped sofa. The gunman stood in front of the television. He turned it on and flicked through the channels until he found a local news station.

It was a live broadcast from nearby Hillsdale. A gaggle of reporters surrounded a police spokesman.

"Is it the Hillsdale rapist?" a journalist called out.

"It's too soon to say," said the spokesman. "But we do have a lead. A man was seen running away from the vicinity."

He held up a photofit of the man's face. The cameras zoomed in on the image. Brenda leaned forward, already knowing whose face she was going to see. It was the gunman. Not an exact likeness, but close enough. The Hillsdale rapist. Five women beaten, raped and murdered in a matter of months. And now here he was - in her home! - holding her hostage.

"Fuck!" said the gunman, starting to pace. "Fuck!"

He turned on Brian. "This is all your fault. How the fuck can you run out of gas?"

Brian melted into the back of the sofa. "I uh I ... I...." He looked too terrified to speak.

"I-I-I what?" said the gunman. "I shit myself? I too fucking stupid to see the warning light?"

"You put a gun in my face! I couldn't think straight."

"You couldn't think straight? You only had enough gas to drive eight miles! You should have seen the warning light before I flagged you down."

The police spokesman flashed back on screen talking about how there'd been a chase, but the killer had given them the slip.

"He won't get away. We've set up roadblocks around Hillsdale and Richwood. There's no way he's getting out."

The gunman turned and swore at the television before starting pacing again, prowling the area in front of the TV.

Another picture flashed on screen. The victim – twenty-four year-old nurse, Gabriella Czerna – pictured from happier times when she could still smile. When her face wasn't bruised, her dress torn and blood-spattered, and her ghost wasn't a see-through wraith hovering above the broken shards of Brenda's mirror.

The wraith began to pulse against the wall, brightening and fading in time to ... to what? A ghostly heart beat? Had anger, the sudden sight of her former self on the television, imbued her spectral form with some remnant of life?

The pulsing began to diminish and with it went the anger in her face. Replaced by tears. A low sobbing accompaniment to the news report of her death.

"Why don't you take my car?" said Brenda. "They can't be watching every road out of here."

"No. Best to stay here and wait," said the gunman. "Tomorrow this'll be old news."

Tomorrow? He was staying *here* – in her house – for twenty-four hours?

"Don't look so worried. Do what I say and you'll both get out of here alive. You never know – you might start to enjoy it."

He smiled – a serial-killing rapist's smile. *Are you having a good time? I am.*

A small sad voice sounded from the ghost by the wall. "He never leaves loose ends."

Brenda closed her eyes. *He never leaves loose ends.* She wasn't going to get out of this alive. He was going to hole up in her house until the roadblocks were lifted then make a run for it in her car. Either he'd take her with him as a hostage, or he'd kill her here. He wouldn't care. And when he wasn't killing her, he'd be raping her.

He never leaves loose ends.

"I'm sorry," said Brian. "It's all my fault. I should never have let him hijack my car. I should have fought back. I could have saved you from this."

"Shut up," said the gunman. He smiled at Brenda and rolled his eyes. "Of all the cars to hijack I had to hijack his. You'd be a better driving buddy, wouldn't you? I bet you wouldn't run out of gas. I bet you could go for hours."

He sauntered towards her, smiling his serial-killer rapist's smile. He probably thought himself irresistible. Brenda glanced towards the ghost by the wall. The ghost who'd found enough power earlier to dislodge the mirror. Wasn't it about time...

The ghost vanished. No goodbyes, no 'I'm going for help.' She just vanished.

"How much do you want?" asked Brian. "I'm a rich man. I can raise a ransom. Just let us go. You won't get a penny if we're dead."

He had the killer's interest. "How rich?"

"Very. Look, take my wallet. It's full of platinum cards. I can raise hundreds of thousands. Let me call my wife. She'll get it for you."

The gunman took the wallet and opened it. He pulled out a number of credit cards and pocketed them. Then stopped dead, his eyes narrowing.

"Where'd you get this?" he shouted at Brian, pulling a photograph from the wallet and thrusting it at him.

Brian pulled away, flattening himself against the back of the sofa. "It's Tina, my wife. It was taken–"

"Is this some kinda joke?" He stood over Brian, gun hand drawn back ready to strike. "This is Tina Murphy!"

Brian brought his arms up to protect his face. "I know. I'm Brian Murphy."

The gunman brought his arm back further, held it there, quivering. Then turned away. "Fuck!"

Brenda watched, confused. Who was Tina Murphy?

The gunman paced, shaking his head. The picture had unnerved him. He was already unpredictable. He could snap at any second.

He charged at Brian, grabbed a fistful of hair with his left hand and shook the man's head, his gun hand held high, threatening to come smashing down on the side of Brian's face.

Brian wailed, both hands coming up to claw at the killer's left hand. But with no strength or conviction.

Brenda's hands flew to her face. He was going to kill him. Beat him to death in front of her. And all for what? A picture of his wife?

The gun hand continued to hover. The fingers of the killer's left hand continued to bite. "Were you following me? Is that why you were there when I needed a car? Did you let me hi-jack it?"

"No! I don't understand."

"*You* don't understand. Tina Murphy is fucking dead. I killed her last month!"

"No! I talked to her this morning. I can phone her if you like. She's alive."

"Can I see her picture?" asked Brenda. The words came out of her mouth before she could stop them. Curiosity, the cat killer, had struck again. She flinched in her seat, not sure if she'd just tipped him over the edge, not sure if he was going to come racing over, flailing and shooting.

He stopped shaking Brian. And stared at Brenda. Then back at Brian. "Are you in this together? Did you bring me here on purpose?"

"No! We've never met. I ran out of gas. You can check."

The gunman let go of Brian, let him slump back in the sofa and moved towards Brenda. "Why do you want to see the picture?"

He stood in front of her, daring her to say something he didn't like.

And what could she say? That she thought the face might

belong to one of the many ghosts who floated through her home. Maybe the one who'd warned her earlier?

"Sorry. I thought I might recognize her from the TV. I was only trying to help."

She pitched her voice calm and businesslike. *I'm not a threat. I'm not trying to provoke you. I'm trying to help.*

He handed her the picture. "Well?"

It wasn't the woman from breakfast. Or anyone she recognized. Not that she'd been following the Hillsdale case closely. She tried to avoid that kind of news.

"She's not dead!" shouted Brian. "Let me call her. I can prove it! Give me my phone back!"

Brian was getting up. He'd leaned forward, planted both hands on the rim of the sofa ready to push off.

The gunman erupted. In two strides he was across the floor, gun arm pulled back and swinging towards the side of Brian's unprotected head.

And then Brenda's life changed forever.

Chapter Two

There was a sickening crack. The worst sound she'd ever heard. Followed by the worst sight she'd ever seen. Brian's head came off. It actually came off! Like a cartoon head in a cartoon world. It couldn't be real, but ... there it was - arcing through the air, bouncing, rolling across the floor towards the bookshelf in the corner behind the TV. And that wasn't the worst of it. His body was still moving - twitching, jerking, spasming - blood welling from the red, ragged mess of a neck.

The killer recoiled. "Jesus motherfucker!"

Brenda froze, too shocked to move, too stunned to look away. Until the body jerked to its feet.

She had to look away. Bile rose in her throat. She'd heard stories about headless chickens taking ages to die, but this... It was still moving. She could see it out of the corner of her eye. Arms waving in a demented jerky fashion, legs attempting to walk. One step, two. It was closing on its killer, its hands reaching out.

The gunman jumped back, fell over the arm of Brenda's chair, hit the ground, propelled himself backward on hands and heels towards the door. Brian lurched after him - a headless, arm-waving zombie. Brenda pulled her feet up onto the chair, tried to bury herself into the foam back as the 'thing' stuttered by.

Two shots rang out, the noise deafening, echoing around the room. Brian staggered backwards with each shot. Then crumpled to the floor.

A stunned silence swept in, punctuated by ragged breaths. Then a scream. Not from Brenda. Or the gunman. But from the head lying on its side against the bookcase in the corner.

Brenda joined in. She couldn't help it. Brian's eyes were

moving. She could see them! He was still alive! His mouth full open.

"Shut up!" screamed the killer. He was back on his feet, over by the front door, frightened, confused and waving his gun.

Brian's screams faded.

"Is he dead yet?" barked the killer, peering towards the bookcase, but not getting any closer. He couldn't see the head from where he was. The television and the cabinet it sat on blocked his view. But Brenda could. It had stopped screaming at last. And the eyes were...

Brenda jumped. It blinked! Brian blinked. How could he still be alive?

Brian spoke. "What happened? I can't feel my legs. I can't feel anything! Am I ... am I paralyzed?"

The gunman turned away. "Fuck!" He screamed at the carpet, bending forward, both hands ripping through the air as though he was tearing out his hair.

Brenda was in a daze. Brian was looking at her, worried, imploring. Could he really be still alive? Could he not know what had happened? The television cabinet blocked his view of ... the rest of him.

"I can't move my neck! I really think I'm paralyzed."

She had to answer. "I think you're a little bit more than paralyzed."

"Is something broken?"

"You could fucking say that," shouted the gunman. He'd started to prowl the small area between the front door and the kitchen, his eyes downcast, not looking once at Brian.

"Wait," said Brian. "I think I can feel something. I'll try and wiggle my toes."

Brenda wasn't sure how much more of this she could take. He was dying. He had to be, but ... the way he spoke – so calm, so innocent.

A clunk sounded to her left.

"Fuck!" The gunman jumped back against the wall as Brian's right foot jerked, banging the heel of its shoe against the floor. Not just once, but twice.

"I do *not* fucking believe this!"

Brenda didn't either. She stared at the foot. Then at Brian. *How?*

"Can you see it?" he asked. "Is it moving?"

Brenda opened her mouth, hoping something cogent might come out. It didn't.

Clunk. Brian's foot rose again, higher this time. And again. The entire right leg lifted off the floor, bending at the knee now, slapping the sole of his foot against the carpet. The left leg joined in.

"Is that me?" said Brian. "I can hear it, but ... I think there must be something wrong with my ears."

The gunman jerked away from the wall, leveled his gun at Brian's body and held it there, both hands clamped to the gun, both hands shaking. "You ... are ... dead!"

He was losing it, going to shoot, maybe spray the entire room with bullets. Brenda had to do something.

"Is that someone outside?" she asked.

"What?"

She had his attention. "Someone must have heard the shots. It's Saturday morning. All the neighbors are home."

"Shit!" He ran to the window and peeled back the near curtain. "I can't see anyone."

Brian's feet tapped twice on the floor. "This is really strange," he said. "I can hear where both your voices are coming from perfectly, but my feet seem miles away."

Brenda shook her head. What could she say?

The gunman had no such qualms. He strode from the window, swept past Brenda and stopped a few yards from Brian's head.

"You're dead, don't you get it! You're a fucking head. The rest of you is lying over there!" He pointed behind him, sweeping his left arm around and jabbing it towards the body.

"Show me," asked Brian.

The gunman backed away, waving 'no' with both hands. "No way am I picking you up. You're dead. You're gone."

Behind the gunman, the body on the floor rolled over.

"Please," said Brian. "I need to see."

Brenda watched. The gunman was distracted, too busy arguing with Brian the head to hear what was happening behind him. Brian's body had pulled itself up onto its knees. His hands were feeling towards his neck.

"You are sick!" shouted the gunman, pointing his gun

once more at Brian's head, shifting his weight from one foot
to the other. "You are *fucking* sick."

Brian's body moved silently to its feet. Was he going to
creep up behind the gunman and make a grab for the
weapon? Brenda shifted in her chair, grounding both feet.
She had to be ready to help. It might be their one chance.
She had to be prepared to do anything – gouge, shoot, kill.

"I need help that's all," said Brian, looking directly at
Brenda. She nodded. She was ready.

Brian's body began to walk – hesitatingly, sliding each
foot a few millimeters off the ground like a blind ice skater,
feeling his way, hands outstretched. Brenda steeled herself,
reached up and grabbed his right hand, gave it a squeeze,
guided it around her chair. Then took his index finger and
pointed it at the gunman's back.

He was a few feet away, closing...

Then Brian screamed.

Brenda couldn't believe it. Why? Why had he screamed?

"What's that behind you!" cried Brian.

The gunman swiveled round, took one look at headless
Brian and lost it. He half jumped, half fell over backwards,
arms flailing and eyes bulging. He fired once, then again.
One bullet hit the ceiling. One must have hit Brian – his body
lurched backwards, toppling towards Brenda. Who couldn't
move, her eyes transfixed – those windmilling arms trying to
regain balance, that raw stump of a neck leaning ever closer
towards her.

It slumped on top of her. A dead, dying, putrefying,
'wouldn't stay dead' lump sprawling in her lap. And it was
still moving. Squirming, shifting its weight, gurgles and
guttural noises coming from its chest. *Get it off! Get it off!*

She pushed and pummeled at his back.

"Ow!" said Brian. "That hurts."

"I do not fucking believe this!" said the gunman, hunched
over now, both hands on his thighs, breathing hard. "You've
lost your fucking head, you moron. Of course it hurts!"

Brenda stopped pummeling, but not pushing. She wasn't
letting that oozing stump of a neck get any closer. She
arched her back in the chair and pushed, holding him away.

But why had Brian screamed? He could have locked both
arms around the gunman. He could have wrestled him to the

ground. He'd had a chance. Maybe the only chance they'd ever get.

The body in her lap stirred, leaning forward and shifting its weight onto its feet. It was still alive – no surprise there – and getting up.

"Is that me?" asked Brian, calming down.

"I need a drink," said the gunman, turning away.

Brenda brushed at her clothes – not sure what Brian might have left in her lap now that he'd regained his feet. Severed fingers? Pieces of flesh? Goo? She looked down at her T-shirt and jeans – not even a bloodstain.

Which was strange. He'd been shot several times and his head had come off. There should be blood everywhere. But there wasn't. Not on his clothes nor on the carpet. And the blood welling in that stump of a neck was doing just that – welling – not overflowing, not pumping, not even dripping.

He continued his stuttering zombie walk until he was standing over his head, then he bent down, reached out, patted along the floor and picked it up.

"Do you think it'll stick back on?" he asked Brenda.

Brenda shrugged. After what she'd seen in the last ten minutes nothing would surprise her.

In the kitchen, cupboard doors clicked and banged as the killer searched for something to drink. Rat poison, hopefully. And in the living room, Brian's head, clasped tightly between two hands, was hoisted back onto his shoulders.

"What do you think?" he asked.

"It's usually better facing front," said Brenda. "Unless you're auditioning for *The Exorcist*."

"Fuck!" The gunman had chosen that moment to return from the kitchen. "I mean – fuck! – what *are* you?"

"I don't know," said Brian, smiling as he turned his body around to match his head. "It's got to be a miracle, hasn't it?"

He stood facing Brenda, his head still clasped between both hands, making slight adjustments to the left and right. "Is it centered?"

The gunman took a swig from a bottle of tequila. "You think that's going to grow back? You're a crazy man. You're a dead fucking crazy man."

"Do you think I'm immortal?" Brian asked Brenda, his

eyes sparkling. "Like one of those superheroes on TV?"

It made about as much sense as anything else. "I think you need to move your head a little to the right."

"Or maybe I'm a zombie," said Brian. He sniffed the air twice, then looked at the gunman. "Can I smell brains?"

The gunman blanched. He was standing motionless in the doorway, a gun in one hand and a bottle in the other.

"I'm not sure if I could eat brains," continued Brian, now turning to Brenda. "Do you think its compulsory? I mean, wouldn't you catch CJD eating all those brains? Of course that would explain why zombies are so slow. Their brains would have turned to mush."

He turned back to face the gunman. "I think I'd avoid brains. I could eat liver though. Maybe a leg."

For a second Brenda thought the gunman was going to lose it again.

"Shut up!" he screamed, jabbing the gun at Brian. "You're *not* a fucking zombie. You're a *freak*! A *fucking* freak!"

He was breathing fast, shifting his weight from foot to foot, as he spat out the words.

"Stop looking at me!" He jabbed the gun at Brian again. "Go back to the sofa and sit down. Now! I don't want to see you, okay?"

Brian obeyed and the gunman stomped to the table in the dining area behind the sofa. He pulled out a chair facing Brenda and slammed the bottle down on the table. Followed by the gun, slapping it down hard on the highly polished wood. Brenda winced. The table was an antique. The gun might have gouged the wood – they had sharp pointy edges, didn't they? The last time it had been damaged she'd had to call out a French polisher. And why couldn't he use a coaster for that bottle...

Well isn't that just great, thought Brenda. You're trapped in a room with a serial-killing rapist and a headless zombie and all you can think of is French polishing.

"Do you think I'll have a scar?" asked Brian.

Brenda burst out laughing. Uncontrollable, nervous laughter at the absurdity – the innocence – of the remark. He looked so serious, so hopeful. Sitting there, one hand holding his head in place. A ragged seeping collar of a wound below.

"Shut up!" screamed the gunman.

Brian began to cough. A congested, chesty cough.

Brenda stopped laughing. "Are you okay?"

He looked far from okay. His head was jerking forward with each cough. Even with both hands holding it on, she could see daylight at the back of his neck with every lunge forward. Was this it? A delayed but inevitable death?

Brian's eyes began to bulge. He leaned forward, coughed something up onto the floor. And again. Something reddish and ... metallic? There was a faint clink as one struck the other. Were they bullets?

One more cough and it stopped. Brian leaned forward, one hand holding his head, one hovering over the mess on the floor.

"It's a bullet," he said, rolling the slimy piece of metal between finger and thumb. "I've coughed up all three bullets."

"I'm not listening," said the gunman, his ashen face streaked with sweat. "You're a crazy fucking dead man."

Brian wiped his mouth on his sleeve, and smiled. "I really am immortal. I coughed up the bullets. My head's back on."

He took his hands away and tried a slight shake of his head. Brenda went bug eyed. The head teetered on his shoulders. It looked like it was going to fall off again.

"I wouldn't move around too soon." She looked to the gunman. "He needs a hospital."

The gunman took another long drink from the bottle. "He needs a morgue."

Brian got up. Carefully. He was trying so hard to keep his head level, he looked like a student at a zombie deportment class.

"I think we'll be going now," said Brian. "There's nothing you can do to stop us."

The gunman was across the room in an instant, upturning the dining table in his wake, the bottle of tequila sent flying. "Sit down!"

"Or what?" asked Brian. "You're going to knock my head off again? Shoot me?"

Brian didn't cower, or step back, or flinch. He just stood there.

The gunman couldn't stop moving. One moment he was in Brian's face, the next he was stepping back, his weight shifting from foot to foot. He looked lost, unsure whether to strike out or run. "Yes, I'm going to shoot you. And throw your fucking head out on the lawn."

"You'll have to open the door to do that, but ... what if the door won't open? What if you're trapped in here? With me."

This was a totally new Brian. All fear had vanished.

The gunman raised the stakes. Still looking at Brian, he swung his arm round and pointed the gun at Brenda.

"Sit down, or she gets it."

Brenda felt the blood drain from her face. She could die in the next second. Did either of them care? The gunman didn't. Did the new Brian? He was too busy playing superzombie to think straight. She could feel things sliding out of control. A bloody conclusion imminent.

"I wouldn't do that if I were you," said Brian. "What if she's like me and something weird happens?"

"Like what?"

"Can't you guess? After all, you must know by now that I led you here."

Brenda's mouth fell open. Did she hear that right?

"What ... what are you talking about?" asked the gunman.

"You don't really think I ran out of gas?"

"*Who* are you?"

"Someone who wanted you here. In this house. With her."

This was not just a new Brian, this was a *Hammer House of Horror* Brian. Menacing and creepy. He spoke slowly, he looked the gunman in the eye and ... there was more than a hint of madness in that face - the eyes, the smile. He'd transformed.

The gun swung back to point at Brian.

Who welcomed it. "Every time you shoot me I get stronger. I feed on it. Are you going to feed me?" He took a step towards the killer and leaned forward, his head teetering as only a partially severed head can, until his forehead rested against the gun barrel.

"Let's see what'll happen next, shall we?" he said.

The killer took a step back, swinging the gun around to face Brenda. Brian's head toppled forward - the angle impossible, his nose swinging down towards his chest, a slooping, tearing sound from the back of his neck...

Then both hands came up and pushed it back into place.

"Go on then," he said. "Shoot her. My powers are nothing compared to hers."

What little blood Brenda had left, fled. Brian was playing Russian roulette with her life.

"I don't believe you," said the gunman, his voice saying otherwise as nerves lifted it half an octave. He took a step backwards, his right heel hitting the skirting board beneath the window.

"Do you want her to prove it?"

"Yeah, prove it. Come on, lady, show me what you got?"

Crap. Brenda closed her eyes and shook her head. She still wasn't sure if Brian was insane or playing a clever game. Trying to get her killed or protect her. Did he really think she was a zombie too?

On the other hand...

Could she have superpowers? She saw dead people.

"You never looked upstairs, did you?" said Brian.

A thump sounded from upstairs. The killer jumped. "Who's up there?"

"Her children. Tiny misshapen children." He spoke slowly, pausing between each word, twisting them into the ebbing confidence of the killer. "Hungry children with lots of little, sharp teeth."

Something skittered along the floor upstairs. It sounded like tiny running feet. And was that laughter? Distant, muffled, childish laughter.

More skittering. Both Brenda and the gunman had to look up, following the sound as it traversed the ceiling. Which was impossible. On so many levels. There were internal walls upstairs. No one could run from the front of the house to the back in a straight line.

Except ghosts.

Was that it? Ghosts? Were they helping her? Was Brian a ghost too? It would explain the head and the bullets. But could ghosts take corporeal form?

The gunman edged along the window towards the door, his hands shaking, the gun pointing at Brenda then Brian.

"Give me your car keys," he told Brenda. "Do that and I'm out of here."

"Do you want to let him go?" Brian asked Brenda.

Yes! The sooner the better. This was their chance. He

wants to go. We want him to go. So let him go!

"But he's a murderer, Brenda. He'll kill again. And rape. Until someone stops him."

Which is why we have police. Come on, Brian! We can end this.

"It never ends," said Brian. "Until it ends."

Shit! He was answering her thoughts. Could he read her mind? And what did he mean? It never ends until it ends? What kind of gibberish was that? Uh ... sorry, Brian, no offence.

There was a commotion at the door. The killer was trying to unlock it, but the catch wouldn't budge. He hit it with his gun, rattled the door, kicked at it, swore.

"You can't escape," said Brian.

The killer took a step back, aimed at the lock, fired once, twice. Wood splintered, but the door still wouldn't open. He pulled at it, kicked at it, threw himself at it, shoulder first.

'Let him go!' Brenda framed the thought and flung it at Brian. She wanted the killer out of her house and gone. 'Can't you call the police? Or immobilize him? He won't be able to hurt anyone in prison!'

'His kind can inflict pain wherever they are.' Brian's voice resounded inside her head. Except that it wasn't Brian's – not the one he was speaking with. This one had an English accent. Did all ghosts think with an English accent?

'Only the really old ones. And what if a clever lawyer gets our friend here off with a lighter sentence? Or there's not enough evidence? Or he brokers a deal?'

'So what would you do? Torture him?'

'I strive to make the punishment fit the crime.'

The gunman gave up on the front door and ran through the house to the back. The kitchen door rattled. It hadn't been locked, but now...

"Fuck!"

Thumps and thuds came from the kitchen. And screams – both of rage and fear. He was kicking at the door, beating on the glass, screaming at them to break. Two shots rang out, but there was no sound of breaking glass. Was the whole house magically sealed? The glass in the kitchen door was nothing special. A gun butt should have shattered it easily.

The front doorbell rang.

Brenda jumped. The banging from the kitchen stopped. Were the police at the door? A neighbor? There'd been so many gunshots someone must have got curious.

"Would you like to open the door, Brenda?" asked Brian.

"No!" screamed the gunman, emerging wild-eyed from the kitchen. "Stay back, both of you."

He started to run towards the door. Brian lunged forward like a swordless fencer, stamping his lead foot on the floor in front of the gunman, then jumped back.

The killer ignored him, running for the door, one stride, two then....

Brenda blinked. Even after all she'd seen she couldn't quite believe it. The killer's feet stuck to the carpet where Brian had stamped his foot. Except it wasn't really carpet any more. It stretched and clung like sticky toffee. The killer was leaning forward, straining, panicking, his breathing ragged and loud, his arms waving wildly as he tried to keep his balance and pull his feet clear. One foot was six inches off the ground, a sticky fibrous goo stretched between the carpet and the sole of his shoe.

Brian stepped forward, having no such trouble, and twisted the gun free from the killer's right hand.

"The door, Brenda," he said. "I think it's time you found out who's on the other side."

Brenda slowly lifted her right foot – testing to see if the carpet came with it. It didn't. And the door latch behaved itself too, sliding back as easily as ever. Then Brenda paused. Whoever was going to be on the other side of that door had only rung the once. Why? If it had been the police they'd have banged on the door until they had an answer. A concerned neighbor would have shouted through the door, asking if she was all right. They wouldn't ring once and wait.

Could the killer have an accomplice? Had Brian lured another serial killing rapist to her house?

"You're perfectly safe," said Brian. "She's expected."

She? How many more people were there?

Brenda gripped the door handle, turned it and slowly pulled the door open.

It was a hooker.

Brenda's jaw, which over the last hour had been getting closer and closer to the ground every time she opened it, set a new record. A hooker?

"Hello. I Luljeta," said the hooker in a heavily accented east European accent. Beneath the make-up she could have been any age. Mid-twenties, mid-teens. The little clothes she wore were garish, revealing and straight from the shelves of HookerMart. "I very pleased to meet."

She grabbed Brenda's hand and shook it, her eyes filling up. "You make me very happy."

What? How? Brenda was approaching 'who?' when Brian spoke.

"Come in, Luljeta. It won't be long now."

What won't be long? Brenda stood back to let Luljeta inside.

"Who's she?" said the gunman, his voice shaking.

"Who do you think she is?" said Brian. "One of your victims perhaps? It would be poetic justice, would it not?" He circled the mired killer. "Do you think I should give her this gun? Or maybe a knife? Let her carve her own form of justice into your murdering rapist hide."

"I've never seen her before!"

"Are you sure? Take a closer look. Think of all those girls you raped before you got the taste for killing. Could she be one of them? Or maybe a sister?"

Brenda stood by the open door, glancing outside. Maybe this would be a good time to leave?

"Close the door, Brenda, and come inside. You have to see this."

She felt compelled to close the door. She looked at Luljeta. There was real hatred in the girl's eyes. She stood there, arms folded, weight resting on her right foot, watching Brian taunt the killer, waiting.

"But I'm far more creative than that," said Brian. "You see, Luljeta here sold everything she had in Albania for the promise of a better life in the West. And guess what? The gang who arranged her trip sold her to the Albanian Mafia. Now she's a sex slave with no hope of escape. They give her food, accommodation and clothes and keep all the money she earns. She ran away once, but her handlers tracked her down and dragged her back. She still has the scars. If she tries it again they'll kill her. No way out. Unless – and this is where you come in...."

He stopped circling.

"You help her."

"How?"

"Empty your pockets. Give her all your money, all those credit cards. My car keys. Everything."

The killer agreed in an instant. He emptied his pockets with shaking hands, passing everything to Brian and watched as he, in turn, filled Luljeta's open palms.

"You're free now," Brian told her. "Take the money and my car – the black BMW outside. Go as far away as you can. No one will follow."

Brenda didn't understand. But then she'd understood very little all morning.

Luljeta started to cry. She thanked Brian. She thanked Brenda. She went back and hugged Brian. Then left, the door clicking shut behind her.

"Okay, you've had your fun. Now let me go," pleaded the killer.

Brian began circling again.

"I haven't said how you're going to help her yet."

"I gave her money!"

"A few dollars. That's not going to keep her safe. There's only one thing that will."

"What?"

A thought echoed by Brenda. Was he going to kill him after all?

"You're going to trade places," said Brian.

The killer looked confused, then horrified. "What are you going to do?"

Brian rolled up his right sleeve and flexed the fingers of his right hand.

"No!" screamed the killer. "Keep back!" He swung at Brian, missed, tried again, grabbed hold of his hair, tugged. But Brian's head stayed on. And Brian's right hand reached forward and slowly pushed inside the killer's chest.

Brenda swallowed hard. Brian's hand was inside the killer. She could see it! It was up to his wrists, the killer's flesh parting as though it was made of soft cheese. There wasn't even any blood. The killer was struggling and screaming and...

Changing. His clothes, his features. He was shrinking

into ... Luljeta. A perfect replica. Even his voice had raised an octave. And that accent.

"What you do to me? You crazy motherfucker!"

"I'm giving you a fresh perspective on sex and violence."

And with that, the Hillsdale Rapist vanished.

Brenda blinked. "Where did he go?"

Brian reverted to his English accent. "A massage parlor downtown. She doesn't look very happy."

"You can see him ... her?"

Brian's eyes had become unfocussed. He stared past her right shoulder into space.

"I can see her," he said. "And so can her pimp."

"What *are* you?" she asked.

Before Brian could answer, a woman materialized behind him. The dead woman from breakfast, her eyes blacker than ever, her face set in a tight-lipped scowl.

"You wouldn't listen, would you?" she snapped. "Don't look at me. He can't read your mind at the moment – magic takes it out of him – but don't let him know I'm here. He's a Vigilante Demon."

"Me?" said Brian, oblivious to the ghost behind him. "I'm the third arm of the justice system. Law, Order and Vengeance. And I'm looking for a partner."

"A partner?"

"He means bait," said the woman. "He may be in-vulnerable, but we're not. I was his last partner."

"Yes," said Brian. "A partner. Someone who can see and hear the dead. I can't, so I need someone who the dead come to. Someone who'll listen to them, look out for the ones who were murdered and question them – try to find out who killed them. You pass the information to me and we ... we bring them to justice. Find a fitting punishment."

"Like turning a rapist into a sex slave?"

"Exactly. We bring the bad guys to justice and have a little fun doing it. Our serial killing rapist friend had a penchant for violent horror films, so I chose a zombie theme for his takedown. Considerably more gory than my usual takedowns but, I hope, as inventive. What do you say? Are you interested?"

The dead woman shook her head. "He'll use you like he did today. Dangle you in front of every sick killer in the country and get you killed like he did me. He takes too many risks."

"Come on, Brenda. It's your chance to make a difference. Get killers off the streets."

Brenda didn't know what to say.

"You *can't* do it!" said the ghost. "You're not ready. You're not even a proper medium! You could never replace me!"

Then a second ghost materialized – floating, shining – a few feet to Brian's left. The ghost of Gabriella Czerna, the killer's last victim, her clothes no longer ripped or blood stained, her face no longer bruised. "Thank you," she said.

Just the two words.

And, sometimes, two words are enough.

Chapter Three

And sometimes they're not.

"Wait!" Brenda shouted. "I've changed my mind! I don't want to be a crime fighter. Come back!"

She couldn't believe it. How could everyone vanish like that? One minute she was the center of attention, everyone and her ghost offering advice, the next - poof - she was on her own. No Brian, no ghosts and no idea of what was supposed to happen next.

"Brian!" She shouted at the ceiling, swung round and yelled at the windows. "Brian!"

Where had he gone? And why so suddenly? Had he sensed she was having second thoughts? Was that the way demons negotiated - close the deal, then shoot off before the poor sap of a human could change her mind?

Brenda slumped into the nearest chair. She'd been set up. The man had brought a serial-killing rapist into her home for Chrissakes! Deliberately! The whole thing must have been some kind of test - an audition - to see ... to see what? If he could work with her? If she could watch someone's head fly from their shoulders without freaking out?

Incredible!

And what if it had all gone horribly wrong? Would he have apologized to her dying body? Sorry, Brenda, things got a little out of hand, but don't worry, I'll find another partner.

And how did he know she could see the dead? He must have been spying on her. Watching her for weeks without her knowledge. Reading her most private thoughts.

Brenda shuddered. She felt cold, used, and violated. This was her home. Her refuge. Bad things weren't supposed to happen here. Not here! She'd left all that behind.

Back came the memories - the ones she'd been burying for the past four years - rising up out of the ground like coffins in a waterlogged cemetery. London. Her apartment. That day in June when she felt unwell at work, took the afternoon off to go home and recover...

And walked in on her husband and her best friend. A best friend who she worked with! Who she shared her innermost secrets with!

And now, apparently, her husband too.

Brenda had died that day. The young, optimistic, fun-loving Brenda. Other Brendas crumbled in quick succession. The career girl Brenda – how can you go to work when the woman in the adjacent desk is sleeping with your husband! The rational Brenda – how can you think or concentrate when your mind is forever stuck on replay? That day, that scene, those words, those looks. The trusting Brenda – how can you trust anyone when the two people you trusted most in the world had deceived you so badly?

And how can you live in an apartment that would forever smell of *her*?

Marriage, home, best friend, job. All swept away. She couldn't stop crying long enough to risk a job interview. She couldn't face her friends, and as for her family – that wouldn't be a refuge, that would be hell.

All through her teenage years she'd been told that women in her family didn't get divorced. They worked at their marriages. And they didn't have breakdowns, they coped. Her sister and mother would have sat her down in the big armchair by the fire and talked 'sense' at her until she'd lost the will to be unhappy.

And then there were the dead people. She'd forgotten when exactly they appeared. Week three, week four of her breakdown? They seemed drawn to her. Not that they'd offer comfort – far from it – they were too obsessed with their own plight. *You think you've got problems? Look at me. I was sick for years. You young people don't know what real pain is.*

So Brenda ran away, turned her back on London, her career, her friends, and ran back to the U.S.A. But not to her hometown. She wanted somewhere far away – somewhere she'd never been, a place with no memories, a town plucked blindly from a map on a wall.

It was to be her retreat. The place where she'd settle

down. The new Brenda. The low-expectation Brenda, who'd swaddle her life in protective folds, who'd look for a stress-free job close to home. Something routine and repetitive that she could leave behind at the end of the day. And she wouldn't have friends any more. She'd have acquaintances. People you smiled to in the street. People you shared a joke with in passing. Not your husband.

And she would rekindle her love of books. Spend long evenings curled up inside their pages, live life vicariously, safe behind the heroine's eyes. And she'd watch more films and immerse herself in soaps. Who needed the real world when fantasy was so much richer?

And safer. She'd tried the real world, and it hurt.

Then along came Brian.

For four years she'd lived in peace and contentment, living life at arm's length, never allowing anyone too close, dipping into the outside world, but never letting anything penetrate her rose-tinted firewall. Then Brian tricks his way inside her home and suddenly she's neck deep in the real world and treading water.

How could he!

But...

Brenda closed her eyes. A small part of her welcomed the idea of becoming a crime fighter. If this were a book she'd be shouting at the heroine to stop obsessing and get out there and kick ass. It was the opportunity of a lifetime. A chance to use her skills and make a difference. A real difference. Save people's lives, give people closure, make the streets safe again.

But...

She liked her stay-at-home, risk-free life. She needed it. A fallow time while she let herself heal. And she was still healing. She didn't have the confidence to trust another person and if she and Brian were to become partners, trust would be paramount. Her life would be in his hands, and from what she'd seen, he was someone who would be forever taking risks.

Brenda sighed. What the hell was she going to do?

Ten minutes of pros, cons, if and buts later, Brenda was still in a quandary. Perhaps there was no decision to make? Perhaps it had all been a dream?

Brenda didn't need to be drowning to recognize a stout length of straw when she saw one floating by.

She glanced around the living room. No blood on the carpet. No signs of a struggle. And the door – it looked pristine – but she was sure she'd seen wood splintering from around the lock when it had been shot at.

She walked over to investigate. The door was unmarked. She slipped the latch and opened it to check the other side. Both sides were undamaged, but ... the door felt different. More substantial, heavier. And had there always been that strip of material around the doorframe?

She pressed her index finger into the strip. It felt soft. Some kind of draft excluder?

Or soundproofing?

She hurried through to the kitchen. She was sure she'd heard the killer try to smash the glass in the back door. She ran a finger over the door's glass panel. It was unmarked. But different. It looked thicker. She opened the door, swung it back and forth. It felt different too. Heavier, smoother. The old door had caught occasionally. This one fit like a glove. And there was the same soundproofing strip around the doorframe.

She checked the windows. Triple glazed. In both the kitchen and the living room. She'd never had the windows triple glazed! But now they were. He'd soundproofed her home. But why? Why this way?

He'd said he'd used magic, but this ... this looked real.

She was about to slump back in her chair when she remembered the carpet. Brian had turned a patch of her carpet into glue. Was it still glue?

She fetched a mop from the kitchen and inverted it, using the wooden handle as a prod to poke at the carpet. The mop didn't stick. She patted at the area with her right foot, pressing her shoe hard into the pile. Her shoe came away with no resistance. Whatever Brian was, he tidied up after himself.

Brenda bent down to take a closer look at the carpet. It looked clean, but ... anything could be on it – from invisible demon blood to ecto-glue. The same for the sofa and the cushions. She'd have to clean the lot.

Hours passed. Brenda stripped the furniture, shampooed the carpet. And dug a bullet out of the ceiling with a knife. It hadn't been a dream. Real bullets had been flying around her living room and this one could have penetrated her body just as easily as it had the ceiling.

She shuddered. She had to find a way to get in touch with Brian and tell him she'd changed her mind. Maybe she'd be ready to help in a year or two, but not now. Now was too soon.

Days passed. The hunt for the Hillsdale Rapist slipped down the news schedules and Brenda settled back into her routine. As much as she could. She still jumped every time she heard a noise, wondering if it was Brian, wondering if he'd appear out of the blue with a new serial killer in tow.

But it never was. Towards the end of the week trepidation gave way to disappointment. Maybe he'd found someone else? Maybe her life *could* do with a little more excitement? Her job as a school secretary had begun to look dull and unfulfilling. She'd been on the verge of being a crime fighter. A sidekick to a superhero!

Back came the counter argument – Brian not coming back was a good thing. She wasn't cut out for crime fighting. Partnering up with a demon would be a huge mistake, and as for quizzing dead people – what was she supposed to do? Ask them to form lines? Murdered people over here, accidents in the kitchen, communicable diseases outside and *way* down the block.

There was a lot to be said for living a quiet uneventful life.

And yet...

Chapter Four

By Saturday Brenda had put the excitement of the previous weekend behind her. Brian had found someone else and that was an end to it. And besides, she had something else to worry about – her mother's birthday party. Three days to go and she was running out of excuses not to attend. The fact that it involved a three-hour drive was lost on her mother. *A three-hour drive's nothing to a daughter who loves her mother. Your cousin Emily's flying in from Hawaii to be with her mother at Thanksgiving.*

Good for Cousin Emily. Cousin Emily wouldn't be pinned in a corner and lectured for two hours about the mess she'd made of her life and how it was time to get up off her ass and do something about it. Stop being a school secretary and find a proper job – one with prospects. Find a man – any man! Move closer home. Give me grandchildren!

The latter was left unspoken, but conveyed eloquently by her mother's eyes every time the subject of children came up. Brenda's sister, Susan, had a nine year-old daughter, but couldn't have any more. A situation made worse by the rabbit-like fecundity of all her cousins. Brenda's mother had armfuls of great nephews and great nieces, but just the one grandchild. A predicament that only Brenda – the thirty-one year-old, resolutely unattached disappointment – could rectify.

Aaaarrgghh! Brenda screamed at herself. *Stop this! You're on vacation. School's out for the summer. You promised you wouldn't let Mom spoil it this year!*

An hour later Brenda was sitting on her sofa, daydreaming about the new teaching assistant at school – all thoughts of interfering mothers and demons flushed completely away – when the doorbell rang. Slightly annoyed at the interruption, she left the extremely athletic, extremely accommodating, young man bronzing on the beach and opened the door.

There is shock and there is *shock* – the wide-eyed 'Oh. My. God. Let the ground open up and swallow me whole?' variety.

Brenda experienced a touch of the latter.

He was standing there. On her porch. Jason, the male lead from her daydream.

Her face began to flush. What was he doing here? They'd never spoken, never been introduced.

"I've got to see you," he said, brushing past, inviting himself into her home as she stood frozen in the doorway.

"You do?" She pinched herself. If he took his shirt off, she'd know she was dreaming.

"Do you want me to take off my shirt?"

"No!"

Brenda closed the door – swiftly – she didn't want her neighbors to see him. She wasn't sure if *she* wanted to see him. He was barely out of his teens and ... what did he want?

She turned and found him standing a few feet in front of her, arms open wide and a strangely impatient look on his face. "Come on," he said. "Grab hold. Let's get going."

"What?" She'd heard some pick-up lines in her time, but 'grab hold and let's get going?'

He smiled and waggled his eyebrows.

"Had you going for a while, didn't I? It's me. Brian. Your friendly neighborhood Vigilante Demon. I thought this shape would please you."

She couldn't talk for a while. Relief, anger, trepidation, embarrassment – she cycled through all in quick succession. He had to have been inside her mind. Watching her dreams, watching her...

"What do you want?" she asked. "And don't ever do that again."

"Sorry," he said. "I wasn't prying. It was just that you were very loud. I couldn't help but overhear."

He smiled, that same boyish smile he'd tried on her last week. It hadn't worked then either. She crossed her arms and gave him the look her ex-husband had named the Medusa. "What do you want?"

"You, of course. There's a bank siege nearby. It's all over

the TV."

"So?"

"So we can use it to practice. A valuable training exercise."

"Why do we need a training exercise?"

"Because we're a team and teams need to practice. Don't you watch any sports? And, besides, people are in danger. Someone could get hurt. Killed even. We can prevent that and have some fun at the same time."

Brenda knew Brian's idea of fun. He'd laugh his head off – literally – and delight in freaking people out with his headless zombie act until everyone was banging on the doors to be let out.

"Why not just teleport the bad guys out."

"In front of all those witnesses? Not to mention the cameras. We have to be subtle, Brenda. When confronted with the unexpected, you humans tend to run screaming to the nearest shop and loot everything electrical."

He strained his voice into something approaching, but never quite reaching marrying distance of a mock hillbilly accent. "Help, help the aliens are a comin' an' I needs me a giant plasma TV."

Beneath the humor, he had a point. A depressingly accurate one. Reports on the TV that a gang of criminals had vanished in front of dozens of witnesses would be an invitation to every nut job in the country to add their two cents: *It's the gummint testing their secret weapons. No, it's not. It's God cleaning house. What god? It's aliens, I tell you – haven't you heard there's a galaxy-wide shortage of anal probe subjects?*

Everyone would have a theory and every news channel and tabloid would find room to air it.

"Best to find a quiet corner and teleport in," said Brian. "Then we can practice our skills."

"What skills? I'm a medium. I see dead people. I'll ask around and pass on information, but that's it. I don't 'do' danger."

"There'll be no danger. As long as you come along. I can disable their guns, but I need a second pair of eyes. Someone to watch my back and stop any of the hostages from doing anything stupid. I can defuse the situation, but it takes time."

He looked at her pleadingly. For all she knew he was messing with her mind as well – making her feel guilty. *Think of the hostages, Brenda. They're terrified. Not knowing if they'll live or die. Not knowing if they'll ever see their loved ones again. How can you not help?*

"I could make things worse," she said. "I'm a school secretary, not a SEAL."

"Nonsense. All you lack is confidence. And this is the ideal situation to rectify that. None of the gang are killers. Well, not unless pushed. And I'll disable their weapons. We'll save people, have fun, and bond at the same time. What do you say?"

'No' was a good candidate. Sensible, short and to the point. He might say he needed her to come along, but they both knew he didn't. He had the power. She was just another damsel in distress – or, more accurately, a red cape that Brian the matador could flutter in front of the nearest charging felon only to snatch away at the last second to the appreciative gasps of the cheering crowd.

And one day he'd miscalculate and leave Brenda dangling there for one fraction of a second too long. As his last partner had told her – his dead last partner – *he takes too many risks.*

"All life's a risk," said Brian. "It's how we learn. Now, come on. There's people to save. Grab hold."

He opened his arms again. Brenda shook her head, tried to take a step back, but he was faster, lunging forward and grabbing her shoulders. The earth moved, and not in a nice way. Her living room shimmered and shook as though it was being bombarded by hundreds of micro tremors. Silent micro tremors. There wasn't a sound anywhere. Her ears felt like they were going to pop, and a thick cloying silence pervaded the room.

And then the room began to change. The far wall started to recede as though it was painted on plastic wrap and a giant invisible finger was pushing into it, forming a funnel, everything stretching and elongating and ... they were moving. Fast! Into the tunnel. Streaks of blurred color washing past them, but no physical sense of movement. No wind in her hair, no G-force throwing her back. If it wasn't for the dizzying blur streaming by she'd have sworn she was standing still. Maybe she was. Maybe it was the world flying past her.

'It is,' said Brian, his voice inside her head. 'Imagine a giant hand taking two points in space between finger and thumb and squeezing the two together. We'll be there soon.'

She was beginning to feel sick, disoriented. The streaking blurs rushing past her face were making her eyes hurt.

And then the streaks began to slow and take form. At the end of a long narrow tunnel a room was racing towards her. A white wall, a picture, strip lighting, blue carpet, an office...

And stop.

For one second she thought she was going to lurch forward into the wall opposite, but she didn't. She had no momentum. She was standing opposite Brian in a sparsely furnished, windowless office. Or was it a storeroom? There were boxes in the corner, a stack of old printers and telephones, and a desk that looked as though it hadn't been used in months.

"Where are we?" she whispered.

"In an empty upstairs room at the bank. Everyone else is downstairs."

She looked at the door and listened, suddenly very aware that she was in a bank during the middle of an armed robbery. "Are you sure?"

"Reasonably," he said. "And you don't have to whisper. I've sealed the door. No one can hear us and no one can get in."

She listened just the same, straining for the slightest sound of a footstep or a voice.

Nothing.

"The hostages appear to be in a single group," said Brian, his eyes unfocussed as he – presumably – projected some kind of inner eyeball through the floor. "There's about twenty of them lying face down on the floor in the lobby."

"And the robbers?"

"Two are in the lobby. I think the others are in the back."

"Think?"

She heard her voice wavering. Anger, fear, trepidation.

"I can't see through walls, Brenda. I have to visit each room in turn."

Brenda took a deep breath. She had to stay calm. No amount of argument or histrionics would persuade him to send her back home. She was here. And she'd have to deal with it.

Another deep breath. *Come on, Bren. People's lives are at stake. You've got to stay calm.*

She closed her eyes and offered up a prayer.

Then opened her eyes to a surprise, and not one she'd prayed for. Brian - still in his Jason guise - had lost his shirt. His lean torso glistened beneath the bare strip lighting. Muscles flexed.

"What ... where's your shirt?"

He winked at her. "I thought you needed something to take your mind off the robbery."

He stood there smiling - perfect teeth, taut abs, tight trousers. And was that sweat or oil glistening all over his upper body?

She shook her head. "I find this *really* unsettling. Can't you change into someone else?"

Hunky Jason began to age in front of her eyes. And change. Radically.

Brenda blinked. It wasn't?

It was.

"In nomine patri...."

It was the Pope, in full regalia, going through the motions of blessing her, his right hand moving from forehead to chest.

"Do you find this shape less unsettling?" he asked, raising both arms and turning slowly like a geriatric fashion model.

Brenda was about to answer with something cutting when he reached the midpoint of his twirl. His white cassock was split open at the back like a hospital gown.

"You are going straight to hell," she said, looking away.

"What makes you think I don't live there? Can't you just smell the sulfur?"

"Only the bullshit. Change into someone else. Please!"

He morphed into Bruce Willis, disheveled, barefoot and straight out of *Die Hard*.

Brenda shook her head. But at least it was apt.

"I won't be long," he said. "I need to take a closer look

downstairs. Remote viewing can only show you so much."

And with that he vanished.

Seconds passed, long seconds which Brenda filled by listening and wishing she were somewhere else. What had possessed her to hook up with a crime-fighting demon? She could have said no. Or would he have ignored her answer and used her just the same – teleporting her into dangerous situations until she either agreed to help or died along the way?

More seconds passed – even longer ones. What was taking him so long? Had he lost one of the robbers? Was he frantically searching the rooms below, but not finding him because the cackling, demented, gun-toting psychopath had moved upstairs – maybe he was outside the door now, one hand on the door handle, the other cocking his gun...

Brenda held her breath, froze every muscle in her body and listened. Was someone out there? She couldn't hear anything, but Brian might have soundproofed the room. The entire gang could be gathering out there now, signaling to each other. One to open the door, one to go high, one to go low...

Brenda! she mentally shouted at herself. She was being stupid, frightening herself for no reason.

No reason! Brenda's internal voice – a woman of great perspicacity who tells it like it is and has known for a fact that the entire world has been participating in a conspiracy against Brenda since the age of four – couldn't stay silent any longer.

You're on your own, Brenda. In a bank. During a robbery! What if Brian doesn't come back? What if *this* is the training exercise? Drop Brenda alone in the bank and see if she can come out alive? Die Hard 5 – No Bruce, just Brenda.

And you need to pee. What were you thinking? Allowing yourself to go undercover at a bank robbery – a potentially long bank robbery – on a nearly full bladder!

More seconds passed, maybe minutes. It wasn't just her bladder now. She was sure she could feel a cold coming on – her throat had that dry feeling at the back and her sinuses didn't feel right.

"And you look spotty," said Brian, materializing in front of her, still in his Bruce Willis form. "Come on. Time to go. Lie down on your stomach. I'll put you at the back. All the cameras have been disabled and I'll make sure the gang are distracted."

"Wait! Shouldn't we have a plan?"

"We do. It's called playing by ear. We go in. We observe. We look for a weakness in the gang, exploit it. Get creative. Have fun. Undermine them and persuade them to release the hostages. Your job is to keep the hostages alive and be my second pair of eyes."

Audience more like it. He needed someone to see how clever he was. It had to be galling – saving people every week, performing incredible feats, but never being able to claim the credit.

"You're more than an audience, Brenda."

She didn't reply. Grudgingly, she lay down, trying to find a comfortable way to lie on her stomach. Should she keep her head down or propped up on her elbows to get a better view?

"Where will you be?"

"Around. See if you can spot me."

She lay there, waiting. She felt the light touch of his hand on her head and then everything began to shake. Including her bladder.

"Wait! I need to go...."

She didn't have time to finish the sentence. The floor began to fall away, forming a funnel beneath her that stretched through the ceiling into the large lobby below. She could see the hostages spread out beneath her. Men in black with guns. And then a spire of tiled floor shot up to meet her and dragged her down.

She braced herself. Even though there was no sense of falling or motion whatsoever she couldn't help herself. Her eyes told her she was falling twenty feet. She closed them.

And felt the soft carpet replaced by hard, cold tile. And there was a shout. A man's voice. "What was that?"

Brenda flattened herself against the floor. Had someone seen her beam in? Brian said he'd create a diversion, but Brian said a lot of things. She closed her eyes and counted through the seconds. She couldn't hear footsteps running towards her. Maybe she'd got away with it.

"It's okay," said another male voice. "It's only a box. It

must have fallen off the desk back here."

Brenda opened her eyes and raised her head. She was at the back of a group of hostages – about twenty in all – lying in a haphazard group on the lobby floor. She slid her forearms beneath her and pushed up to get a better view. The teller line was in front of her – about thirty feet distant – and there was an open door to an office on the right-hand side of the lobby. Behind her and to the right were double doors to the street. Wooden doors with glass panels.

And there were four – no, five – men in black with guns. Three were in the lobby and two were in the back office behind the teller lines. One carried a heavy duffel bag and hoisted it next to three others already positioned on the teller counter. They'd obviously had time to clear the vault.

'Brian?' Brenda formed the word as a thought and fired it into the ether. 'Where are you?'

He didn't answer. She looked from face to face. Had he beamed in with her? None of the hostages returned her look. Most were staring at the ground. Some had their eyes closed. Others appeared terrified or shell-shocked. An elderly woman was whimpering nearby.

"Shut up!" shouted one of the gang members, striding towards the old woman. He wore a black ski mask, a baggy black top and black sweat pants. Only his eyes were visible. And he carried a shotgun. "I said *shut up!*"

He kicked her. He actually kicked her! Not hard, but the woman must have been over seventy and frail. She didn't even have the strength to scream. Or cry. She just folded in upon herself, clasping a bony hand over her mouth in an attempt to stifle the whimpers she couldn't stop.

Brenda had to bite her tongue. Why hadn't Brian stopped that?

The thug stood over the old woman, menacing, looking around, daring any of the hostages to speak up. *I'm in control. Don't forget it.*

Come on, Brian! Intervene. Do your stuff.

Silence. Brenda took a longer look at the old woman. Could she be Brian? She couldn't see Bruce Willis or any prominent members of the Catholic hierarchy lurking in the lobby, so becoming an old woman would fit his modus operandi – the little she'd seen of it. Become the weakest person in the room, the one no one would suspect, and turn that weakness to his own advantage. Push, prod and finally gross everyone out.

A phone on the teller counter rang.

One of the gang – the granny kicker – moved gingerly towards it.

"It'll be the cops," said another. "What do we do?"

"Shut up! I'm thinking." He hovered by the phone. Several times his hand moved to lift the receiver, several times he pulled it back.

Then he snatched at the phone. "What do you want?"

Somehow he must have switched the phone's loudspeaker on as everyone heard the reply.

"This is the FBI Hostage Negotiations Service. Press one if you wish to surrender. Press two for a getaway car. Press three for a helicopter. Press four for a pizza."

"What the hell's that?" said one of the gang.

Granny Kicker shrugged. "They must have one of those automated switchboards."

"Let's take the helicopter," said a third member of the gang, eagerly rushing over to join his colleague by the phone.

"Can you fly a helicopter?" asked Granny Kicker.

"Well, no," said Eager.

"Then shut the fuck up. They'd have to supply a pilot and he'd trick us somehow. We'll take the car."

He pressed two.

"You have selected the getaway car. Press one for an SUV. Press two for a sports model."

"Sports," said Eager.

"Are you an idiot?" asked Granny Kicker. "We need room for us, the money, and a couple of hostages. We'll take the SUV."

A tone sounded as another button was pressed.

"Good choice. You have selected the SUV. Press one for a black SUV. Press two for powder blue. Press three for bright orange with the 'caution: bank robber on board' bumper sticker."

"What?"

Granny Kicker stared at Eager, who shrugged.

"You have selected the bright orange–"

"No!" shouted Granny Kicker. "I didn't! I didn't press anything!"

He stabbed his index finger at the phone pad, repeatedly hammering down on one of the numbers. The loudspeaker tone rang out with each depression.

"Good choice. You have selected the orange SUV with the tracking device-"

"No! I pressed one! I pressed one!"

"Excellent choice. You have now selected the model with the nearly empty gas tank. Less weight for a faster, smoother ride."

Granny Kicker slammed the phone down. "What the fuck was that?"

He walked away, angry. Swung back. Shook his head. "What are they playing at? Don't they know we've got hostages? We've got guns!"

He emphasized the point by holding his shotgun aloft and shaking it.

Brenda watched, wondering if Brian had pushed Granny Kicker too far. She loved the idea of an automated hostage negotiator, but ... an orange SUV with a 'bank robber on board' bumper sticker? Had Brian's sense of humor gotten the better of him?

"It's gotta be a mistake," said Eager. "Try it again. There's gotta be a button for talking to a person."

Granny Kicker hesitated. He stared at the phone. He walked away. He came back. He kicked at the wooden panel that ran along the base of the teller counter.

Then snatched up the phone.

"We want an SUV with a full tank outside the bank in thirty minutes. Get that?"

"Press one if you wish to speak to a negotiator."

Brenda waited. Was he going to bite, or slam the phone down? It was difficult to tell, not being able to see his face.

He pressed one.

"Please hold."

There was a long pause, and then music blared out of the phone's loudspeaker: *The Clash* belting out *I Fought The Law And The ... Law Won.*

Granny Kicker shook his head. He turned to Eager. "Are they fucking with us? Why are they fucking with us?"

Eager shrugged. "I like *The Clash*."

The music stopped and an Indian voice answered. "Hello, Sanjay here, how may I be helping you?"

"We want a car out front in thirty minutes. An SUV."

"Okay, name please?"

"Ji .... Do you want me to shoot one of the hostages?" Granny Kicker snapped. "I got twenty here. I don't need them all."

"No! No shooting please. I am apologizing if there is any misunderstanding. My job is to keep everyone alive and happy. Now, let me see." There was a rustling of paper on the other end of the line. "Ah, yes, would you be liking food? I can send out for pizza if you release three hostages. Four hostages will get you extra topping."

"We don't want any food! We want a car out front."

"Very good, sir. We will be sending SUV to you straight away. Now, tell me please, on my screen it say Second National Bank, Main Street, Greensboro. Is that correct?"

"Yes."

"Very good. Now, is this Greensboro in the North or the South America?"

Brian was pushing it again. There was a pause while Granny Kicker shook his head.

"It's in Ohio," said Eager, leaning forward to speak into the phone.

"Ah, yes, of course," said Sanjay. Then there was a pause. "And is Ohio in the North or the South America."

If Brenda hadn't been lying on a cold dirty floor in a bank full of armed raiders, she'd probably have giggled. But she was, so she didn't. But she had to applaud Brian's comic timing. The pauses. The deadpan delivery. The use of an Indian call center. It was inspired.

If it worked and Granny Kicker didn't slam the phone down and start shooting people.

"Ask to speak to an American," said Eager.

"I was about to!" snapped Granny Kicker, cupping his hand over the receiver.

"I want to speak to an American," he said.

"Very good, sir. Please hold."

Back came *The Clash* – still fighting, still losing.

"Hello, I am American," said a voice which sounded

suspiciously like Sanjay. "How may I be helping?"

"Are you Sanjay?"

"No, I am entirely different person. Very American. I am knowing the Tom Cruise like my own brothers."

"Then you'll know where Greensboro is. And you can tell Tom if I don't see a truck outside this door in thirty minutes, I'm going to start filling the street with dead hostages."

He slammed the phone down.

"Do you think they'll give us a car?" asked Eager.

"They'd better."

Granny Kicker strutted across the lobby towards the hostages and stopped a few feet in front of the group. He just stood there, glaring at them, his head turning as he looked from one frightened face to another.

Brenda tensed. Was he going to pull one of the hostages out? Prepare for his threat to fill the street with dead hostages? She could feel the tension rise. Twenty terrified hostages bracing themselves for the worst.

And then a little red dot danced onto Granny Kicker's chest. He couldn't see it. None of the gang could. They were all behind him.

"Who wants to be first?" he said.

No one answered. No one was even looking at his face. Everyone was staring at the tiny red dot. And then another. And another. Soon his chest was alive with dancing lights.

Brenda fought the desire to glance over her shoulder. Were the lasers real, or something Brian had dreamed up? She couldn't remember if there were windows at the front or not. Or what the field of view was like from the door.

"What about you?" said Granny Kicker, pointing his gun at a uniformed security guard. "Do you want to go out a hero?"

The security guard didn't answer. And the red lights stopped dancing ... they formed a pattern. A large X on his chest.

Then the telephone loudspeaker crackled into life.

"Where are we going to find getaway SUV this time of night, Sanjay? It is midnight here in Mumbai. No one is open."

Granny Kicker swung round. Eager shrugged. "It wasn't me. I never touched the phone."

"Relax, Radhesh. Number one rule for hostage

negotiation is never give them what they want. Number two rule is keep fool talking long enough for SWAT sniper to get bead on him. You watch. I expect fool standing by big window this very minute with little red dot on his chest."

There was a long pause while Granny Kicker digested what Sanjay had said. A tilt of the head as his little masked grey cells thought, 'no, surely not....'

Then a glance down at his chest, his chin jutting forward in shock. A long bug-eyed stare and...

Panic. He threw himself backwards, swatting wildly at the lights on his chest as though somehow they had a physical presence that he could bat away with his hands.

Cue gravity. In his haste to lean back and protect his chest, he began to lose balance. His legs made a valiant effort to catch up with his toppling shoulders, but failed, succeeding only in propelling him backwards faster in a series of stuttering steps until...

Splat. He toppled backwards, slid along the floor on his back, discharged his weapon and shot the ceiling directly above him.

Cue gravity again. White plaster descended like a personal snowstorm covering his head and torso. He coughed, spluttered and swatted at the plaster which, no doubt with Brian's considerable help, continued to fall in prodigious quantities.

One of the hostages laughed, then quickly covered his face as panic replaced hilarity. Brenda wasn't laughing either. Suddenly her bladder felt very tight.

'What are you doing?' she hissed into the ether. 'You told me you'd disabled all their guns!'

Brian didn't answer.

The other four gang members rushed over to help, but Granny Kicker shrugged them off, tossing his gun aside as he staggered to his feet, brushing and beating at his chest, head and arms.

Until he suddenly froze. "Get back!" he yelled, shouting at his gang. "All of you."

"What's the matter?" asked Eager.

Granny Kicker didn't answer. He grabbed for his gun, pumped another round into the chamber, leveled it at his comrades and slowly backed away.

"There are five of us," he said.

"Don't be stupid. There's four... Shit!"

All five masked men backed away as one, tensing, leveling their guns at each other, heads and guns jerking left and right as they turned from face to face. They were all dressed identically, all clutching identical weapons.

Brenda swallowed hard. How was Brian going to talk his way out of this one?

"How can there be five of us!" said Eager. "No one's come in or out since we got here. The door's locked." He sounded agitated. He shifted his weight from foot to foot, his left hand sliding along the barrel of his shotgun. Was he going to shoot?

One of the gang raised a hand. "Sorry, Jimmy. But I had to come along."

"Mom?"

"It's your first bank heist, son. I couldn't sit at home and worry. I had to come and help."

"But ... but...." Jimmy, aka Granny Kicker, was speechless – about as speechless as any son would be upon finding his mother had accompanied him to his first bank heist. "How did you get here? How did you know?"

"A mother knows these things, Jimmy. You put your favorite ski mask in the wash. And I heard you talking to Mikey."

"Mom! Don't use our real names!" hissed Jimmy, then paused. "Not that my name's Jimmy."

"No, and I'm not Mikey," said Eager. "I'm ... Sebastian. Or I would be. If my name *was* Sebastian, which it's not. Either."

Mikey, having dug a hole large enough for two people – neither of them called Mikey – wisely decided to stop digging and played with his gun instead – pointing it, gangsta style, at the hostages and mimicked firing it.

Brenda had to look away. Her body was shaking with silent laughter. She had to cover her mouth with a hand. *You put your favorite ski mask in the wash*. Brian had excelled himself.

'And now, Brenda, it's your turn.'

Brenda's smile morphed into wide-eyed shock.

'What? What do you want me to do?'

'What I told you. Work on the hostages. They're ready. The gang's hold over them is waiting to be broken. Once that's gone everything changes.'

Brenda closed her eyes. What the hell was she going to do?

The phone rang.

Jimmy and the gang looked at each other.

"You've got to answer it, son," said Brian. "They might have the car ready."

Jimmy wasn't convinced. He stared at the phone, but made no move towards it.

With the gang's attention focussed on the phone, Brenda took the opportunity to slide forward, reaching out with her hands and pulling herself alongside the hostage in front of her.

"I think we're on TV," she whispered. "You know, one of those spoof reality shows."

"Really?" the woman whispered back.

"Yes. I recognize one of their voices. He's an actor."

"I thought so!" hissed the hostage on Brenda's other side. "It's been way too weird – first that Indian guy, then the mother."

"Shut up!" shouted Jimmy.

The hostages shut up. The phone continued ringing.

"You've got to answer it," said Mikey.

Jimmy looked torn. He took two steps towards the phone, turned away, swung back, shook his head. Then ran forward and snatched up the phone. "What?" he shouted.

Sanjay's voice crackled over the phone's loudspeaker. "What is going on? I am hearing report of gunshot. Is anyone hurt?"

Brenda slithered forward again, squeezing between two surprised hostages. "We're on a reality TV show," she half whispered, half mouthed to them. "It's all a spoof. Tell the others."

"It was a warning shot," said Jimmy. "The next one's for real."

"Sorry. Repeat please, you are breaking up. Who have you shot?"

"I haven't shot anyone!"

The loud speaker hissed and crackled. "I am not hearing very well. My ears are full of crackling. Are you hearing this, Radhesh? I think he has shot Mr. Warning."

"You are right, Sanjay. And now he is threatening to shoot an eel."

"An eel?" asked Sanjay.

"That is what I am hearing. He say next one's an eel."

One of the hostages stifled a giggle into a cough. Others nudged the person next to them. "It's a hoax. We're on TV. Pass it on."

Jimmy was shouting down the phone, enunciating each word. "No one has been shot!"

The phone crackled some more before Sanjay replied. "How many eels are you holding hostage?"

"I didn't say eel. I said FOR REAL!"

"You are holding four eels?"

"He is very, very sick man, Sanjay."

Jimmy slammed the phone down, angry and confused. "What the *fuck* is going on?"

Several of the hostages were laughing. Jimmy turned on them.

"You think this is funny?"

He ran at them, incandescent with rage. The laughing stopped, but not the whispering.

"Shut up!" he screamed. "The next person who makes a noise will be shot."

The whispering stopped. Brenda waited. This was either the moment she did something very, very clever or very, very stupid.

"Me! Me!" she shouted, waving her hand high over her head. "I'll do it. Shoot me! I don't mind."

A large black woman three bodies over was the first to react. "No, choose me! I volunteer. I *demand* to be shot."

"No, me! I'm prettier!" said a blonde-haired teen.

Within seconds all the hostages were either sat or standing, some were shouting, most had their hands raised, several were jumping up and down.

And some were arguing.

I volunteered first! No, you didn't! Yes, I did! You're too fat to be on TV! Who you callin' fat, you dumb bitch? Don't you call me a dumb bitch, you...."

Only Jerry Springer was missing. And, knowing Brian, there was still time.

Jimmy just stood there, too confused to do anything other

than point his gun from one hostage to another. The rest of
the gang were equally perplexed. They ran forward to join
Jimmy. "What's going on?" said one. "What's happening?"

Jimmy didn't answer. No one did. A tussle had broken out
amongst the hostages. There was hair pulling and a bout of
purse slapping.

"You've got to do something, Jimmy," said Brian, still in
the guise of Jimmy's mother. "Get their attention and show
them you're in control."

And, with those words, Brian stepped back.

"Shut up!" Jimmy shouted at the hostages at the top of
his voice. "Sit down!"

And then he fired his gun.

At the ceiling, directly above his head.

The hostages stopped arguing and turned to look at
Jimmy. A small white cloud drifted down from the ceiling.
Brenda narrowed her eyes. Why so little plaster? Why no
chunks? It was unlike Brian to miss an opportunity.

Then she heard the squawk. And saw the dead pigeon. It
plummeted from the hole in the ceiling and struck Jimmy on
the head, bounced once, somersaulted, then settled there,
beak forward and wings spread out like a second pair of
ears. Above the scene, and almost in slow motion, a dozen
feathers floated leisurely towards the ground.

Brenda started laughing. Someone on her right began to
applaud. Others joined in. It *had* to be a spoof television
show.

"What the...." shouted Jimmy, crouching down and
swatting at his head.

The pigeon fell to the floor. Jimmy stared at the pigeon.
Then at the laughing hostages. Then up at the hole in the
ceiling ... in time to see a large lump of plaster fall from
above and strike him squarely on the forehead. More
laughter, even louder applause.

Jimmy was not amused, or entirely coherent. "What?
What?" he spluttered until Brian tugged at his sleeve.

"Forget it, Jimmy. I've got an idea. Follow me."

"What?"

"Come on," whispered Brian. "All of you. I know how we
can get out of this."

Brian's real voice sounded inside Brenda's head.

'You know I spoke earlier about you being my second pair of eyes?'

'Ye-es.'

'Well, it's time to step up. I've had to send my eyes elsewhere and I'm walking towards the door next to the teller line blind.'

Chapter Five

Brian's eyes lingered outside the bank. The SWAT team had just arrived. How much longer could he hold the police off? He'd blocked all their attempts to phone the bank. He'd disabled their megaphones. He'd soundproofed the lobby so no one heard the gunshots.

But from the way the SWAT team was deploying, someone was considering storming the building.

Which made his current journey all the more important. He had to find a toy store.

'Right a smidge,' said Brenda. 'Not that much! Straighten up. Why are you swinging your head from side to side? You look like Stevie Wonder.'

Brian locked his neck. He'd never been good at multi-tasking.

'You try walking in a straight line while your eyes are zigzagging across town searching.'

Somehow he made it through the door into the back office behind the teller line without walking into anything.

'Point me towards Jimmy,' he asked when he was in position.

'He's at your seven o'clock.'

Brian turned and began to whisper, hoping he was talking to the gang and not empty air. "They think they're on TV," he said. "On one of those reality spoof shows and we're a bunch of actors."

"Oh, right," said Mikey, his voice betraying the moment the one cent coin – which was definitely not called Penny – finally dropped. "That explains it."

"And we can use that to get out of here," said Brian. "With all the money. And without the need for a getaway car."

"How?"

"Easy. That crazy bunch'll volunteer for anything. So we

dress five of them up as us and send them out to surrender. Then we walk out – with the money – dressed as hostages. The cops won't give us a second look and none of the hostages will give us away if we tell them not to. By the time they realize they've been had, we'll be long gone."

"Sounds good to me."

"And me."

"Wait," said Jimmy. "We can't all walk out carrying duffel bags. It'll look suspicious."

"You're right," said Brian, injecting just the right amount of dejection into his voice as he guided the conversation to where he wanted it to go. "Wait a minute! Did you see those stuffed bears in that room off the lobby? Some charity event the bank is sponsoring."

"No," said Jimmy. Which was hardly surprising as Brian was still looking for them. He'd found a toy store, but did they have enough bears of the right size?

"We can pull out the stuffing and fill them with bills. No one'll think the money's inside the bears."

"Won't it look kinda odd?" asked Jimmy. "Five people all carrying bears out of a bank?"

"Not in this town it won't. Not this week. They're staging a big charity event for kids. It says so in that room. They're selling bears all over town."

"I think it'll work, Jimmy," said Mikey. "And we can keep the bears, too."

Now came the problem. He'd sold them his plan, now he had to show them the bears. Which would be difficult – even for a demon. He couldn't teleport anything without being in physical contact. And inner eyes didn't count.

"I'll keep an eye on the hostages," he said, thinking quickly. "You four stuff the money in the bears. They're in the room off the lobby."

He thought of waving an arm in the general direction of the room, but decided against it. The chance of accidentally hitting someone in the face was too high. He used a restrained finger instead.

And then waited, listening for their footsteps.

'Have they all gone?' he asked Brenda.

'Yes. They're picking up the bags.'

'Okay. It's back to you. Stall them. Don't let anyone in the room off the lobby until I say it's okay.'

He didn't give her time to object. He transformed the fabric of his clothes, hardening them, making them rigid and self-supporting. No one would know they were empty. Unless someone came up close and looked into the ski mask's empty eye slits.

Then he was gone, sending his naked body racing along a tunnel he'd created between the bank and his eyes in the toy store.

He materialized in a storeroom at the back of the shop, his eyes snapping back into his head. He crouched down and listened. He couldn't hear anyone. And a naked man materializing in a toy store was usually worth a scream or two.

He clawed at the stack of boxes in front of him, ripping them open and freeing one bear after another until he had the four he needed.

A last look round. Were four bears going to be enough to take all the money? He couldn't see anything bigger.

And then he gathered all the bears together in one large communal bear hug and created a tunnel back to the bank.

He froze his journey the moment the bank began to take shape. He hovered in mid-materialization, his clothes lay a few meters below him at the base of a shimmering funnel. He nudged the funnel base away from his clothes and through the teller line into the lobby. The funnel moved below him like a slow motion tornado. He *had* to materialize in the room on the far side of the lobby.

And it had to be empty.

~

Brenda's brain was in danger of overheating – not from overactive little grey cells, but from the friction generated by fleeing ideas. She was on her own. One woman against four armed bank robbers. How was she supposed to stall them?

To make matters worse the only idea that refused to flee – having hooked a leg around a pole in her brain – involved losing her top.

"Excuse me," she said, running over to block their way. "Um ... um...." Her mind went blank – even the pole dancer had fled. She attempted a smile, aiming at winsome and overshooting into crazed beauty contestant territory. She twirled a strand of hair, felt the other hand reach down for the hem of her T-shirt...

"Get out the way," said Jimmy, shoving her aside.

"Wait!" she said. "There's something you should know about the police."

All four robbers stopped and turned. "What?"

Good question. The words had sprung from her mouth without a clue as to what came next. She opened her mouth hoping another sentence was lurking behind her tonsils. No such luck and she could feel her right hand straying towards the hem of her T-shirt again.

That's when she saw it – over the bank robbers' shoulders and to the right. It was pink. It had bears and ... oh my God!

"What's the matter?" asked Mikey.

Brenda tried not to stare. The door to the room was open. She had a clear view inside. Too clear a view. All that pink wobbly skin and far too many hairy bits.

She swung back to face Mikey and glazed a smile onto her face. "That money," she said.

"What about the money?"

Another search of the tonsil area and still no sign of a telling sentence.

Out of the corner of her eye she noticed Brian wipe his hand over a poster and transform it into one with a bear on it. Then he turned and gave her a thumbs up sign – at least she hoped it was a thumb.

Brenda took a lungful of air and launched into the nearest thing she found to a coherent exit strategy. "I was thinking you might want volunteers to help smuggle the money out the bank. I've done some acting."

~

Brian teleported across the lobby, funneling through the ether and back into his clothes. This time he remembered to de-starch his trousers a microsecond *before* he fell inside them. He'd almost yelled out in pain the time he'd returned with the pigeon.

He watched Brenda rejoin the other hostages. She was

looking daggers at him.

'What do you think you're doing?' she hissed. 'Why are you always taking your clothes off?'

'It's a demon thing. Which I'd love to explain, but I've got to leave again. I want to make sure the police are still behaving themselves outside.'

He cast his inner eye across the lobby and out through the door. The police lines were much the same as before. A few more cars perhaps, but ... where were the SWAT teams? He looked up, down and around, but couldn't see them. Which was worrying. If they weren't out front where were they?

He circled the building twice before he saw them. They were on the roof. They'd found a skylight and were cutting a hole in the glass.

Shit! Brian dived back into his body. Time to take control of the phone lines again. He patched a call through to the police outside, modulating his voice into a passing impersonation of Jimmy.

"We surrender. We're coming out in ten minutes with all the hostages."

He cut the line and hoped that would be enough to hold the police back.

Five minutes later Jimmy and the gang returned clutching four oddly shaped bears who each looked as though they'd gone ten rounds with Pablo Tyson - the impressionist boxer.

"Now," said Brian, addressing the hostages. "Who'd like to swap clothes with us and pretend to be bank robbers?"

A dozen hands shot up. *Me! Me! I can do it! I am SO a bank robber!*

Brian raised his hands to quieten them. "Okay, everybody form a line and we'll come and choose you."

"What about our masks?" asked Jimmy. "We can't take them off."

"We've got to eventually," said Brian. "We can't walk out wearing ski masks. And the five bank robbers we send out have got to look the part."

"She's right, Jimmy," said Mikey.

Jimmy agreed - reluctantly - and each member of the gang selected a hostage to swap clothes with. Brian chose

Brenda.

'Are you sure you're going to look like Jimmy's mother when you take your mask off?" asked Brenda.

'Positive. I've taken her image from Jimmy's mind. She's a bit taller and broader than you, but Jimmy won't notice. And I'll make your clothes fit.'

~

Stripping down to her underwear in a bank full of strangers had only featured once in Brenda's rich tapestry of fantasies, and then it hadn't involved swapping clothes with a bank robber's masked middle-aged mother. She gritted her teeth, thanked God she'd put on clean underwear that morning, and wondered if Brian's powers stretched to magical liposuction – she could do with losing an inch or two.

A fact not lost on a few of the female hostages who considered themselves unfairly passed over for the role of Bank Robber Babe.

"She is SO fat," said a horrified teenager in spray-on jeans.

"You talkin' outta you skinny white ass, girl. She not fat enough. No cop gonna believe she some bad ass bank robber."

Then Brian stripped off.

"Whoa! Now that's one bad ass bank robber. They's prison tats?"

Brenda could barely look. There were folds and bulges and tattoos of pirates. And God knows what those parrots were supposed to be doing...

She threw him the thought. 'What *are* you doing?'

'I'm having to use my imagination. Jimmy hasn't seen his mother in her underwear for years.'

Lucky Jimmy.

But, at least, people had stopped staring at Brenda.

She grabbed the sweat pants and baggy top and pulled them on, turning away so she didn't have to look at Brian's bank-robber-mom-from-Hell squeezing into her new jeans and top.

"Okay," said Jimmy. "You five put your masks on and line up over by the door."

"No," said Brian. "Not yet. We've got to tell the cops first so they don't start shooting. And we've got to give them our guns."

Jimmy shook his head and tightened his grip on his weapon. "No. We keep the guns."

He looked so young. Late teens, early twenties. Stripped of the mask and the anonymous black uniform he suddenly looked ... human. And vulnerable.

"We can't, son," said Brian. "We've got to walk out as hostages. And the cops have got to see five shotguns thrown onto the sidewalk to know we're giving ourselves up."

"Okay, but we're not giving them loaded weapons."

He ejected the magazine and the chambered cartridge. The others did the same.

Brian collected them and handed them to Brenda and the other volunteers. Brenda took the gun gingerly. Knowing Brian, he could have done anything to them. Reloaded them with blanks, or converted them to water pistols.

Now came the dangerous part. Pretending to be an armed robber walking out of a bank surrounded by SWAT teams and nervous deputies. While accompanied by four excited, armed wannabes who each thought they were appearing on a TV reality show.

'You're going to throw some kind of protective shield around me, right?' she framed the thought and sent it to Brian, who smiled.

'You don't need a protective shield. You've got your wits.'

Brenda preferred the protective shield. 'Do the cops have any idea of what's been going on in here?' she asked. 'I mean, did they hear the gunshots?'

And was a SWAT team massing for an assault this very second?

'Don't worry. I soundproofed the bank. They didn't hear the gunshots and we couldn't hear their loudspeakers.'

One problem eliminated, only another thousand to go.

"Come on," said Brian, switching effortlessly back into the voice of Jimmy's mother. "Time to go. Tell them you're coming out and do what the cops tell you."

Five masked and armed hostages started to walk towards the door. Slowly at first, excited and nervous...

And then competitive. Their pace quickened, there was

jostling, grabbing and the occasional flying elbow. *I should be first, I'm Jimmy! No you're not. Let go! You let go...*

Brenda jostled back. She was the only one who *had* to be first. Someone could get killed. If these four ran out the building waving guns and showing off for the cameras there'd be a blood bath. She had to prevent that.

Up ahead, the doors beckoned, the view through the glass panels growing. She could see police cars on the other side of the street. Helmeted officers peering from cover. Real guns, nervous trigger fingers.

She broke into a run. So did everyone else and they were faster. Someone grabbed for the door handle and tugged, but the door was still locked. And everyone else piled into the back of them.

"Wait,' said Brenda, but no one was listening. She was helpless as the key was turned. Three pairs of hands reached for the handles, tugged, both doors opened inward an inch before hitting feet and forearms as everyone pressed forward, trying to push their way through.

"Wait!" shouted Brenda. "We've got to do this properly. There'll be agents and producers out there. If we run out like a rabble it'll ruin our chances."

"She's right," said one of the men. "I'm Jimmy and I should be first."

"No! It's not about being first. It's about being good. Anyone can show off in front of a camera. What they want to see is talent."

"Talent?"

"Yes, they want to see people who can think themselves into a role. Who walk out that door as real bank robbers. Who look like real bank robbers and act like real bank robbers. Not a bunch of kids showing off for their friends."

"Should we try and shoot our way out?"

"Yeah, like Butch Cassidy!"

"No! The script says we're going out to surrender so we open the door slowly, tell them we're coming out, then do as we're told. The director's out there. He'll be looking for people who can follow direction and have a good profile. So get the masks off and move slowly so the cameras can pan in for a close up."

"Right," said one, nodding. "That make sense." The others

agreed. A close up was far better than a masked blur.

Thank God, thought Brenda. *Now all I have to do is open the door and hope no one's trigger happy out there.*

She opened one of the doors.

"We're coming out!" she shouted.

"Throw your guns onto the sidewalk."

She threw hers and stood back for the others to comply.

"Now come out, one at a time, with your hands above your head."

Brenda stood back. "You go first, Jimmy. And remember – walk slow and keep your head up so the camera can zoom in on your face."

'Jimmy' walked out. The others followed at one-second intervals. Brenda took a deep breath and walked out last.

"Down on the ground! Slow! On your stomachs. Arms and legs spread."

Another of Brenda's fantasies ruined for all time. Though the SWAT uniform might be a keeper.

Police swarmed in from all directions. Brenda was prodded and patted and began to relax. Her part was over. But what had Brian planned?

~

Brian nodded to himself as Brenda left the bank. She was a big improvement on the last one. Tonya had been a mistake. And he'd told her far too much. But Brenda...

She had potential. She was quick. She was fun, and she didn't ask too many questions.

"Okay," said Brian, addressing the remaining hostages. "We're going to walk to the door. No running! You're going to walk outside and when you reach the edge of the sidewalk you're going to run – as fast as you can – across the road, along the street, wherever you want. Remember, you're hostages who've just been released and you want to rush over and see your friends and family."

He turned to Jimmy and whispered. "We'll walk out last. The cops'll be too distracted by that lot to pay us any attention."

The hostages milled around the door then, on Brian's signal, spilled outside. The gang followed, each carrying a bear. Brian held the door for them and made a point of touching each of them, lightly, on the shoulder. "Make for the car," he said. "I'll be right behind you."

Brian stayed behind the door, out of sight and, a second later, out of the physical world.

~

Brenda watched the first wave of hostages rush across the street. They made enough noise for fifty hostages. Fifty stage-struck hostages in search of a camera. There was screaming, there were histrionics, there was overacting. And a fight.

Get outta my face, you dumb skinny ho! Stop blocking the camera, you fat bitch! Who you callin'...

At the back, keeping quiet and clutching their bears, walked the four young robbers.

Then Brenda heard a hiss from one of the SWAT officer's radios, followed by a voice. "It's a set up! The five who surrendered are hostages. I repeat, the five who surrendered are hostages. The real gang are the ones with the bears. The money's inside the teddies!"

Brian must have cut into the police feed. Heads were turning. Suddenly no one was interested in the spread-eagled hostages on the ground. Guns were being drawn again, faces were being scanned. Where were those bears?

And it wasn't just the police. Behind the barriers at the far end of the street the press erupted. Brian must have tipped them off as well. The cameras swung from the hostages in the road to the four men walking along the sidewalk towards them.

"Freeze! Drop the teddies!" Probably the first time that line had been used in law enforcement circles outside of a bachelor party.

The gang froze. They dropped the bears, raised their hands and – on live TV, right in front of the cameras – four pairs of trousers dropped in unison to reveal ... four matching pairs of brightly colored underpants – all bearing a striking teddy bear motif.

A strange hush descended upon the scene. Then cameras clicked and flashed and hardened crime reporters giggled. Those hostages who didn't have a handful of someone else's hair in their hands, applauded. The *Teddy Bear Gang* had been apprehended.

Brenda drifted to the back of the crowd and ducked under the police tape when it was safe. Where was Brian? Wasn't it about time he whisked her back home? And returned her clothes.

'What's the point in having a partner if you can't swap clothes?' said a familiar voice in her head.

'Where are you?'

'In the alley to your right.'

She found the alley and ducked down it. The moment she did, the alley fled away from her – all the dumpsters and brick walls whooshing down a long bizarre tunnel into the distance. Brenda shot after them, picked up and blurring through several counties until the familiar surroundings of her living room materialized around her.

Brian was still wearing her clothes. But not as a woman. Thankfully not as the Pope either. He'd returned to his own form – or what Brenda assumed was his own form – that of an unassuming fortysomething male.

Brenda made a mental note that here was one top and pair of jeans that she wouldn't be wearing for some time. "Can I have my clothes back?"

"You want me to take my trousers off? Is this what crime fighting does to you, Brenda? Turns you into a raving sex maniac?"

Brenda closed her eyes. What had happened to her quiet, uneventful life?

She trudged upstairs to the bathroom – bliss – then returned to find Brian watching television.

"Come and have a look at our reviews."

A smirking news anchor was reporting on the events at the bank. Apparently there was still some confusion. Was it a bank robbery, or a hoax? The police were adamant it was a robbery. The hostages were convinced otherwise. No gang could be that dumb.

"See," said Brian. "That's where we score over the justice system. The courts would send them to prison and in a few years they'd be back on the streets. A little bit meaner and a little bit craftier. Me, I look at the long term. They're not bad boys – well, apart from Jimmy. The others just fell into the wrong company. So, let's deprive them of that company.

Who'll team up with a gang of incompetents who wear matching underpants to a bank heist, can't keep their trousers on, and whose hostages laugh at them? They'll be forced to find other employment."

Brenda hoped he was right, but it sounded too simplistic.

"Not everything has to be complicated, Brenda."

"Hah! You can talk. You could have ended that robbery in a second, disabled the gang and freed everyone. And still made them look stupid."

Brian shook his head. "You're using hindsight. When we went in, we had no idea what we'd find. Sometimes you can use humor, sometimes you have to use fear, or trickery, or force. Each job's different, and the skill is in selecting the right approach.

"Plus you've got to have fun. Can you imagine doing this for hundreds of years if all you did was turn up, catch the bad guy, then go home? You'd die of boredom. Anyway, look at what we did. We foiled a bank robbery, no one got killed, a gang of criminals were brought to justice, and we turned what could have been a traumatic situation for the hostages into one they'll all look back on with happy memories. They had a great time."

And they still were. Queues of them were lined up giving interviews to anyone with a microphone.

"Does it bother you, never getting the credit?" she asked.

Brian shrugged. "It used to. But think of the alternative. I go public and everyone will want to know why I didn't save their family. Humans are fickle."

The news anchor turned to the mystery of the missing gang member. Somehow she'd got clean away. But not for long, said a police spokesperson. They knew she was the mother of one of the gang.

Brenda suddenly saw a huge flaw in Brian's plan. Jimmy's mother was innocent. And yet twenty witnesses would swear they saw her in the bank.

"They're going to arrest her, aren't they?" she said. "She's not going to have a chance."

"Perhaps she needs a scare. It might make her take more interest in what her children are up to."

Brenda was surprised. "That's a bit harsh."

"I'm a demon, not a social worker. But ... if she's truly an innocent, I can always sabotage the case against her. And she'll probably have an alibi anyway, so it'll be a matter of which witnesses the jury believe."

The news switched from the police spokesperson to a replay of the gang's arrest. Jimmy, a whistling Mikey, and their two friends were walking nonchalantly along the sidewalk holding their bears. The news station had added a soundtrack. *The Teddy Bears' Picnic.*

"Now why didn't I think of that?" said Brian. "I could have taken over a loudspeaker and had that playing as they dropped their trousers."

And then, as the trousers dropped, Brian began to sing along. "If you go down to the bank today you're sure of a big surprise...."

Chapter Six

"Wait! If we're going to be partners, there's a lot more I need to know."

For a second Brenda thought he was going to ignore her and teleport off into the distance.

"Such as?" he asked, still standing in the middle of the living room, his hands slightly raised, looking like a male version of Wonder Woman about to spin into her costume.

"Such as are there any other demons are out there? Am I going to be in danger from them as well as serial killing humans?"

He smiled. "Do you know, I haven't met a single demon on this planet for years. I think they find it boring."

Brenda was surprised. "But you don't?"

"Not at all. But then I'm an atypical demon. I was always the odd one out at school."

"You went to school?"

He placed his hand over his heart – or at least the place his heart would have been if he'd been human.

"Hades High, class of 1317. While all the other kids were out tormenting minor civilizations, I preferred to stay at home and read a good mind."

She waited for him to smile. Or waggle his eyebrows. But he did neither.

"You're joking, right?"

"High School is never a joke, Brenda. It's hell. Literally in my case. All those demons flexing their adolescent powers, all vying with each other to catch the recruiters' eye."

"Recruiters?"

"Demon Lords, Magical Universities, Demonic corporations. Microsoft."

She laughed. "You are so full of bullshit."

"Okay, so perhaps not Microsoft – not back in 1317 – but

I'm painting a picture for you here. The universe is a huge place, millions of civilizations and you humans–" He grimaced apologetically. "You're not that much of a challenge for the modern demon. There are some frighteningly rational civilizations out there which require a lot of skill to manipulate. But you lot ... I could fly downtown and magically etch a face in a pizza and within minutes half the town would be venerating it. All hail the wondrous pizza face! And don't get me started on vegetables that look like Elvis."

She didn't have to, he was already well away.

"I mean," he continued. "You've got to be a pretty messed up god to communicate with your congregation via vegetables and pizza topping. Me, I'd go for the colossal head and shoulder shot over the skies of New York. Big booming voice, easy to understand message."

He rose up on tiptoe, cupped his hands around his mouth and strained his voice into a toned-down yell towards the carpet. "Stop killing your neighbors. Be nice to everybody and learn to get along." He removed his hands and winked at Brenda. "Simple isn't it? But then I'm a demon. We're practical."

"Could you really do that? Appear over New York and make an announcement?"

He shook his head. "I'm not that powerful. And besides, the immortal sphere is heavily unionized. If a demon started to dabble in god work there'd be a galaxy-wide demarcation dispute."

"You have got to be kidding."

"I wish I were. You wouldn't *believe* how petty those minor gods can be. It's one of the reasons we cast them out of Hell. Always on the picket line. And that Kali can hold a lot of placards."

Brenda had to smile. She was reminded of the Harriet Vane quote about Lord Peter Wimsey. *If anybody does marry you, Peter, it will be for the pleasure of hearing you talk piffle.*

"Piffle?" said Brian. "Here I am giving you the low-down on Heaven and Hell and you call it piffle?"

"It's entertaining piffle. But tell me one thing – truthfully – you call yourself a demon, but you...." She searched for a good way to phrase the next part. "You don't act like a demon. You fight crime. You do good."

"Demons can be good." He sounded hurt. "There's an old saying in Hell, 'The Devil has the best tunes and the worst publicists.' Which is sad because Satan's a really good bloke."

"A good bloke?"

"One of the best. He doesn't impose his will on anyone, or pass down any laws. Unlike the gods, who can't pass a rock without feeling the need to chisel out another command- ment. Do you know they once had eighteen thousand? It took us ages to get them to whittle it down to ten. Thou shalt not wear white after Labor Day – that was one of theirs. Control freaks, every one of them.

"Whereas Satan's more practical and less hands on. He helped you out of Africa, gave you fire, and apples, and pyramid erector sets for your leaders on their birthdays."

Brenda snickered. "So he doesn't torment souls and seduce people to the dark side and make them evil?"

"Brenda, we demons *live* in Hell. Why would we fill it with evil human souls, wailing and gnashing their teeth all day? The property values would crash overnight."

Brenda had to smile. It was complete bullshit, but ... it had been years since anyone had talked to her like this. Not since college. Not since those carefree days when she'd sit up to all hours talking nonsense and putting the world to rights.

"And anyway," continued Brian. "Far more killers claim to hear the voice of God or angels than the devil. Satan doesn't care what you humans do. Go and enjoy yourselves. And if you have financial problems and have the odd soul you want to mortgage, in he'll step and help you out. He'll even handle the souls no one else'll touch – the sub-prime souls. What a mensch!"

"You are so full of bullshit."

He smiled. "Prime bullshit, I hope."

This time he did waggle his eyebrows. "Is that it? Can I go now?"

"No! How do I contact you?"

He looked surprised. "Didn't I say? I'm in the Yellow Pages."

"I'm serious. If I find a murder victim how do I contact

you?"

"I really am in the Yellow Pages. Have a look if you don't believe me. I'm under 'D' for Demons: friendly."

He pointed at the phone directory on the small table by the door and crooked a finger at it. The phone directory jumped from the table, began to fly towards Brenda then fell to the ground a yard short.

"Sorry. I'm weaker than I thought. Magic takes it out of me."

Brenda retrieved the directory from the floor and started to flick through the pages, unsure if she were going to find a phone number or the set up for another joke.

She found both. A phone number – HELL 666 – and a half page picture of a smiling Brian, looking like a used car salesman with horns.

"You've just done this, haven't you?"

Brian raised both hands, palms out. "Haven't got the energy. It really has been there all week. I conjured it last Saturday. I have my own call center."

"With Sanjay no doubt."

"He likes to keep busy."

~

The next day, Brenda was feeling guilty. She'd been a fully-fledged crime fighter for twenty-four hours and not one ghost had been to see her. Where were they all? She hadn't seen a ghost in eight days. She'd never gone that long before without a visitation. Most days she'd have several. Had Brian scared them all off?

Or had Brenda lost her ability to see the dead? That would be typical of Brenda's life. Give her a talent she doesn't want, then take it away the moment she finds a use for it.

Brenda paddled in the shallow end of the depression pool for a while, splashing around with 'why me?' and 'God, my life sucks.' She couldn't even get into her book – *Strong Poison*, the first of Dorothy L Sayers' Harriet Vane books. She had all four Harriet Vane novels set aside for the first week of her summer veg-out re-readathon. She'd been looking forward to it for months. But now she couldn't get past the first chapter. She'd read the current page three times and nothing had stuck. Her mind was elsewhere, starting at every noise and imaginary shimmer glimpsed from the corner of her eye.

Even *The Rich, The Spoiled, and the Surgically Enhanced* failed to lift her spirits. Celeste had forsworn sex and fled to an exclusive recovery clinic in Tibet where she was being looked after by a hunky lama called Darley. With Celeste's track record, Darley would either turn out to be her long lost brother – kidnapped by a gang of rogue lamas as a child and raised by Yeti – or the reincarnation of her grandfather – the one who'd died in the Turkish bordello knife fight.

Normally an episode like that would have had Brenda speculating for days. But today she was too preoccupied. Maybe if she could summon a ghost...

Could she? She didn't have the power to send them away – she'd tried often enough.

But how difficult could it be? The dead knew where she lived. Half the astral plane had popped in for a whine at one time or the other.

Brenda dimmed the living room lights. Should she put on some mood music? A few Gregorian Chants. A dash of Leonard Cohen.

She decided to forego the accompaniment. Silence was good. She'd be able to hear better.

She sat down on the floor in front of the sofa and closed her eyes. A few deep breaths. A shake of her arms and shoulders. Flex and relax.

What next? Should she light a candle? Or fetch a pen and paper?

The pen and paper sounded good – she'd need something to write the victim's details down.

Back she came with a notebook, two ballpoints, a can of air freshener and a large glass of wine. Be prepared, the motto of boy scouts and psychic investigators everywhere.

She closed her eyes again, another deep breath, more loosening up exercises, a quick slurp and...

Now what?

How about 'Is anyone out there?'

Not specific enough.

"Are any murder victims out there?"

She listened, hardly daring to breathe. Not a sound. She opened her eyes. Still nothing. Should she keep her eyes open? All the mediums she'd seen on television closed their eyes, but then they were trying to channel the dead which Brenda definitely did not want to do. She wanted her ghosts out in the open, not poking about inside her.

Brenda took a couple of long looks over each shoulder. She didn't want to be crept up upon either.

"Hello," she said. "Anyone out there? Anyone with a grievance?"

Not a sound. Not a shimmer. Was it lunchtime on the astral plane? Was something good on TV up there?

She took another slurp of wine before trying again, adding a pleading tone to her voice, then a friendly tone, and finally an authoritarian bark.

"I command thee! Any spirit who hears my voice. If you've been killed step forward!"

There was a shimmer to her right – by the bookcase. An outline of a child rippling against the book spines. Building, fading, pulsing slowly in and out of phase.

"You're safe here," said Brenda. "Step forward so I can see you."

A small girl drifted out of the bookcase. The temperature dropped immediately. She couldn't be older than seven. Her hair was long, dark and unkempt. She looked lost. And her face was streaked with tears.

Brenda shuffled to face her, not wanting to make any sudden movements in case she frightened the girl off.

"Hello. My name's Brenda. What's yours?"

The girl looked away. Her fingers were nervously playing with the hem of her blue T-shirt.

"I expect you have a pretty name," said Brenda.

"I don't have a name."

Her voice was small and strangely distant as though it wasn't coming from the girl, but from some place further off. A place with an echo.

"You've got to have a name. All little girls have names."

"I don't."

She still wouldn't look at Brenda. She showed no interest in her surroundings at all. Her eyes downcast, staring vacantly at the carpet.

"What does your mother call you?"

"Don't have a mother."

The echo was becoming more pronounced – as though the girl's voice was coming from a large empty room.

"What does your father call you?"

"Sacrifice."

Sacrifice? Brenda had heard some strange girl's names before, but Sacrifice?

"That's a ... that's a nice name. What do your friends call you?"

"Don't have any friends."

"But you must go to school."

"No."

Brenda paused. "How old are you?"

"Don't know."

Goosebumps. Brenda had never met a child who didn't know their age to the nearest three months. And the matter of fact way the girl was speaking. She wasn't frightened or shy.

"Where do you live?" asked Brenda.

"Don't know."

"Is it in a city?"

"Don't know."

"Do you live in a house or an apartment?"

The ghost shrugged, her eyes now riveted on her fingers and the tiny piece of T-shirt wrapped around them.

"What can you see out of your bedroom window?"

"Don't have a window."

Double goosebumps. Brenda had a very bad feeling about this.

"Why were you crying?"

"Because it hurt."

Brenda took a deep breath. If this were a living child she'd stop at this point and hand everything over to an expert. The girl had probably been abused. God knows what memories she had festering below the surface. Did Brenda have the right to force her to relive them?

Or were the dead inured to trauma?

She studied the girl, shuffling closer, bending down to look up into her face. She didn't seem agitated in any way. There was no quiver in her voice. If it wasn't for the tear-stained face and what she had to say, Brenda would have sworn she was fine.

But...

What if the girl started to cry, or became hysterical? Brenda couldn't hug her, or provide any form of physical support.

But if she let her fade away, which was the norm for all the ghosts Brenda had met – they rarely stayed for more than ten minutes – a child torturer could get away.

"Did your daddy hurt you?" asked Brenda.

The girl didn't speak. She just nodded.

"What's your daddy's name?"

"Daddy."

"What do other people call him?"

The girl shrugged.

"Do you see him with other people?"

"No."

"Are you allowed out of your room?"

"Never."

Brenda shivered. What should she do now? She had no idea of the girl's identity. Sacrifice didn't sound like a real name. She had no surname, no address. She couldn't even place the girl's accent. It might be local. It might be anywhere in the country.

A photograph! Brenda got up slowly and walked – fighting the urge to break into a run – to the drawer where she kept her camera. She pulled it out, fumbled with the controls, switched it on, turned, pointed it at the little girl and...

There was no little girl in the viewing screen. Brenda could see her, but the camera couldn't. She took the picture just in case, but held out little hope.

Frustration. There had to be something else she could do. But what? She couldn't take fingerprints. She couldn't make a sketch – she was useless at drawing, always had been.

'Brian!' She framed the thought and gave it as much power as she could, firing it through the ceiling and beyond. Surely he had to be somewhere out there. 'Come on! You wanted a murder victim. Here she is. Come and get her!'

No answer. The girl continued to play with the hem of her T-shirt. Brenda ran for the phone. Was there time to call Brian? Was HELL 666 a real number? She grabbed the phone, turned to check on Sacrifice and...

The girl was fading. Her outline blurring into its

surroundings.

"No! Sacrifice. Don't go! You're safe here."

The girl looked up, her features transparent and fading.

"Are you my mommy?" she said, her voice trailing away.

Then she was gone.

Chapter Seven

Brenda was still shaking five minutes later. She'd seen hundreds of ghosts, but none had touched her like Sacrifice. What the girl must have gone through. And for so long. Had she lived her entire life in a windowless cell?

She tapped Brian's number on the phone pad and waited. After three rings there was a click on the line, then a woman's voice in a slow and heavily accented eastern European drawl began to speak.

"You have reached switchboard from Hell. If you sold soul and now have question, press one. If you have soul and want quote, press two. If you want speak Satan, press 666. If you want speak Brian, press three."

Brenda shook her head. She was in no mood for jokes. But she pressed three just the same.

The Rolling Stones cranked out the opening bars to *Sympathy for the Devil*. Brenda rolled her eyes.

Then Sanjay's voice came on the line.

"Brian cannot be coming to the phone at this moment. Please be leaving message after the scream."

Scream?

Even with the warning it was still a shock when it came. A scream-queen ear-splitter that nearly knocked the phone from Brenda's hand.

"Brian! Stop messing around and get over here now. I've found a victim."

She slammed the phone down.

"Thank you for calling," said Sanjay. "Have an evil day."

She waited for Brian to call back. Made herself a cup of coffee. Waited some more. Where was he? Out on a case? Asleep in his coffin? Recharging his magical batteries?

She eschewed a second cup of coffee in favor of some

hardcore pacing, wearing out a channel between her bookcase and the door. What should she do next? Call the police? Wait for Brian?

She paced. She thought. She argued with herself.

Then she had an idea. The internet! Maybe she could trace the girl online?

She pulled out her laptop and started searching. She Googled murdered children. She Googled missing children. She Googled dead children – accidents, fires, anything.

And found a depressingly large number of hits. She tried to cut the numbers by adding the name 'Sacrifice' to the search. And found hundreds of links to ritualistic murders – most of them in Africa. She skimmed and searched, typed in new keywords, experimented with new combinations. An hour passed. Two. No picture of Sacrifice, but thousands of depressing stories. Every day over two thousand children went missing in the US. Nearly 600 infants under the age of five were murdered every year. She could surf for days and barely skim the surface.

And what if Sacrifice's body had never been found? What if she'd been locked in a windowless room all her life and the authorities never even knew she existed?

She switched the laptop off. And cursed Brian. Didn't they have pagers in hell?

She called HELL 666 again and received the same message from Sanjay and his Transylvanian sidekick. After the scream, she added her own.

~

The next day came and still no Brian. Did he only work on Saturdays? Brenda thought about leaving another message on his answering machine, but decided against it. For all she knew, HELL 666 could be another of Brian's little jokes – a dummy call center set up for comic relief, not for taking messages.

She'd go to the police instead.

And say what?

Hello, I'm the neighborhood psychic and I'd like to look through your files.

How far would that get her?

I'm a witness to a possible abduction.

She liked that better. It would certainly get their attention, but ... how would she follow it up? She had no idea when Sacrifice was killed, or where. It could be yesterday, it could be years in the past. And the first question the police would ask would be 'where and when did this abduction take place?' Brenda didn't have a clue.

Despondency. She had important information in a murder case and no way to impart it – without sounding like a crazy person and tainting every word that came out of her mouth.

Could she make up a story?

That improved her mood. She could invent a location. Tell them it happened locally just to get a look at their files.

Doubt swept back in. What if they only showed her pictures of local missing children? She needed to see pictures of every missing or murdered child from across the country.

She thought about it some more. She needed a good reason to access every file they had. Research? How about *I'm doing research for an article on abused children?* It was vague enough to give her a reason to look at all their files. But would she need ID? Some kind of reporter's accreditation, or letter from a university?

Time to blame Brian. Where was he? This was exactly the kind of thing he should be helping her with. He could fashion accreditation out of thin air.

Doubt, an ever-present in the Steele household, hopped back onto Brenda's shoulder. It whispered in her ear. She wasn't cut out for crime fighting. Four years ago the confident, adventurous Brenda had crashed and burned in the outside world. How could stay-at-home Brenda hope to fare any better? Stay home. Do what you're good at. Do what you enjoy. A month ago you were looking forward to the summer break. The Harriet Vane books are there – on the bookcase – waiting. Go on. You've already read the first chapter of *Strong Poison*. Pick it up.

No! Harriet Vane wouldn't have turned her back on a mystery and neither would Brenda. She'd drive to the police station now and ... bluff her way past the desk sergeant. She wasn't sure how, but women had been charming their way past men for thousands of years and Brenda could do charming.

As she drove to the police station, her plan grew flesh.

She was a freelance reporter researching for a book. A charming freelance reporter prepared to flirt, pout, and – if the situation called for it – burst into tears if she didn't get her way.

Brenda Steele, intrepid reporter, strode into the police station, crossed the small lobby, and headed straight for the desk sergeant.

"Good morning," she said, showing plenty of teeth, a winsome smile and a couple of buttons worth of cleavage. "My name's Brenda Steele and–"

Before she could finish a man interrupted her from behind.

"Sorry I'm late, Miss Steele. I was stuck in traffic."

Brenda swiveled on her heel. The man was a stranger. Twentysomething, dark suit, clean cut, embarrassed smile.

And he was holding an FBI badge.

He addressed the desk sergeant. "Hi, I'm agent Mulder. Miss Steele is assisting the FBI in a missing persons investigation."

Agent Mulder? Brenda and the desk sergeant both stared at the badge. And then at Brian – because it had to be Brian. Who else would turn up at a police station claiming to be Agent Mulder? At least he hadn't made himself look like David Duchovny.

"Agent Mulder?" said the desk sergeant. A smile had insinuated its way onto his lips.

"I know," said Brian. "It's a cross I bear every day. I thought of changing my name, but ... why should I? It'd be like disowning my parents."

'Brian?' Brenda poked the thought through the ether between them. 'It is you, isn't it?'

'Call me Fox,' came the reply.

Brenda mentally rolled her eyes.

'Where have you been! I've been calling since yesterday.'

Brian ignored her. "Miss Steele's helping us with a missing person investigation. We need access to your files."

"Don't you have your own files at the FBI?" asked the desk sergeant.

"This is closer. And, believe me, time is critical."

The desk sergeant shrugged. "Okay, I'll find a detective who can help."

Detective Sjoberg was a man in a hurry. He had five cases
on his desk. All of them far more important than babysitting
an FBI agent. Even if he was called Mulder.

'I think you should have come as Scully,' said Brenda via
the ether.

Sjoberg hurried them upstairs, taking the steps two at a
time. He bustled them through a large open plan office,
found a room they could use, logged them in to the state's
Missing and Exploited Children database and left.

"You can access the NCIC from there, too," he said from
the door. "I'll be next door if you need me."

He'd turned away and pulled the door closed before
Brenda or Brian had had time to thank him.

"Okay," said Brian. "Bring me up to speed."

"Can't you just read my mind?"

"I can only read surface thoughts, Brenda. So, if you're
not thinking about it, I can't hear it."

Brenda recounted her story. And how she tried to call
Brian several times with no response.

"What's the point of having a phone number if you never
answer?"

"I couldn't," said Brian. He looked embarrassed. Which
wasn't one of his usual looks. "Every time I use magic it ...
has a cost."

"What kind of cost?"

"It drains me. Not too much, but if I do a lot of magic over
a short time – especially the complex stuff – it can be
debilitating. More so the following day. It's like performing a
strenuous activity. You feel tired at the time, but it's not until
the next day that your muscles seize up. Except with magic
the pain's worse and your brain feels like it's been
carbonated under pressure and given a good shaking. Ever
had migraine?"

"No."

"Well, imagine the worst headache you've ever had and
throw in simultaneous bouts of toothache, earache, eyeball
ache and nausea. And the knowledge that there's nothing
you can take to dull the pain."

"You can't magic the pain away?"

"That's the last thing you'd want to try. Unless you're into exploding heads. No drugs or meditation technique can help, either. We demons have a devil of a life. Now, find me some paper."

She rummaged in her bag, pulled out a notepad and handed it to him.

"Do you want a pen?"

"Not yet."

He tore the front sheet from the notebook and pressed it flat against the desk. "Okay, think of Sacrifice. Bring her image to the front of your mind. That's it. Now zoom in on her face. Excellent. Hold it there."

His right hand moved over the paper, barely brushing its surface. A picture appeared, an almost perfect rendition of the image in Brenda's mind. Sacrifice. He'd even captured her faraway look.

"What do you think?" he asked. "Does that look like her? Anything need changing?"

"It's amazing," said Brenda. It could have been a photograph from last night.

"It's magic," said Brian.

He fed the picture into the document scanner attached to the computer terminal and tapped away at the keyboard.

"This might take a while," he said. "Without a name or date we're going to have to spread the search pretty wide. And hope Sacrifice wasn't abducted as a baby – that would stretch the photo recognition software beyond breaking point."

It did take a while. Brian fed the picture into both the state system and the FBI's National Crime Information Center. Long minutes passed. Eventually potential candidates began to appear on the screen. Brenda leaned closer for a better look. It was difficult. Some of the girls were four or five, some younger. All of them had a look of Sacrifice – around the eyes or the mouth – but none *were* Sacrifice. Or, at least, not that she could tell.

Doubt. After ruling out the first ten candidates she had to go back and look at them all again. Children could change so much. And pictures could lie. The angle the picture was taken from, a chance expression – all could combine to make one person look like another and vice versa.

But when the twelfth picture flashed on screen there was

no doubt. Brenda's voice caught in her throat. The girl's hair was different. Her face younger. But the features, that look...

"That's her," she said, pointing at the screen and backing away at the same time.

Brian clicked on the picture. The screen filled with details. Mary Alice Cassini, aged four, abducted from a park in Stamford, Connecticut, thirteen years ago. No witnesses, no suspects.

"What do we do now?" asked Brenda. "Visit the parents?"

"We need to find them first. This file's thirteen years old."

He typed and clicked, navigating from one screen to another faster than Brenda could keep up.

"You've done this before," said Brenda. The second the words were out of her mouth she felt stupid. Of course he'd done this before. He was a crime fighter. He'd have needed to trace thousands of people over the years. What better way to do that than hacking into the FBI?

"Even Santa does it," said Brian.

"What?"

"Santa. You don't think he really keeps his own book on who's been naughty or nice."

A new page flashed on screen. The FBI's Naughty or Nice Child Register.

"Do you want to see what it says about you?" asked Brian. "I can go back to any year."

Brenda shook her head – in disbelief. If Brian ever tired of crime fighting he had a ready-made career in television. Candid Camera with Brian – he'd make a fortune.

"But I wouldn't be happy, Brenda. All that attention – it's too dangerous for us demon folk."

He tapped and clicked some more, tracking down both parents – they divorced two years after Mary Alice went missing. Was that significant? The mother remarried and now lived in Greenwich and the father, Frank Cassini, appeared to be living over the family store.

Brian printed off details of both parents, then went back and printed off three pages of the investigation into Mary Alice's abduction.

"Now, I think we visit the father," said Brian. "If anyone's a strong candidate for 'Daddy' it has to be him."

Chapter Eight

They drove back to Brenda's house to drop off the car. During the drive, Brian took the opportunity to send his inner eye roving across the countryside in search of Frank Cassini.

Brenda was intrigued. And jealous. Being able to project your sight must be like being able to fly – without the fear of gravity to send you crashing into the ground. You'd be able to soar like a bird and fly unconstrained – no seat belt, no engine noise, no ears to pop.

"Do you follow roads?" she asked.

"How do you mean?"

"When you're projecting your eyes. Do you follow the roads, or cut across country like a bird?"

"A bit of both. If I get a good bearing on where I want to go I set off fast across country, climbing to about ten thousand feet if there's not too much cloud. But it's easy to get lost so you need to drop down low and find a road sign occasionally."

She stopped at the lights and turned to watch him. She found it fascinating. The idea of having your body sitting in a car while your eyes roamed elsewhere. What would it be like? One sense telling you you're flying, the other four filling your brain with contradictory information. If he had a brain, that is. Maybe he had several?

Brian's head rolled slowly to the right. Was he following his eyes as they dived out of the clouds? His head straightened, then turned sharply towards her. His eyes were unfocussed and...

A car horn from behind informed her that the lights had changed. Reluctantly she turned her eyes back to the road and pulled away.

"Found him!" said Brian a minute or two later. "He's in his shop. I'll find a quiet place nearby and wait. How long until you're home?"

"Two minutes tops."

"Excellent. We'll set off as soon you get the car in the garage and out of sight."

"No," said Brenda firmly. "I'm going to the bathroom first. I'm not going to get stuck like last time."

They arrived in Stamford behind a dumpster in an alley off a busy street. Once more Brenda felt like she was about to pitch forward and once more she didn't. Not that it stopped her from pushing both arms out in front of her just in case. One day she'd get used to it.

She took a deep breath, inhaling an exotic mix of fried food, spices and something unpleasant which hopefully was coming from the dumpster and not from something she'd stepped on.

She checked just in case, lifting one shoe, then the other. Both clear.

"Come on," said Brian. "The shop's just round the corner."

Brenda followed Brian out of the alley into one of those run-down, low-rent streets often seen on the edge of large towns. Small stores, lots of ethnic restaurants, large immigrant population, graffiti. And there, three doors away, was Frank Cassini's convenience store.

Brian handed Brenda a black wallet. "Here, take this. You're Watson and I'm Agent Holmes, Cold Cases."

Brenda flipped open the wallet. It looked official – to her untrained eye. There was a badge, an authentic looking FBI logo, her picture. But the name...

"Shouldn't it be Agent Watson not Doctor Watson?"

Brian waved her objection away. "He'll never notice."

"Why take the risk? Why not be Agent Smith and Jones."

Brian looked hurt. "I am *not* a Smith or a Jones. I'm a Maigret or a Poirot. But if you're really worried I'll drop the Sherlock." He brushed a hand over his FBI badge. "There, I'm now Hercule Holmes. Do you think I should add a moustache?"

Brenda rolled her eyes. If she ever got through this day...

They stopped outside the convenience store and looked in the window. Four narrow aisles of packed shelves with one

Frank Cassini – Brenda recognized him from his picture – sitting behind a single till. He didn't look like the kind of man who'd imprison his child and kill her, but then, who did? According to his file he was thirty-nine and five ten. He'd filled out some over the last thirteen years, and his once-black, curly hair was now flecked with grey and receding.

"Okay," said Brian, putting on a Belgian accent. "The game, she is afoot."

They went inside. The store wasn't busy. There were a couple of women browsing in the far aisles. Brian ambled over to the till and flashed his badge while Brenda hung back and tried to exude an aura of sensible law enforcement.

"Can we have a word?" said Brian, ditching his Belgian accent in favor of a soft southern drawl. "It's about Mary Alice."

"Have you found her?"

Brenda wasn't sure if she sensed hope in Frank Cassini's voice or fear. He was nervous – that was obvious – the second Brian flashed his badge the man's breath caught and his eyes darted towards the door.

"Not yet," said Brian. "Can we talk in private?"

Frank Cassini called to an assistant in the back room and asked her to take his place at the check out. She didn't look happy about it. She glared at Frank.

"It's nearly eleven," she said.

"I know," said Frank. "I won't be long."

Brenda hung back as Frank led Brian into the back of the store. She watched the assistant take her seat behind the till. She was in her early thirties, dark haired, and thoroughly pissed off. Why? It wasn't as though the store was busy.

Brenda caught up with Brian, who'd been shown into a small cluttered room at the back – a cross between a kitchen and a stock room. It had a sink, a table, a couple of chairs and piles of crates and boxes.

"Sorry about the mess," said Frank, dusting off one of chairs.

"About Mary Alice," said Brian. "Did she have many friends?"

Brian's delivery was slower and more considered than his usual quick fire banter. Maybe he was taking his time while he read the man's mind? Or maybe this was Brian playing good cop?

"What's this all about? Are you re-opening the case?"

"We're from Cold Cases, Mr. Cassini. Your daughter's is one that we're considering re-investigating. Did she have many friends?"

Cassini looked confused, glancing from Brian to Brenda and back again. But he answered the question.

"Yes, she had lots of friends."

"Friends from school?"

"From kindergarten. And from the neighborhood. We lived in Southfield then."

"You moved house?"

"Yes. Susan and I. My wife. My ex-wife. We got divorced ten years ago. She – we – never got over losing Mary Alice. I live over the store now."

"On your own?"

"Yes."

His reply was fast. And he glanced towards the door. Was he living with his assistant? Miss Marple would have known. She'd have been reminded of someone she knew from St. Mary Mead. But Brenda wasn't Miss Marple. She was no expert at reading body language. She hadn't spent a lifetime observing others.

But she could learn. And she would learn. If she wasn't so nervous, this would be fun. Her very first interview with a suspect. It was like stepping inside the pages of a book.

Brian switched his attention to the piles of boxes lining the room. "Don't you have a cellar?"

"No."

Brian looked puzzled. "I thought all these buildings had cellars."

"No."

Cassini didn't look fazed by the question. Brenda wondered what Brian was picking up from his thoughts. Was Frank picturing Mary Alice imprisoned in her windowless room?

"Did your old house in Southfield have a cellar?"

This time there was a reaction.

"No! Why are you asking about cellars? Have you found something?"

"We're following up on a lead, Mr. Cassini. There are

similarities with another case we're working on where a girl
was abducted. That girl was held captive in a windowless
room."

Brian paused and watched Cassini, who swallowed hard.

"What happened to the other girl? Is she alive?"

"I'm not at liberty to say, but do you know of any cellars or
windowless rooms? In a neighbor's house maybe? Or a
friend of the family? An old workplace, or a cabin you took
your family to?"

"No."

His answer was quick. Very quick. Brenda couldn't work
him out. Was he a grieving father struggling to keep his
emotions in check? Or Daddy, the child murderer trying to
blot out what he'd done? Brenda couldn't tell. And why did
he keep checking his watch?

"Sacrifice," said Brian – completely out of the blue.

Frank Cassini looked confused. But not shocked.

"Pardon?" he said.

"Sorry, I was thinking aloud. Thinking of all the sacrifices
that parents make for their children. I expect you made
sacrifices too."

"Yes."

Now he was looking even more impatient and glancing
towards the door.

"What happens at eleven?" asked Brian.

Frank's eyes widened. An instant of startled rabbit fear
and then it was gone.

"Nothing," he said, his face softening into a smile. "She's
worried about her coffee break, that's all."

Brian slapped his hands on his thighs and rose from his
chair. "Thank you, Mr. Cassini. That'll be all for now."

"Well?" asked Brenda the moment they'd left the store.

"Walk with me," said Brian.

They headed back to the alley.

"Something's wrong back there," said Brian. "I don't know
what, but it's going to happen at eleven."

"Couldn't you read his thoughts?"

"It doesn't work every time. It's easiest when people are
calm and concentrating – like when I ask you to think aloud.
But when people are nervous, or distracted, their thoughts

can be all over the place – nothing more than a jumble of scrambled words and images."

"You didn't get *anything*?"

"I got snippets, but nothing concrete. My badge panicked him. *Really* panicked him. But it didn't appear related to Mary Alice. As soon as I mentioned her name – a new set of thoughts swirled in. Flashbacks, disjointed memories, images of his daughter. But none of her being locked in a cellar or abused. Then he started to panic again – he thought we'd found her body. But whether that was the natural fear of a parent or the guilty fear of a murderer, I couldn't tell. And from then on his brain was all over the place. I didn't even get a reaction when I said 'Sacrifice.' The only constant was a wish for us to be gone and out of the shop as soon as possible. That and the number eleven. Something is going to happen at eleven o'clock and it's scaring the crap out of him."

Brenda checked her watch. It was five to eleven.

"Do we stay and watch?"

"Indeed we do. Though not like this. I think a disguise is called for."

He changed before her eyes. Years dropped off him – and pounds – he morphed into a gangling adolescent – thirteen, fourteen – with acne and lank, greasy hair.

"Do I get a disguise too?"

Brenda's vanity had wrested control of her vocal chords before her sensible genes could react. But now they were reacting. Having years and pounds stripped away may be a huge tick in the plus column, but Brian had a puckish sense of humor which was an even bigger tick in the minus column. And wouldn't it deplete his magical reserves?

"I think I can risk a minor makeover," said Brian, leaning back and tilting his head to one side in an appraising stare.

Before she could react Brian's hand darted out and closed around her left hand. Instinctively she struggled to pull free, but he held on, staring into her eyes for two whole seconds while her flesh tingled and burned.

"There," he said. "I think that should do."

Shit! Her clothes had changed. Some hideous dress that looked like it had been spawned by a pair of mutant bathroom curtains – bright colors, huge flowers and … giant lobsters! What the hell were giant lobsters doing on chrysanthemums?

Her hands flew to her face. No beard, so that was a plus. But something felt different. Her nose! It was smaller. And her hair! It was big and falling around her face in curls.

Instinctively she looked for her purse, but she'd left it back at the house. So much for travelling light. She needed a mirror. She needed a mirror now!

"Will this do?" asked Brian, holding up his right hand. He'd flattened and glazed his palm into a hand shaped mirror. Brenda grabbed it and stared.

It was like seeing a stranger. A big-haired blonde with too much make-up.

But...

She liked the nose. Back in her teens she'd even considered having a nose job. Until her best friend, Jackie Lowell, had filled her head with Michael Jackson horror stories. *First the nose, then you turn albino and your ears drop off.* But now...

Maybe she *should* have a nose job. Maybe Brian would let her keep the nose! Lose the hair and clothes, but the nose was a keeper.

"You want to lose your clothes?"

"No!" She let go of his hand and wrapped her arms tight around her body. And felt ... different. Bigger. She looked down, her eyes widening. Are my boobs bigger?

"I thought they went with the character."

Brenda was incandescent. She'd been violated. "You can't touch my boobs!"

"I didn't. I just thought them larger."

"Thought! You shouldn't even think about my boobs." She paused to take a breath. "Did you think my boobs were too small? No! Don't answer that! Don't even think about that."

She backed away from him, holding her arms out as if somehow that would fend him off.

He looked confused. He flexed his right hand and morphed it back to a human hand shape. "Do you want me to put you back as you were?"

"No! No touching. No thinking." She wanted desperately to have a look at what he'd done to her. Knowing Brian he might have given her five nipples.

"I didn't."

"You're *thinking*! I said *no* thinking. My nipples are not a topic for conversation."

Especially from a fourteen year-old boy.

Brian checked his watch and thankfully changed the subject. "It's nearly eleven. We've got to go. I'll take the shop. You find somewhere close by."

Brenda lingered in the alley for an extra second or two to check on the girls.

'Mmmm, nice,' echoed a voice in her head.

'Brian!'

'Just getting into character. I'm a fourteen year-old boy, remember?'

Brenda stormed out of the alley. The dress was too tight. The hair too big. The shoes didn't match anything, and the least said about the lobsters the better. She looked like she'd just stepped out of an eighties trailer park seafood restaurant.

'You'll pay for this.' She threw the thought at Brian's disappearing back as he jogged along the sidewalk. He didn't react. He didn't even glance her way when he turned into Cassini's convenience store.

"Urrrgh!" Brenda was about to stamp her foot too, but thought better of it. Her dress was already attracting too much attention – people not wearing dark glasses were having to shield their eyes. The sooner she got the lobsters off the street the better. She noticed a cafe opposite. She'd nip over there and wait.

As soon as she ordered her coffee, two large men – neither of whom Brenda would have wished to meet in an empty parking lot – entered the convenience store over the road.

Chapter Nine

Brian was standing by the comic rack at the back of the shop when they came in. The sense of fear from Frank Cassini was palpable, his thoughts condensed to the words 'oh, God' repeated over and over again.

"Have you got it?" asked the older of the two men. He was in his late twenties, six two, well-built, expensive suit. He looked like a Mafia enforcer – dark hair, designer stubble, and giant hands. His friend just looked like a thug – six four, broken nose, tracksuit, and tattoos. He stood by the door, arms folded and feet planted slightly apart.

Frank Cassini handed over an envelope. A payment? The furtive way he produced the white envelope from beneath the counter suggested as much.

"It feels light," said the Enforcer clone, hefting the envelope.

"It's been a bad week. I'll make it up next time."

"You'll make it up now."

Brian kept perfectly still. He was behind a comic rack at the end of one of the four small aisles. The top shelf was at shoulder height, the comic rack a foot higher. It wasn't the best hiding place, but neither of the newcomers had given the aisles more than a cursory glance. Which was strange. Everything about the transaction cried out shakedown. Why weren't they concerned about witnesses?

He tried to scan the men's thoughts, but they were at the edge of his range. Only Frank was readable, but the adrenaline that magnified his thoughts garbled them as well – running them together into an over-amplified mess. What had Frank gotten himself mixed up in? Blackmail? Protection racket? Loan sharks?

Could someone have found out about Mary Alice and started blackmailing him?

Brian had to get closer. He stepped out into the center of the aisle. "What yer doing?" he asked.

Enforcer turned and glared. Most street-wise fourteen year-old boys would have taken the hint. Brian stuffed his hands in his pockets and ambled forward.

"What yer doing?" he repeated.

"Beat it, kid." Enforcer hooked a thumb towards the door. Thug opened it for him.

Brian walked closer, smiling innocently. He was within range now. He focussed his mind on Enforcer and asked, "Are you blackmailers?" He added a wide-eyed excitement to his delivery. This would be his role – the star-struck teenage wannabe hoodlum.

"I'm not telling you twice, kid. Fuck off."

Enforcer was annoyed and impatient, but there was no reaction to the blackmail question – not physically nor mentally. Brian moved to the next question.

"I bet you're loan sharks, aren't you? I can help if you want. Let me hold him down while you hit him."

Disbelief from Enforcer, sprinkled with a growing anger, but no reaction to the loan shark comment.

There was, however, a reaction from Thug. He'd moved away from the door and was now striding down the next aisle. He was going to block Brian's escape, come at him from behind, sweep him up, give him a couple of slaps and throw him onto the street.

Brian was running out of time. "Is it protection money?" he asked. "I bet he can't pay. Shall I start pulling food off the shelves and smashing the place up?"

That got a reaction. Protection money, can't pay, smash the place up. Frank spiked on all three. And kept on spiking. *No, no, no! What are you doing, kid! Don't wind these guys up. I could have found the extra hundred. Now they won't stop.*

The two hoods did their share of reacting too. Rage, exasperation. It came off them in waves. Brian was going to get more than a slap. Enforcer moved to block one end of the aisle while Thug covered the rear.

"Aw, come on," said Brian, still smiling, still radiating a childlike enthusiasm. "Cut me in on the action. I can be your apprentice. Like on TV."

A large hand grabbed him from behind, scrunching his jacket up just below his neck and hoisting him off his feet. He dangled for a second, the tips of his toes just touching the floor, listening – listening to the thoughts of the man whose breath he could feel on the back of his neck. Thug was a killer. Images of previous victims flashed through his mind. Men begging for their lives. Men kneeling on the ground. He could snap Brian's neck without hesitation.

Which would open up a restaurant size can of worms. Brian didn't want to reprise his headless zombie act. Or be rushed into anything precipitous. He hadn't finished probing these men's minds and one thing he'd learned over the years was that humans tended not to think straight when placed in close proximity to a headless zombie.

"Get him out of here," snapped Enforcer.

Brian was carried up the aisle, then thrown towards the check out desk. Thug intended it to hurt, pitching Brian off balance hoping he'd hit his head or a shoulder on the sharp wooden edge. But Brian had read the thought and threw out his arms, cushioning the fall.

Thug kicked him – hard – below the ribs then picked him up, marched him to the open door and threw him out. This time Brian couldn't keep his balance and hit the ground hard, landing on his shoulder and hip. He rolled once, then flung out an arm to stop to himself. The shop door slammed shut behind him.

No one came to help him. The street was busy, but only a few people even glanced his way. He scanned their thoughts. *Walk on. Don't get involved. Stupid kid. Bet he was stealing.* And other thoughts in languages he didn't understand which probably distilled down to the same collective thought. *Walk on by. Don't get involved. It could be dangerous.*

This was not a neighborhood with a strong sense of community.

Brian jumped to his feet and looked towards the shop. The two hoods were at the till talking to Frank. Any second now they were going to hurt him.

They weren't even watching the door.

Which meant they didn't care. The street was busy. There were hundreds of potential witnesses. They'd even drawn attention to the shop by throwing Brian out onto the street.

And yet... he hadn't picked up one concerned thought from either of the two hoods about being observed. Yes, they'd wanted Brian out of the way. But only after he'd spoken up. No one had bothered to search the shop for customers before that, or lock the door to prevent anyone else coming in. The door was still unlocked now. Anyone could walk in.

Which meant they *really* didn't care. The whole street was probably in fear of them. Every business paying them protection money. They could do what they wanted with impunity knowing that no one would testify or call the police.

And where was Frank's assistant? She'd been in the back of the shop ten minutes earlier. She obviously knew the men were coming at eleven. Was she still in there, hiding?

Brian had to act. He'd made things worse. Innocent people could get hurt. And there were several questions still unanswered.

He ran over to the door and opened it. Thug had a gun pointed at Frank Cassini's head. Enforcer was taking money from the open till drawer.

"Wow!" said Brian. "Is that a Glock?"

The Glock turned Brian's way. "Get out!"

"Can I hold it?" said Brian, playing for time as he desperately tried to think of a plan that didn't involve anyone getting shot in the head.

Enforcer was on him in two strides. One ape-like hand folded around Brian's face and shoved him into the street while the other slammed the door shut behind him.

Brian hit the sidewalk hard, first with the seat of his pants, then his back and head. But this time someone offered him a helping hand.

~

Brenda had been watching from the cafe opposite. The first time Brian had been thrown onto the sidewalk, she felt he'd probably deserved it. But the second time – well, he probably deserved that too, but she was his partner and partners had obligations.

"What happened?" she asked, pulling him to his feet.

Brian filled her in as quickly as he could, breaking off every now and then to run over to the store door and bang on the glass, or give them a smile and a thumbs up sign. Anything to keep them distracted.

And all the while a plan was forming, deep in the sneaky half of his brain.

"You want me to do what?" asked Brenda.

"Play my mother."

"I'm too young to have a fourteen year-old son!"

"The new you isn't. Come on! We don't have much time. We've got to get those thugs out of the shop and onto the street."

Brenda looked at the store, then back at Brian. "You *have* placed a bullet-proof shield around me?"

"Like I said, it's an *everything*-proof shield."

Brenda thought about it for another second. She could do this. She was angry enough. This would be a chance to vent. She took another look at the mutant dress Brian had inflicted upon her. Then she grabbed his hand and tugged him towards the store. Two thugs were about to come face to face with the pushy mother from trailer park hell.

She threw the door open.

"Why won't you let my boy be in your gang?"

Three heads turned her way. One red Frank Cassini head – which was wrapped in an arm lock – and two startled hoodlum heads.

"Well?" she said, tapping her right foot. "I'm waiting. And put that man down when I'm speaking to you."

The two hoods exchanged confused looks. Thug maintained his grip around Frank's neck and Enforcer pulled his jacket back to show the gun holstered at his hip.

"Beat it, lady," he said.

Brenda leaned forward, screwing up her eyes in a myopic stare. "What am I supposed to be looking at? Are you trying to show me something in your trousers?"

Enforcer blinked. He was disconcerted, and at the same time struggling to control his anger. He pulled out the gun and pointed it at Brenda.

"It's a gun, lady, now beat it-"

"Call that a gun? My grandmother's got a bigger gun than that."

"It's a Glock," said Brian, still clutching Brenda's hand. "He wouldn't let me hold it."

"Is that true? You wouldn't let my boy hold your gun?"

"Lady, get the fuck out. Now!"

Brenda recognized the 'you've pushed me too far' look on Enforcer's face.

She sent a thought to Brian. 'How do you know if a protective shield's working? Is there a battery full light?'

'Don't worry, Bren. You're doing fine. He's thinking about scaring you, not shooting you.'

Brenda changed tack. She craned her neck and made a show of staring at Thug and Frank.

"What are you doing here, anyway? Robbery?" she asked.

"Lady–"

"With no look out, or anyone on the door. You guys must be real amateurs."

"I'm not telling you twice."

Enforcer stepped forward and leveled his gun at Brenda's new, improved nose. His eyes burned.

The old Stay-at-Home Brenda would have turned and run. Even London Brenda would have been cowed. But Trailer-Park Brenda stood her ground. She had a protective shield, and a mission.

"Or what?" she said. "You're going to shoot me in front of a street full of people? Take a look behind me. See the woman with the camera phone?"

There wasn't a woman with a camera phone – not as far as Brenda knew – but there could have been. There were enough people in the street – walking by, milling around store doorways, chatting. Enough to make Enforcer look. And think twice.

"Get out!" he said. "Or...." He turned the gun on Brian, keeping his eyes locked on Brenda. Back came the cool killer confidence as he spoke. "Or I'll find out which school your boy goes to."

The same thought arose simultaneously in Brian and Brenda's minds. Mary Alice Cassini. Had she been abducted to put pressure on her father? Maybe to teach him a lesson?

Another thought entered Brenda's mind. This time from Brian. 'Time to leave,' he said. 'We need to regroup outside.'

"What about Frank?" asked Brenda once they were back on the sidewalk. "We can't leave him in there."

"We're not going to. This is just a time out. We need to get them outside and the best way to do that is to make them come to us."

"How?"

"By standing outside the shop and making a nuisance of ourselves."

"Do you think they abducted Mary Alice?"

Brian shook his head. "Not this crew. They're too young to have been active thirteen years ago. But the people they work for could have."

"But Sacrifice was imprisoned by one man."

"Did she tell you that?"

Brenda couldn't remember. The girl had only spoken about 'Daddy', but had Brenda asked the right questions?

"Did you pick anything up from the two men?" she asked.

"Enough to know that the threat to abduct me was real. They've taken children before. When Enforcer made the threat, I saw an image of a boy climbing into their car. And it wasn't me."

Chapter Ten

"Hey," shouted Brenda, pointing theatrically at the door to the Cassini convenience store some eight feet away. "There's a couple of guys in there robbing the store. Call 911!"

Up and down the street, people stopped what they were doing and looked her way. None reached for a phone.

The door to Cassini's flew open and out came Thug, six foot four of tattooed attitude. He glared at Brenda, then up and down the street.

"Nothing's happening here," he shouted. "The woman's crazy." He pointed at his temple and did the finger twirl.

Brenda didn't appreciate the finger twirl.

"Who you calling crazy, big nose?"

Thug didn't appear to appreciate the allusion to his broken nose.

"Shut the fuck up, you crazy bitch."

"Or what, big nose? You gonna come over here and hit me with your trunk?"

Thug produced a gun from his waistband and pointed it at Brian. "You've five seconds to fuck off or the kid gets it."

Brenda folded her arms, right over left, then - thinking that left over right felt more menacing - switched.

"In front of all these witnesses? Are you an *idiot*? Has that nose sucked all the sense out of you?"

She was enjoying this. There was something exhilarating - cathartic even - about hurling insults at a street thug. Never in a million years would she have dared to even look someone like Big Nose in the eye and yet, with Brian's protective shield, she could do anything she wanted. As long as Brian wasn't lying about the protective shield...

'It's operating at maximum power,' said Brian's voice in her head. Disconcertingly it had the slippery tone of a used

96

snake oil salesman.

"One," said Thug.

A small crowd was beginning to gather, most people stayed well back, those close by stood and stared. Only one man tried to intervene – a short, middle-aged man who'd been standing in the neighboring doorway. He sidled up to Brenda, glancing nervously at Thug with every step, nodding his head to him like a vassal to his master.

"Lady," he said in a heavy Italian accent. "Please come away. This man he dangerous. He will hurt you and your son."

"Two."

Brenda shrugged him off, not taking her eyes off Thug. "Not yet," she said. "I'm waiting to see if Big Nose can count to five."

Big Nose, aka Thug, almost lost it. He bared gritted teeth and narrowed his eyes in a feral glare.

"Three," he spat.

Brenda's middle-aged Italian grabbed her arm again. "Please, lady! Come with me."

A woman from the crowd joined in. "He's right. It's not worth it. Walk away."

Brenda shrugged them all off and pulled Brian towards her, pushing him behind her.

Thug's gun swung to point at Brenda. He was beginning to sweat. He shifted his weight from one foot to the other.

"Four," he said. "Standing in front of your kid won't help. I'll shoot you both."

The small crowd, which up to that point, had been growing, split. People nearest turned and ran. People over the road, behind Brenda, dived for cover. Others crouched, or pulled their children close.

Only Brenda remained calm. "Hey!" she shouted. "You in the store. Your boyfriend's out here making a fool of himself."

Time, as it does during moments of extreme stress, slowed to a geriatric crawl. Brenda's internal voice, which for the past ten minutes had been hiding speechless with her hands welded in front of her eyes, screamed at Brenda in disbelief. *What are you doing? Are you insane? You're staring down a gun barrel thinking that bullets are going to bounce off you!*

Well, wake up, Brenda! Bullets don't bounce off human flesh!

Brian interceded. 'You're doing brilliantly and you're safe. The man's bluffing. He wants to shoot, but he knows there's too many witnesses. He wants you to back down. Follow the plan and everyone wins.'

The plan. She couldn't believe Brian's plan when he'd first told her a couple of minutes earlier. They were in the middle of a case trying to track down the killer of a murdered girl. They had a lead that maybe the girl had been snatched by a gang to put pressure on the father. A sensible plan would have been to phone the police, let *them* save Frank Cassini, then have Brian follow the two hoods back to their base and...

That's where her sensible plan had petered out. If only Brian had an inner ear he could project to listen to remote conversations. But no, he'd said, we've got to visit the gang in person and question them. And just because we're on a case doesn't mean we look the other way if we see another crime. We're crime fighters, Bren, we don't get to pick and choose. This neighborhood needs our help and my plan achieves that *and* gets us an invite to see the gang's boss.

As long as Brenda wasn't dead. Or fending off the media after a hundred witnesses reported seeing bullets bounce off her face.

Brenda was still arguing with her various selves when the store door burst open and Enforcer ran out.

"What the fuck is going on out here?" he said. "Put that gun down and get back inside. And you assholes, beat it! There's nothing to see."

Big Nose didn't move. His gun remained leveled at Brenda.

"Scott! Inside!"

"Go on, Big Nose," said Brenda. "Your boyfriend's calling."

Brenda felt Brian's hands encircle her waist and lock together. His body pressed tighter against her back too.

'What are you doing?' she asked.

There was no reply. Had he sensed that Big Nose was about to shoot? Was he strengthening her shield? Preparing to teleport? Preparing to shapeshift her into an armor-plated beetle?

"Scott!"

Big Nose lowered the gun. His scowl morphed into a sneer. "I've seen your face, bitch. One night soon you're gonna see mine."

He ran a finger across his throat.

"I'll leave the door unlocked," said Brenda.

Big Nose didn't just reach the end of his tether, he overshot it at a gallop. Up came the gun, his face contorted in rage. Enforcer grabbed him from behind and tried to wrestle his gun arm down.

"No!" shouted Enforcer as they struggled, faces reddening. "We'll deal with her later. Come inside!"

He pulled Big Nose back towards the store.

"Go on," said Brenda. "Run inside and hide. You hoods are all the same. Pathetic!"

For a moment it looked as though both men were going to charge Brenda, but Enforcer maintained his grip on his colleague.

"Lady, you are *really* pushing it," he said. "Now fuck off before I let him loose on you."

"What, him?" She stared Big Nose in the eye. "Take away his gun and he's nothing. Come on, Big Nose. You and me. No guns, no knives."

She stepped forward, breaking Brian's hold around her waist and beckoned at the six foot four struggling mass of muscle. "From what I hear you only hit old men when your boyfriend pins their arms back. You can't hit a moving target."

Brenda put up her fists and danced in front of him. Brenda's inner voice hung her head in her hands. Brenda, Brenda, Brenda.

But Brenda was enjoying this. Invulnerability was such a wonderful thing to have. Now all she needed was Brian to make good with his other promise.

"I'll kill you!" shrieked Big Nose, struggling wildly. Enforcer had given up trying to pull him inside the shop. He was having enough trouble preventing him from flying at Brenda.

Brian sidled up to the rear of the struggling pair, reaching tentatively towards Enforcer and touching him ever so lightly on the elbow.

"Do you want me to help you get him back inside?" he asked.

"Fuck off, kid," snarled Enforcer.

Brian let his outstretched hand linger, brushing the tips of his fingers against Big Nose's arm, before standing back.

The crowd, which had run for cover earlier, was now back and growing. People were coming out of doorways all along the street. Traffic was stopping. People were asking what's happening? Who is she?

And Brenda was dancing. She'd seen footage of Muhammad Ali. She knew how to float like butterfly – even in a tight dress and heels. And she knew how to goad an opponent.

"Big Nose is going down in five. He too ugly to realize."

Brian knew a thing or two about goading, too.

"It's not too late to run, Mr. Nose," he said. "No one'll blame you for being a big girlie chicken."

Big Nose broke free and charged at Brenda ... like a toppling redwood. Brian had tied his shoelaces together.

Big Nose's gun bounced out of his hand and skittered across the road. With a timely telekinetic shove from Brian it not only changed direction slightly, but maintained its speed all the way to a drain at the curb opposite. Splash.

Brenda stopped dancing to peer down at Big Nose. "Boy, you are one pathetic hoodlum."

Big Nose jack-knifed on the ground, his hands wrenching at his shoelaces, pulling and prying. Brenda used the time to move into the center of the road and Brian snuck into the restaurant next door.

Try as he might, Big Nose couldn't undo the laces. Brian had fashioned a knot fused at its core.

Brenda milked the situation, turning to the crowd. "Is there a grown-up who can help Big Nose with his laces?"

A few people laughed. Most kept quiet. There had to be around three hundred people watching from various vantage points. Most of them looked confused. Unsure if they were watching an unlikely reincarnation of Joan of Arc, or an impending train wreck. Brenda wondered if anyone had called the police. She hadn't seen one person with a phone to their ear.

Over to Brenda's right, Enforcer bent down to help his

friend. Big Nose pushed him away. Then started loosening the laces on each shoe, yanking one off then the other.

"You are going to pay big time," he shouted to Brenda as he jumped to his stockinged feet.

Brenda braced herself. And that's when she noticed she was on her own.

'Brian! Where are you?'

No answer. He'd left her in the lurch again.

She disguised her panic with a breezy smile and danced up onto her toes.

'Brian!'

Big Nose charged across the road towards her, his face contorted into a growl, his enormous arms protruding from his shoulders like a couple of giant pincers.

'Duck left!' came a shout emanating from the center of her brain. She ducked left. Big Nose's huge right arm swung prematurely as though he was trying to grab someone standing in front of Brenda and over to her right. The whole top half of his body followed this wild lurch, spinning him counter-clockwise. He lost his balance, tripped over his legs, shot past the ducking Brenda and crashed to the ground.

'Get ready to catch,' said Brian.

'Catch what?' Brenda straightened up to look for Brian. Just in time to see a red bottle flying towards her from the sidewalk. She caught it. Just. It was a squeezy bottle of tomato ketchup.

'Remember,' said Brian. 'The plan is to ridicule not maim. If you beat him up, people are going to think *you're* special and nothing changes. But if you make *him* look a fool, then they're going to think *he's* a joke and away goes the fear and the wall of silence that keeps these gangs in business.'

That was the elegance of Brian's plan. Now came the fun part.

Big Nose was incensed. He'd risen to his knees and had just slapped the ground hard with both hands when Brenda struck. A one second burst of ketchup to the back of his neck. He swung round, startled, red-faced and soon to get even redder. A half-second burst of red gloop to the eyes.

Brenda danced backwards out of range of a blindly swinging Big Nose, her steps, by necessity – thanks to the dress – short and fast, her thumbs squeezing the bottle, a red stream arcing from her hands to his face.

'Throw the ketchup to the crowd,' said Brian. 'And get ready to catch.'

Brenda lobbed the ketchup towards a group of women to her right. Most recoiled as if thrown something radioactive. But one reached out and caught it. Brenda noticed Brian out of the corner of her eye and turned towards him. He was in the road now, moving behind the first rank of onlookers. He tossed a yellow bottle towards her. She caught it. Another squeezy bottle. This time mustard. Nice.

Big Nose was on his feet, blinking. He'd rubbed most of the ketchup away from his eyes, but from the way he was flexing his shoulders most of the ketchup on his neck was now dribbling down his back.

He charged, but this time slowed a yard or two short from Brenda and adopted a boxer's stance. He wasn't taking any chances. Brenda was on the balls of her feet too, waiting for instructions.

She never heard Enforcer come up behind her. She didn't have time to react when his hands dug into her biceps and squeezed her body together like a vice. Where was her protective shield? 'Brian? What's happening?'

Big Nose smiled and drew back his right shoulder ready to unleash a punch to her face.

'Don't move,' said Brian.

Don't move! She was about to get her nose broken. Her nice new nose. Shouldn't she kick out with her feet? Move her head to the right or left?

Big Nose swung, stepping into the punch and unleashing his full weight behind it. It hit Brenda hard – in the hair that cascaded around and above her left ear – but hit Enforcer harder, crashing into his jaw. Something had deflected the punch wide. Whether it was the late activation of her protective shield or Brian's telekinesis she didn't care.

Enforcer staggered backwards, releasing the startled Brenda who ducked to her right before bouncing back up with both hands clenched around fifteen ounces of hot, tangy mustard.

The even more startled Big Nose, who was staring alternately at his right fist and his fallen comrade, received a one-second burst to his ear.

Someone in the crowd laughed nervously. Others less so. Someone clapped.

And Brenda danced. She threw the mustard bottle into the crowd. Several hands reached for it. Brian tossed her a new bottle. Mayonnaise.

Big Nose flapped at the mustard dripping from his left ear, but he was more concerned about his friend, who was lying on his back, mouth open and looking suspiciously unconscious.

"Sorry," he said to his prone companion. "I don't know what happened."

Brenda glooped them both with salad dressing.

Big Nose exploded. Growling, he came at her, swinging blindly, his face streaked and dripping, his hair lightly tossed in a mustard vinaigrette.

That's when the Black Forest Gateau hit him – thrown out of the crowd by Brian – plenty of cream and, from what Brenda could see, quite a bit of jam and chocolate too. It hit Big Nose square on the side of his face and showed considerable adhesive qualities. Big Nose tried to scrape it off, but strangely experienced a breakdown in hand eye co-ordination – or, more accurately, finger eye co-ordination. His right eye, which one-second earlier had been full of cream was now accommodating an index finger too.

"Ow!" he shouted, followed by "ulpffft." Moral: it is never wise to open your mouth wide whilst standing within squirting distance of an opponent with a 15 ounce squeezy bottle of salad dressing.

The crowd went wild. A woman ran out of the crowd and hit Big Nose with a stream of ketchup. A man followed suit with mustard.

"Anyone have any rotten fruit?" Brenda shouted. "Gotta be some slops from those restaurants."

Scores of people ran towards the stores. An excited buzz ran through the crowd.

'And now the finale,' said Brian. 'Pull down his trousers.'

'What?' said Brenda.

'His trousers. Before he gets completely covered in gloop.'

Brenda paused. He was wearing sweats so it should be a simple tug. But she'd have to get past those long flailing arms. He couldn't see much – every time he wiped his face someone glooped him again – but he could still grab her by random chance.

She circled behind him ... and darted in. A quick grab and ... tug.

He was wearing the briefest and brightest neon yellow thong.

Shrieks erupted from the crowd. One woman may have wet herself. Camera phones snapped and Big Nose, with his trousers wrapped around his ankles, tripped and toppled backwards.

What happened in the next three minutes could have come straight from a Laurel and Hardy film. No custard pies, but surprising quantities of hummus, eggs, coleslaw, sauce and noodles. Scores of people ran from stores, their arms full of things to throw and squirt. Storekeepers followed them, reveling in a chance for revenge. And, as everyone knows, revenge is a dish best smeared in your tormentor's face. Or, in the case of chili sauce, squirted inside his thong.

Brian and Brenda stood and watched from the sidewalk as the two hoods were pelted, splatted, glooped and smeared.

"Do you really think the gang's hold over this neighborhood has been broken?" asked Brenda.

"I don't think these two will work this town again. Street thugs are like Regency heroines. Reputation is everything. And these two are thoroughly compromised."

"But won't the gang just send in another two hoods?"

"Definitely, but an event like this changes people. It emboldens them, gives them hope. *You've* given them hope. And, maybe, one or two will now come forward and testify to the police."

It sounded too good to be true.

"You have to start somewhere, Bren. A march of a thousand miles begins with a single step. Or, in this case, a canary yellow thong."

A police siren sounded in the distance. It was hard to hear at first amidst the shrieks and laughs of the street wide food fight. But it soon grew louder. And it was coming from more than one direction.

"Time to leave," said Brian. "Let's get back to the alley and change our appearance before the media arrives. Then we'll see who comes to bail these two thugs out."

This was the second part of Brian's plan – the sketchy part he'd glossed over earlier with an impatient wave of his hand and an 'it'll work, trust me.'

But Brenda still had her doubts. "What if the police don't arrest them?"

"Then we follow the trail of mayonnaise back to the gang's hideout."

Brenda had to laugh. "I'm being serious," she said, playfully punching his arm.

"So am I. Look, we've got both bases covered. If they get arrested, someone's going to bail them out or send in a lawyer. We follow that lead back to the gang leader and knock on his door as detectives investigating today's disturbance. If they don't get arrested, then the two thugs'll lead us back to the gang leader's door. Same door, same result. We're police detectives investigating a disturbance outside Cassini's convenience store. I'll drop Mary Alice's name into the questioning, probe for a reaction and – voilà – we move the case forward."

"Do I get a say in what I wear this time?"

"Of course."

"And you're not touching my boobs."

Brian raised his hands. "Hell forfend."

Brenda was still smiling when they turned into the alley and noticed a large black town car parked behind the dumpster. They both stopped. The car windows were black. They couldn't see inside.

"Crap."

Brian's voice was the last thing Brenda heard before pain exploded at the back of her head and everything went black.

Chapter Eleven

Brenda drifted towards consciousness. Patches of light and dark swam in front of her eyes, pain stabbed at the back of her head, her arms ached, and someone was calling her name.

Except it wasn't her name. It was Harriet Vane's.

"That's your name," said a voice. An English voice. "You're Harriet Vane and I'm Peter."

Peter? Lord Peter? Suddenly she was on the beach, running barefoot across the sand. Or was it through a meadow? She could feel grass between her toes, see cornflowers and poppies and ... was that him? Lord Peter? In the distance running towards her. His blond hair teased by the wind, his monocle glinting in the sunlight...

"Peter," she gasped.

"Yes, Mom," said Brian.

Reality hit Brenda like a jet-propelled brick. Away went the sun swept meadow, away went Lord Peter Wimsey, and in came bare concrete and broken glass, the sound of dripping water, and the smell of dust and decay. She was in what looked like an abandoned warehouse. Tied to a wooden chair, her arms bound behind her, her feet tied at the ankles. A man stood in front of her, staring. A man in his fifties, bald, overweight, shiny silk suit, cruel eyes. He was leaning forward, looking into her face. Two men stood further back, one black, one white, both huge, both standing impassive, watching. Brian was a few feet to her right, bound to an identical chair. He was still a teenager.

He turned his face towards her and beamed her an update. 'We're experiencing the hospitality of Big Nose's boss a little earlier than planned. His name's Bruno Abbiati and he's not best pleased.'

Bruno Abbiati leaned closer and slapped her. Not a hard

slap – more of a 'waking up the drowsy prisoner' kind of slap.

"Who are you?" he demanded.

Brian's voice sounded inside her head. 'You're Harriet Vane and I'm your son, Peter – your love child from a dalliance with an English Aristocrat.'

Brenda closed her eyes. Oh, crap.

"Hey, I'm talking to you."

Another slap, harder this time.

"I'm Harriet Vane," she said, glancing down at her dress, wondering if Brian had shapeshifted her into a 1930's heroine in tweeds and brogues.

He hadn't. The same mutant curtain spawn radiated back at her, threatening to burn out both retinas. And what had happened to her protective shield? Why was she being slapped?

'I can't shield you at the moment,' said Brian.

What? Brenda heart skipped several beats. She was tied up in an abandoned warehouse, about to have bamboo shoots shoved under her fingernails, and now she had no shield!

"Who sent you?" asked the bald man.

Brenda ignored him. She had a far more pressing question of her own. 'Why can't you shield me?' she asked Brian.

'Because if his hand bounces off an invisible force field he'll notice.'

'Then deflect his hand like you did with Big Nose.'

'It's not the right time.'

'Not the right time!' She was incensed.

And, a second later, slapped.

"Ow!" She turned on Abbiati, scowling. "Will you *stop* doing that."

"*Who* sent you?"

'Well?' she asked Brian. 'Who sent me? Or isn't it the right time to answer that either?'

"Daddy sent us," shouted Brian. "I already said."

"Shut up, kid. I told you one more word out of you and I'm going to let Dwayne break both your legs. Understand?"

Brian nodded and sent a thought to Brenda. 'Whatever you say, keep mentioning Daddy and Mary Alice and watch for a reaction. I can't read this man's mind.'

'You can't read his mind?'

'No. It's shielded somehow. I've never seen anything like it.'

Oh, great. She had no protective shield. A bamboo manicure was imminent, and now the gang's boss had superpowers. He might even be a demon.

The bald supervillain grabbed hold of Brenda's face, digging his fingers and thumb into her cheeks, and jerked her head round to face him.

"*Who* sent you?"

"Who do you think sent me?" she snapped, playing for time. What was she going to tell him? And what if he could read her mind?

'He can't read our minds,' said Brian. 'If he could, he'd have reacted by now.'

Brenda looked into Abbiati's eyes, waiting for a reaction. "Daddy sent me," she said.

She saw impatience give way to anger. "Who the *fuck* is this Daddy? What's his name?"

"That *is* his name. At least that's what he calls himself. He said he wanted another little girl."

Was that a reaction? It was difficult to tell. Abbiati looked surprised, but it looked more like puzzled surprise than shock.

"What little girl?"

"Mary Alice something. He said you'd know."

"What the fuck are you talking about?"

There was anger in his voice. Confusion, impatience, frustration. But no guilt. No telltale sign of recognition.

Brian added a nudge of his own. "Mary Alice Cassini," he said.

This time there *was* recognition.

"The storekeeper's daughter?"

"That's right. Daddy wants another one just like her."

Abbiati turned and looked at his men. "Do you know what she's talking about?"

Both shrugged. Then one spoke. "They were at Cassini's store today."

"That's right," said Abbiati turning back to Brenda. "Did Frank set this up?"

"Who's Frank?" said Brenda. "Daddy told us you were the one to see. He wants you to find him another sacrifice."

"Sacrifice?"

More brow furrowing. Either he was a very good actor, or he really had no idea what Brenda was talking about.

"That's the message he gave us."

Abbiati stood up and shook his head.

"If you had a message for me why didn't you come and see me? Why all that shit with my boys outside Cassini's?"

'I think it's time to teleport out,' said Brenda. 'I've run out of names to drop and things can only go downhill from here.'

'There's too many witnesses,' said Brian.

'He's a demon! He doesn't count.'

'All the more reason not to tip our hand. He might be able to come after us.'

Shit! She hadn't thought of that. Abbiati might be able to teleport after them. He might be stronger than Brian. He might...

Slap!

"I asked you a question! Why all that shit outside Cassini's?"

"They wouldn't let me join your gang," said Brian. "There wouldn't have been any trouble if they'd said yes."

A small vein in Abbiati's left temple throbbed into prominence.

"Dwayne, break one of his arms."

He kept his eyes on Brenda, not a single glance to his right as his minion strode forward to grab hold of Brian's left arm. He just watched her, the edges of his mouth curling into a self-satisfied smirk. "Well?" he asked. "Are you going to answer now?"

Brenda's brain atrophied. What *could* she say? She'd dug herself into a cesspit of a conversation with no hint of a way out.

'Get him angry,' said Brian. 'I don't know if he's a demon or not. Or how he maintains that shield. But it may be something that requires concentration so break that concentration and maybe I can read him.'

Dwayne worked at the knot securing Brian's hands. Abbiati continued to smirk.

And Brenda tried hard to keep herself together. Brian had

assured her he was the only demon on the planet. What else had he got wrong? Shouldn't they be looking for a way to withdraw and regroup?

'Can't you throw your voice?' she asked Brian. 'Make a noise outside? Something to make them go outside and look. Then we can teleport out without any danger of being seen or followed.'

'We've got to find out more about Abbiati. I'll protect you.'

'What if he's more powerful than you?'

Brian didn't answer. The rope securing his hands fell to the floor. Dwayne grabbed Brian's left wrist and twisted it, straightening the arm and pulling it up and back. It looked excruciating.

"Don't worry, Mom," said Brian. "I can take it. You wait. These guys'll see how hard I am and they'll *have* to let me join their gang."

"Well?" said Abbiati, staring into Brenda's eyes. "I'm waiting. One word from me and Dwayne will snap the brat's arm in two."

Brenda closed her eyes, took a deep breath, and came out fighting. Trailer Park Mom From Hell Part Two: The Teenage Years.

"Go on then," she said. "I double dare you."

Abbiati's smirk melted, the ends of his mouth curled down. His eyes widened.

"What?" she said. "Cat got your tongue? Go on Dwayne, snap away. Baldy's getting squeamish."

Abbiati recovered his composure. "Break it," he said, locking his eyes on Brenda. Brenda stared back, tilting her head to one side, and crossing her eyes.

There was a grunt from Dwayne and a large amount of straining, which Brenda could just see out of the corner of her less crossed eye.

"He's doing it all wrong," said Brian in a whiny-teenager-knows-best voice. "He'll never break anything like that."

"You only employ amateurs, Baldy?" asked Brenda. "You get a job lot off the internet?"

Baldy broke eye contact with Brenda and straightened up.

"What's taking so long?" he snapped at Dwayne, who was straining so hard his face was contorting and reddening under the strain.

"I'd've used a baseball bat," said Brian. "And look." He waved his right hand. "He's left my other hand free. I could be doing anything with it."

"Michael!" Abbiati called over his other minion.

"I'd phone out for some more," said Brenda. "You three pussies are no match for a fourteen year-old."

Abbiati was close to apoplectic. He grabbed Brenda by the face again, digging his fingernails deep into her cheek and yanking her face towards him. "I haven't started with you yet." He shoved her face away. "When I've finished, your own mother won't recognize you."

"She never could. Bad eyesight. That and the drink."

The inner Brenda crossed herself. Bad mouthing a mob boss and potential demon was bad enough, but *her mother*? That was asking for trouble. Brenda's mother had a sixth sense. She'd know exactly what Brenda had said. She was a walking guilt detector who could read her daughter like a large print book.

Slap!

That one really stung. Abbiati was putting considerably more meat into his swing.

Brenda smiled back, wondering how much more she could take. And what if he started using magic on her? He could be holding back like Brian. Fearful of witnesses. But if she pushed him too far...

'Is he angry enough yet?' she asked. 'He looks angry.'

'If he was going to use magic against you, he'd have done so by now,' said Brian. 'It's *his* interrogation. *His* rules. There's no need for him to hold back. He can send his men outside any time he wants.'

'Yes, but is he angry enough yet? Are you reading him at all?'

Brian didn't answer. Both minions were busy with his left arm. Both straining and both failing to make any headway.

"You're still doing it all wrong," said Brian, his voice portraying no sign of pain or fear. "You need to focus the pressure on a single point. Try one of my fingers. You might find it easier."

"Shut up!" shouted Dwayne, the sweat beading on his forehead and dripping from his nose.

Abbiati's eyes darted between Brenda and the huffing and

puffing to his right. He balled his fists. It was a toss up who he was going to hit first. Brenda, Brian, or one of his minions.

Brenda helped make up his mind. "Hey, Curly," she said. "Tell Larry and Moe to hurry it up."

Abbiati lost it. His whole head went red. He stabbed a finger at Brenda, spitting out the words.

"You think this a joke? You think this is a *fucking* joke? You've just signed both your death warrants, you dumb bitch."

"Oh noes," said Brenda, slipping into lol-speak. "I can haz ghost?"

Abbiati's head discovered a hitherto unknown shade of red. He spluttered, words simmering in his throat. His index finger continued to stab through the air. Then back came a semblance of control. His face set, he turned to his men and shouted.

"Leave it! Both of you. Dwayne, tie him up. Michael, with me."

Abbiati stormed off towards the outside door. Michael hurried after him.

"We'll see if you're still laughing in five minutes," Abbiati shouted over his shoulder.

'Great,' said Brenda. 'Tell me you read his mind. I don't think I can get him any angrier.'

'Sorry,' said Brian. 'I don't know how he's maintaining it.'

Brenda closed her eyes. If her feet hadn't been bound, she'd have kicked something – probably Brian.

Brian's chair scraped against the rough concrete as Dwayne yanked Brian's arms behind the back of the chair.

"You think you're funny, kid? You wait 'til we've finished with you."

He wrapped a cord tight around Brian's wrists and lashed them to the chair back.

'Okay,' said Brenda. 'This has gone far enough. Distract the goon and let's get out of here.'

'No. We haven't finished. I've got to break through that shield.'

'How? I've got him as angry as a person can get without spontaneously combusting. He's coming back to kill us and – oh, yes – I don't have a protective shield!'

'You will when you need it.'

'I need it! Like I needed it in the alley when I got whacked from behind!'

'I wasn't expecting it then. I am now.'

Dwayne walked between them, brushing against Brenda's left shoulder as he took up his old position standing guard about ten yards in front of them.

Brenda ignored him. She was too busy arguing with Brian.

'It's okay for you. You don't need a shield. You're immortal.'

'What makes you think that?'

'Um ... your head comes off? I'd call that a give-away.'

'That doesn't mean I can't be killed some other way.'

What? Brenda turned to stare at him. Was he joking? 'You can be killed? How?'

'Do you know, I've found it an extraordinary good policy never to divulge that information.'

That was all Brenda needed. 'Teleport us out now! You can come back later and investigate as much as you like. By yourself.'

'We might never find him again. He might go into hiding.'

'We could get killed!'

A shadow cut into the rectangle of light that was the door to the outside. Abbiati and Michael had returned. Michael was carrying something large and red. Brenda screwed up her eyes and peered. It looked like a gas can.

'Oh,' said Brian, sounding worried. 'You know I was saying earlier about how I could be killed?'

Brenda froze. 'Fire? You can be killed by fire?'

He didn't answer.

Chapter Twelve

'Teleport now!' Brenda shouted. This had gone far enough.

'Just a little longer,' said Brian. 'I have a plan.'

'So've I. It's called: Get the hell out now.'

'Which we'll implement the moment my plan's finished. We've got minutes before Abbiati's going to do anything.'

Brenda hung her head. What could she do? Brian had all the magic. If he didn't want to teleport, she couldn't force him. But if his plan involved her getting anyone angry...

'Don't worry. This one's all me. I need to get Abbiati to touch me.'

Brenda lifted her head. 'Then what? You're going to teleport him?'

'No.'

'Shapeshift him?'

'No.'

"You look worried, Harriet," said Abbiati. "Have you come to your senses at last?"

Brenda took a deep breath. Watch this for teamwork. "Okay," she said. "You were right, Mr. Abbiati. We were paid a thousand dollars each to bait your guys this morning. I never saw the guy, but Peter did."

"Mo-om!"

"We've got to tell him, Peter. He's going to kill us otherwise."

For the first time that morning Abbiati looked pleased. He walked over to Brian and stopped a yard in front of him. "What's the guy's name?" he asked.

"If I tell you will you let me be in your gang?" said Brian.

"Of course."

"Can I have *his* job?" said Brian, nodding at Dwayne. "I can break arms much better than he can."

Abbiati grabbed hold of Brian's face and tugged it towards him.

~

Brian acted immediately. He stretched out with his mind, concentrating on the area of cheek where Abbiati gripped him. He had to be subtle. He couldn't afford to let Abbiati notice even a tingle until he'd finished. He began altering the skin where they touched, fusing the outer layers, creating microperforations so small that only a nerve fiber could pass through.

He stretched his mind again, visualizing the nerve fibers in his cheek, growing them, guiding them through the tiny skin perforations into the tips of Abbiati's fingers and thumb, seeking, probing, pushing, finding other nerve fibers on the other side until...

Connection. A direct link between their two brains. Abbiati might be able shield his brain from telepathic probing, but could he block a physical brain to brain transfer?

Brian had no idea. He'd never done this before. He wasn't even sure how to proceed, or what the repercussions might be – would his own mind be opened up to Abbiati?

He squeezed his eyes shut, concentrated hard, imagined his mind being split in two – his thoughts and memories blockaded behind an impenetrable firewall; a second part, an inner Brian, slipping out, like an inner eye, but with far less freedom, using the neural bridge to cross over into Abbiati's body.

Everything went black, and silent. He was cut off from his own senses, straining to see, to hear, to feel his way into Abbiati's mind.

And stay hidden. He couldn't risk being detected. He had to shield his thoughts, his purpose, his very existence.

A distant sound – like tinnitus – a white rushing noise of random nothingness. He moved towards it, the sound increasing, other noises wrapped in the stream – Voices? Rain? Applause? – it was all so confusing. He paused, concentrating, picking something that sounded like a voice and tuning everything else out. It was Abbiati. Shouting. He could almost make out what he was saying.

Moving again, dragging himself towards Abbiati's voice, feeling his way and...

"Tell me his name, or I'll let Dwayne set you on fire."

Almost there, Abbiati's voice was so close and suddenly there were swirls of shapes and shadows and...

Light. Crisp and clear. He was looking at himself through Abbiati's eyes. The other Brian, autonomic Brian, his eyes tight closed and no one home. It was bizarre.

Now came the next part – accessing Abbiati's memories. More seat-of-the-pants experimentation. Would suggestion work? Would an unexpected voice in the head cause a psychotic break?

Only one way to find out.

"Mary Alice," he whispered, concentrating on the words, imagining them spoken softly into Abbiati's subconscious mind, so softly spoken his conscious self would be totally unaware.

No reaction. No sudden movement of Abbiati's head. No scream of shock or torrent of words.

Until: "Why doesn't he say something! Can't he see we're going to kill him?"

It was faint, slightly muffled, thoughts not speech and coming from somewhere else. Brian flowed towards the sound, the light fading, everything turning dusky orange.

"It's got to be the Russians. They're the only ones mad enough. But why send a woman and a boy? She doesn't sound Russian. She sounds crazy."

Louder now. And there were patterns in the burnt orange, shapes and figures – people maybe – that came and went and morphed in a dizzying array of light and dark.

Brian tried to imitate Abbiati's voice. "Mary Alice Cassini," he said.

A shape that could have been a little girl flickered then began to fade. He pursued it, hanging on to it, whispering her name, "Mary Alice, Mary Alice Cassini."

The shape swirled and billowed then eventually slowed, sharpening and gaining color. It was her. The same picture he'd seen in her police file. The smiling four year-old as she'd been a month before she'd disappeared.

Now what? Brian had no idea where he was, what he'd be able to do, or how long he had before Abbiati broke the contact. The fusion of skin between fingertip and cheek had been subtle rather than permanent. Abbiati could snap it if he pulled hard enough.

"What happened to Mary Alice?" Still a whisper, but this time Brian concentrated harder, imagining it a command, imagining himself a stage hypnotist with Abbiati, wide open to suggestion, plucked out of the audience and ready to obey every command. "Show me, Bruno. It's important. Everything hinges on what happened to Mary Alice."

A giant newspaper page appeared with a picture of Mary Alice on it. *Girl abducted in Cummings Park* ran the headlines in bold black type, everything sharp and clear.

"I need more. Show me everything you have on Mary Alice Cassini."

Other images flooded in. Mary Alice on the television news. Mary Alice in another newspaper. Snatches of commentary from a newsreader. *It's been a week since four year-old Mary Alice Cassini went missing. Police are still looking...*

Then a surprise. Frank Cassini appeared. Frank Cassini as he looked thirteen years ago. And he wasn't framed by a television set or a page of newsprint. He was 'live' in what looked like a large study – antique furniture, oak paneling, shelf after shelf of leather bound books. Frank was standing in front of a desk. The whole scene viewed through the eyes of the person sitting behind that desk – presumably Abbiati and presumably a memory from thirteen years ago.

"Please, Mr. Abbiati," said Frank. He looked a mess – dark rings around his eyes, hands shaking. He couldn't even look Abbiati in the eyes. "You have contacts. Can you ask them if they've heard anything about Mary Alice?"

Abbiati's voice replied, a slight echo giving it a strange, otherworldly feel. "I'll help in any way I can, Frank. I've already instructed everyone to keep their ears open. If anyone in the city is holding your little girl, we'll find out about it."

The scene faded. And with it Brian's theory that Mary Alice had been abducted to put pressure on Frank Cassini.

If he was being shown a real memory and not some fake to throw him off the track.

Brian tried something else. "How do you shield your thoughts?"

A woman's voice answered. It was faint and slightly distorted as though she were a long way off on a windswept cliff. "Get out!" she cried. "Get out, now!"

Was she warning him off?

"Who are you?" he asked, peering at the swirling orange mist that flowed all around him.

"Get out!" This time it was a scream. A long, distant scream and ... pain! He was hit by a sudden jolt of electrifying pain. Had he tripped some kind of defense mechanism? Was Abbiati, or whoever this woman was, aware of his presence and fighting back?

Or was it Brenda? Screaming at the Brian sat in the chair that Abbiati was trying to remove his hand and had noticed it was stuck.

He tried to reel himself back, hoping there was some link, some memory of the way he'd come. Pain! Another jolt reverberated through him. Something was wrong. Very wrong. He could sense something terrible about to happen. A feeling, a certainty, a foreboding. He had to get out. He had to get out now!

But...

What if this was a trick? Part of Abbiati's defense mechanism? Brian's direct brain-to-brain link had been discovered and Abbiati was forcing him out. And, once out, Abbiati would know to keep his distance. Brian would never be given this chance again.

"How do you shield your thoughts? I command you to tell me."

No answer just pain – sharp, sustained and debilitating. He had to get out. The pain could be coming from his own nerve endings as Abbiati tried to rip his hand free.

But there was one last question he had to ask.

"Gene therapy. Have you ever had it?"

He tried to blank out the pain. He tried to peer through a sudden jagged mess of flashing lights. He tried to tune out the ear splitting white noise. He tried...

He fled. Pulling back on himself, not sure of the direction, but trusting to instinct. All around him a migraine storm of flashing lights and pain raged and seared. Noise like static from a bank of million watt speakers. *Back, back the way you came. Find the nerves, find the bridge.*

Pain, confusion, blind flight. He tried to blot everything out, to relax, to imagine himself a long elastic band under tension and snapping back. But shouldn't he be out by now?

How long could it take?

Explosions, pops, snapping, tearing sounds. He was falling, spinning out of control and...

"What the *fuck* have you got on your face, kid? Glue?"

The real world ballooned up from nowhere. Abbiati filled most of it. He was pulling away, staring at his fingers, shaking them. The world shook in sympathy. Brian swayed, his head felt like a lead cannonball – dense, heavy and rolling beyond his control. He slumped forward.

'Are you all right?' asked Brenda. 'What happened?'

He tried to reply, but couldn't remember how. He couldn't even lift his head. It just hung there.

And the room wouldn't keep still. The concrete floor pulsed and swayed.

'Brian! Answer me!'

He tried to turn his head towards her, but it wouldn't move. Everything else moved – the room, the chair – but not his head. He tried again, straining. The room moved faster. Nausea, pain, confusion.

He closed his eyes. That made it worse. Nausea and the feeling his head was on a thousand rpm spin cycle.

He tried to ignore it all. He tried to push all his physical sensations to a spare room at the back of his mind and lock the door. But they wouldn't go. He couldn't even think straight. In some ways it felt like he was suffering magic fatigue, but in others it didn't. And he couldn't focus his mind long enough to work out what the differences were. His thoughts echoed and slurred and wandered off at a tangent.

'Brian!' Brenda shouted.

"Stop fucking about and give me his name, kid," shouted Abbiati.

Nausea gave way to a light-headed sensation. He could feel the world receding. He opened his eyes and saw his chest, the floor, everything sliding away down a long dark tunnel. He closed his eyes. Tried to claw himself back, tried to think, to concentrate, but he was too drained, too tired, too confused. And it had started to rain. Either that or the tunnel was damp and running with water. He felt wet. His clothes, his hair. His skin felt cold and clammy. And some woman was screaming at him. "Teleport! Teleport now!"

Danger. Darkness. Warm inviting sleep. Danger again. He

was drifting between sleep and waking. He so wanted to sleep, but ... why was he wet? He couldn't sleep in wet sheets. And there was that woman again – screaming at him to teleport. Teleport where? Teleport how?

Danger. There was that feeling again. A warning at the back of his mind. And a strange smell. Petrol?

He opened his eyes, rocketing back to something approaching consciousness. He was in a warehouse, lashed to a chair. His clothes were wet. His face too. The smell of petrol was everywhere. Abbiati was speaking.

"This is your last chance. Give me a name!"

Fingernails dug into his scalp, grabbed a fistful of hair and yanked his head up and back. He couldn't see who the hand belonged to. Abbiati was standing in front of him, a cigarette lighter in his hand, the open flame flickering a foot in front of Brian's face.

It was mesmerizing. So pretty. The flame curling and smoking, blue and yellow in ever-changing patterns.

'For God's sake, Brian. Do something! What's the matter with you?'

'Brenda?'

'Brian! He's going to set you on fire!'

Fire. She used the word like it was bad. How could anything so beautiful be bad? And yet ... something nagged at him from the back of his mind. Some kind of warning. If only he could think straight.

Abbiati started shouting at Brenda. Something about making her kid see sense and was he on drugs. But Brian only saw the flame as it danced in Abbiati's hand. The flame was important. He knew that now. And dangerous. Yes! That was it! Dangerous. He had to get the flame away from Abbiati, as far away as he could.

He stared at the flame, staring so hard his eyeballs almost crossed with the effort. One mental tug and he could rip the lighter from Abbiati's hand and send it flying. If he could remember how it was done. And the lighter kept still.

Think, concentrate, pull!

The lighter broke free of Abbiati's grip. It started to fly. It started ... but then lost momentum. And began to fall. A slow motion descent into Brian's petrol soaked lap.

Chapter Thirteen

Brenda watched in horror.

Whoosh! The gas ignited in a flash of flame five, six feet high. The fire spread fast – racing up to Brian's head, down to his feet. He was engulfed, his entire body shrouded in flame.

'Brian!'

He wasn't moving. He wasn't doing anything to stop the flames. Abbiati looked stunned. He stared at the hand that had held the lighter. He stared at Brian. He looked as surprised as Brenda by what had happened.

Heat. Brenda was only a yard away from the inferno. Her face felt seared. She had to turn away. The entire left side of her body felt scalded. Her hair, her dress could catch fire any second.

She threw her weight to the right, tried to topple the chair. It rocked, but not enough. She tried again. Harder. Throwing everything she had into it. She could smell burning hair.

The chair fell. Abbiati had backed away too, still looking stunned. Dwayne and Michael had moved alongside him.

"What do we do?" asked Dwayne.

Abbiati didn't answer, he couldn't take his eyes off Brian who still wasn't moving. No screams. No frantic pulling at his ties, or attempts to kick his legs free.

Could he have teleported out? Like he'd done at the bank? Starched his clothes to make it look as though he was still there while his naked body flew free?

But he had no ski mask this time. His face was exposed. Could he have turned his head into a mask? Could he have teleported out earlier? He'd barely said a word since Abbiati grabbed his face.

'Brian, are you there? Are you anywhere? Speak to me!'

The fire continued to blaze. A human shaped golden inferno. Even the chair had started to burn.

"We'll have to kill her too," said Abbiati. "She's a witness."

Brenda closed her eyes. Was this how her life was going to end? Trussed up on a grubby floor in a grubby warehouse.

"Shall we burn her too?" asked Dwayne. "We could put them in a car and make it look like accident."

"I don't drive," said Brenda. "All my friends know that and they'd tell the cops."

She looked Abbiati in the eye as she lied, playing for time in the forlorn hope that something might come along. A passing squad car, another vigilante demon, something.

"We could shoot her and feed them both to the pigs," suggested Michael.

"If my boss doesn't hear from me in the next hour you've got a gang war on your hands," said Brenda. "He's been waiting to take over your territory for years."

Abbiati gave her a look – one that showed her credibility had sunk towards zero.

"Yeah? What's his name?"

"You know," said Brenda, wobbling into the penalty shoot-out phase of the playing-for-time gambit.

She continued to look Abbiati squarely in the eye – or as squarely as a person lying on their side tied to a chair could manage – while her mind frantically raced. And wouldn't it be a good time for a really powerful ghost to appear? One who could make himself be seen. One who could freak Abbiati and his goons out. They must have killed other people here. The whole warehouse should be teeming with dead hoodlums thirsting for revenge on Abbiati.

She closed her eyes and tried to summon one up. Anyone out there with a grudge? I've got Bruno Abbiati here. Come and get him. Anyone? Anyone at all? Paging Jack the Ripper.

"Shoot her," said Abbiati.

Brenda pulled furiously at the rope binding her wrists, hoping to access that inner reserve of super strength you hear about. The mother who lifts a car to free her trapped child. Surely this was a time as desperate as that?

An unexpected voice broke the silence.

"Hey, look at me," said the teenage Brian. "I'm on fire and

it doesn't hurt!"

Everyone turned. Brian was still swaddled in fire, but the flames were lower now, his human shape more discernible. He moved his head, looking down at his body. He snapped the cords binding his wrists – they must have burnt through – and raised both arms, stretching his shoulders at the same time.

"That feels better," he said. "Anyone got a camera? Come on! Someone's gotta have a camera. I must look way cool."

Brenda stared at him. He was alive. 'I thought you said fire could kill you?'

'I don't think I did. You may have inferred that, but ... truth is, I didn't know. I've never been set on fire before.'

Abbiati and his two minions stared open-mouthed. Dwayne's gun, that seconds before had been pointing at Brenda, turned to point at Brian. Michael was scrambling for his weapon too.

Brian ignored them both. He leaned back and kicked his feet free of the ties binding his ankles to the burning chair and stood up.

"Wow," he said, staring down at his arms. "It doesn't hurt a bit and...." He started swinging both arms, striking poses, marveling at the way the flames cut through the air in an almost stroboscopic light show.

Dwayne looked to Abbiati, his question unvocalized, but obvious to everyone in the room. *What do we do?*

Brian took a step towards Abbiati, who recoiled. "Keep back," he said, fumbling for his own gun.

"Aw, come on. You gotta want me in your gang now. I'm Flame Boy. I can burn stuff. I'm a regular firestarter."

He took another step. Abbiati fired. Dwayne and Michael joined in. Brenda flinched on the floor. Bullets were going everywhere. Eight or nine shots must have hit Brian. He staggered back with each impact...

But didn't fall.

The firing stopped.

"Wow!" said Brian. "Did you see that? Even bullets can't stop me."

Brenda looked at the flaming boy wonder and narrowed her eyes.

'Have you been compos mentis all the time? Has this

been another test to see how I cope on my own while you sit there giving me the silent treatment and pretending to die?'

'No,' said Brian. 'I tried a kind of mind meld and something went wrong. But I feel better now, thanks for asking. There's nothing like being set on fire to clear the head.'

Abbiati turned and ran. Dwayne and Michael followed. The three of them circled past Brian and sprinting for the door.

"Wait for me!" shouted Brian heading after them.

Brenda watched, expecting Brian to turn back for her the moment Abbiati and his men left the building. But he didn't.

'Brian? What about me? You're not going to leave me here tied up on the floor. Brian!'

'Won't be long,' he said. 'There's something more I need from him.'

'Brian!'

Brenda couldn't believe it. It wouldn't have taken him more than a few seconds to free her. Or at least put her upright. The floor was filthy. There were undoubtedly rats in the building. Maybe roaches.

'Brian!'

~

Two cars were parked outside – the black town car and a black SUV. Two men were crouched by the SUV their guns drawn.

"What's happened?" shouted one as Abbiati, Dwayne and Michael sprinted towards him. Then he saw Brian behind them. "Fuck! What's that?"

Abbiati didn't answer. He was pumping hard and heading for the rear door of the town car. Dwayne already had the driver's door open and Michael had thrown himself into the front passenger seat.

Abbiati threw himself into the back seat. "Drive!" he shouted, reaching to close the door.

Too late. Brian grabbed the door and jumped in next to him, bouncing on the sumptuous, and soon to be charred, leather upholstered seat.

Abbiati slid over and wedged himself against the far door. Dwayne and Michael turned in unison to stare at the flaming passenger seated within a few inches of the petrol tank.

"Phew," said Brian. "Nearly missed you. Where we going?"

Three people threw open their doors and tumbled outside. The padded roof above Brian's head had caught fire and the smell of burning leather was everywhere.

All three scrambled to their feet and ran after the SUV – which was now thirty yards away and accelerating – shouting and waving for it to come back and collect them. Brian lingered in the back of the car long enough to run his hands over anything he thought flammable then, with the rear of the car pleasantly alight, climbed out through the flames to jog after his new friends.

"Wait," he shouted. "I'm one of you now. I'm not going to hurt anyone."

The town car exploded.

Up ahead, the SUV had been thrown into reverse and was fishtailing back towards Abbiati at speed.

"Aw, come on, let me be in your gang. I'll be your best friend."

The SUV rocked to a halt and three men jumped in the back. Brian was twenty yards away and not going to make it in time.

Not on foot. So he sent his eyes on ahead, found a suitable spot under the chassis of the SUV and bent the space in between, sucking his body forward in a blur of fast extinguishing flame. Blackened, charred, but no longer burning, he clung to his new hiding place beneath the SUV, waiting and listening.

The road below flashed by disturbingly close. Hopefully they weren't heading for a speed bump.

"Can you see him? Is he following?" Brian could just about recognize Abbiati's voice from the interior of the SUV. He sounded out of breath and shaken.

"Can't see him," said Dwayne. "What was he? No one can burn like that and survive."

"We must have hit him a dozen times," said Michael. "I never missed. I know I shot him."

"We all shot him," said Dwayne. "The kid's a fucking freak."

Brian listened. He was intrigued by Abbiati. He'd never met anyone who could shield his mind before. How did he do it? And what else could he do? He hadn't tried anything in the warehouse. He hadn't tried to counter Brian's powers.

He'd resorted to a gun and, when that didn't work, he'd run.

Was the mind block his only power, or was he ultra careful about using magic in front of witnesses? Listening to the present conversation, it was obvious Dwayne and Michael had never encountered anyone like Brian. Abbiati gave the same impression, but was he playing along? Playing the shocked human to keep his identity secret?

Brian probed the other men's minds – Dwayne, Michael and the two in the front – looking for a hint of recognition, a jogged memory of a similar event, a strange, inexplicable incident they'd witnessed. Maybe Abbiati being shot and miraculously surviving. Or everyone thinking he'd been shot, but somehow every bullet fired from point blank range having missed.

But he found nothing. Their thoughts were all over the place. Flashbacks of flaming Brian, fears that he was after them, a desperate search for ways to kill him. Dwayne was actually considering silver bullets soaked in holy water.

And Abbiati's mind was a total blank. It was as if he wasn't there.

The SUV put in a tight turn at speed. Brian gripped tighter as he was thrown to one side. And cursed the fact that superstrength had never featured in his catalogue of powers. Maybe he should morph suction pads onto his fingers to improve his grip? Or maybe not. In the coming hours he might need all the magic he could channel. Best to conserve his energy and observe.

Abbiati was on the phone now, talking to someone called Johnny. "Lock the place down," Abbiati told him. "I want two people on the gate at all times. And bring everyone back. We'll be there in ten minutes."

Ten minutes. Brian had ten minutes to work out what he was going to do when the car stopped. Should he try to take Abbiati down? Attempt another mind meld? Stay hidden and observe? None were ideal. And he was losing focus. What had started out as a quest to track down Daddy was splintering into three separate investigations – the search for Daddy, the enigma of Abbiati and the desire to bring him and his crime empire crashing down. And Brian didn't have a clue which was the more important. The businesslike, neat and tidy Brian said, Concentrate on one case at a time. The search for Daddy was the original case, so stay with that and stop getting sidetracked. Flying off at a tangent every time something interesting came along was a sure way to failure.

But Sacrifice had been dead for years. What were another few days to her? Abbiati was a current threat. His men were out there now, extorting, threatening, beating people up, maiming and murdering. It made sense to deal with him first and take down his empire.

Unless Abbiati had superpowers and Brian was being lured into a trap. There might be a whole nest of demons waiting for him the moment the car stopped.

Abbiati was on the phone again.

"Hey, it's me," he said. "You know you said to call if ever I had an emergency?"

There was a pause, presumably while the person on the other end of the line replied.

"Well, I have one now," continued Abbiati. "There's a kid about fourteen years old. He took a dozen bullets without flinching and fire can't kill him. I can't see how he does it. Even if he was wearing treated body armor his face was unprotected. Now he's a human fireball and I think he's after me."

Another pause. Brian listened, waiting for a name. If only he could project an inner ear into Abbiati's phone.

"Okay," said Abbiati. "I'll be at the house."

The last sentence had a hint of finality about it. Brian couldn't see or hear the call being disconnected, but it felt like it had.

"Do you think we should try different ammo?" said Dwayne. "Maybe tell everyone to switch to armor-piercing?"

"Do it." said Abbiati.

This was turning into a day of firsts. Brian had never been set alight before, and he'd never had to face armor-piercing bullets either.

Chapter Fourteen

The SUV slowed, turned and then stopped, its engine idling. Abbiati must have opened a window as his voice was suddenly louder and clearer.

"Anyone been watching the place?" he asked.

"No one," said a voice from outside – presumably a guard on the gate.

"Good. Lock everything down. If you see anyone – especially a woman with a teenage boy – tell me immediately."

The SUV pulled away. The ground changed from black top to ornamental pink. Brian lowered himself as far as he dare to get a better view of his surroundings. It looked like a parkland estate. Extensive well-kept grounds – lawns, shrubs, mature trees – sweeping up to a large, sprawling house. It had to have at least fifteen rooms. He could see a group of people waiting there. More guards, no doubt. The whole estate was probably crawling with them. A private army. He'd never taken on an army before.

And he still didn't have a plan. That last phone call was worrying. Who did a man with his own private army turn to for help? It didn't sound like a request for legal advice. And whoever it was – he, she, or the demonic hordes – they were on their way here.

So, did he act now while the odds were better, or wait and observe?

"Stop!" came a shout from up by the house. "There's someone under the truck."

Well, that about killed the 'wait and observe' option.

The SUV screeched to a halt. Brian almost lost his grip. Then the truck accelerated. Brian clung on. It was heading for the house at speed. Why? Were they looking for something painful to drive over? A cactus bed, nettles, blocks of rubble? The driver slammed on the brakes again.

Brian absorbed as much of the forward momentum with his arms as he could, but was still launched like a human torpedo from the front of the SUV, skidding ten feet on his back across the drive in front of the house.

"Ow, ow, ow!" he said.

Six men - some with rifles, some with pistols - charged towards him. The doors to the SUV flew open. More men, more guns - all of them pointing in one direction. Brian's.

"Stay down. Hands where we can see them."

Brian tried a smile and raised two charred stumps.

No one smiled back. Most of their faces were set, emotionless and hard. Except the ones revolted by the blackened, flaking - and occasionally smoldering - body lying on the ground before them.

Abbiati marched into view. He stared down at Brian, grimacing.

"What do you want?" he demanded. "And no more bull-shit."

"To get your attention."

"Don't trust him," said Dwayne. "Look at him. He's not even human."

"I'm *super*-human," said Brian. "Just what your gang needs. Unless you've already got some of us superhuman dudes working for you?"

He tried to sound innocent as he reached out with his mind – probing, listening, flitting from head to head searching for that one incriminating thought. Did anyone here have superhuman powers? Had they seen such powers used? Had they heard rumors?

And was anyone else's mind shielded from Brian's view?

A fat 'no' to all four questions.

"You've got my attention. Now what do you want?" said Abbiati.

"A million dollars," said Brian. His new plan - hatched a matter of microseconds before he started speaking - make yourself invaluable to Abbiati, go undercover, infiltrate his organization and observe from the inside. It actually made sense. Everything would be easier without the constant threat of being shot, burned alive, or tortured. He'd be able to take his time, come and go as he pleased, maybe try another mind meld. And he'd be able to see whoever it was

Abbiati had phoned. Up close with all his senses turned to the max. No hiding in the shrubbery, unable to hear or pick up surface thoughts, having to view everything through a projected inner eye and attempt to lip-read.

"Why should I pay you a million dollars?" said Abbiati

"For my services. Got a building you need burned down? I can do it without accelerants. No one'll even know it was arson. You want someone taken out? I can get to anyone. Bullets can't stop me."

"Don't trust him," said Dwayne. "He's playing mind games like he did back at the warehouse."

"I don't," said Abbiati. "But there is a way he could earn my trust."

"How?" asked Brian.

"Kill your mother. If she is your mother. Do that in front of witnesses – me and some of the boys – then I'll trust you."

Brian tried not to show any emotion as his brain steamed through every option he could think of. How could he appear to kill Brenda in front of witnesses? He couldn't get her to play dead – they'd check. Could he manufacture a fake Brenda? From what? A spare corpse he'd prepared earlier?

"Make him cut off her head to prove she's really dead," said Dwayne.

"Yeah, and put the rest of her in acid just in case she's the same as him," added Michael.

"What about some holy water," added Brian. "Do you want her sprinkled with that too?"

Dwayne, Michael and several of their colleagues nodded.

Brian took a deep breath. Time for the ever-popular Plan B. He'd noticed the remains of his right shoe still smoldering. Perhaps with a little help...

"Deal," he said, as he re-hydrated the skin around his feet and ankles – not so much with water but with fatty oils. Lots of oil. And he created pockets in what was left of the heels of both shoes. And filled them with methane.

His right foot went first. The methane exploded, creating a small fireball that engulfed his foot.

"Ow!" he said, sitting up. "What happened? I thought I'd put that out."

He started slapping at the flames. The men surrounding him jumped back. So far so good. No one had shot him –

which was always a plus – and he still wasn't sure how his body would handle armor-piercing rounds.

He conjured oil into his hands. Not as good as petrol, but it would it have to do until he could reach the SUV. He kept slapping at the, by now, low flame around his right foot. Both hands caught fire and his left foot exploded as the methane ignited.

He jumped to his feet, stamping them on the ground.

"What's happening?" he said, injecting just the right note of panic into his voice. "I can't put them out!"

He ran towards Abbiati. "Help me," he said. "Is there a fire extinguisher in the truck?"

Brian didn't wait for an answer. He turned, stamping and flapping, and ran for the passenger side of the SUV, the side with the petrol tank.

Still no one had opened fire. From the thoughts he'd sampled, they were more taken aback than feeling threatened. *What the hell was happening? Was he dying?*

"Don't get in the truck!" shouted Abbiati, no doubt remembering the last time Brian had climbed inside one of his vehicles. "Get away!"

Brian obeyed, veering away from the open front passenger side door, clutching the door's edge as he, somewhat theatrically, spun and stamped and whirled and finally slumped against the side of the SUV. Just by the petrol tank.

Brian acted immediately. Turning his body to block everyone's view, he used his inner eye to visualize the locking cap to the petrol tank. Then he focussed his mind, turning the lock telekinetically. One hand grabbed the cap, turning and pulling. The other he extinguished before reducing its size – extruding both hand and arm until they were thin enough to pass through the opening into the petrol tank. Then, before plunging his arm inside, he covered it in a tight fitting toweling sleeve. All the better to soak up the gas.

Time dawdled. He was moving as fast as he dared. Swirling the coils of his snakelike arm around the insides of the petrol tank, sending out fronds of toweling fingers to soak up as much petrol as he could. Growing a black toweling skin over the obscured parts of his thighs, torso and face. Keeping the petrol away from his burning feet until he deemed the moment right.

But he could hear the thoughts percolating behind him.

What's he doing? Is he all right? He's doing something to the truck!

He wouldn't have enough time to soak up all the petrol he'd need.

"Get away from the truck!" shouted Abbiati and Dwayne in unison. One of them slammed the front passenger door shut. Guns were pointing at Brian. Several people were poised to shoot. He could hear their thoughts. *Shoot the freak! Why doesn't he give the order? Count to two and drill the bastard.*

"I feel sick," said Brian, trying to buy time, his face still turned away, his body slumped against the car. "I'm not sure if I can stand up by myself."

The first bullet ripped into him. He swayed with the impact, holding onto the truck with his extruded arm, bracing his feet. The second went straight through him. Both armor-piercing and Brian-piercing. A searing pain erupted in his chest. He had to let go. He had to act now!

He drew his arm back at speed, coiling it in, swaddling his body with the soaked toweling, pressing it next to the flame at his feet and...

Whoosh! Flame shot past his eyes, the roar, the heat, the pillar of fire. And soon a bigger explosion. He was already pushing away from the truck with his good arm when the pressure wave from the exploding SUV hit him. He flew through the air, rolling on impact, trying to focus his eyes, his mind, trying to see where the others were.

Several were on the ground. Some had been close to the SUV, others had been luckier.

"Don't shoot!" shouted Brian. "You'll make me explode. It'll take out the entire house and grounds! I don't want to hurt anyone."

He staggered to his feet, a ball of flame, hoping his lie had bought himself more time. The pain in his chest was becoming manageable – just – but he wasn't sure how many more Brian-piercing bullets he could take. He'd never experienced pain with a bullet before.

He raised both hands and tried to look less threatening – as less threatening as any flame covered bulletproof freak could in the circumstances.

Two of the men were still down, but the others were either on their feet or getting there. And far too many pistols and assault weapons were pointing at him. He walked towards them, hands held high.

"Don't shoot," he reiterated. "I just need help putting out these flames. If I get too hot I'll blow."

"Keep back!" shouted Michael. He'd run forward to help Abbiati to his feet. The aging mobster had been caught in the blast when the truck exploded. His clothes were torn and blackened and he looked out of it.

Dwayne fired. A non Brian-piercing round thankfully. It smacked into Brian, knocking him back slightly, but his body absorbed it.

"No!" shouted Brian, putting on a panicked expression, even though he wasn't sure if anyone could identify a panicked expression through a veil of flame it helped him drop into character. "You've made it worse! I can feel the bullet heating up. I'll blow any second unless someone can help put me out. Aaaagghhh!"

It was a good scream, blending pain with a hint of Hammer hysteria. The kind of scream a B movie actor of the sixties would emit upon encountering Christopher Lee on a dark night in a graveyard. And Brian threw in some silent film over-acting – staggering forward, clutching his chest, the occasional beseeching swing of an arm, as he blundered towards them like a ham actor putting his all into his final death scene.

One of the men broke and ran for the house. Another preferred the scenic route across the lawn. One more push...

Brian stopped dead, looked down at his chest and roared. "Nooo! Run for it! I'm going to blow."

Even Dwayne turned and ran. Some threw their weapons down. Abbiati showed a remarkable turn of foot for a man with a limp as he half-ran, half-hopped for the front door of the house.

Brian hurried after them, hoping he could stay alight for the next stage of his plan.

The six men who'd run for the house reached the front entrance – an impressive arched set of wooden double doors. They pushed one open and piled through, slamming the door behind them.

Brian increased his pace. He didn't want to give them time to think. Luckily no one had thought to lock and bolt the door. They probably saw it more as a blast door – something they had to close rather than lock against a pursuer.

Brian opened the heavy door and rushed through. Four men were still in the hallway. All turned in shock as Brian burst through.

"Where's the bathroom?" shouted Brian. "Quick! If I can get to water I can put this out."

Four arms pointed up the stairs. Brian raced past them, grabbed the rolled end of the ornate banister and used it to swing round onto the stairs. Up he went without breaking stride, scorching the thick carpet as he ran. He scanned behind him, listening for the merest thought of someone shooting him in the back. No one had the slightest inclination. They were confused, frightened, and already heading for the back door.

Brian kept going, looking for anything flammable. Curtains would be ideal, a gas stove even better. He took the first door on the landing. A bedroom. Not bad. Long ceiling-to-ground curtains and plenty of bedding. He made for the curtains first, hoping they hadn't been treated with fire retardant. They hadn't. He made for the bed, then the walk-in wardrobes, pulling clothes off the racks, setting them alight and flinging them around the room.

A good blaze, but not good enough. He had to create an inferno. He had to make Abbiati and his goons evacuate the house and stay clear until he'd finished.

There had to be a boiler room. Oil, gas, something flammable, something he could rig to explode.

And it would be downstairs. On the ground floor or in a basement. He ran for the stairs. He could see the flames on his body dying down. Had to run faster. He took the stairs two at a time, jumped the last three.

And ran smack into the gun sights of Abbiati and Dwayne. Both were standing some ten feet away in a doorway off the hall. Both had machine guns. Both were ready to fire and both guns were undoubtedly crammed full of Brian-piercing bullets.

Chapter Fifteen

"Don't shoot!" shouted Brian skidding to a halt on the wooden floor. "It'll make me explode."

"Bullshit," said Abbiati.

Brian didn't need to read minds to know exactly what was going to happen next. He reacted instinctively, not pausing to weigh any pros or cons, or worry about the consequences. He broke his number one rule and teleported in front of witnesses. He tried to hide the fact by collapsing to the ground the moment before teleporting – an action which cost him at least three bullet holes in his upper torso – and then teleporting downwards in a blur through the wooden floor. He hoped it might look like he'd collapsed and died under the hail of bullets. And, being supernatural, his body had evaporated. Just like in the movies.

He broke through into what he hoped was a cellar, still not materializing, but hanging instead in the ethereal void between the dimensions. It was difficult to concentrate. The entire upper left side of his body felt like it really was on fire. The pain was excruciating, but he had to try and blot it out somehow. For the next few minutes at least.

And it was dark. Hopefully because the cellar was dark and not because he'd teleported into bedrock, or his inner eye had been shot out. He flew frantically left and right, fighting back the pain, trying to find some hint of definition in the blacks and greys. He flew towards the lightest patch of grey. It grew in brightness. He was in the cellar. There was an open door up ahead and ... light. As he passed through the door, the light hit him. There was a single window, high on the wall to his right. He materialized beneath it. And peered at his chest. Even through the low flame he could see the holes. Three of them. The skin red and streaked with purple around the edges. He looked for the other hole. The one he'd taken earlier. It was less angry. Still noticeable, but smaller and less painful. Would they all heal with time? Could he speed up the process?

He concentrated hard, thinking the wounds gone, thinking the surrounding tissue fluid and flowing in to fill the holes. But nothing happened. He concentrated harder, tried to visualize the affected areas in his mind, but couldn't. It was as though they were dead to him – not even part of him – black holes in his personal matrix. He could visualize the rest of his body no problem. He could alter its shape, do anything he wanted with it. He grew an extra arm from his right shoulder. He inflated his chest.

But whatever shape he tried those four holes remained.

Shit, shit, shit! This was all he wanted. A glimpse of mortality in the middle of a case. He morphed himself back to his original charred and smoldering form. He'd continue with his plan – execute it as quickly as he could – and worry later.

He found a light switch and combed the cellar, looking for a boiler, or better yet a fuel tank. He found the former. A gas boiler. Could he make it explode?

He poked and peered, tapped and pulled. The unit was enclosed. He had no tools, he was losing feeling in his left arm, and his telekinetic abilities couldn't even turn a screw, everything was so well fastened.

Next stop: the kitchen. There had to be a stove. He sent his inner eye up through the basement ceiling and ranging through the house. Abbiati was on the phone. Dwayne was poking gingerly with his foot at the spot Brian had disappeared from. Brian swept past. The kitchen had to be close. A room off the hall? Somewhere at the back? He found it, swung his eye around the room, checking it was clear, then materialized by the stove. The kitchen door was open so he had to be quick. And quiet. The kitchen door opened onto the hall.

He turned the oven and all the rings on without igniting them. He wanted the room to fill with gas. And he wanted Abbiati out of the building, not inside making phone calls.

He teleported again. Blind, stepping into the ether before releasing his inner eye to sprint ahead. There had to be a garage. A large one. A house like this would garage more than one car. And there had to be petrol cans. An acre of lawns didn't cut themselves. There'd be a lawn mower.

He found the garage block behind the house. One of the doors was open. Maybe some of Abbiati's men had grabbed a car to escape in. Maybe they were still inside?

Brian's eye swung under the door. The garage was large enough to house six cars. Three were inside. Another SUV and two large sedans. All of them black – obviously the house color. Brian swung his eye up and down and around. The light wasn't too good – all of it bleeding through from the one open door and a few small windows. He couldn't see any of Abbiati's men. The cars looked empty. But he was finding it difficult to concentrate – the searing pain from his shoulder and chest was coming in waves. There was a tractor mower in the corner and was that a couple of five-gallon plastic containers? They looked like they might contain petrol.

Brian joined his eyes in the garage, materializing by what were indeed two five-gallon plastic containers. He hefted one with his right hand. It was half full. He unscrewed the top and sniffed – carefully as parts of him were still smoldering. Petrol. The other container was three quarters full. He took them both, carrying the lighter one in his left hand, flexing his fingers to try and encourage life back into them. Then he was teleporting again, blind, leaving his body hanging in the ether as his inner eye raced back to the house. He'd find somewhere nice and flammable. The roof maybe. Or next to a gas pipe.

He chose the roof, materializing – petrol cans in hand – in the attic. Wooden joists, wooden floorboards, roof timbers, some old boxes of assorted flammable cast offs. He dragged all the boxes into one place, then emptied the fuller of the two containers, splashing and sprinkling over the boxes and floorboards while being very careful to keep his smoldering feet out of the way. Until the last moment.

He took one last admiring glance at his handiwork, grabbed the other container, then dabbed a foot onto the nearest box. Whoosh. He teleported out, dropping through the floor into a bedroom at the back.

He materialized, staggering under the pain. Was it getting worse? Was all his teleporting making it worse? No time to think. He emptied the last container, splashing petrol over the bed, the furniture, the curtains. Then ignited it all, teleporting a fraction of a second later, heading back to the garage. He had three cars to blow up.

He found a couple of oil-stained rags and used them as fuses – dowsing the rags in petrol, then stuffing them inside the petrol tanks. For the third car he lit a scrap of paper and dropped it inside the tank. All three cars exploded within seconds of each other. If that didn't get Abbiati running outside to check, nothing would.

Brian flew back to the house. The kitchen and hall were empty, so he could close the kitchen door unseen. Give the gas in the kitchen more time to build up an explosive concentration. One more spin around the house for his inner eye to check on the fire's progress – it was beginning to take hold – then off to find Brenda before Abbiati or his crew beat him to it.

~

Brenda was lying on her side, trussed up, abandoned and debating which insect was going to crawl over her face first – a spider or an ant. The spider was the favorite ... by a long hairy leg.

And she was hungry. She hadn't eaten since breakfast. Not to mention a certain tightness in her bladder from something else she hadn't done since breakfast.

All in all, the day couldn't get much worse.

That's when she saw a shape out of the corner of her eye. Someone was watching her from an overhead walkway.

Crap. Had Abbiati left one of his goons behind? Or could it be a child, a vagrant, someone who could help?

The figure moved. It was a fair way off, but – Brenda strained to get a better look – it didn't look like one of Abbiati's goons. They were all six foot plus and built like wrestlers on steroids. This shape looked slight. And Abbiati's men didn't skulk around hiding. They swaggered.

"Hey!" she shouted. "Over here. Help untie me."

The figure moved again, catlike, and silent. Which was strange. The empty warehouse seemed to amplify sound and the walkway was metal. But this person didn't make a sound.

And then they jumped. Brenda couldn't believe it. The

walkway had to be fifteen feet off the ground. But the person
didn't fall – they glided – and Brenda suddenly understood.
She was looking at a ghost. A woman by the looks of it. She
floated closer. A frail old woman with gnarled arthritic hands
and a faded black dress which seemed to hang limp on what
was left of her bony frame. A slightly putrid smell came with
her.

"Ya can see me?" she said. Her voice betrayed none of
the signs of frailty that her body did.

"Yes, can you untie me?"

The woman tilted her head to one side and peered down
at Brenda's dress.

"Are they lobsters?"

"Yes, they're lobsters. Can you untie me, please?"

"What are they doing on flowers?"

"Who knows? They're lobsters. Now, please. If you can,
untie me."

The woman's attention switched to Brenda's feet. "Why're
ya tied up?"

Brenda closed her eyes. This was going to be a long conversation.

"I was being tortured."

The woman paused, her expression slowly changing from
mild confusion to one of comprehension.

"Tortured, eh? Wish I was being tortured. Be a change
from being dead."

Brenda wasn't sure if she'd heard correctly, but then she
remembered she was talking to a ghost. They couldn't help
it. All those years living – well, existing – all by themselves.
It couldn't help but make them slightly batty and self-
centered.

"Can you untie me?" she asked again, pushing her wrists
out to show the ties.

The ghost shook her head in slow motion and raised a
spectral, gnarled hand. "Sorry, dear. It's my hands. They'd
pass right through ya. Can't touch a thing. Not even myself.
I've had an itch on my neck for seven years. Seven years!
What I'd do for a good scratch."

The woman's skin looked dry and paper thin – a good
scratch would probably rip it to shreds.

"Could you go outside and take a look for me?" Brenda

asked.

The woman looked towards the door. "Out there?"

"Yes," said Brenda. "I want to know what's out there. I heard an explosion and my friend was outside. I want to know if he's okay."

"An explosion, ya say?"

"Yes, I really need to know."

The woman stared vaguely at the door, then began to drift towards it. She took an age. Surely ghosts could move quicker than that. Even old ones. Couldn't she teleport? The ones in Brenda's kitchen were always flitting in and out.

It must have been three minutes before the ghost returned. Via the door and a slow drift across the warehouse floor to where Brenda was lying.

"There's a big black car on fire," she said.

"Any bodies?"

"Not that I could see."

"Not even a charred body? A big black husk?"

"Ya want me to look in the car?"

"If it's no trouble." And you could move a little faster.

Five minutes passed this time. Brenda counted the seconds, wondering if the ghost had faded into the ether, or forgotten why she'd gone outside.

Neither was true. The ghost appeared in the doorway and began her funereal glide across the concrete.

"Anything?" shouted Brenda.

"Nope," said the woman. "No one in the car. I even looked in the trunk."

The inner Brenda, always ready to chime in with a happy thought during times of stress, added her two cents. *Brian's dead and not coming back, and you, Brenda, are staring at your future. A dried up old ghost with an itch it can't scratch.*

"Feeling hungry?" asked the ghost.

"Yes," said Brenda who, up until that point, hadn't thought about food for a solid ten minutes. As if to make a point her stomach chose that moment to gurgle.

"Ya'll be a sight hungrier tomorrow. Place like this. No one'll find ya for weeks. Unless kids come along at night to run wild and shoot up them drugs and do their vandalizing. Huh, kids these days. Got no respect. They're as likely to cut ya throat as call for help. That's if they don't rape ya first."

"Haven't you got somewhere you've got to be?" asked Brenda.

"Don't worry, dear. I won't leave ya all alone. I'll stay and keep ya company. Ya look like ya need cheering up."

"I won't be alone for long. My friend'll be back soon."

"Yeah?" she said, tilting her head back. "A man is he?"

Give or take a chromosome or two. And maybe a horn and a cloven foot. "Yes."

The ghost smiled, a knowing toothless smile. "Men," she said, disparagingly. "Mark my words ya'll never see him again. Men say they'll come back, but they never do. I should know. I've had three husbands – all of them upped and left. Good riddance if ya ask me."

"Couldn't you haunt them? Get your own back that way?"

Like now? Don't worry about me. Off you go. There's a good ghost. Shoo.

"Wouldn't waste my time on them. They're all most likely dead anyway. Never was any life in any of them. Uh-oh."

The ghost's demeanor changed. She stared behind Brenda.

"What?" said Brenda. "What is it?"

"There's a big black rat behind you."

If Brenda hadn't been lying on her side lashed to a chair she'd have jumped. She strained her neck instead, twisting it violently in a vain effort to look behind her. The chair rattled and scraped on the concrete.

"Don't do that! Ya'll frighten him."

"Frighten *him*!"

The ghost shook her spectral head, wafting it from side to side. "Ya don't want to go frightening no rats. Never tell what they might do. Unpredictable is rats. And where there's one, there's always others."

Inner Brenda agreed. *And it's all your fault, Brenda. You had to ask if the day could get any worse. Sensible people don't ask questions like that. Sensible people don't hook up with Vigilante Demons and spend their vacations being tortured in smelly warehouses. Look at you, Brenda. You're tied to a chair, lying on a cold, filthy floor. Your legs and arms are cramping. Your neck's about to go into spasm and now you've upset a rat. A hungry rat, and you're dressed like a seafood platter!*

'But look on the bright side,' said a familiar voice in her head. 'You'll get to wear that lovely dress forever in the afterlife.'

"Brian!"

He appeared in front of her. A black husk with white shining teeth and eyes and ... was he naked?

"Where's your clothes?"

"What?" said Brian, looking down. "Oh, they must have burned off."

He looked like a lava-grilled stripogram beamed straight out of Pompeii's red light district.

"Where have you been? Are we safe? Get me out of this chair."

He bent down to untie her, grimacing slightly and ... was that a hole? She caught a flash of daylight – three flashes of daylight! – as his chest passed in front of the door.

"Does that hurt?" she asked. The area around the three holes were streaked with purple and appeared to be weeping. "I can see right through you."

"It's nothing. I can either absorb bullets, or let them pass straight through. Think of it as extreme body piercing."

He started picking at the knot securing her wrists. "And don't worry. We're safe. For the moment. There's one little thing we need to do then we can go home."

"What little thing?"

"A small little thing."

He was infuriating! But at least he'd untied her hands. She flexed her shoulders, rubbed her wrists and inspected the raw red line the cord had left.

"Did you find out if Abbiati's a demon?" she asked.

Brian shrugged. "That's one of the small little things we've got to do next."

"What? No! I'm not going near Abbiati again. I'd rather stay here!"

"Don't worry." He pulled and picked at the knot securing her legs. "Abbiati's not going to be around. He's um ... experiencing the insurance protection industry from the client's perspective. He'll be too busy dealing with that."

The cords around her legs loosened at last. She staggered to her feet, massaging life into her thighs, brushing the dust from her hideous dress, inspecting her over-the-top hair for singed ends.

"You *are* going to tell me where've you been and what happened?" asked Brenda.

"As soon as we get this last job done. It's time-critical and there's a lot to tell. Now grab hold."

He held out a blackened stick with fingers on the end. Brenda hesitated. She wasn't sure what to grab hold of. His hand looked like it'd snap and his skin ... she wasn't sure if it would flake or smear. And if she got some on her clothes would it still be part of him? A little shapeshifting remnant that she might never get rid of?

"Come on," urged Brian. "There really isn't much time."

"That him?" asked the ghost, nodding a spectral head towards Brian. "I'd've stayed with the rats."

She had a point. But Brenda was a crime fighter and crime fighters had to grab hold of black flaky things now and then. It was in their job description.

She held out a tentative hand and let Brian grab it. His fingers felt remarkably strong. Then the warehouse blurred to grey dust...

Chapter Sixteen

The grey dust picked up streaks of blues and blurring browns and greens as they raced across town. Brenda felt dizzy and disorientated. And then hot. They materialized in a burning room. A study by the look of it. A paneled wall was on fire. Part of the ceiling too. Smoldering flakes floated down from above. Smoke seeped under the closed door.

"Oh God, this isn't Hell, is it?"

Had Brian taken her to his home?

"Don't be silly, Brenda. We don't have flammable furnishings in Hell."

He hurried to the window and sneaked a look outside. "This is Abbiati's study. We're here to search the place before the fire department – or anyone else – gets here. Can't see anyone yet. So get searching."

"What for?"

He turned away from the window. "Anything unusual or incriminating. That computer will do for a start. Any address books, medical files, a nice gleaming safe."

"Medical files?"

"Especially medical files. I want to see if Abbiati had any medical procedures in the last ten years."

She was about to ask why when his voice sounded inside her head.

'No time to explain. Someone very nasty could arrive any minute.'

"Who?"

"Could you start looking?" He tapped his left wrist where a slight lump was all that remained of his watch. "You might not have noticed, but the room's on fire."

Brenda gave him a hard stare. And then noticed something smoldering float past her face. She jumped back, then glanced up to see a flame shoot out from the burning wall behind her and lick across the ceiling directly overhead. The desk on the far side of the room suddenly seemed a much safer place to be.

She picked her way across the room to the desk, ducking and dodging, while Brian moved along the walls, looking behind paintings and tapping his feet on the floor. She'd disconnect the computer and search the desk.

"Found it," said Brian.

Brenda glanced over. He'd found a wall safe behind a square of paneling. He swayed in front of it. Which looked ... odd. Was he conjuring some kind of opening spell? He almost fell over, throwing out a hand to grab the wall just as it looked certain he would topple sideways.

"Are you all right?" she asked.

"I've felt better. Keep looking. There's not much time."

She continued disconnecting leads from the desktop computer, glancing over at Brian whenever she could. There was definitely something wrong. He wasn't using his left hand. His arm just hung there. And the way he was standing – at times he looked hunched.

"I'm fine," said Brian, his voice sounding far from fine – tired and tetchy. "Just search the desk."

Brenda obeyed. Was this what he was like when he'd performed too much magic?

She pulled the top right-hand drawer of the desk open and began to rifle through it. Pens, business cards, scraps of paper, elastic bands and paper clips. She flicked through cards, speed read the papers. Nothing interesting from what she could see. She moved to the next drawer.

Magazines and correspondence. She went through them as fast as she could, rarely reading more than an opening sentence or a title before throwing them aside. She could smell smoke and the fire was spreading – spitting, crackling sounds coming from the burning paneling along one wall. And other sounds – muffled crashes and bangs – from the rest of the house.

Brian was staring at the wall safe, his right hand pressed against its door. His head glistened like lacquered metal – whether by effort from his task, illness, or heat from the fire she couldn't tell.

A siren sounded in the distance.

Brenda pulled out the next drawer and the next, setting them on the desktop. She emptied the larger of the two, throwing the contents out. They could use it as a box to carry stuff back with them. If Brian was strong enough to carry it.

She shot him another look. He'd barely moved and his eyes were closed. And the smoke was getting thicker.

Shit! Shit! Shit! She sped up her search, barely looking at papers and envelopes before throwing them into the keep or discard pile. No medical files. No correspondence from doctors or hospitals. Maybe he kept them elsewhere?

She ran her eyes around the room. The smoke was pouring in from around the door. That whole area was a cloud of fog.

"Done it," said Brian. There was barely any triumph in his voice. He had the safe door open. He was reaching inside. The ceiling above him was ablaze.

"Hurry up!" shouted Brenda. "Grab what you can and let's go."

He didn't answer. He was sifting through the material one-handed. Come on, Brian!

Outside, the sirens were getting louder. She picked up her keep drawer and ran towards him. "Throw it all in here."

She tried to push him aside, but he wouldn't budge. But he did start shoveling the contents into the drawer she'd jammed between them. Lots of large brown envelopes, folders, a gun and stacks of money. Her eyes went from the gun to the bundles of bills. There had to be hundreds of thousands of dollars. Maybe a million. She felt excited and dirty at the same time.

"I've got this," said Brian. "Help me tuck it under my right arm, then grab the computer."

A shred of burning flotsam landed in the drawer. She hooked it out, using an envelope, then pulled the drawer away from Brian. "Come on," she urged. "It's safer over here."

She hurried back to the desk, coughing. Smoke was everywhere now and she was sure her hair was burning. Brian staggered against her. She gave him the drawer, helped him tuck it under his right arm, then turned and grabbed the computer.

"Put my left hand on your shoulder," said Brian.

She looked at his left arm hanging limp by his side. How was he going to teleport them through space when he couldn't even lift his own arm?

"We can leave this stuff behind," she said. "It's not important-"

He cut her off. "Just do it."

She grabbed his left hand and placed it on her shoulder, holding it there. Now go!

Something major exploded in the house. The door and windows shook. Smoke stung her eyes and throat.

"Come on, Brian! Now!"

The room blurred, then sharpened again. She wasn't sure if it was Brian or her eyes. Come on, come on! A siren wailed nearby. Wood crackled and spat. Smoke billowed. She held her breath. Everything turning white, then grey, then white again.

The featureless white dissolved into greens and blues. They were outside, floating slowly across a lawn. The house was behind them, flames licking from upstairs windows and the roof. Two fire engines were racing up a long drive. And then gone - blurred into a visual soup as they picked up speed, the greens and blues blending together in a streaky mess. Seconds passed. Brian's eyes were closing. His head dropping forward...

"Brian!" she shouted, but no sound came out. She was in a silent noiseless bubble shooting across country. Or into space. Or God knows where. Was Brian in control any more?

'Brian!' She formed the word in her mind and fired the thought at his sinking head. 'Are you all right? Wake up! Brian!'

No answer. No eye flickering open. He was slumping forward. She squeezed his hand, pushed her left elbow forward to support his chest then...

They materialized. Brian started to fall sideways. She tried to grab him, but she had the computer under one arm. He fell, dropping the drawer and spilling its contents.

It was only then that Brenda became aware of her surroundings. They were by the side of a long, straight road. Cornfields stretched for miles in all directions. Not a car, not a person in sight. Wherever they were it wasn't home.

~

Two men stood under a stand of ornamental maples watching the fire trucks arrive at Abbiati's burning home. They were alone and unobserved, a quarter of a mile from the house at the edge of the grounds.

"I see what you mean," said one to the other. "We have a problem."

The air around the two men shimmered, then both figures disappeared.

Chapter Seventeen

Brenda swept the horizon. It could be Ohio. There was corn. Acres and acres of it. But, equally, it could be anywhere in the Midwest. Or the Steppes for that matter. She didn't recognize a thing. She was miles from anywhere, and lost.

She knelt next to Brian. His eyes were closed and he wasn't moving. Should she feel for a pulse? Would he have a pulse? She didn't even know if he breathed.

She watched his chest, looking for a rise and fall. If there was any movement, she couldn't see it.

She grabbed his wrist, felt for a pulse – nothing – peeled an eyelid back...

Dead eyes stared back. She held the palm of her hand over his nose. Was that breath? *Something* tickled at her palm. She looked around for a mirror, a cold surface, a feather. Something to prove he was breathing.

She looked further afield, combing the grass verge that ran between the road and the corn. And found a feather. She held it against Brian's nose and watched. The feather moved. Not much, but every six seconds or so, it moved. Something in there was breathing.

But for how long? He had three holes in his chest. One where his lungs should be. She leant over his chest and looked closer. There was no blood – red, green, or any color. Nothing was seeping out. The wound looked clean. Horrible, tinged with reds and purples, but clean. For all she knew, he was healing fine and the real problem was overexertion through too much magic. He might sleep for a few hours, then wake up perfectly restored.

Or he might die in the next minute.

She growled in frustration. Why hadn't he prepared her for this? If he was hurt, he could have said, and given her instructions.

149

She narrowed her eyes and gave him a long hard look. Could he be faking? Another test to see how she coped under stress?

She sighed long and hard. And to make matters worse, she *really* needed to pee.

She cast a furtive eye up and down the road. Not a car, not a house, not a person in sight. She looked at Brian. Gave him a poke. Waved her hands in front of his eyes. Well...

She walked off to find a spot, stopped, took another look at Brian, then ran back and turned his head away. Thinking that might not be enough, she put a large manila envelope on his face. Satisfied that her modesty had been afforded an adequate level of protection, she stood up, gave the road another horizon to horizon peer ... then knelt down to rummage through the drawer for a non-important piece of paper or two.

Now all I need is for a car to drive by while I'm in mid-squat. Look, mommy, there's a dead body and a lady peeing. How many points do I get for that?

Luckily, no points had to be awarded. But that was about as lucky as Brenda felt. She had no phone, and she was in the middle of nowhere with a char-grilled Brian. How was she supposed to get them back home? Stand by the road and dazzle drivers with her radioactive lobster dress? Wait for them to crash into the cornfield, then steal their car while they lay unconscious?

She took the manila envelope from Brian's face. Who in their right mind would stop to give the pair of them a lift? One look at Brian and they'd either drive off, or insist on calling the police or an ambulance.

Of course there was the gun ... and the money. The inner Brenda came spluttering to life. *Are you mad? You can't hold up a car? Where are they going to drop you? Outside your home? Or are you going to take their car and leave them here so they can flag down the next car that comes along and call the police?*

She had a point. And if the police found her, how would she explain Brian and the gun and the million dollars? If the money wasn't hot, the gun would be. Why else would Abbiati keep it in his safe? It was probably used in a murder and Abbiati was either hiding it, or holding it for leverage against the murderer. Neither possibility would do Brenda any good. She'd be in possession of a murder weapon!

She heard a car in the distance.

Panic. She had to get Brian out of sight which meant ... the cornfield! She grabbed him by the shoulders and dragged him in – one row, three rows, seven rows deep. Was that far enough? She ducked down. And remembered the computer and drawer full of money. If a driver saw that by the roadside they might stop.

She ran out. The car was visible now, a quarter of a mile away and closing. She knelt down and scrabbled at the envelopes and papers, the money and the gun, stuffing them back into the drawer and resting the computer on top. It was heavy and awkward, but she picked it up and hurried back into the corn, keeping as low as she could. She reached Brian and dropped down even lower, keeping her back to the road and her head tucked in. The car drove past. Then slowed. Shit! Shit! Shit! The driver had to have seen her. It was a straight road in the middle of nowhere and her dress was so bright it could be seen from outer space. Even if they drove off now, they might come back later to look. Or tell a friend.

The car stopped. She couldn't see it, but it had to be forty, fifty yards away. If it began to reverse...

She had to act quickly. She couldn't let anyone see Brian. Or the gun. Or the money.

A car door opened.

Brenda took a deep breath. What if the driver was a cop? Or a felon. She had to have a story...

And she'd need money. She took the computer off the drawer and placed it carefully on the ground. Then grabbed a large manila envelope and emptied its contents into the drawer. That should do. It was large enough to take a stack of bills without drawing too much attention. She stuffed forty, fifty, sixty thousand dollars inside. Then stood up, brushed herself down, patted her hair, and stepped out of the corn.

The driver was middle-aged, short and squat with a red weather-beaten face. He was wearing overalls and driving a pick-up. Probably a farmer, thought Brenda. Followed by a more worrying thought. Maybe the farmer who owned the cornfield she'd just walked out of.

"Are you all right?" he called.

Brenda slipped into character, while putting as much distance and corn between her and Brian as she could without breaking into a run. She bit her lip and clutched nervously at her envelope.

"Not really. I had an argument with my boyfriend and he pulled over and left me here." She let her bottom lip quiver. "I thought you might be him, so I hid."

"He left you here?" He looked up and down the road. "To walk home by yourself?"

"Yes, sir." Brenda sniffed back a tear. "He ... he gets angry very easy. I don't ... I don't even know where I am. He's been gone thirty minutes."

She lowered her head and had a stab at crying.

"I can drop you off at the next town if it's any help," he asked.

"Could you?" she said, raising her head and pitching a brave smile.

"Of course." He smiled too. A fatherly smile. Brenda had her lift.

Now all she had to do was figure out what she was going to do when she reached town. Look for a phone? Who would she call? Not her family. They'd ask too many questions. Even if they did drive across two states to collect her, how would she explain the new nose, boobs and hair?

Not to mention Brian.

And as for friends – the only people she knew well enough to ask would have the same set of questions.

She climbed into the pick-up, still wondering. The only thing she was certain of was that she had to memorize this location. She'd have to come back later and pick Brian up. But the place was so featureless. She took a long last look from the window. Corn for miles. Lines of trees in the distance. A road without a bend or a useful pothole. A grass verge without a distinctive tall weed...

Then she saw it. About thirty yards away on the other side of the road there was a patch of earth about the size of car where the corn was small or had failed to germinate. She committed it to memory. And checked the pick-up's odometer. Now all she had to do was find a way to return.

"Is the nearest town far?" she asked as the driver pulled away.

"Wellesley's about ten miles."

Wellesley? That was miles from home – an hour and half's drive at least. Bang went the idea of hiring a taxi. By the time she'd got home and driven back in her car, more than three hours would have passed. She hadn't hidden Brian that well.

"Is there a car dealer nearby?" she asked.

Good plan. She'd rent a car. Drive straight back and pick Brian up.

"There is. I can drop you there if you like."

"That would be very kind." She dabbed at her eyes with the side of her index finger, keeping in character as the sad, abandoned heroine while memorizing the route for later.

Everything was going well until the driver sniffed the air for the third time and shot Brenda a curious look.

"Have you been near a bonfire?"

"We went to a barbecue," said Brenda thinking quickly. "It was more smoke than steak."

She let her lower lip tremble and turned away, stifling a bogus sob. She didn't want to engage in any more small talk just in case her imagination developed a conscience and stopped furnishing her with appropriate lies.

And she needed to concentrate. She'd just had a worrying thought. She'd need ID to rent a car. A driver's license and proof of insurance. All she had was sixty thousand dollars and a cute smile.

She controlled the urge to bang her head on the dash-board. Could she even *buy* a car? Wouldn't they insist on ID for that too? Was she going to have to hire a taxi after all?

Thoughts tumbled and churned inside her brain. She had sixty thousand dollars! That ought to solve any problem. She'd find some college kid and offer him ten grand to borrow his car, no questions asked. Except that usually guaranteed plenty of questions asked. He might follow her in a friend's car, watch her drag Brian out of the cornfield and blackmail her for the rest of her life.

By the time she was dropped off at the dealer's lot, she'd exhausted every possibility. Except one.

Brenda thanked her good Samaritan and, as he drove

away, switched – goodbye tearful, abandoned girlfriend, hello rich, confident lottery winner. She ran a hand through the outer margins of her eighties hair checking for singed ends and sniffed her dress – not too smoky. And so what if it was – she was a woman with sixty thousand dollars in cash. She had a right to be eccentric.

She eyed the car lot. Small, but select. Two dozen or so used cars outside, maybe seven or eight new models inside. She'd need to find the owner. Someone who could make decisions without clearing it with someone else first.

She sashayed into the building, using her dress to its maximum effect – while hoping it didn't set off the sprinkler system – and made her way straight to the most expensive car in the showroom. A Winter Gold Jaguar XF. Price tag: $49,975.

A salesman came rushing over. Just the one salesman in the showroom from what Brenda could see.

"Are y'all the manager of this fine establishment?" asked Brenda affecting a generic southern drawl.

"I have that honor." He was in his early fifties, dressed in a sharp suit and if he wasn't wearing a wig, then someone had been doing some serious experimentation on his hair follicles. His hair shone as black and shiny as tar.

Brenda turned to admire the golden Jaguar and ran a hand over its bonnet. "I jess *lo-ve* this here car."

"It's a beauty," said the salesman. "Four-point-two liter V8 engine–"

Brenda waved away the technical spiel.

"I *have* to take this car for a test drive."

"Certainly, madam."

"Now y'all might think I'm some kinda crazy woman, but I *only* buy cars that I feel one hundred per cent comfortable with."

"I quite understand." He wasn't exactly rubbing his hands together, but he was coming close.

"And the only way I can know – I mean *really* know – is to take them on a long test drive ... by myself."

She could hear the first chime of a warning bell as it swung behind his eyebrows. She held up her hand.

"*Stop* right there," she said. "I know exactly what y'all gonna say. Which is why I *always* bring a li'l something with me for a deposit."

She flashed twenty thousand dollars, waving the two bundles enticingly in front of his face.

"I *ain't* no time waster and I *ain't* no thief. I'm just mighty particular in my purchases."

He brightened, mesmerized by the sight of so many Ben Franklyns.

"I understand. If I may have your details...."

What name would she be this afternoon? She didn't want any paper trail leading back to Harriet Vane.

"Jessica Fletcher," she said.

"Like the TV detective?"

"My mom's favorite," she said, adding a beaming smile.

"May I see your driving license?"

"Of course."

She made a play of looking inside her envelope. "That's strange. It ain't here. Why ain't it here? Carl *said* he'd put it in with the money. Can you believe that?"

She turned and gave the salesman her best pout. "My stupid husband's taken my driving license to Cincinnati. And I *so* wanted this car."

She gave it her fondest look, then bestowed the salesman with an even fonder one. "Is there *any* way I can test drive this wonderful car without a license?"

"Well...." He looked apologetic. "I could always sit in the back."

She shook her head. "It wouldn't be the same. Do y'all believe in auras?"

A moment of doubt crossed his face before the lure of selling a fifty thousand dollar car brought him to his senses.

"Then y'all can see why I jess *have* to be alone with this car. Otherwise I can't tell if she's right for me."

She dropped her head, crestfallen. "I guess maybe this Jaguar and me jess weren't meant to be."

"Could you come back tomorrow?" asked the salesman.

She shook her head, adding a sniff for effect.

"No, sir. I'm joining Carl in Cincinnati tomorrow. Then we're heading west. Do they have Jaguars like this in California?"

The salesman was wavering. Brenda beamed him encouraging thoughts. *Take the risk. What harm can she do?*

Ask for the full purchase price of the car as a deposit. You'll lose her otherwise.

And she nervously fingered her manila envelope, folding it to show the contents inside were substantial and money-shaped.

"Maybe we ... could work something out?" he said.

She raised her head slightly, going for the hopeful puppy dog look. She thought about batting her eyelashes, but wisely refrained.

"Y'all could?"

"Yes, um, maybe if you left a more sizeable deposit?"

"How much?"

"For an unaccompanied test drive with no documentation...." She could see the calculation going on behind his eyes. "I'm afraid head office would insist on the full purchase price."

He sounded more hopeful than insistent, but Brenda wasn't going to waste time haggling.

"Done. Hold this." She gave him the twenty thousand and rummaged in the envelope for another three bundles. She handed them over. "Keep the change."

The Jaguar drove like a dream, with its push button starter and a gearshift that looked like it came straight out of a spaceship. I could get used to this, she thought.

A thought that was too much for the inner Brenda. *Are you mad? You've practically stolen it! With money you stole from a crime lord! Did you check the serial numbers to see if they were consecutive? The FBI probably have whole teams doing nothing but waiting for that money to surface.*

Brenda wasn't handing over her conscience without a fight. She was *borrowing* the car. She'd give it back. The money, too. Not to Abbiati, but to a good cause. She wouldn't benefit in any way.

You say that now, but ... it's addictive, Brenda. You haven't had the money an hour and already you've blown fifty grand on a test drive. You'll be tempted again the next time you're in trouble. And the next.

Brenda disagreed. She was stronger than that. Though a small part of her thought Abbiati owed her at least the fare home. After all, he'd abducted her and tied her to a chair. If she took him to court she'd be awarded far more than fifty grand. He *owed* her a Jaguar.

There you go! Justifying your actions. You've watched Charmed. *You know the danger of using magic for personal gain. Brian used magic to open the safe. The money came from the safe and you're sitting in the proceeds. How do you think The Powers That Be are going to view that?*

Suddenly Brenda became very aware of the traffic on the road. Would Fate tamper with someone's steering and brakes, sending them hurtling towards her head on? Or tamper with her own steering and make her drive straight into a tree? Like that big one over there.

She gripped the wheel tighter, fighting the siren call of the magnetic oak. She'd be extra vigilant. And hand back the car as soon as possible.

Maybe.

Then the trip odometer approached ten miles and Brenda eased off the gas. That hole in the corn couldn't be far.

She saw it up ahead on the left and slowed even more. Brian had to be about sixty yards away on the right.

She pulled over, stopping part way on the grass verge. She waited until a car passed, unlocked the trunk and the rear right door, then ran for the corn. It didn't take long to find him – just long enough to have a mini-panic and convince herself that she was looking in the wrong place, the police had already discovered Brian, and her face was plastered all over the local media. In other words – about twenty seconds.

Brian was still unconscious, still breathing, and still sur-rounded by large piles of exquisite looking – and exceedingly spendable – money.

Brenda!

She took another look up and down the road, grabbed Brian by the shoulders and hauled him over to the car. So far so good. At least neither of his arms had fallen off. She propped his shoulders against the lip of the rear seat, then pushed, shoved, slid and squeezed him aboard. Not exactly the recommended procedure for transporting injured and unconscious patients, but she was under severe time constraints. Any second someone could drive by.

Someone did.

Chapter Eighteen

Brenda had closed the back door and was readying herself for a run to the corn when she heard the car. Panic and guilt took it in turns to wring her insides. She had a charred corpse stuffed in the back seat and a million dollars in the cornfield! And an overpowering urge to put her hands behind her back and saunter along the grass verge whistling nonchalantly. Drive by, drive by. Don't look!

They slowed – probably dazzled by her dress – but they didn't veer into the cornfield, or stop. Brenda waited for them to drive out of sight before rushing into the corn. She grabbed the computer, placed it carefully in the trunk, then ran back for the drawer, taking special care of the gun. She wasn't even sure if it was loaded. And she wasn't going to risk covering it in fingerprints to check.

The trip home was uneventful – as journeys in an appropriated car with a charred corpse, one million dollars and a murder weapon go. Brenda only had the one coronary, and a ninety-minute panic attack.

She didn't think Brian was visible in the back seat, but she wasn't sure. A bicyclist might see him if one pulled up next to her at an intersection. Perhaps she should stop somewhere and put Brian in the trunk? A thought that came to the fore every time she approached an intersection or saw a cyclist. And promptly disappeared every time she found a stretch of quiet open road. Wouldn't the Powers That Be be waiting for such a moment? Lure Brenda into thinking she was unobserved, then produce the squad car just as she had the trunk open and the charred corpse in her arms.

The same went for if she stopped to buy a coat or a blanket to throw over him. Wherever she parked, she'd return to find a cop staring into the back of the car.

Even the sight of her house didn't make her feel any

easier. She'd have curious neighbors to contend with. Who *was* that woman in the toxic dress and new car?

She pulled into her driveway, sinking lower in the seat. Some kids were playing in the yard three doors down, but they looked more interested in each other. She took a deep breath, opened the car door, and talked herself into the role of Candy – an old school friend coming to stay. Brenda was going to be out, so she'd told Candy about the garage key she kept under a stone in the flower border by the house. Candy walked confidently from the car to the flowerbed. She didn't act furtively. She didn't glance left or right before scrabbling in the dirt. She didn't run to the garage upon finding the key. She did just what she had to, placing a firm lid on her nerves until the garage door closed behind her and manic Brenda could re-emerge and show headless chickens what real hysteria looked like.

First, she had to get inside her house. She kept a spare key under a flowerpot on the top shelf of the garage. Once inside the house, she had to grab her car keys, move her own car out of the garage and swap it with the Jaguar. Only then, away from the watchful eyes of her neighbors, could she drag Brian into the house via the garage door.

Brenda executed a slightly longer version of the above – with extra running caused by frequent changes of mind – and bouts of hyperventilation. *Should I ditch the dress? Ditch the Candy persona? No! Yes! No! Hide Brian upstairs? Drag him to the sofa? No! Yes! No! Breathe!*

Only when she'd sat Brian in her armchair could she relax – using a definition of 'relax' only found within the pages of the Bipolar Dictionary. She was totally wired and there was still so much to worry about. Top of the list being – what if Brian never recovers? She'd be stuck with her new nose and boobs for life. Unless she used part of the million dollars to pay for cosmetic surgery to put her back to how she used to look?

Slippery slope, Brenda. Personal gain. You're going to go through that million within the week.

It's not personal gain! It's putting everything back to how it was. How it *should* be!

The inner Brenda shook her inner head. *Sophistry, Brenda. As long as you have access to that money, it'll be a temptation.*

Brenda turned to the body slumped in her armchair. Was he looking any better? The three holes in his chest weren't so noticeable. She moved closer. They were definitely smaller and not so angry looking.

Brian stirred. His head moved slightly and his chest rose. He coughed.

"Ow," he said in a small, tired voice.

Brenda moved closer still. "Are you okay? Do you need anything?"

"Food." His eyes still hadn't opened and his lips barely moved.

"You eat?" Brenda was surprised, and drawn to the three holes in his chest. Was there an alimentary canal in there somewhere? Would food fall out of the holes?

Brian smiled weakly and opened half an eye. "Better stand back while I drink."

He tried to sit up, straining under the effort before falling back. Brenda darted forward to help him.

"Do you want to sit up?"

"Please. And food. Lots of sugar." He spoke between gasps, wincing with the effort each word was costing. "Have you ... Grape Nuts?"

"No. I have granola."

"Have to do ... big bowl ... plenty milk ... extra sugar. And chocolate ... with nuts."

"Will that make you better? Are you ... sick?" She looked at the three bullet holes. Did they need dressing, antibiotics?

"Apparently I'm allergic ... to armor-piercing bullets ... And I overdid the magic ... head killing me."

"So you'll recover?"

"Hope so ... never been shot before ... like that. I'll ... I'll know more tomorrow. Assuming I eat."

He attempted another smile and made it about half way. Brenda headed for the kitchen. She was hungry, too. Too hungry to spend time preparing a proper meal, so she went to the freezer and pulled out a pizza.

She carried Brian's bowl of extra sugary granola through to him and held it for him while he ate. His left arm was use-less and he ate slowly as though every chew was an effort.

"Can you tell me what happened?" she asked. "You don't

have to talk. You can send me your thoughts."

He waited until he'd finished chewing before replying. "Can't. Need magic to send thoughts."

"Oh." Brenda's curiosity would have to wait.

Another bowl of granola – with an extra sprinkling of sugar – two bars of chocolate and a packet of peanuts later, he at last began to tell her what had happened. His attempted mind meld with Abbiati. The recovered memories that appeared to show him helping Frank Cassini rather than threatening him. Abbiati's intriguing phone call for help, the fire, and how he'd got shot.

"You teleported in front of witnesses?"

"No choice. It was that or ... die. Maybe?"

His speech became less labored with time. But he'd still sometimes stop in mid-sentence, his eyes screwed up in pain for several seconds.

"Who do you think Abbiati was calling?" she asked.

"Don't know. That's why we need all this." He pointed to the computer and the drawer of papers. "Must be something in there. Address book. Phone numbers."

"What if Abbiati's human, but he's working for a demon?" said Brenda. "Can a demon shield a human's mind, or do something to it to stop another demon from subverting them?"

Brian shrugged – a lop-sided one shouldered shrug.

"But you're a demon. Shouldn't you know these things?"

"I think I must have missed that class."

"Can't you call home and find out? Doesn't Hell have a library?"

"Only a horror section."

She had to smile but... "I'm being serious. Can't you find out if there are other demons on Earth?"

He grimaced – maybe from pain, or maybe from a desire not to answer the question. "Demons are inherently secretive. I've looked for others on this planet, but ... never found one."

"So you *do* know what to look for? If you met one, you'd know?"

He closed his eyes. Another grimace. "Sometimes. Perhaps. I don't know. I don't even know about Abbiati and ...

I've been inside his mind."

He opened his eyes and stared at Brenda. "Check his files ... look for medical procedures ... make a list."

"What kind of medical procedures? Is there something specific?"

His eyelids drooped. His voice began to fade. "Make a list. Wear gloves. Anything incriminating goes to the police."

He passed out. Or feigned passing out. She considered rolling his eyelids back to check but, other than watching people do that on TV, she wasn't sure what it was supposed to achieve. Would the words 'out cold' be written on his eyeballs?

She went to the kitchen and checked on her pizza. It was almost ready, which was good enough. She was starving.

She spent the first part of the evening wearing pink kitchen gloves - they were the only ones she had - sorting through Abbiati's papers. She found share certificates, bonds, mortgages and deeds. Abbiati certainly owned a lot of property. Or held the deeds to them. She found over thirty bank accounts. Some in Abbiati's name. Some in family members' names. Some in names she didn't recognize, and the rest belonged to a series of companies. Millions of dollars, euros, and Swiss francs, in accounts based all over the world.

But no medical files. No hospital admissions and no doctor's letters.

She organized everything into piles and made a list of any names she came across - both people and companies.

And she counted the money. Seven hundred and fifty thousand dollars. Eight hundred thousand if you counted the money spent on the car - which she supposed she had to. She let it all sit on her carpet for a while, all neatly stacked and shouting 'spend me!' to the ceiling. She'd never seen so much cash.

With help from her inner Brenda she tore herself away from the shiny money mountain and assembled Abbiati's computer. She plugged in her screen and keyboard, switched it on and ... she was in. No obscure operating system, no password protection - maybe he thought having his house patrolled by armed guards was protection enough? Either that or there was nothing incriminating to protect.

She checked his email account, saving all the files to a memory stick. And had a cursory glance through the names and titles. None stood out – no obvious messages from demons, crime boss newsletters, or cryptic notes from people called Bugsy.

And nothing medical either. No emails from doctors or hospitals. She checked his documents folder, downloading everything. No folders called medical, no obvious correspondence with doctors or hospitals.

She remembered the search facility and went back and used it on his email folders – trying 'doctor' first, then 'hospital', then 'operation' and 'procedure.' Dozens of irrelevant hits that wasted fifteen minutes wading through emails to check the context. She tried the search facility on his document folders next and found the same.

Brenda rubbed her eyes. File checking was boring when there was nothing to find. She bet Batman never did any filing. He'd have the Bat Computer programmed to do the searches for him. And he had a proper crime fighter's car.

Brenda daydreamed for a while, wondering if she could carry off the black leather look. CatBrenda? CatBrenda in her Winter Gold Jag. Maybe she should dress in gold to match? And dye her hair. GoldBrenda. She could have a theme song. Shirley Bassey would sing it. *GoldBrenda! She's the girl, the girl with the Midas touch.*

Even the inner Brenda sang along for a few bars, before gently reminding her host that she had a crime to solve. Several crimes, in fact. Had she forgotten about Sacrifice and the search for Daddy?

She had. She typed in 'Daddy' and 'Sacrifice' and searched Abbiati's files again. Another wait, another screenful of hits to search through, another series of dead-ends. There had to be something else she could do!

There was. She could summon Sacrifice again and ask her what Daddy looked like. She already had a picture of Frank Cassini. If she could find a picture of Abbiati she could show them both to Sacrifice and solve that part of the mystery once and for all.

She checked through Abbiati's picture folders. He didn't have many photographs, but he was in a few. She connected

her printer and printed them off. Some of the pictures
showed Abbiati at what looked like business events – posed
pictures with men in expensive suits and women in evening
gowns. What if Daddy was one of them? He might have hired
Abbiati to abduct Sacrifice. She took a print of them all and
checked back to see if she could attach names to the faces
or a venue. But found nothing in the file names or the
folders.

She saved the pictures to her memory stick. Then
wondered if she should expand the search. Might as well
make the most of her time with Sacrifice and show her as
many pictures as possible. Abbiati was a rich man. He
attended business functions. Just the kind of person who'd
show up on an internet search.

Brenda disconnected her keyboard, screen and printer
and reconnected them to her own desktop. She typed in
'Bruno Abbiati' and searched for other pictures, preferably
from thirteen years ago.

She found one from ten years ago. *Prominent Stamford
businessman Bruno Abbiati receiving an award* –
presumably not for artistic maiming. And she found a group
picture, with names, from a function eight years ago. She
printed them off.

Now all she had to do was summon Sacrifice.

She sat on the floor as she'd done the previous summoning. Though, then, it had been a general call for murder
victims. She wasn't sure if it would work for a specific spirit.

But she had to try.

She took a deep breath and cleared her mind.

"Sacrifice," she whispered, echoing the name in her mind.
Sacrifice.

Her eyes scanned ahead, looking for the merest hint of a
shimmer.

She called again – louder – elevating her whisper into a
soft-spoken call, boosting her mental echo into a full-blown
yell.

Still nothing. She focussed her eyes on the bookcase,
imagining it was more than just a repository for books. It was
a portal to the astral plane, and Brenda had the power to
fling that door open and shout a message through.

Sacrifice!

She concentrated harder, screwing her eyes tight shut and clenching her teeth.

Sacrifice! I summon you here, now'

"Yes," said a voice.

Brenda jumped, almost falling over backwards. The sound came from behind her. A girl's voice. She swung round...

And saw a different girl. Similar – slim, long unkempt dark hair, brown eyes – but older. Thirteen, fourteen. She was wearing what looked like a white shift, and barefoot.

"Is your ... is your name Sacrifice?"

"Yes."

She stood by the edge of Brenda's sofa with what appeared to be a gentle wind blowing into her face. Her shift rippled slightly and clung against her body. Her long hair moved as if alive. And her eyes bore into Brenda's. No tears, no outward sign of fear, or any emotion at all.

How many dead girls called Sacrifice were there on the astral plane?

"How old are you?"

The dead girl shrugged.

"What's your mother called?"

"I have no mother."

The air suddenly felt distinctly chilly.

"What's your father called?"

"Daddy."

Deja vu with a double dose of industrial strength goose-bumps.

"What school do you go to?"

"I don't need to go to school."

"Why not?"

"Because I'm Sacrifice."

The girl smiled. She looked so proud. *I'm Sacrifice. Look at me.* Was this something Daddy had taught her? Some story he'd made up to explain why she never went to school?

"What's the last thing you remember?"

"Being injected."

"Injected with what?"

The girl shrugged. "Some kind of poison."

Brenda swallowed hard. The girl spoke of being poisoned as though it was an everyday occurrence. Dear diary, woke up, went to school, got poisoned.

"Who injected you?"

Brenda was sure she knew the answer, but she had to ask.

"Daddy."

Brenda reached out for her stack of pictures, her hands starting to shake.

"What does Daddy look like? Can you describe him to me?"

Another shrug. "He looks like Daddy."

She showed her the picture of Frank Cassini first, holding the picture out, firmly clamped with two hands. "Is this Daddy?"

For a moment it looked as though the girl wasn't interested. She continued to watch Brenda, her expression a mix between bored disinterest and amused aloofness.

Then she lowered her eyes and looked at the picture.

"It's not him," she said immediately.

"Are you sure? Look closer." The girl had barely glanced at the picture.

This time the girl floated closer. As she did so, the astral wind blowing against her appeared to strengthen. Her hair tumbled away from her face, her shift outlined every inch of her slim adolescent body. And her face ... it shone as if illuminated by some spectral light as she leaned forward, her nose inches away from the picture.

Brenda clutched the paper tighter, trying to make sure it didn't shake.

The girl stared at Frank Cassini. Was there a hint of recognition? If there was, it was fleeting.

"No. I've never seen this man before."

Brenda swapped pictures, thrusting one of Bruno Abbiati towards Sacrifice before she could pull away.

"Is this Daddy? He may be older in this picture. Or younger." She suddenly realized she had no idea when this Sacrifice had been murdered.

The girl studied the picture. "That's not him either."

Brenda grabbed the next picture – a formal dinner with Abbiati and assorted colleagues. The girl didn't recognize any of them either.

"Are you sure?" Brenda asked. "Have you ever seen

Daddy with another man. Or a woman."

"Daddy only needs me. I'm Sacrifice."

Back came that look of pride. Total confidence.

"Do you know what year it is?"

"2005. Or 2006. Time is unimportant. I'm Sacrifice."

Brenda showed her another Abbiati group picture and another. The girl recognized no one, and was becoming bored. She barely glanced at the last picture.

"Where did Daddy keep you?" Brenda asked, scratching around for pertinent questions. Ghosts didn't hang around for long and she knew she'd be kicking herself in a few minutes time for not asking the right questions.

"In my room," said Sacrifice, pulling back. Already she was beginning to fade. Even her voice had lost that crystal clear clarity.

"Did your room have a window?"

"No."

"Do you know what city your room was in?"

"The City of God."

She was already transparent. Her face, her shift, her hair rippling like a two-dimensional image projected on the surface of an undulating sea.

"What state is the City of God in?"

"A parlous one."

The girl disappeared.

A parlous one? Not the kind of state Brenda was inquiring about. And not the kind of word a thirteen year-old American girl would routinely use.

Brenda gathered her pictures from the floor and stacked them. Her hands had begun to shake again. Who was this Daddy? A brainwashing serial killer with a penchant for pre-pubescent dark haired girls and religion. She dredged up all her television psychology – culled from every mystery series she'd ever watched. Was he fixated on girls who reminded him of someone in his past? A sister, a daughter, some poor girl that in his sick twisted mind had done him wrong?

And were there others? If he'd killed in 1998 and 2005, what had he been doing in between? Was he still active today? Was there another Sacrifice in that windowless room, waiting for Daddy to visit her?

Chapter Nineteen

Brenda couldn't sleep. Every time she closed her eyes, she imagined some poor frightened girl locked in a windowless cell, waiting to be killed. Sacrificed. Was that the origin of the name? They were sacrifices? Girls abducted and held for days, months, years against their will, isolated and brainwashed by that sick bastard until they accepted their fate. They were sacrifices who wouldn't scream or struggle. They'd roll back their sleeve and let Daddy inject them.

Why? What pleasure could he possibly get from seeing them die? Luckily Brenda couldn't answer that question. Some people were too sick to be understood. Drawing pleasure from other people's pain, from breaking their spirit, from exercising total control over another person's life, from watching them die...

The list was as endless as it was sick.

And there had to be other girls. Perverts like Daddy didn't stop until someone stopped them. He had to be have been active for at least thirteen years. Thirteen years! It beggared belief. Why hadn't anyone noticed? Was he covering his tracks? Hiding the bodies? Abducting girls from different cities? Maybe different states?

They *had* to catch him. *Had* to. No playing for laughs. No amusing sidetracks. Track the bastard down, catch him and...

Let Brian find a punishment that fit the crime like a spiked glove.

Brenda awoke late the next morning – the result of a night tossing and turning. When she wasn't worrying about Sacrifice she was worrying about Brian or burglars. What if Brian never recovered? What if a burglar broke in and stole all the money, or the car? At one point she had to climb out of bed and creep downstairs – to check on Brian, the car, and to bring the money upstairs and hide it under her bed.

So it was a scratchy-eyed Brenda who descended the stairs later that morning. A scratchy-eyed Brenda who froze halfway down. Brian wasn't where she'd left him. The armchair was empty. She went from half-asleep to wide-awake in an instant. Where...

There he was. In the far corner of the room, slumped over her computer keyboard.

She ran to him. "Brian! Are you all right?"

He didn't answer. He didn't move. The three bullet holes were still visible – smaller and less colorful than the night before, but still very much there. She placed her hands on his shoulders and eased him upright, gently propping him against the back of the chair. His head lolled against his chest. And was that a snore?

"Are you asleep?"

It looked like he was. She could see his chest slowly rising and falling. And that was definitely a snore. She could hear it over the noise from the computer fan.

Her attention moved from Brian to her computer. It was on. Brian must have got up in the middle of night to use it. And then fallen asleep at the keyboard.

She leaned over Brian and refreshed the computer screen. A website appeared. A medical website discussing advances in cancer treatment. Cancer treatment?

She looked at Brian, then back at the screen. He needed to drag his body across the room to read this?

She rolled her Brian-laden office chair to one side and fetched a wooden dining chair to sit on. What had he been looking at last night?

She saved the current page to disk and pulled up the internet history file. He'd accessed about a dozen sites. Some of them she recognized. She'd accessed the same sites when she'd been searching for Bruno Abbiati. But others were hospitals, news sites, and medical journals.

She clicked on the first site. An article about the treatment of neck cancer. Did Abbiati have cancer? She skimmed the article. No mention of Abbiati and no hint why Brian might have found it interesting.

She saved the page and clicked to the next. Another

cancer site. This time at a hospital listing their various treatments for head and neck cancer. She could see a pattern developing, but not the reason. Why the interest in neck cancer? None of the sites mentioned Abbiati. Could he have found the hospital's telephone number amongst Abbiati's papers from the drawer?

She saved and moved on to the next page. Another article on neck cancer. But this one had a picture.

A photograph of Brian.

Brenda stared at the image. It was definitely Brian. It even had his name underneath. Brian Trafford, the first patient to benefit from the revolutionary new treatment for neck cancer. Gene Therapy.

Brenda devoured the article. It was from 2004. A gene therapy trial on twelve patients in England. Six of the patients had been cured completely – Brian Trafford had been one of them.

She looked at Brian. His face was charred and unrecognizable, but ... could he be this Brian Trafford? And if so ... what did it mean?

She saved the page to disk and clicked on the next site. More gene therapy trials – this time in the US. No mention of Brian or Abbiati. She clicked on the next and the next. More cancer, more gene therapy trials.

Her phone rang.

Reluctantly, she pulled herself away from the computer and answered it.

It was Susan, her sister.

"You are coming tonight, aren't you?"

Tonight? Brenda's brain wobbled into a state of fogged paralysis.

"Coming where?"

"Ha, ha. Very funny." Susan was not laughing. Neither was Brenda. She'd just remembered. Her mother's birthday party! How could she have forgotten?

"Consider this your ten hour warning," continued Susan. "Dinner's at eight and we're expecting you at seven."

Brenda shifted her voice a notch or two into the sick register – aiming for weak with a suggestion of hoarse.

"I'm not feeling too well. There was a bug going through school last week. I thought I'd escaped it, but ... you know what these bugs are like."

"You're not getting out of this, Brenda. When's the last time you saw Mom?"

"I'm three hours away, Sue. It's a long drive."

"Emily lives in Hawaii, but she visits Aunt Donna three times a year."

Cousin Emily again. Weren't their any matricides in Susan's circle? Where was Lizzie Borden when you needed her?

"It's a long drive, Susan. I'm really not feeling good, and I don't want to give you all my cold."

"Bullshit! You haven't got a cold. And why don't you stay for a few days. Mom would love to see you."

Brenda closed her eyes. What could she say? There was no way she'd stay overnight at her mother's. She'd find bars on her bedroom window and wake up to a team of deprogrammers sitting at the breakfast table. *It's for your own good, Brenda. We've sat on the sidelines far too long. You're a vibrant, intelligent woman who's wasting her life. You had a career, a husband ... and now look at you! Living on your own in a dead-end job. You've got to snap out of it, my girl. You're not getting any younger.*

"I'll see," she said.

Susan sighed. One of her big sister exasperated sighs. "Oh, you're coming, Brenda. If you're not here by seven we're moving the party to your house."

They would too. And if Brenda didn't open the door, they'd set up camp on the lawn.

Susan hung up before Brenda could prevaricate further. She was probably on the phone to Mom already.

Brenda slumped into the nearest chair. What was she going to do? She couldn't *not* go to her mother's and yet ... if Brian didn't recover pretty damn soon, how could she? Her mother would have a fit. *How could you have plastic surgery and not tell me? Your own mother!*

Brenda's head found her hands. Could she feign an accident? Hide her nose under a bandage? It might work. With a sports bra and a lot of tape she might be able to hide her boobs. She'd find something loose and voluminous to wear. And she'd have her giant eighties hair cut and dyed back to its original brunette.

Could she have her hair cut and dyed? She knew nothing about magic, but she'd seen *The Fly*. Did shapeshifting work on the same principles? Had that extra hair come from the skin and bone shaved off her nose? Would she be cutting and dyeing her nose?

Her head sunk deeper into her hands. If she dyed her hair, she'd have a shiny black nose for the rest of her life.

Brenda waited until she'd had breakfast and two cups of strong coffee before she tried to wake Brian. As curious as she was to find out about Brian Trafford and gene therapy, she also wanted him fully rested. She needed him to change her back.

"Brian? Are you awake?"

No answer. She gave his shoulder a gentle shake.

A singed eyelid fluttered. "What?" he said sleepily.

"Are you ... feeling better?"

"I feel terrible."

"Will you have your powers back by this evening?"

He tried to shrug and screwed his face up in pain.

"Is there anything I can get you? Granola? Chocolate?"

"Hot sweet tea. Three sugars. No, make that four. And biscuits."

She fetched the tea and cookies, wondering how to frame the next series of questions. Perhaps he'd be more malleable on a sugar high?

She let him drink half a cup before broaching the question. "Who's Brian Trafford?"

He took another sip of tea. A long sip. "Who?"

"You know," said Brenda. "The man you were Googling last night. The Brit who had the gene therapy."

"Ah, him. I met him once. He had a face I thought I could use. Nondescript and instantly forgettable. Ideal for our line of work."

"So why were you Googling him last night?"

"I wasn't. I thought maybe Abbiati had gene therapy, and that page came up."

"Why do you think Abbiati had gene therapy?"

Another attempted shrug, another grimace, another long sip of tea. "A hunch. We demons are always having them. Sometimes they're spot on, sometimes not."

Brenda didn't believe a word of it. But she wasn't sure if she should press him. He could turn her into a frog if she annoyed him. A frog with eighties hair and a large chest.

Maybe it would be safer to try again later – slip it casually into conversation when he was being less guarded. In the meantime...

"I talked to Sacrifice last night."

That got his full attention. No long pauses while he sipped his tea or nibbled on a cookie. He wanted to know everything, interrupting frequently with a question or an observation.

"Summon her now," he said when she'd finished.

"Why?"

"I can help. I ... I have some power back. Not much, but ... enough to alter a picture. If you get Sacrifice back I can do a photofit. And if we get a picture of Daddy...."

He didn't need to finish the sentence.

"Are you sure you're up to it? It won't knock you back or anything?"

"It'll hurt, but ... it has to be done. Chances are he's got another girl. The longer we delay, the worse it'll be for her."

He tried to get up, leaning forward, grimacing. Brenda noticed he was using his left arm – not very well, and it collapsed under the strain of trying to push himself up from the chair. But at least he could move it.

"Do you need any help?"

"We need pictures. Lots of them. And I need to be close ... when you talk to Sacrifice ... so I can alter the faces."

She helped him onto the sofa, then went searching for magazines. She'd need a good selection of faces. Old, young, tall, short, fat and slim. Though not too young – if Daddy was active thirteen years ago he'd have to be at least thirty. Unless he started young. She'd play it safe and collect the largest cross-section she could find. Best not to overtax Brian if she could help it. He had to be awake, fit, and fully functional by seven that evening.

She tore pictures from women's magazines, TV guides, and newspapers. She combed her bookshelves for suitable covers, pausing for a moment's contemplation of how she'd feel if Daddy turned out to look like Fabio. And she grabbed the pictures of Frank Cassini and Bruno Abbiati – just in case.

Then she looked at Brian – the chargrilled, skeletal, naked corpse sitting on the sofa. Would one look at him send Sacrifice screaming back to the astral plane? She decided not to take the risk and turned the sofa round so that its back was facing the bookcase.

Now came the hit-and-miss part – summoning Sacrifice.

She sat on the floor next to the sofa and spread the pictures out over the carpet. She closed her eyes, flexed her arms and fingers, took a deep breath. Then cleared her mind, wiping away any negative thoughts. This was going to work. She'd done it before, she could do it again. Even with the added pressure of an audience and a young life at stake.

Backtrack that thought – too negative – there *was* no extra pressure. She was a medium. Ghosts came to her all the time. This was merely an extension of a natural process. A request for a specific spirit to step forward and be heard.

She formed an image in her mind – imagining the boundary between the real and spirit world to be wafer thin. Imagining it as a membrane stretched tight like a drum skin that could take sound and amplify it ten, twenty, thirty-fold. She touched her lips to the membrane and whispered. *Sacrifice.*

She called again and again, the name resonating through the spirit world like a siren call. *Sacrifice. I need you here. Come to me now.*

She added her voice to the summons. "Sacrifice. I summon you. Appear before me now!"

Silence. She tried again, imagining the membrane ripped in two, pushing her mind through the gap, shouting Sacrifice's name at the top of her voice. *Sacrifice! I summon thee!*

"I'm here."

Brenda opened her eyes. The girl was standing some six feet away, her eyes cast down, her hands clasped in front of her. She was nine or ten this time. Another Mary Alice Cassini lookalike. Small and waif-like with hair that looked like it hadn't been brushed for days or professionally cut for years. Her clothes looked clean, though. Blue jeans and a green top.

"What's your name?" Brenda asked.

"Sacrifice."

Her voice was thin and small. And the resemblance between her and Mary Alice was uncanny. Did Daddy have to comb several cities to find the 'right' girl? Was that why no one had made the connection? Every abduction occurred in different states?

"Do you go to school?"

"No."

"Does your bedroom have a window?"

A shake of the head.

That was enough of the preliminaries, now Brenda had to get her to identify Daddy before she faded away.

"Can you see these pictures on the floor?" she asked.

The girl hesitated. She looked reluctant to move her eyes away from the floor by her feet.

Brenda pushed the pictures closer, reaching out and sliding one, two, three across the carpet towards Sacrifice's feet.

"You see the pictures now?"

"Yes."

"Let's play a game then. Let's see if we can find a picture of Daddy. Can you see him down there?"

The girl didn't just shake her head, she shook her body, swinging from her knees, suddenly looking far younger than the nine or ten physical years her height suggested.

Brenda pushed the remaining pictures closer.

"What about these? Is he here?"

The girl took her time, leaning theatrically from the waist to peer down at the ones furthest away.

"No."

"Which one looks the most like him?"

Another long pause as Sacrifice scrutinized each picture in turn. Some she returned to.

"That one," she said pointing to a picture of an almost bald Sean Connery from a few years ago, with a greying goatee beard. Picking Sean Connery was bad enough, but thank God it wasn't Fabio.

Brenda picked up the picture. "How could we make him look more like Daddy?" She asked Sacrifice. "Change his hair?"

"Daddy has no hair. Only a beard."

"Is the beard like this? Or is there more of it? Or less?"

"Like that."

"And the same color?"

"Yes."

She turned to Brian. "Lose the hair. The beard's fine, but the rest goes."

Brian took the picture, held it in both hands and concentrated. His hands shook with the effort. "Done," he said handing it back.

They continued in that vein. Brenda asking Sacrifice if the shape of the nose was right, the eyes, the jaw line, the outline of the face. Brian made the alterations, his blackened forehead glistening. Sometimes he had to stop mid-shift and rest. Sometimes he had to curl up in a ball, head in hands.

"Are you sure you can continue?" Brenda asked him. "The likeness must be pretty close as it is."

"No," he said, his teeth clenched. "Got to get it right."

"What's the matter with him?" asked Sacrifice, leaning to her right to peer towards Brian, but showing no inclination to move any further from her spot by the television.

"He has a bad headache," said Brenda.

"Daddy gets those. They make him angry."

Brenda shivered. She could imagine – in graphic detail. From his picture, Daddy was a thickset version of Sean Connery – probably six foot plus and approaching two hundred and fifty pounds. Sacrifice was a waif-like nine-year-old. It would be terrifying.

"I don't like it when Daddy gets angry."

"No, I don't expect you do. But Daddy's not angry at the moment. See, look at his picture. He's not angry at all, is he?"

The girl shook her head, but didn't look convinced. She looked afraid. The thought of an angry Daddy had unsettled her.

Brenda tried to press on and finish the photofit before she lost the girl completely.

"What about his eyes? Do they look like Daddy's eyes? Or should they be closer together? Or larger?"

"Don't know."

"Close your eyes and think, Sacrifice. Think about a time

when Daddy was happy. And you were ... happy."

Brenda could feel she was digging herself into a very large and inappropriate hole, but felt powerless to avoid it. How do you try and lead a girl, who's been locked up and murdered by a sadistic pervert, to a safe place in her past where she could think calmly and describe her abductor? For all Brenda knew, Daddy smiled most when he was torturing her.

Brenda persevered, giving Sacrifice time when she felt she needed it, and pressing when she thought she could take the risk. It was slow and painstaking work. But, together, they refined the picture, adjusting Daddy's eyes and nose, and thickening his lips.

Then Sacrifice began to fade.

Brenda slipped into panic mode. Think of a question! Quick! She's going!

"What year is it?" she asked.

Sacrifice was barely visible. Her mouth moved, but her answer – if it was an answer – was too quiet too discern. It was more like a sigh.

And then she was gone.

Brenda's annoyance was short-lived. She had a picture. Anyone as sick as Daddy had to have a record. Or have been noticed. Even if he'd never been convicted, his name would appear in reports as a person of interest. His face would be in the FBI database. It had to be!

And she could find it today. In the next hour if she was quick. The desk sergeant downtown knew her from yesterday. He'd let her access the FBI computer. All she'd have to do was input the picture and out would come Daddy's name and address.

Reality lobbed a brick in Brenda's direction. The desk sergeant wouldn't recognize her, because yesterday she'd had a different face.

Brenda dropped her head, then raised it to look at Brian who was staring vacantly into space.

"Brian? Brian! Can you change me back? Just the nose. I'll disguise the rest. I need to get into the FBI computer."

He stared at her through hooded eyes. He looked exhausted. He hadn't said a word since Sacrifice left. And, maybe she was imagining it, but for someone char-grilled black, he looked surprisingly pale.

"Can't," he said. "Living flesh too hard. Paper easier."

"Paper?"

He held out a shaking hand. "Fetch paper. Those pictures."

He pointed a shaky finger at the magazine pages on the floor. She collected them up and handed them to him.

He screwed the pages up between both hands. Then smoothed them together, rubbing the flat of his right hand over his left. All the time he stared at Brenda intently. It was unsettling.

"You'll need a password too," he said. "It's inside."

Then his head rolled back and he passed out, dropping what looked like a black wallet from his hands.

Brenda bent down and picked it up. As she did so, a scrap of paper fell out. She picked that up too. It had an agent number and a password scrawled on it. Then she opened the wallet and found an FBI badge with her picture and ... a new name. Agent Jane Marple.

Chapter Twenty

Agent Marple was ready. She had ID. She had two pictures – one of Daddy, and one of Mary Alice, so she could search for other victims. And she had a plan. She'd tell the desk sergeant she was a colleague of the FBI agent who'd requested access to their computer yesterday. A plan which sounded much better when she left out the names Mulder and Marple. The desk sergeant had already picked up on Agent Mulder, would Agent Marple tweak his curiosity enough to call FBI headquarters?

Brenda convinced herself it wouldn't. Miss Marple was unassuming and in her seventies. Agent Marple was a thirtysomething blonde with a distracting chest.

And, on the subject of distraction, should she wear *that* dress to complete the effect? On the plus side, it was difficult to call Quantico if your eyeballs had been burnt out at the roots. But on the minus side...

No, she'd wear a T-shirt. A tight T-shirt. Not that she had a choice since her unasked-for augmentation.

Ten minutes later, Jane Marple – in tight jeans, T-shirt and enough hair to cover a small planet – sashayed out the door. And looked at her 1999 Ford Contour and thought...

What if they recognize my car from yesterday? Shouldn't I drive something else to keep my cover?

You thought nothing of the kind! tattled the inner Brenda. *You just want an excuse to drive the Jaguar.*

Brenda turned longing eyes towards the garage door. It wouldn't be *her* driving the Jaguar. It would be Agent Marple...

Are you completely *mad? You want to drive a stolen car to a police station! And, oh, what about the forged FBI badge? Do you* want *to draw attention to yourself?*

Agent Marple sighed. The Ford Contour it was. She

climbed inside and drove away.

The same desk sergeant was on duty as the previous day. Agent Marple smiled, walked confidently over and flicked open her badge.

"I believe my colleague was here yesterday. Agent Mulder?"

"Yes," said the desk sergeant, carefully checking Agent Marple's chest against its picture.

"I need access to a computer terminal, too. This case is moving fast and I need to run a suspect's picture through the system now."

"Really?" he said, his eyes moving up to her face before being waylaid by her hair.

"I'm undercover," said Brenda feeling the need to explain her eighties look.

What as? A time-travelling trollop?

Brenda ignored her repressed inner self and furnished the sergeant with a confident smile. And a request.

"Is Detective Sjoberg on duty?"

The sergeant rang to find out and a minute later a harassed-looking Detective Sjoberg came hurrying downstairs.

"Yes, what is it ... Oh." His face brightened. "Good morning, Miss um...."

"Marple," said the desk sergeant.

"No!" said Brenda. "Not Miss Marple. I'm um Mrs. Agent Marple."

The Inner Brenda cringed.

Detective Sjoberg smiled. "Well, Mrs. Agent Marple, would you like to follow me?"

Brenda trudged after him, her head metaphorically in her hands. How not to draw attention to yourself, lesson one – don't speak and panic at the same time.

Detective Sjoberg showed her to the same room as before, but this time he was in no hurry to leave.

"What case are you working on?" he asked.

"The Daddy investigation."

"Daddy?"

Brenda showed him the picture. "We think he's been abducting girls for at least thirteen years. He takes them, holds them in some underground dungeon, then kills them."

"You think he lives around here?"

"We don't know where he lives. It's likely he's been taking girls from all over the country to avoid detection. We're only just beginning to tie the pieces together. Which is why I need to run these pictures."

"Right."

He leaned against the door, still showing no signs of leaving.

Brenda considered asking him to help. He'd know his way around the system far better than she would. But...

He was already curious and Brenda had a few extra searches in mind which would be difficult to explain.

She grimaced, bending slightly and placing a hand on her abdomen.

"Are you okay?" he asked.

"It's just cramps. I started my period this morning. Is there somewhere nearby where I can buy tampons?"

Detective Sjoberg suddenly found urgent business in another room. If he'd been a cartoon character, he'd have left behind an open mouth.

Brenda used Brian's ID and password to access the FBI database. No sirens sounded and no warning message flashed on the screen about unauthorized access. So that was a plus. The FBI database could have been a little more user friendly – a help screen for inexperienced hackers would have been good – but she tapped and clicked her way through a series of screens until she found a place where she could upload a picture. She placed Daddy's photofit on the document feeder, waited an age for it to be digitized, then fired off the search.

Hit after hit appeared on the screen – hundreds of near matches. She sifted through them one by one. They all exhibited some resemblance, but ... none of them *was* Daddy. Assuming Sacrifice's picture had been accurate. And if she doubted that, then the whole exercise was doomed.

She played with the search criteria, extending the search into victims and suspects and agents and police officers. More hits, more possibilities, but no one who cried out 'Daddy.'

She narrowed the search to violent crimes, deciding to print details of anyone who came close. After all, Daddy could have altered his appearance.

And what about the name Daddy? What if it was a nickname?

She searched on the name Daddy, found a few Big Daddies and one Puff Daddy, but no one who looked anything like the picture.

Time to try something else. She noticed there was a search for matching similar crimes. You input some or all the details of your crime and the system looked for matches. Brenda filled in the victim type – female child, brunette. She added the abduction, the imprisonment in a windowless room. The names Daddy and Sacrifice. And murder by lethal injection.

She found no close matches, but thousands of partials. Over two hundred children were abducted and murdered each year. Some had been imprisoned in basements. But no mention of death by injection, or the name Sacrifice.

She kept skimming through the partial list, looking for similarities, looking for something close enough to at least print. But nothing came close.

Then she tried searching just on the name Sacrifice. She found a few hits where children – usually recent immigrants from Africa – had been ritually murdered. And she found two cases where the word sacrifice had been scrawled on a bedroom wall at the murder scene. Both cases involved young girls. One was seven, the other nine. Neither resembled Sacrifice. They lived fifty miles apart, a couple of hundred miles from Mary Alice and Stamford. But the dates...

Both murders were thirteen years ago, a few months apart. The second had occurred two months before Mary Alice Cassini was abducted. Was this Daddy in his early years, before he found it safer to abduct the girls and dispose of their bodies later?

It could be. No one had been charged with either girl's murder. She pulled up more details. None of the suspects looked anything like Daddy, and the girls were killed by having their necks broken. Did that rule Daddy out? Didn't serial killers stick to the same MO?

Or was Daddy just starting out thirteen years ago? Experimenting. He didn't like the fact that the bodies were discovered so quickly, so he moved them to his basement. And he didn't like the way they died so quickly. He liked having them around, so he built a special room where he could keep them. Then when Mary Alice died, he was so fixated on her, he had to replace her. Hence the need to find girls who looked the same. He was recreating her.

Brenda printed off everything she could find on the two cases, then uploaded the picture of Sacrifice. She'd search for matches again, but this time she wouldn't stop when she found Mary Alice.

One by one, the lookalikes appeared on screen. She scrutinized them all. Again, none of them looked familiar, but then these were pictures provided by their families. The girls were clean, well-fed, and well-dressed. The Sacrifices were rail thin and had hair down to their waists. Plus some of the Sacrifices she'd seen could have been kept for several years. Children change.

But not that much. She stared at the gallery of missing and murdered children. Could Daddy have altered their appearance to make them look like Mary Alice? Dyeing their hair wouldn't be enough. But if Daddy was a plastic surgeon...

Brenda considered that for a while, wondering if she'd just crossed the line into bad TV movie territory or made a real discovery. She was looking at the FBI database of all the missing or murdered children whose face resembled Mary Alice in any way. She should have found more than one positive match. She'd met three Sacrifices. There were probably more.

So why weren't they showing up here? Was he targeting girls who wouldn't be reported? *Were* there girls who wouldn't be reported? Surely even street kids had a missing person report somewhere in their past. Or was he going abroad for his victims? Into Canada or Mexico or further afield? But the girls all spoke English. They had no discernible accent. He couldn't be going that far.

Could he be a plastic surgeon?

It might explain the hypodermic and the poison. As a doctor, he'd have ready access to lethal drugs.

She typed in cosmetic surgery and murdered children and ran a search. Had any post mortems found the victim had had cosmetic surgery? No hits came back. She stood back and rubbed her chin. She was running out of ideas. Daddy was a doctor. He killed by lethal injection. Could he do that in such a way that the death wasn't picked up as a murder? An air bubble into a vein? A heroin overdose that looked self-inflicted?

She liked the latter. The Sacrifices could pass as street children. He could dump their bodies on waste ground or in abandoned buildings. Leave the syringe, create a series of track marks to make it look like they were long term addicts. They might not even get a post mortem. They might not be found for weeks.

She typed in drug overdose and children – girls under twelve. There couldn't be that many pre-teens overdosing on drugs, could there?

There weren't. Brenda did her best to scrutinize the pictures, but one was partly decomposed and another was bloated. They could be Sacrifices, they could be anyone. She cleared the screen. This was getting her nowhere. He might be burying the bodies, disposing of them at sea, or feeding them to pigs for all she knew. Was she going to search for cosmetic surgeons who kept pigs next?

Well...

The FBI database didn't appear to have such a search facility. But it did have a person search. Should she enter Bruno Abbiati and list off his associates?

Then she had a better idea. What if she typed in Brian Trafford?

There was a box for nationality so it might link to data-bases in England, or even Interpol.

She tried it. And back came a very different picture from the one she'd been expecting. It was a bruised and battered Brian Trafford from eleven years ago. He'd been attacked while on vacation in Florida. His wife and child had been killed. The attackers – one white, one Hispanic – had never been found.

Brenda read open-mouthed. It was definitely the same Brian Trafford who later contracted neck cancer. Even with his face swollen and bruised she could still recognize him.

And his address was given as Reading, England.

So, Brian Trafford was a victim of crime. Was that why Brian had chosen his face? Or was this *her* Brian – Brian the Vigilante Demon on one of his takedowns that went horribly wrong?

And was his dead wife one of Brenda's predecessors?

Chapter Twenty-One

Driving home, Brenda eyes kept straying towards the stack of papers on the passenger seat next to her. Angela Trafford's picture lay at the top. She'd been shot five times in the head and chest. Her daughter's body lay beside her, shot once in the face. Their bodies found in a Florida parking lot next to Brian, who'd been beaten, shot, and left for dead.

According to Brian's statement, they'd been returning to their car when two men came up to them and demanded money. Brian handed over what he had, but the men thought he was holding out on them and started beating him. His wife intervened, was knocked to the ground, then shot. Their daughter became hysterical and she got shot, too. In the mouth to shut her up. It was brutal and totally unnecessary. The Traffords weren't a wealthy family. They'd handed over their money and their one credit card. The men just kept shooting. Not in panic or drug fuelled rage, but in cold blooded spite. Neither killer was ever apprehended.

Brenda shivered. There were no other witness reports. Only the husband's. It didn't sound like one of Brian's takedowns, but if he was the only witness, that meant nothing – he might have bent the truth to placate the police. Had he misread the robbers' intentions – failed to stop the first bullet hitting his partner, then everything went to hell in a handbasket? And the men were never apprehended for the simple reason that Brian had shapeshifted their asses to bugs and stomped them flat.

But...

Where did the daughter fit into this crime-fighting scenario? Brian used a medium to find murder victims. He didn't need anyone else. And it said in the report that Brian had been treated in hospital. Wouldn't they have noticed he wasn't human? He'd been unconscious when they'd found him. They'd operated on him to take two bullets out. They'd X-rayed his broken arm.

So...

What if Brian the Vigilante Demon and Brian Trafford the human were one and the same person? What if he'd been human eleven years ago? What if he'd been human five years ago when along came gene therapy and – zap – suddenly he wakes up with superpowers? What's he going to do with them? Join the circus, save the world, or go after the murdering bastards who killed his wife and child? It fitted. His need to fight crime. His reckless behavior. His interest in gene therapy. He wasn't a demon. All that bullshit about Heaven and Hell was exactly that – bullshit. He was a vigilante with superpowers – a grieving husband and father still lashing out at the men who'd murdered his family, seeking revenge by hunting down killers and switching roles – making them feel as impotent and frightened as he'd done that evening in Florida. And when he'd discovered that Abbiati could block his telepathic eavesdropping, his first thought hadn't been 'he must be a demon too.' It had been 'has he undergone gene therapy?'

And how many people in the world had undergone gene therapy? Hundreds? Thousands? Had they all developed superpowers?

When she got home she found Brian still slumped on the sofa.

"Brian?" she called. "Brian! We need to talk."

He didn't so much as open an eye. He looked like he was asleep. After his recent exertions fabricating pictures and FBI badges, he could very well be asleep. But ... it was all too convenient. Whenever she had something important to ask him, he passed out. Was that one of his superpowers? The ability to faint when confronted with a difficult question?

The day dragged itself towards afternoon. Brian slept and Brenda stared at pictures of dead and missing girls, trying to see some resemblance to one of the Sacrifices. Imagining a nose job here, a cheek implant there. Then she decided the whole process was a waste of time, as any one of them could be fashioned into a Mary Alice clone by a skilled plastic surgeon.

Should she summon another Sacrifice and ask? They'd know if they'd been operated on.

She tried. Several times. But no one appeared. Maybe they really did have a lunch hour on the astral plane. Or Brenda was too tense. She was finding it difficult to concentrate on anything. She had to leave for her mother's in two-and-a-half hours and Brian was still out cold. What was she going to do?

The afternoon dragged even slower. She'd have to take Brian with her in the car. Put him in the trunk so he wasn't seen. And if he hadn't recovered by the time they reached her mother's, she'd keep on driving and go into hiding until he had. Maybe she could persuade him to give her a few facial scars? Make it look like she'd been in an accident. Yes! She could see a viable Plan B. She'd turn up at her mother's door the next day covered in cuts and bruises. *I was tired and I had this splitting headache, but I couldn't miss your party so I drove for hours to get here and then this car came out of nowhere and hit me. I've been in hospital ever since.* She'd get sympathy, maybe even make her mother and Susan experience a pang of guilt or two. *And* her car would have to be totaled. She could keep the Jag!

It was a win, win, win scenario.

As long as she could fool her mother – the mother with a built-in lie detector.

Four o'clock arrived with Brian still unconscious and no freak storm having washed away all the roads between Brenda's house and her mother's. She'd have to leave. Unless she took the Jag. It was bound to be faster. If she took the Jag she could wait another fifteen minutes at least. And the new car would completely throw her mother. *Look, Mom, I told you my life was turning round. I've got a new job and a new car!*

The deprogrammers could be sent home.

That is if her mother – the one with the built-in lie detector that never ran low on batteries – actually bought the story. Reality check time. Both her mother and Susan would want to know everything about the new job. The pair of them would cross-examine Brenda all through dinner. They'd want details. They'd want her work phone number.

Could she use HELL 666?

"Sanjay would charge."

"Brian! You're awake. Can you change me back?"

He sat up, not exactly moving spryly, but without grimacing or slumping backwards.

"I'll try myself first."

He changed in front of her, morphing slowly from naked charred corpse to ... well, he *was* clothed. And he looked like Brian, but ... his skin. It was flaky and blotchy. His face, his hands, and probably the rest of him too, looked dry and sunburned. Even his hair, which looked as dry as tinder and ready to fall out by the roots the moment a comb went anywhere near it.

"Is that because of the fire?" she asked.

He stared at his hands. "I don't know. I'm not feeling one hundred percent yet. It might be an idea to wait a while before I change you."

Brenda didn't need any convincing. Turning up at her mothers with giant hair and fake boobs would be bad enough, but looking like someone who'd then been locked inside a tanning bed for twelve hours would be far worse. Luckily, seven o'clock was still three hours away. And she had a lot of questions to ask Brian on the drive down.

First she told him about her failure to find Daddy in the FBI database. Then she moved onto the two murdered girls with 'sacrifice' scrawled on their bedroom walls. That interested him. He studied the pictures and read the case details for ages.

"If this is where he started, it might be close to where he's based," he said. "Somewhere in central New York State. It's not that far from Stamford."

"What about him switching MO?" she asked. "Do you think that's a problem?"

"I'm not sure. Looking at these PMs, he broke both their necks, but not expertly. He's not one of those trained killers who snap people's necks with ease. He used brute force. Maybe in panic, maybe trying to keep them quiet. So, maybe later he found that by keeping the girls locked up, he could brainwash them, and no longer needed to get so physical. Who can tell with psychos?"

He was less convinced about Brenda's plastic surgeon

theory.

"Of course there's one way to prove it," he said.

"How?"

"We hack into some computer somewhere that has a list of all plastic surgeons and look for a picture of Daddy. If the surgeon files don't come with pictures, we cross-reference their names against the DMV. I can't imagine a plastic surgeon who doesn't drive."

That's when Brenda decided to raise *the* question. Brian was relaxed, open and, hopefully, not reading her mind.

"How long were you and Angela married?"

"What?" He didn't exactly blanch, but he came close.

"You were talking about her in your sleep–"

"No, I wasn't. I can read your thoughts, Brenda. You saw Brian Trafford's case file and you're curious. But you're wrong. Angela Trafford came to one of my previous partners and ... it's a case I never solved, okay? It niggled. It still does. So I adopted Brian's face to remind me that I'm both fallible and have unfinished business. I *will* find Angela and Julie's murderer."

It had an annoying kernel of plausibility. But...

"So why the interest in gene therapy? Why were we searching Abbiati's home for medical files?"

"Because there was a good chance he wasn't human, and what better way to determine that than to get hold of his medical files? If he's a demon, he'll steer clear of all hospitals, X-ray machines, and blood tests."

He looked her straight in the eye. He had to be reading her thoughts, too. Which made it even more annoying. He'd be able to gauge how well his explanation was going down and modify his story accordingly. But he *did* sound plausible.

She tried one more question. "You were specifically looking at gene therapy."

"To see if he'd had his DNA tested. Look, if you want, I can take you to see this Brian Trafford. After we've caught Daddy that is. I expect Brian'll be easy to find."

Brenda stared at the road ahead, while trying to mask her prime thought: *Oh, you're good, Brian. But I don't trust you an inch.*

Soon Brenda was trusting him concerning several inches.

Namely her bust size. They'd just pulled into her mother's street and, knowing her sister, Susan would be at the window, curtain pulled back, mouth set and toe tapping on the floor.

So Brian had better make the change and disappear before the car came into Susan's radar range.

Brenda pulled over several doors down.

"You *can* do this, can't you?" she asked. "If you're not fully recovered, we can turn round."

Brian cracked his knuckles. "Relax. I'll have you presentable in seconds."

"And you're not going to do anything weird, are you?" She had visions of arriving on the doorstep with an extra boob on her back. "Because this *really* means a lot to me. It's my mother. It's my family. And it's going to be hell anyway without you making it worse."

He sat back, giving her a mock startled look. "You have my word as a spawn of Satan."

Brenda rolled her eyes.

Her eyes were still in mid roll when Brian reached out and touched her arm. Her body began to tingle. She looked down. Her clothes were changing. *No, Brian! You promised!*

Shock gave way to amazement. He'd changed her clothes, but in a good way – he'd given her that dress she liked in *Chantal's* store window. The expensive one. The one she was thinking of saving up for.

"You haven't stolen this from the store window, have you?"

In her mind she could see a brick lying on a sidewalk, shattered glass, alarm bells ringing...

"Of course not. The only place I stole it from was your mind. I knew you liked it, so I gave it to you as a present. And I've restyled your hair."

Aaaaarrrggghhh!

She couldn't reach the mirror quick enough. What was it going to be? A Mohawk? A blonde afro?

Neither. It was a style she'd considered a few months back, but wasn't sure she could pull off. She moved the mirror to the left and right. It ... it looked great. It really suited her. And together with the dress and her old boobs and ... well, forget the nose, she couldn't have everything.

But still, she looked great. She looked elegant and confident. She looked like a person who could out-Susan Susan.

"Thank you," she said, not knowing what to say. "It's...."

"It's nothing," said Brian. "You have a great night. You deserve it."

And with that unexpected compliment, Brian vanished.

Brenda spent a few seconds just sitting there, hands on the steering wheel, psyching herself up. Even with the new hair and dress this was going to be a stressful evening. Eventually she slipped the car into gear and drove the extra hundred yards to her mother's house. Bob and Susan's giant Hummer loomed in the driveway. For a second Brenda wished she'd brought the Jag. Or at least a photo she could show everyone when Susan started sniping.

Calm down, advised the inner Brenda. You're dressed to kill. You're on time. And no one – not even Susan – is going to rattle your confidence tonight.

She walked up the drive, rang the doorbell, took a step back, smoothed her dress, patted her hair, whipped up a confident smile and...

Her mother opened the door. And, as she did so, the biggest bunch of flowers Brenda had ever seen appeared magically next to her. They were being thrust towards her mother by ... Brenda could not believe it.

Fabio!

Chapter Twenty-Two

Brenda's heart reached speeds that had been known to kill lesser individuals. But then they hadn't been standing next to Fabio. Brenda was. And it was a young Fabio. In his prime. Early thirties. All hair and muscles.

He looked fabulous. Book cover fabulous. Fashionably windswept and disheveled as though he'd just stepped from a sword fight on a wild Scottish moor. His frilly white shirt was more unbuttoned than buttoned, and his jacket struggled to contain his bulging shoulders.

"You must be Susan, my Brenda's beautiful sister," he said in a lyrical Italian accent. Brenda's knees almost gave way.

So did her mother's. Brenda had never seen her so shocked, or so girlish. It was a toss-up which was open the most – Mom's mouth or her eyes. She looked from Fabio to Brenda, to the flowers, then back at Fabio. And almost melted on the doorstep. Years fell away as she transformed into a giggling schoolgirl.

"I'm Brenda's mother, silly."

Silly? Brenda couldn't believe the transformation. Who was this impostor standing on the doorstep, pretending to be her mother? Her real mom would never fall for the 'you look like sisters' line in a million years.

But it *was* Fabio.

"No!" said Fabio, affecting a style of shock that only a Mediterranean heartthrob could carry off. "You no look one day over thirty."

If Brenda's mother had been made out of chocolate, there'd have been a gooey mess on the doorstep by now. She giggled, she simpered, she buried her face in the mass of flowers and inhaled deeply. And then she turned to Brenda.

"Who is he?" she mouthed, and then regained sufficient composure to smile and ask, "You never said you were seeing someone."

"I am Fabio," said Brian before Brenda could answer.

Brenda clung to the same bemused smile she'd been hiding behind since Fabio's materialization. 'Why do you always push it, Brian? Why couldn't you call yourself Bruno or Rafael? You're impersonating a real person!'

Whose picture was undoubtedly adorning at least one of the books on her mother's bookshelf.

Brian ignored her and bent forward, his eyes never leaving Brenda's mother's. He swept up her right hand in his, and kissed it.

"Holy shit!" said Angelica, Susan's nine year-old daughter, who'd just appeared in the doorway. "Auntie Brenda's brought a man with her, and he's kissing grandma!"

Teams of wild horses couldn't have dragged Susan to the door quicker. The door flew open. Susan's mouth followed suit. And then her brain must have overloaded. There was just too much to take in at once. Brenda looking like she'd stepped off a catwalk. The most gorgeous man she'd ever seen standing next to her. Her mother holding the biggest, most exotic bunch of flowers imaginable. And Angelica had just said 'shit' in company.

"This is Susan," Brenda told Fabio. "And she's not my daughter."

Brenda and Fabio – mainly Fabio – were ushered inside. A movie star couldn't have received more attention. Vases were found for the flowers, then Fabio was guided into a sofa, and Brenda was thrust next to him. Angelica sat at their feet and Susan and her mother hovered in front – alternately offering them drinks and nibbles and firing off questions.

"How long have you been seeing each other?"

"Where did you meet?"

"Why didn't you tell me you were bringing someone?"

Meanwhile Bob, Susan's husband, manned the spotlight shining into Brenda's eyes. Well, he didn't, but Brenda felt like someone was. They'd barely fielded one question when the next was shot towards them. There was a limit to how fast Brenda could lie.

Not Brian though. He was loving the attention. Hamming it up with the occasional hair toss and an Italian accent to die for.

"Where do you work, Fabio?"

That was Brenda's mother. Pleasantries over, now time for the bottom line. How much do you earn, and are you fertile?

"I am doctor."

Brenda thought her mother was going to swoon. Handsome, Italian, *and* a doctor.

"A doctor!" She interrupted her swoon to give Brenda a knowing look. What are you waiting for, Brenda? There's a bed upstairs. Go get me grandchildren!

"Your mother must be so proud," she continued.

"No," sighed Fabio. "It is long story. Very sad. Many castles."

"Castles?"

Brenda didn't think Fabio's fan club could get any more excited, but they just had. Angelica was practically cuddling his shins. Susan was on the edge of her seat and Mom was designing wedding invitations. Even Bob, who rarely got excited about anything other than work and Angelica's school reports, had a glint in his eye – though that was probably down to the prospect of having a well-connected brother-in-law in need of financial advice.

"Si," said Fabio. "Very sad. My father he want me marry *la Marchesa Luisa*."

"What's a *Marchesa*?" asked Angelica.

"A duchess," said Susan, almost shushing her daughter with the speed of her reply.

"But I say," continued Fabio, lapping up the attention. "Papa, when I marry, I marry for love, not castles."

Brenda's mother shot her new favorite daughter a look, her eyes brimming. *Could this man get any better?*

Brenda had a sneaky suspicion that he would. Brian never knew when to stop. Just as she knew that she was the person who'd have to pick up the pieces when Fabio disappeared into the sunset. And put up with years of put-downs from her mother. *Why did you let that lovely man get away, Brenda? What were you thinking?*

'Don't go too far over the top, Brian. I have to live with these people.'

"My papa," said Fabio, suddenly looking as downcast – and twice as cute – as a very large abandoned puppy. "He very proud man. He say I spit on eight hundred years of family tradition. So...." Fabio shrugged, one of his giant elbows nearly knocking Brenda's cognac out of her hand. "He disinherit me. I have to find job. I study hard to become doctor. I do a leetle modeling in Milan to ... how you say? Put bread all over the table?"

"You modeled in Milan," said Susan, using the same hushed tones that her mother had used at the news he was a doctor.

"Si. Giorgio is good friend. I know him many years. He say, 'Fabio, you come Milan and work for me. I design special clothes just for you.'"

"Giorgio *Armani*!"

Brenda thought Susan was going to stand up and applaud. She'd put her hands together and almost bounced into the air.

"Si. I work three, maybe four year in Milan then, when I become doctor, I come to United States." He sighed again, and back came the big, sad puppy.

"I no talk to my mother, *la contessa*, for five years. Still. No worry. I think Doctor Fabio sound better that Count Fabio. Yes?"

The jury was out on that one.

"What do you do in your spare time?" asked Bob. "Do you play golf?"

Brenda waited to hear the name Tiger dropped casually into the conversation, but Brian must have learned restraint.

"No. I no play golf. All my spare time I spend with my Brenda." He flashed Brenda the kind of smile that could undo a bra strap from fifty paces. Brenda was sure she heard two twang close by.

"And my second job, of course," continued Fabio.

"You have a second job?"

"Yes. I am volunteer fireman."

There went the third bra strap.

"You're a fireman, a doctor, a model, *and* a count?" asked Angelica, her eyes widening so far that her eyebrows were in danger.

"And he's Italian," said Brenda. "Which, in poker terms, I think ranks as a royal flush."

Only Bob and Fabio laughed. Angelica didn't get the poker reference, and Susan's and her mother's eyes had glazed over as their thoughts drifted perilously close to a full-on Fabio fantasy daydream.

"It hard work being fireman," said Fabio. "But I love it. Yesterday I have to climb tree to save leetle kitten." He turned to smile at Brenda. "I love pussy."

Brenda had been sipping on a particularly fine cognac. Not any more. It left her mouth in a fine spray of remarkable force. Some may even have taken the scenic route via her nostrils.

"Auntie Bren!" cried Angelica, jumping up and swatting at her clothes. "You got that all over me."

Brenda apologized, in between the choking, the blushing, and the mental scream of: 'Brian! What are you doing? You can't say pussy in front of my mother!'

Brenda's mother, who had taken most of the cognac spray, looked like she needed the dowsing. It wasn't just embarrassment that was reddening her face. She looked uncomfortably hot. "I think I'll check on dinner," she said, getting up.

"I'll join you," said Susan.

The interrogation settled down as the evening progressed. Brian was over the top and fabulous, fielding every question with wit and charm, inventing amusing anecdotes and flirting outrageously. He'd always been funny, but there was something about the Fabio persona that really made him shine.

Was it just his looks? Looking like Fabio, he could probably recite the telephone directory and make it sound sexy. Or was it the accent? Or the easy charm? The smile. His *naïveté*. Brian's Fabio was like a big handsome innocent who seemed genuinely charmed by everyone around him. He asked as many questions as he fielded. Which was probably a good stratagem. The fewer facts he let slip about his history, the better. Susan was an inveterate Googler.

And he'd taken the family spotlight away from Brenda. No one was interested in sniping at her dead-end secretarial job any more. Her mother even commented on her hair. How it suited her. And her dress. Brenda hadn't received a compliment from her mother in four years. Not since her divorce.

Which made the evening almost enjoyable. Brenda could relax – up to a point. However restrained Brian was being at the moment, she knew he was only ever one heartbeat away from another pussy moment. Or worse.

With dinner ready the party moved through to the dining room and still everyone was enjoying themselves. The food, as usual, was superb. Steak with mole sauce and a lime honey vinaigrette.

"I *must* have this recipe," said Fabio.

"You cook?" said Brenda's mother.

"I am Italian. We *love* food. Tell me. This sauce. I can taste chocolate, no? And cumin. Cinnamon, I think. And a leetle nutmeg."

Brenda was impressed. He was reading her mother's mind, getting her to think of the recipe and reeling off the ingredients. She'd be his forever. Food may be the path to a man's heart, but it was an eight-lane freeway to her mother's.

Not that her mother needed much encouragement by this stage. Brenda had never seen her so girlish. It was like the second coming of Tom Jones. Another minute and underwear would be flying across the dining room table.

The only person for whom Fabio's spell appeared to be wearing off was Susan. She'd become noticeably quieter during the past ten minutes. Was she jealous? She was certainly used to having her side of the family center stage at these get-togethers. Bob would have won another promotion or a big fat bonus. And Angelica would have moved up another belt in some obscure oriental martial art, or have just passed a piano exam, or be auditioning for the lead in the school play.

"Brenda?" said Susan as the main course concluded. "Can you help me in the kitchen?"

It was not a request.

Brenda followed her sister into the kitchen. Susan found the sink, turned round, folded her arms, and glared.

"He's an escort, isn't he?"

"Who?"

"Him! Count doctor fireman Fabio."

"Of course not!"

"Yeah, right. What are you thinking, Brenda? Bringing a ... *gigolo* into Mom's house! Are you *that* desperate? Are you paying for sex, too? Is he going to strip during dessert?"

"If we're lucky."

Brenda thought Susan was going to explode. Her arms reached for the ceiling and clawed at the air.

"This isn't a joke, Brenda!"

"No, it's not, Susan. Every year I come here and every year you put me down. Well, not this year. And if you want me and my boyfriend to leave, then you can explain to Mom why."

"Explain what?" Both sisters turned at the sound of their mother's voice. She was standing in the doorway holding a tray full of plates.

Brenda glared at her sister, daring her to speak up. "Well?"

Susan backed down. "Nothing," she said and left.

Brenda drifted past Brian as she returned to her seat and sent him a thought. 'Susan thinks you're a prostitute.'

'Really?'

'Apparently I'm so sad and desperate I have to pay male escorts to accompany me to my mom's.'

'So, you're not paying me?'

Brenda kicked him under the table.

Dessert passed off without incident. Susan put on her party face, and with the exception of a few hard stares at both Brenda and Fabio, no one could tell she'd just accused one of the guests of being a prostitute. Even her mother's usually infallible radar failed to pick up on Susan's behavior, dazzled as it was by the brilliance of Fabio's hunky Mediterranean charm.

And later, when the meal had been cleared away and the party had moved back through to the living room, Brian caught Susan's arm and asked her to walk with him.

~

"You can't con me," she said. "I know what you really are."

Brian led her through the French Windows onto a deck at

the back. "You no love your sister?"

"Of course I do."

"Then why you say these things?"

"Because they're true! Brenda needs help, not a ... gigolo."

Brian went for the hurt puppy dog look. It might not work on Susan, but he was enjoying remaining in character. And by remaining in character he was going to win her round. Eventually.

"Would a gigolo know Brenda's birthday? Or her favorite song? Come, you test me. Ask me any question about Brenda and I prove to you I know her as good as you."

He wasn't sure if she was going to bite at first. But Susan had a competitive streak and loved to be proved right. She bit, and with her thoughts holding the answers as soon as her voice framed the question, Brian passed every test she could throw at him.

Even then Susan wasn't convinced. "Are you wired?" She spoke into his lapel. "Are you giving him the answers, Brenda?"

Fabio shrugged. "I am no wired. You want me take off my clothes to prove it?"

She gave him a withering look – a close relative to Brenda's Medusa. Then peered into the house. "If I find Brenda's lurking in the bathroom, I might take you up on that."

She hurried back into the house where she found Brenda surrounded by witnesses. And not a microphone in sight.

~

It was approaching midnight.

"I think we should be going," Brenda told her mother. "It's late."

"Nonsense," said her mother. "I see you so little. Why don't you stay the night? Two nights. I can make up the spare room ... for both of you."

"No!" Brenda didn't mean to sound so shrill – or so panicked – but her mother had just winked at her.

Brian appeared at her side and draped a long possessive arm around her shoulders. "It is all my fault," he said to Brenda's mother. "I have already booked room. And, of course, I have horse to return."

"Horse?"

"Yes, I tie him outside. You no mind?"

Angelica ran to the window and pulled back the curtains. "It's true! There *is* a horse outside! I can *see* him!"

Brenda gave Brian a look. 'What are you doing?'

'Arranging our exit.'

Bob, Susan and her mother joined Angelica at the window.

"I can't see your car, Brenda," said her mother. "You didn't ... you didn't ride here?"

"I thought it romantic," said Fabio. "I promise my Brenda a moonlight ride along the lake shore."

"You don't even like horses, Brenda," said Susan.

"I do. It's just that I've never ... had the time before."

"Can I feed the horsey?" asked Angelica, bouncing towards Fabio. "Please! Please! Can I?"

"If your mother say so. He like the short sweet grass and keep your hand flat."

Angelica had the door open as soon as her mother reluctantly agreed.

"Come, darling," said Fabio. "Our steed awaits."

Brenda followed, peering not at the horse, but past the Hummer at the empty space by the road. 'Where's my car? You didn't turn it into a horse, did you?'

'I moved it around the block when I went to the bathroom. The horse took a while to find, but ... it's worth it, don't you think?'

The horse was magnificent. A huge white Lipizzaner loosely tied to a tree. Angelica was feeding it with a handful of grass she'd ripped from the lawn.

"That's some horse," said Bob.

"Only the best for my Brenda," said Brian looking directly at Susan.

Then he was walking towards the horse, untying him from the tree, making sure Angelica stood back. Brenda watched. Was he really going to jump on its back? There was no saddle, no stirrups.

He placed one hand on the horse's withers and swung himself aboard. Was riding bareback one of his super-powers? Or was Brian winging it?

And was she going to have to do the same? She hadn't ridden a horse in years. She wasn't dressed for it. Her dress was too tight and there was no saddle.

Fabio circled with the prancing horse. Both looked magnificent, both had flowing manes. She could have been staring at a book cover.

Then he brought the horse alongside her and held out his hand.

"Come, darling, the night, she awaits."

The way he said it. The way the moonlight picked out the white of the horse. The clear, cool night. The collective 'aahh' from her mother and Angelica.

She had to take his hand. But first she had to make a slight alteration to her dress. She bent down and ripped a seam.

'I always wanted to do that.'

'I know.'

She took his hand, and he swung her up behind him as though she were no weight at all. She clung to his waist with both hands. And looked over to her mother who ... had her hand in her mouth. She was so happy she was crying.

Then the horse reared. Brenda clung on tighter as the Lipizzaner punched the night with his front hooves and whinnied. She hoped it was Brian being theatrical, but she had a nasty feeling her magic exit was about to end in a Horse vs. Hummer visit to the ER.

"Wow!" shrieked Angelica.

'Wave, Brenda. And don't forget to smile. You're about to make the fantasy exit of all exits. Your family will talk about this for years.'

She smiled – nervous, but fulsome – and gripped extra hard with her knees and right hand while attempting a flamboyant wave with her left.

And then the horse powered forward to the cheers from the doorstep. Brenda clung to Brian as they narrowly missed the Hummer. Even more cheers as they cleared the hedge and galloped across next door's lawn. Another hedge, another lawn, a fence and ... was that a water jump, or a garden pond?

Off they charged, galloping into the night

And Brian was right. *That* was an exit.

Chapter Twenty-Three

"We're not riding all the way back to Ohio are we?" said Brenda as they cleared the tenth garden fence. They had to be out of sight by now.

"No, I've got to return the horse. I'll drop you off at your car."

Five minutes later he materialized in the front seat of her Ford Contour – as Brian.

"You've changed back," she said.

"You're disappointed?"

"No," she lied, then realized he could read her mind and changed her answer to, 'Okay, a little. He's easy on the eyes,' before flooding her mind with neutral thoughts and plenty of la, la, la's.

They shared the driving back. Apparently, teleporting a Ford Contour – even a rusty one – was beyond Brian's powers. By the time Brenda arrived home she was shattered.

"Do you want me to stay here tonight?" Brian asked as Brenda was just about to slip her front door key into the lock.

The key developed a mind of its own and slid across the scratch plate. "What do you mean 'stay here tonight?'"

"So we can get an early start in the morning. There's a lot to do. There's the Abbiati papers to sort out, the Sacrifice case, and I have this strange memory of you stealing a car."

"*Borrowing* a car. I paid for it. Sort of."

Okay the money may have been slightly stolen, but she was going to give the car back! She just hadn't had the time. She'd do it tomorrow. After she'd had some sleep and could think clearly.

Brenda spent a fitful night. Dreaming about Count Fabio was bad enough, but he kept morphing into Brian, which was even more unsettling than when he morphed into the horse. Consequently it was a tired and dreamswept Brenda who dragged herself downstairs the next morning. Brian was already up, sitting at the dining table, busily sorting through papers.

"We seem to be missing something," he said.

"What?"

"About a million dollars. You haven't been shopping, have you?"

It was too early for jokes. "I hid it under my bed for safekeeping. And it wasn't a million. It was eight hundred thousand, fifty thousand of which I had to put down as a deposit on a car to bring your charred, lifeless ass back home. We'll get the money back when I return it."

"Do you want to return it?"

The inner Brenda gave birth to kittens – little black satanic ones with devilish smiles and forked tails. *Watch yourself, Brenda. He's a demon and he's tempting you. That's what they do – lure unsuspecting humans with shiny new Jaguars and drawers full of money. The next thing you know, you've mortgaged your soul and you're taking bribes from criminals instead of putting them away.*

"I've never been bribed in my life," said Brian, hand on heart and looking hurt. "But, seeing as you've brought it up, is there anything wrong with deducting expenses?"

Maybe it was too early in the morning, or maybe he'd caught Brenda at a weak moment, but *was* there anything wrong with deducting expenses?

The inner Brenda produced another litter. *Once you start taking money, you won't be able to stop. You can't trust Brian. For all you know, he's testing you again. Seeing how far he can drag you down his slippery slope to hell!*

"Really, Brenda, everyone knows the path to hell is paved and far from slippery. Besides, Satan has it gritted."

Brenda snorted. It would be so easy to take the money. It would be so easy to justify it, but ... wouldn't it be corrupting?

"Was Robin Hood corrupt? You think the poor got *all* the money he took from the rich? What did he use to feed himself and his merry men? You think he had a day job? You think he lived off Maid Marion? Anyway, if I was only doing this for money I'd be teleporting in and out of bank vaults all day. But I don't. I take what I need. Crime fighting's expensive. We need equipment. And don't forget – the police get paid. Private detectives get paid. But our clients are dead and can't pay. Does that mean they have no rights? Isn't it fitting that we tax criminals to pay for our services?"

He had a point. Several of them.

"How much are we talking about?" said Brenda, shoving her conscience aside.

He shrugged. "Whatever you think's fair. We do need fast reliable transport. If you think you need a new car...."

The inner Brenda was in danger of being buried under small felines. *You don't need THAT car.* She had a point, too. There were plenty of new cars a lot cheaper, and the Jag would stand out.

But it was gold and it had a gearshift that came out of the floor like a spaceship...

"Isn't that breaking the first rule of magic?" she asked. "Using magic for personal gain?"

"What first rule? There are no rules in magic. Anyway, you don't have to decide right now, but sometime this week we've got to hand out that money, and whatever good cause we donate it to, you can be sure that some of it's going to disappear in admin fees."

Brenda ate breakfast while Brian boxed Abbiati's papers – wrapping the gun in a plastic bag before placing it on top of the bank statements with an explanatory note. If nothing else, there should be enough to get him on tax evasion. And keep the local FBI field office in New Haven busy for a month or two.

"I've been thinking about the Sacrifice case," said Brian, sealing the box. "I think the only way to make any real progress is to call up as many Sacrifices as we can and ask them their real names. Then we can track down their cases and see where he's abducting them from and when."

"None of the Sacrifices I've talked to want to give their real names."

"That doesn't mean they all won't. And maybe we can tease it out of the reluctant ones. Be a little more persuasive."

Brenda didn't like the idea of 'persuading' any of the Sacrifices. It was all right for Brian to say 'we,' but it was Brenda who'd have to do the persuading. She was the one who'd have to face the tears and the sobs and feel like an unconscionable bully.

"No," she said. "I've got a better idea. Let's start with the two girls who were murdered before Mary Alice. If they can identify Daddy's picture, then at least we've linked the cases. Maybe they knew him."

Brian agreed and, as soon as they'd cleared away breakfast, they moved through to the area by the sofa that had become Brenda's summoning zone. She sat cross-legged on the carpet, closed her eyes and took a deep breath. What next? She still had no idea how she summoned the dead – whether a simple call was enough, or whether there were mechanisms to boost that call or make it easier for a spirit to slip through from the other side.

"I wouldn't overanalyze it," said Brian. "Every medium I've known has used a different ritual. It's whatever works for you."

Brenda took the case file for the first victim, Ashley Peterson, and concentrated on her picture – the smiling one taken while she was still alive, not the later ones when her bedroom was a crime scene. Brenda closed her eyes and held the image of the smiling girl in her mind.

"Ashley, Ashley Peterson, can you hear me?"

She called out with her voice and with her mind, echoing the words and willing them into the ether and beyond.

She waited. The room silent except for the slow ticking of the wall clock. And the low thrum of her own blood pulsing around her body.

She opened one eye and peered around the room. No Ashley. No ghostly shape shimmering by the bookcase or over by the curtains. She tried again, imagining a rip in the fabric between the worlds, reaching through with her mind and calling through.

'Ashley, Ashley Peterson. I summon you. Follow my voice.'

The clock continued to tick and her blood continued to pulse. But no Ashley. No answering call, no shimmering presence.

She tried again, imagining the rip wider, peeling back the

edges with her mind, amplifying her voice with ten thousand watts of imaginary psychic speakers stacked inside the tear, all volume controls set to max.

'Ashley Peterson! Wherever you are, come to me now!'

Another long wait. Another furtive check of the room. Was she doing something wrong?

"Perhaps if you held her picture," suggested Brian.

She'd try anything. It wasn't quite the same as holding something that had once belonged to Ashley, but ... who was to say that that worked either? Perhaps the important thing was for Brenda to believe.

She took the piece of paper in her hands and placed both thumbs over Ashley's picture, pressing them lightly against her index fingers on the reverse side. Then she concentrated on Ashley's face. Not closing her eyes this time, but calling to the girl with her mind, imagining the picture to be a gateway, the paper a thin membrane separating the physical and spiritual worlds.

'Ashley! You hear my voice and you must come. I summon thee!'

Brenda concentrated harder, her brow furrowing with the effort, a slight pain behind the eyes. 'Ashley. Speak to me. Now!'

Nothing. Brenda let go of her breath, not realizing she'd been holding it for so long. Why wasn't it working? What was she doing wrong?

"Try the other girl," said Brian.

She did, going through the same ritual, holding the girl's picture between finger and thumb, burning the image into her mind, imagining rips and tears and all kinds of tunnels between this world and the next and shouting the girl's name through.

'Lauren! Lauren Stone!'

"Yes?"

A girl materialized by the television set. An eleven year-old Lauren Stone, the girl in the picture. She was wearing different clothes and her hair was longer, but it was her.

"What do you want?" she asked. She didn't seem frightened, or fazed in any way. She stood by the television taking in her surroundings as though beaming into a stranger's lounge was the most natural thing in the world.

"I want to help you," said Brenda. "Are you a brave girl?"

Lauren looked surprised, and a little suspicious. "Ye-es."

Brenda hesitated. This was the tricky bit.

"Good," she said, masking her uncertainty with a smile. "I'm going to show you a picture and I want you to look at it closely and tell me if you recognize the man. Can you do that?"

"Of course. Who is it?"

"Remember, this is only a picture. You're safe here. The man can't hurt you. Do you understand?"

"I'm not a baby."

Lauren sounded so normal, so alive. She barely shimmered and her skin wasn't the slightest bit translucent. She could almost have passed for alive – if you didn't look too hard.

Brenda reached down, picked up the composite Brian had made of Daddy, then showed Lauren the picture.

The girl's face changed in an instant. Her eyes widened and she jumped back – a silent, otherworldly jump, her features shifting and reforming like a girl made of steam caught in a sudden draft.

"He can't hurt you any more," said Brenda. "This is only a picture. You're safe here."

The girl was fading, her face translucent and the edges of her clothes losing coherence.

"Wait!" shouted Brenda. "You *are* safe. See that man over there?" She pointed at Brian, willing the girl to stay for just a second longer and look. "He's a powerful magician. If anyone tries to hurt you, he'll turn them into a frog."

"An ugly frog," said Brian. "With big hairy warts."

The girl's form shimmered and billowed, but was no longer fading. She looked at Brian, then Brenda.

"Is he really a magician?" Her voice was faint and distorted.

Brenda turned to Brian. "She wants you to show her some magic."

In an instant Brian transformed himself into Count Fabio, again looking fashionably windswept, his eyes extra sultry and that smile...

"Wow!" said the girl, both her voice and her shape returning.

Wow indeed, thought Brenda, making a slight adjustment to the collar of her blouse. The room had suddenly become considerably warmer.

"Lauren," said Brenda, "do you know the name of the man in the picture."

Lauren was still staring at Count Fabio.

"Lauren!" repeated Brenda. "Do you know this man's name?"

"No."

"Is he the man who attacked you?"

The girl looked down at her feet, and nodded.

"He's not here, remember. This place is safe. He can't hurt you anymore. Had you ... had you seen him before the night he attacked you?"

She nodded again.

"Where?"

The girl shrugged. "Around."

"Around where? Was he a friend of your parents? A neighbor?"

"No."

"Where did you see him? At school? At a friend's house?"

Another shrug. "He said he'd been watching me. He said he'd seen me in the park, and at the mall with my mom, and going to school. He said I was special."

She looked up, her lower lip starting to quiver. "I don't want to be special. I want to go home."

She started fading the moment she began to speak, her voice trailing away.

"She's gone," said Brenda.

Brian said he wanted to crack on, summon the Sacrifices and quiz them about where they they'd been taken from and when. He wanted to compile a map and look for patterns. But Brenda disagreed.

For one, Brian was still in his Count Fabio guise, but he'd lost his Italian accent. Which was all wrong. It was disconcerting enough having Fabio in the same room, but when he started speaking like Brian...

"You want me speak Italiano?"

He gave her a look. A smoldering fireman Fabio look. Brenda's heart didn't skip a beat – it double-dutched into a palpitating rush.

"No!" she said. "No Italiano and no Count Fabio."

Not until later anyway.

Count Fabio melted into Brian, and Brenda eventually remembered her other objection to Brian's plan. They didn't want to know where he was taking the girls *from*, but where he was *holding* them. Daddy was clever. He'd been abducting children for thirteen years without anyone making even the slightest connection. So why think there'd be a pattern? He'd move from state to state, abducting a girl here, a girl there, and take them back to his bolt hole – which he'd make sure was nowhere near any of the abduction sites.

"So what do you suggest?" Brian asked.

"Daddy's holding these girls for months, maybe years. There's got to be something they know that we can use to find out where they are."

"I thought you already asked them–"

"I did, but ... I didn't ask them everything. I didn't ask if Daddy let them listen to a radio. Or watch TV. Or got them books from a library. I can't believe that he isolates them completely from the outside world. They don't sound feral. They can talk. If we can just get a name of a local radio station or a library, we can narrow the search right down."

"And he'd have no reason to keep their location a secret from them, would he? He wasn't planning on letting any of them go."

"Exactly."

"So get summoning."

"No! I only have a few minutes with each girl, so we need to make the most of that time. We need a complete list of questions to ask. Then I'll summon Sacrifice."

They brainstormed a list, working out all the ways a location might be deduced – local radio, TV, a price tag on a book, a local newspaper. And what did Sacrifice eat? Did Daddy prepare all her food, or occasionally give her takeout and candy? There had to be a certain amount of carrot in his brainwashing – it couldn't all be stick. Would he give her treats when she behaved? Treats carrying a price sticker with the store name on it? Or maybe the store name was on the bag they came in, or the paper they were wrapped with.

And what about clothes? He'd have to buy her clothes. Did they have labels? A brand could be traced and cross-referenced to retail outlets.

There had to be a way. If this was CSI, Sacrifice would be sharing her cell with a rare beetle – something brightly colored and stripy – that only existed in one tiny part of the country.

She summoned Sacrifice, going through her usual routine of summoning trial and error – concentrate hard, envision various breaks, rips and tunnels in the fabric of inner space and persuade like mad.

"Sacrifice, I summon thee!"

"Have you finished?" said a woman's voice.

A sweet sickly smell hit the back of Brenda's nose. She opened her eyes. A dead woman was standing by the bookcase. She didn't look a bit like the other Sacrifices. She was in her forties, well dressed – if not overdressed – and she was wearing a hat. Brenda had never seen a ghost in a hat before. The woman looked like she was attending a wedding. And she was blonde.

"Who are you?" Brenda asked.

"I'm Cynthia. You *are* the medium working with the Vigilante Demon, aren't you?"

"Yes, but–"

"Good. I need you to track down my husband and frighten the crap out of him. Turn that slut of his into an old hag and give her something contagious. Nothing lethal, I'm not vindictive, just something with zits. And hemorrhoids too, if your friend can manage it. Is that him?"

Brenda stared at the woman. Who on earth was she?

The woman waved her hands in front of Brenda's face.

"Hello? Can you still see me?"

Brenda considered pretending she couldn't, but ... was there a chance this woman was connected to Sacrifice somehow? She'd appeared during the summoning.

"Do you know Mary Alice Cassini?" she asked.

"I told you, dear. You need to find my husband. Walt Bryant. He lives in Tulsa."

"Wait," said Brenda, picking up the picture of Daddy. "Is this him?"

"God, no. I'm talking about Walt. Walt Bryant. Are you

really a psychic?"

Brenda gave Brian a look. 'Are you picking any of this up?'

'Unfortunately so. I think you've been hit by a drive-by. Tell her you'll look into it and get rid of her.'

Brenda took another look at the woman. She hadn't recognized Daddy, but could she be the mother of one of the victims?

"Did you have children?" she asked.

"Two of them, but it's Walt and his fancy woman I want hounded first. We can get to the children next week. And I've got a couple of so-called friends we could torment the hell out of, too."

"Right," said Brenda. "I'll get onto that right away."

"Good."

Brenda shuffled position on the floor ... waiting ... rearranging her pen and notepad. The woman showed no sign of leaving. If anything she was glowing brighter.

"Well?" said the woman. "What are you waiting for? Aren't you going to scry for him? The slut's name's Rita. Rita Gonzales. You're not writing any of this down–"

"Go!" shouted Brenda. "You're ... you're blocking my path through the astral plane. I can't get to Walt and Rita with you here in the way."

"Okay. Keep your hair on. You only had to ask."

The woman winked out of existence. Brenda let out a deep breath, cleared her mind and began the summoning process again, adding a new filter – all Cynthias keep away.

She forgot to add mothers.

Her cell phone rang. What was this? A conspiracy to stop her finding Sacrifice?

She took the phone out, stared at the caller's name – her mother – considered switching it off. Then relented.

"Hello, Mom."

"Brenda, are you still in town? Do you and Fabio want to do lunch?"

"Sorry, we've moved on. We're ... on a driving vacation. Taking in the sights."

"Oh." Her mother sounded really disappointed. "Are you coming back this way? Maybe this weekend."

Brenda had known this would happen. Last night had gone too well. But while one dose of Fabio was a blast, two would cause complications. There was a limit to how many times they could change the subject or fall back on Fabio's charm. Her mother would want to know all about his work and Susan would stake out his hospital. It would all end in disaster. Her mother would be devastated and Brenda would be consigned to the doghouse's doghouse.

"We'd love to," she said. "But Fabio's going to be busy at the hospital. He had to swap shifts to get these few days off. God knows when even *I'll* be able to see him again. Is that the time? Sorry, I've got to rush. Talk to you later."

This was not going to end well.

She switched off her cell phone, warded her living room against Cynthias and all forms of distraction and threw herself into summoning Sacrifice.

A minute later, an eleven year-old Sacrifice appeared, dressed in jeans and a Spiderman T-shirt. Brenda was struck by the remarkable similarity of all the Sacrifices. The same face, the same long unkempt hair.

"What do you want?" the girl asked.

And the same voice. Always with that hint of echo as if her voice was being relayed from a large distant room.

"Are you Sacrifice?"

"Yes. Who are you?"

"I'm Brenda. I'm here to help you."

"How?"

This was one of the older, self-assured Sacrifices.

"By finding out where you lived."

The girl shrugged. "I know where I lived."

"Where?"

"In my room."

Brenda decided to start again. This time *she'd* ask the questions. She picked up her list and started at the top.

"Did you ever listen to the radio?"

"No."

"TV?"

"Yes."

"What channels?"

The girl reeled off a list, starting with one Brenda had never heard of – Evangelical TV – then progressing through a strange mix of kids channels, news channels, more Christian channels and ending in what sounded like a list of her favorite shows.

Brenda hurriedly wrote them all down, asking Sacrifice to stop and repeat the one's she'd missed.

"Did you ever watch local news?"

The girl shrugged.

"When you saw a weather report what cities did it mention?"

"Lots."

"Such as?"

"New York, Boston, Miami, Los Angeles."

"Was there one city that was mentioned more than others?"

"No."

This was not going as well as Brenda had hoped.

"I'll Google the TV channels," said Brian. "I might be able to narrow them down to a particular provider."

Brenda was less hopeful. None of the channels sounded regional.

"What's your favorite food?" she asked.

"Pizza."

This was more promising. "Does your pizza come in a box?"

"No-o." The girl looked at Brenda as though she was crazy. "It comes on a plate."

Brenda moved on to drinks and candy. And failed again. Drinks came in glass or a cup, not in a bottle with a price tag on it. And as for candy – if there was a price tag on it, Sacrifice never noticed.

The same went for books. Yes, Daddy gave her books to read. But there were no library marks or anything to identify the store on them.

Only clothes to go.

"I like your Spiderman T-shirt," said Brenda. "And your jeans. Did they have a price tag on them when Daddy first gave them to you?"

The girl shrugged. "Can't remember."

"Did they come in a bag?"

"A green one with a stag on it. Daddy always gets my clothes from Bergmans. He says they're special. Like me."

Brenda had to control her excitement. "Bergmans? Are they a clothes store?"

The girl shrugged again. She was starting to look bored.

Brenda glanced over at Brian, he was hunched over the computer, tapping furiously at the keyboard. If only Bergmans could be a small store in a small out of the way town.

"Is it a long way to Bergmans?"

Another shrug. The girl wasn't even looking at Brenda any more. She was watching Brian.

"What's he doing?"

"He's trying to find Bergmans. We'd like to go there. Do you know where it is?"

"No. Is that a computer?"

"Yes."

"Can I have a turn?"

"Perhaps later. Does Daddy ever mention any places he visits? Other stores, towns?"

Yet another shrug. The girl was far more interested in Brian and his computer. She begun to walk towards it. A flowing, skater's walk.

"I've got it," said Brian. "Bergmans – a regional department store chain with 22 stores. Their logo's a white stag on a green background."

"Where are they based?" asked Brenda.

"Hold on. There's a store locator map."

Sacrifice was standing beside Brian now, her hand reaching out towards the computer screen.

"Central New York State," said Brian. "From Rochester in the west to Utica in the east and down to Binghampton in the South." He turned to look at her. "With stores in both Rome and Syracuse."

Where Ashley and Laura had been murdered. Was this his home base? It was classic profiling. He starts out killing close to home, then moves further afield as he becomes more adept and feels the need to hide his whereabouts.

"How big an area's that?" she asked.

Brian looked at the screen, inclining his head to one side. "I'd say about hundred miles by seventy-five."

"Why can't I touch anything here?" asked Sacrifice. Twice her hand had passed both through the screen and the keyboard. "What is this place? Who are you?"

"I'm Brenda and this is my home."

The girl pushed at the sofa, both hands passing straight through. She was becoming distraught.

"I want to go home!" screamed the girl, her body pulsing between dense and bright and wispy and faint. Her voice was drawn and distorted by some strange, ethereal wind.

She was leaving, rising towards the ceiling.

"Wait!" shouted Brenda. "You're safe here. Don't go."

The girl was fading.

One last, desperate question thrust itself into Brenda's mouth.

"Are there any strange beetles in your room?"

Chapter Twenty-Four

Brenda stared at the computer screen. Twenty-two Bergmans stores, seventy-five hundred square miles, probably nearer ten thousand when you took each store's catchment area into account.

"Call up another Sacrifice," said Brian. "See if we can cut the search area down further."

"What more can they know? I asked every question on the list."

"You didn't ask how they got there. If we can find out where they were abducted from, and how long it took to drive to Daddy's, we can narrow the search area down."

"They won't even tell me their real names. I doubt if they'd even admit they were abducted."

"But they might. Ten thousand square miles is a hell of an area to search. You can cut that down dramatically, and it'll only take ten minutes."

They made another list. Where were you abducted from? How long did it take to get from there to Daddy's? Did you see anything along the way? A landmark, a town name? Was Daddy's hideout in the town or the country? In a house or a barn?

And how were you transported? Did Daddy have a car or a truck? What make was it? What color?

Brenda jotted all the questions down. She doubted if any of Sacrifices would answer. The memories would either be too painful or suppressed beneath years of brainwashing. But Brian was right – there was always a chance.

She took up her position on the floor, went through her various routines, and then pushed all doubt aside. She was going to find a Sacrifice who had refused to be broken. One who'd pretended to go along with Daddy, but had kept hold of her memories.

217

"Sacrifice! I'm calling you. The strong one. The brave one. The one who remembers a life before Daddy."

No answering call came. She called again. She pleaded, she cajoled. "Sacrifice. I summon thee. Here! Now!"

"What do you want?"

That voice again – distant and windblown. And this time she was six or seven, dressed in pajamas covered in pictures of Tigger and Roo.

"What's your name?" asked Brenda.

"Sacrifice."

"What's your other name?"

"I don't have another name."

"Not even when you were very young?"

"No."

"Do you remember when you were very young? When you first met Daddy?"

"No."

A more emphatic denial this time, her face turning serious – almost a frown.

"What's your oldest memory?"

The girl shrugged and looked away, leaving Brenda feeling lost and out of her depth. There was undoubtedly an art to questioning child ghosts that Brenda didn't have. Should she press harder, ease off, skirt around the subject? Were there special techniques? It would help if she was used to interacting with young children, but she wasn't.

She tried again.

"What kind of car does Daddy drive?"

Back came the shrug – something else that all the Sacrifices shared – the silent shrug every time the questioning moved into areas they were uncomfortable with. How was Brenda supposed to break through it?

"You're doing fine," said Brian. "Keep going."

Easy enough for him to say.

Brenda took a long hard look at the girl. She was winding a strand of that long dark unkempt hair around a finger. Strange. The girl's face, her clothes, her teeth – they all looked clean. But that hair – like all the other Sacrifices it looked as though it hadn't been washed for weeks or seen a brush for months. Why?

Was it something to do with Mary Alice, the original

Sacrifice? And how did he find so many girls that looked alike? Did he travel the world? Was he a plastic surgeon? Was he...

She felt stupid when it suddenly came to her. Shape-shifter! It was the logical explanation – once you'd met Brian and seen the ease with which he could transform others.

'Ask her if there's a mirror in her room?' said Brian. He must have been eavesdropping in Brenda's head.

Brenda did. There was no mirror in Sacrifice's room. Was that to stop her noticing her face changing?

'Ask her if her hair's always been that color?' said Brian.

She didn't get the chance. Cynthia materialized in front of her, glaring at her.

"Why aren't you out looking for Walt and Rita? We had a deal."

"I'm in the middle of a case–"

"*My* case!"

Brenda couldn't see Sacrifice. Cynthia was in the way and far from transparent. Brenda leaned to her left and tried to peer around.

"Sacrifice, it's all right."

Cynthia glanced behind her. "Beat it, kid. I was here first."

"No!" said Brenda. "She was here first. I've been working with her since Sunday."

"Then it's my turn now. Go on, kid, beat it before I scare the pants off you."

"No! Sacrifice, don't listen to her. Listen to me."

The girl was fading. "No! Sacrifice. Come back!"

"She's gone," said Cynthia. "Now, about Walt–"

Brenda was incandescent. She turned on Cynthia.

"Screw Walt! I was ready to give him zits. Now, because of you, I'm going to get Brian over there to give him a makeover and shapeshift his body back to that of a firm twenty year-old. Rita too. And it's all because of you."

"Oh, yeah? You do that and I'll haunt you for the rest of your days. How many murder victims are you going to find with me shouting at them to get the hell out the moment they materialize?"

"You couldn't stay materialized long enough."

"Try me."

They stood eyeball to ethereal eyeball.

A minute passed without a single flicker. If anything Cynthia was looking stronger. And the temperature around her was dropping. But Brenda was determined she wasn't going to be the one who backed down first. If she could summon ghosts, she could cast them out as well. Or did you have to be a priest? Brenda's brain raced through all the Exorcist movies – even the really bad prequel – skipping over all the revolving heads and projectile vomiting. Could you use salt to repel a ghost, or was that for slugs?

She was about to ask Brian to put in a call to the local vicar when she heard footsteps behind her.

'Brace yourself,' said Brian. 'Let's see if she can follow us when we teleport.'

One second her vision was filled with the ghastly Cynthia, the next it was as though a giant hand had pushed a pin into Cynthia's hat and kept on pushing until a spectral funnel appeared and – whoosh – Brenda was flying down it at speed.

"Where are we going?" she asked.

"Here," said Brian. They materialized in a room. A bedroom by the look of it. There was a double bed against the far wall, a purple shag pile carpet under her feet and an appalling floral wallpaper assaulting her eyes.

"Can you see her?" Brian asked.

Brenda was still coming to terms with the wallpaper. It looked like a close cousin of her radioactive dress. But there wasn't – she looked around to be sure – any sign of Cynthia.

"Good. She can't follow us then. Grab hold."

Another funnel formed – this time in the wallpaper. She tumbled towards it, falling through and beyond.

"Where are we going now? Back home?"

"A bit further than that. How would you like to go shopping at Bergmans?"

It took longer than Brian's usual journeys as he kept stopping to send his inner eye flying on ahead. He had trouble finding a street map of Syracuse, and even more trouble finding an unobserved spot near the store. Which left the pair of them hanging in the air, a ghostly funnel descending from their feet like a motionless tornado.

Brenda peered past her shoes at the sidewalk below. It had to be more than twenty feet away. She could see the tops of people's heads. What if someone looked up?

"Can anyone see us in here?" she asked.

"No. If someone looks closely they might see a slight shimmer – a bit like heat haze – but no one'll think twice."

"And we can't fall out?"

"Only if you ask too many questions."

Soon they were moving again. Brian had found a place by a loading bay at the back of the mall. They hovered above the gap between a truck and a red brick wall before descending at speed. Brenda bent her knees, her brain expecting her kneecaps to be driven up into her chin with the force of the drop. But once again she found herself devoid of momentum.

"Do we have a plan?" she asked, looking around, expecting five burly security guards to descend upon them any second.

He handed her an FBI badge. "We'll canvass the staff and see if anyone recognizes Daddy's picture."

Brenda flipped open her badge. Who would she be this time? Xena the Agent Princess?

Neither. It was Agent V. I. Warshawski. Crap. Knowing Vic's luck, Brenda could see herself being beaten to a pulp and left for dead in aisle three.

"Who are you this time?" she asked, peering over at Brian's badge.

He showed her. Special Agent Maigret, complete with pipe-smoking photograph.

She shook her head. "One of these days, Brian...."

"But not today, Brenda. Here." He handed her a picture. "That's your copy of Daddy's picture. We'll split up once we get inside. Start with the kids clothing department, then move out from there."

Bergmans was on the ground floor of the mall, a typical department store selling clothes, shoes, jewelry and handbags. Brian and Brenda navigated their way through the maze of special offers and displays until they found the girls' section. No Spiderman T-shirts, but plenty of Hannah Montana and Glee.

Brenda decided to stand back and watch Brian do the first interview – to make sure they kept to the same story. He walked up to the nearest sales assistant and flashed his badge.

"Excuse me, I'm an FBI agent. Do you recognize this man?"

The woman's eyes went from badge to picture and back again. She looked slightly flustered. Which, Brenda supposed, wasn't that surprising. One second you're folding T-shirts, the next you're being questioned by Inspector Maigret.

"No, sorry," she said. "What's it about?"

"We're investigating a series of child abduction cases. Could you take another look? This might be an old picture. It's possible this man has been in here buying children's' clothes. Do you remember stocking a Spiderman T-shirt?"

The woman took a closer look. "He doesn't look familiar. And we haven't carried any Spiderman shirts for years."

Brenda left Brian and branched out on her own. What else would Daddy buy here? Menswear? Would a shapeshifter need clothes? That let in a disconcerting thought – what if he'd only said he'd bought the T-shirt from Bergmans? What if he'd shapeshifted it from an old rag?

Doubt again. This case was full of it. Even Daddy's picture – what use was that, if the man was a shapeshifter? He could have one face for the girls and one for the rest of the world.

Brenda's walk around the store descended into a trudge. The store canvass would be a waste of time. No one would recognize Daddy, and there were another twenty-one Bergman stores to canvass.

But she carried out her allotted task, tracking down sales assistants and putting on a positive face. After all, so many real-life crimes were solved by chance during routine investigations.

Twenty minutes later, and without one positive identification, Brenda emerged from the store.

'Brian? Where are you?' She flashed the thought around the concourse. He said they'd meet outside.

'Over here. I'm outside the electrical store next door, looking in the window.'

She walked up to him. He was staring at a bank of TVs.

"Any luck?" she asked.

"Definitely. I think I've found a way to locate Daddy."

Chapter Twenty-Five

"Are you crazy?"

Brenda still couldn't believe it. "You can't be serious."

"It's the quickest way."

"It's the most reckless way. You'd be sabotaging a murder enquiry."

"I'd be solving an even bigger murder enquiry. How many girls has Daddy killed? Dozens? This one only has two victims, and I can get back to it and sort it out later."

That was so typical of Brian. It was either tunnel vision, or fly off at the first tangent. There was no middle ground with the man.

"What's the alternative?" asked Brian. "We canvass all twenty-two Bergman stores? That'll take a day, and even then we won't reach everyone. We'd miss the sales assistants on holiday, or off sick, or who've changed jobs in the last twelve years. We might miss that one person who can recognize him."

"What about security cameras? Can't we–" Brenda paused, looking around, suddenly aware how loudly they were talking. She toned her voice down to just above a whisper and led Brian away towards a quieter part of the mall. "Can't we hack into Bergmans' security system?"

"And sift through thousands of hours of footage from twenty-two stores? This isn't a TV show. I can't magic up a facial recognition program, and even if I could how long do you think Bergmans keep their tapes for? A week? Two? Certainly not seven years, which was when the first Spiderman movie came out."

"Couldn't we put an ad in the papers? Concoct a story about a missing man who...." She was thinking hard. What kind of story would generate maximum interest? "I know. A missing man who's just come into a fortune, but no one's seen him for ten years."

Brian shook his head. "Wouldn't work. For the story to make the impact we want, the press are going to need more. They'd want to interview the solicitors handling the will. Old friends and family. They'd want to make it a human-interest story, and we'd spend the next week shapeshifting ourselves into solicitors and family friends, and tying ourselves in knots. Far easier to take an existing high profile case and hijack it. That way we have a million eyes all looking for Daddy, and every one of them invested in his apprehension."

That was Brian's plan. The local papers and TV stations were full of the Kayla Anderssen murder. A pregnant woman and her three year-old daughter had been gunned down in their apartment a few miles east of Syracuse. Nobody had heard the shots, and there'd been no signs of a break-in or robbery. The motive was a mystery. Kayla had no enemies and the police had no suspects. Her husband had been out of town, and friends and family were adamant that their marriage was one of the happiest they'd ever seen. And, to cap it all, Kayla, a former Miss Sacramento, was as photo-genic as her curly blonde-haired three year-old daughter. A mixture which added up to blanket media coverage.

Which Brian was about to hijack by coming forward as a witness with a photograph of Kayla and – you guessed it – Daddy.

He'd already started on the photograph, taking Daddy's head and shoulder shot and expanding it, giving him a body, putting a gun in his right hand. And adding a worried looking Kayla.

But the picture didn't look right. Both Daddy and Kayla were standing square to the camera and looking directly at it. The whole scene looked posed – photo-shopped even.

"You need to make it look more natural," said Brenda.

Brian gave it another look before reluctantly agreeing. He'd change it another way. Swap Kayla out and use her daughter instead. Make it look as though Daddy was posing for a photograph to frighten Kayla. A picture of him holding her daughter with a gun to her head.

"That way we can let the police discover the photograph," said Brian. "No need for me to go to them as a witness. And when we eventually capture Daddy we can explain away the photograph by suggesting Chelsea was going to be his next victim. Kayla's murderer just beat him to it."

Brenda could see countless holes in Brian's plan. "What if Kayla's murderer is never caught because the police stop looking for anyone else once they've got Daddy?"

"We give Daddy an alibi. Manufacture evidence. Whatever it takes. Don't worry. We'll sort everything out. Do you want to summon Kayla now and find out who killed her? We could put him in the photograph, too."

"No! You can't keep tampering with everything."

Especially when so many lawyers made careers out of casting doubt on prosecution evidence. Brian was about to hand them a stack of 'Get out jail free' cards – credible alternative suspects, photographs that wouldn't stand up to forensic analysis.

"What gun have you put in the picture?" she asked.

Brian shrugged. "A big one?"

Brenda rolled her eyes. "Yes, but does it exist? Is it a real make, or some gun-like design you plucked out of your head? They're going to have experts blow up that picture and analyze the hell out of it. They'll be looking for clues as to where it was taken, when, what time of day, what film was used. If you stick in a non-existent gun, or put Chelsea in the wrong clothes, or put non-existent buildings in the background, they'll spot it's a fake."

"Again, this isn't TV. Have you seen these news reports?" He showed her the front page of a newspaper he'd bought. "The cops haven't got a clue what happened. They're desperate. The media and city hall are clamoring for results, and when they see this picture they are going to love it. It'll be their only clue. A real live picture they can give to the media and say – help us find this man. The press'll love it. The police'll love it. Everyone'll be happy."

"Until it all falls apart."

"Nothing will fall apart because we'll be on hand to magic it all back together again."

Brenda sighed. Sometimes there was no arguing with the man.

"Where are you going to put the picture?"

"I haven't worked that out yet. The police will have searched her apartment, so I can't really put it there. I suppose I could post it to the lead detective."

"That'll add a day to the investigation – assuming the lead detective has time to open his mail. His desk might be swamped with letters from the public."

"Okay, so I dress it up a little. Send it by messenger and make it look like it was sent by the killer."

Brenda shook her head in disbelief.

"Brian, killers don't send pictures of themselves to the police."

"Not even insane ones? Ones with a really heightened narcissism complex?"

If the mall hadn't been full of shoppers she'd have hit him. "Are you taking this seriously?"

He held his hands up. "I'm brainstorming. Okay, so how about I send the picture to the media?"

"No! If you want maximum impact you can't send the picture anywhere. It's a question of provenance. Imagine you're the detective in charge. If you find the picture yourself, it's an important lead. If it's posted to the press by an anonymous source, you want to know who sent it and why. And are you being conned? It deflects attention away from Daddy and onto the bona fides of the picture."

He gave her a long and slightly disconcerting look – halfway between surprise and a leer.

"You're getting good at this," he said. "And you're right. The police have to find the picture, and we have to lead them to it."

"Which brings us back to square one."

"Not me. I see exactly what we've got to do."

Brenda narrowed her eyes. She had a strong feeling she wasn't going to like the answer, but she had to ask the question. "What?"

"Follow me."

Brenda followed Brian out of the mall. Every time she asked where they were going, or what his plan entailed, she was met with silence, a knowing smile, or a wink. Often all three. He was infuriating. And probably about to lead her into danger. Or acute embarrassment.

They crossed the parking lot at the rear of the mall.

"Are we going to teleport somewhere?" Brenda asked, her

brain already making a list. Where would it be – Kayla's apartment, the police station, an evidence locker? And were they going to need a disguise? She wouldn't mind her nose being changed again, but everything below the shoulders was out of bounds.

"You don't fancy being taller?" he asked.

That got Brenda thinking. What would it be like to be a leggy six-foot tall? The inner Brenda spluttered into life. *You can't trust him. He'll stretch your legs seven inches and make you look completely out of proportion. You'll be a little squat body teetering on a pair of giant legs! And he'll put you in a micro mini with mile-high stilettos to make it even worse.*

"As if," said Brian, looking hurt. "Of course I could always give you a floor length dress if you'd prefer. I've got plenty of that mutant dress material left."

Brenda gave him a look – a half-second burst of the Medusa. 'Just try it, Brian.'

"I wouldn't dare," he said. "Now, take my arm and lead me towards the gap between that lorry and mall wall over there. I'm about to send my inner eye off on a search so I'll be blind for the next minute or two."

Brenda considered leading him shin first into the nearest parked car unless he told her where they were going, but thought better of it. For now.

"Why won't you tell me where we're going?"

"Because there are two places we might be going. As soon as I know which, I'll tell you."

~

"The morgue!"

"You're lucky Kayla's still here. If she hadn't, we'd have been materializing in a rather confined space, six feet under."

Brenda's imagination exploded into overdrive. Where were they? It was dark. Confined. They were scrunched together. And Brian had just informed her they were in a morgue.

Aaaaaarrrgghhh! She tried not to scream out loud.

"We're not in a cold storage locker, are we?"

It didn't feel cold. She wanted to push her hands out and

feel her surroundings, but she was terrified what she might touch.

"We're in a cupboard," whispered Brian. "The clue being that bodies aren't usually stored vertically."

Brenda's heart rate dropped below two hundred per minute. "What are we doing here?" she hissed.

"Adding value to our photo. You're right about all the tests the police will do, so let's get Kayla's prints on it. That's the first thing they're going to test for. And once it comes back a match, they're not going to care so much about what Chelsea's wearing. They'll be too busy celebrating. And once they fail to find Daddy in the NCIC database they'll have to go to the media with the picture. Help us find this man."

"So why are we in a cupboard?"

"You'd prefer I beamed us directly into the cold storage locker?"

"No!"

"Then wait here while I clear the building. Last time I looked there was someone working in the cold storage area."

Brian disappeared. By now Brenda's eyes had acclimatized to the little light that was seeping in from under the cupboard door. It appeared to be some kind of janitor's cupboard. A minute later a fire alarm sounded. Half a minute after that, Brenda heard running feet outside and snatches of conversation – two women wondering if it was a drill.

"No one said there was going to be a drill this week."

The voices faded. No more footsteps. No Brian, either. Was he collecting Kayla's fingerprints without her? Had he been waylaid? Was she going to have to find her own way out of the morgue?

'You forgot: Is there a real fire?' said Brian, beaming the thought into her head before he materialized as a grey shape next to her. And what was that smell? Pipe tobacco?

"Now you know why all the great detectives smoke a pipe," said Brian. "Maigret, Holmes. They all had to set off a smoke detector or two in their time."

Brenda was preparing a witty put-down when he suddenly grabbed her. A pinhole of light appeared in the center of the cupboard door. It grew and brightened, then sucked them straight through. Now they were in a corridor, flying at speed, through a wall, through desks and cupboards into another room and...

Stop. They materialized in a cool, stark room. A refrigeration unit was on one wall. A bank of twelve trays, four by three. Brenda shivered, knowing what was inside.

"Do you need me here?" she asked, hoping for a negative.

Brian swapped his pipe for a pair of white latex gloves. "I need you on look-out," he said, snapping them on. "I think everyone left the building, but you never know."

Brenda positioned herself to one side of the double door. She nudged the right-hand one open a crack and peered down the corridor. It looked deserted. She couldn't hear anyone. Which was lucky, since Brian was making enough noise opening locker doors to wake the inmates. She opened the adjoining door a crack and checked the other side of the corridor. No people and no cameras.

'Found her,' said Brian, pushing the thought directly into her head. Brenda kept her eyes and ears firmly on the corridor, trying hard to block out the sound of a morgue tray being pulled out and whatever else Brian was about to do back there.

Seconds passed. How long did he need to press a photo against someone's fingers?

'I need to do it right,' he said. 'It's got to look natural as though she held the picture and examined it several times. Not dabbed her fingers on the back.'

Now he becomes a perfectionist! Someone could come running along the corridor any second.

There was a sliding, grating sound as the tray was slid back into place, and a thump as the locker door latched firm. Brenda eased the swing door closed and turned.

"Where next?" she asked.

"Kayla's apartment. But first I have to send my inner eye off to find it."

"What? You're leaving me here?"

"It's quicker this way," said Brian, his eyes already taking on that unfocused look and his head beginning to slowly track left and right. "I know her address, but don't have a clue where the street is. So I need to find a street map and get my bearings. Much easier to do that by inner eye than dragging our bodies along in a teleportation bubble."

"But what if someone sees us?" She checked her watch.

How long would the fire truck take to get here? Did the morgue have members of staff designated to check all the floors were clear in the event of a fire?

"If anyone comes in, I'll shapeshift us into firemen. Or corpses. Whichever you prefer."

If anyone came through the door, Brenda wouldn't need shapeshifting into a corpse. She'd already have fainted.

Minutes passed. The really long ones reserved for time spent desperately waiting for events outside of one's control – the interview that was supposed to start five minutes ago, the phone call from the boy who said he'd call.

And the errant eyeball in search of a crime scene.

Outside, sirens blared louder. A fire truck pulled up. Then another. She could hear shouts and whistles and a thumping noise from downstairs. They were in the building. She could hear running feet. More shouts, doors banging.

"Can you teleport without your inner eye?" she asked, barely managing to keep her enquiry down to a whisper.

"Do you want to find out?"

Since he was blind, her Medusa look was lost on him. She was about to resort to verbal abuse when Brian's grip on her arm tightened and the door to one of the storage trays began to warp. A funnel formed. They were being pulled towards it. Into, over and through whatever was lying on the slab – euw! – and beyond, barreling through a dizzying array of greys, whites and hints of blue until...

A room crystallized out of the blur and Brenda could breathe again.

"Is this Kayla's? Have you got your eyes back in?"

"Yes and yes. Now, let's find a good place to hide the picture."

"Are you sure this is a good idea?" said Brenda looking around and trying to avoid the very large bloodstain on the carpet. "You said yourself the police will have searched the apartment. They'll know the picture was planted."

"Which is why we're looking for a place they won't have searched."

"How will we know that?"

He didn't answer at first. He was too busy flitting from bookshelf to CD stack – bending down, peering, carefully lifting items out and putting them back.

"By making an educated guess. Remember, this isn't CSI. The police don't search every inch of a crime scene unless they have to. The paper said that both bodies were found in this room. So maybe they didn't search the others so thoroughly. Come on, let's look."

Brenda followed him out of the lounge along a small hallway and into the rooms at the back. From what Brenda could see, it was a small two-bedroom apartment – one large bedroom, one small bedroom, a living room, kitchen and bath. And it looked so normal. Not at all like a crime scene. Nothing was broken. Drawers were closed, and although some clothes were lying on the beds or on the floor, the scene looked natural – a snapshot of a lived-in home. Toys on the floor, magazines spread out on table tops, dishes waiting to be stacked.

"This looks promising," said Brian.

He was standing in the doorway to the daughter's bedroom. Pink floral wallpaper, pink curtains, dolls and furry animals. It looked like a room fit for a Disney princess. It even smelled of flowers. One of those artificial perfume dispensers was plugged into a socket in the baseboard.

Would the police have performed more than a cursory search of this room? Brenda didn't think so. They'd have no need.

"This'll do," said Brian. He was standing by a shelf with a book in his hand. Chicken Little. "I'll slip the picture inside and put it back."

"What if someone remembers flipping through the pages?" asked Brenda.

"Then someone else'll think they did a shoddy job of it. And photographs can stick. Plus do you *really* think someone stopped to flick through every page of every book in the apartment? They'd only do that if they knew there was something to find."

Which begged the obvious question. "How are you going to ensure they search the book this time?"

"Because we're going to convince them there's something here they have to find. Now, do you want the crow bar or the knife?"

"You don't do subtle, do you?" said Brenda, knife in hand,

sawing at the fabric of the sofa. Her job was to slash her way into every mattress, cushion and piece of upholstery to make it look as though someone had conducted an exhaustive, and violent, search of the apartment. Not that she was going to slash any cuddly toys – there were some lines that could never be crossed. And she wasn't going to smash any framed family photos, either.

Brian had no such qualms. He was in charge of demolition – pulling back the carpet and looking for hiding places under the floorboards. Not to mention the walls and ceiling.

"It's got to look convincing," he said. "And we've got to make sufficient noise to make sure a neighbor calls the police. We want them here re-searching the apartment within the hour."

However logical the plan, it still didn't feel right to Brenda. They were trashing the apartment. Kayla's husband had lost his wife and child, now he was going to come home to this!

"When you lose your wife and child, the last thing you care about is property."

Brenda stopped what she was doing. She'd rarely heard Brian snap like that. There'd been a real edge to his voice. Was he remembering the murder of his own wife and child in Florida?

"If you must know, I was remembering a thousand years of wives and husbands having their families ripped from their sides. Even us bachelor demons can empathize. Now get slashing and make more noise. Thump about a bit."

Brenda stomped to the next room, filling her head with plenty of la la las. That was the trouble with speculating about the true identity of a telepath. They had big ears.

Ten minutes later, Brenda heard the first siren. She wiped her kitchen knife carefully and replaced it in the kitchen drawer. Then waited an agonizing extra minute in Chelsea's bedroom because Brian insisted they wait until the police were at the apartment door.

Next second, she was sucked through the pink floral wallpaper and blurring back to her home in Ohio.

"What now?" she asked as her living room took shape around her.

"You wait here and I'll go back and make sure they find

the picture. If all goes well, I'll come back for you in a day or two when someone IDs Daddy."

"And if it doesn't go well?"

"Then we'll think of something else. After all, we're the psychic Mounties – we always get our man."

Chapter Twenty-Six

Brian delayed his materialization, holding the bubble of potential hanging a few feet above the carpet in Chelsea's room while he worked out what to do next. He had to materialize. If he didn't, he'd be powerless to do anything except watch. He wouldn't be able to hear or pick up thoughts or transmit any of his own. And without his intervention, the picture might never be found.

But if he materialized, he'd be visible.

Could he be a cop, a crime scene technician? Could he carry that off without someone asking who he was? He had no idea how large the Syracuse police department was, or how well they knew each other. If they discovered he was an impostor, it might cast doubt on the picture.

So he made the only logical choice. He took one more spin around the room to make sure no one was about, then headed straight for the toy shelf.

And became a bear.

It was a tight fit. He'd never shapeshifted into a cuddly toy before, and wasn't sure how small he could make himself, but he managed to get down to two feet. Which was a little larger than he'd hoped, and it meant the panda he was squiggling next to had to perform – with a little help – a forward dive off the shelf, without tuck and not too high on artistic interpretation either.

But, looking on the bright side, Brian was now within furry arm's reach of the Chicken Little book.

All he had to do now was wait.

And wait.

The two uniformed cops who'd first responded to the call had taken one brief look around Chelsea's room, then left. They were only interested in making sure the flat was empty. As soon as they'd satisfied themselves that the intruders had left, they called in what they'd found, secured the apartment, and left to interview the neighbors.

It was another ten minutes before the detectives arrived.

Now came the difficult part: how to insert a thought inside the head of a detective without them throwing a Joan of Arc. He wanted the Chicken Little book lifted from the shelf, not the siege of Orleans.

It didn't help that all the initial police activity seemed centered on the living room. All Brian could hear was muted conversation and assorted noises as furniture was moved and drawers unpacked. One detective made a cursory inspection of Chelsea's bedroom, but soon moved onto the next room. He'd been sent to do a brief assessment of the state of the apartment and report back. It was another twenty minutes before anyone else arrived.

Now there were two of them – one in his twenties, one in his forties, both male and both looking tired. It was in their faces and in their clothes. The bleary-eyed, disheveled look of people who'd been working long hours – maybe most of the night. Brian listened to their thoughts. They were con-fused. Yesterday, they'd had Kayla and her husband pegged as ordinary upright citizens. But now, the way the apartment had been pulled apart, it looked like someone had been searching for a stash of drugs or money. It didn't make any sense.

Brian watched them, trying to work out which one to target. Who'd be the most susceptible? Who the least likely to freak out?

Then the younger detective stopped dead and stared at Brian.

"Bob, does that bear look funny to you?"

Bob, who was on his hands and knees peering under the bed, looked up.

"In what way?"

"His eyes seem to follow you around the room."

Shit. Brian fought the desire to stare dead ahead and kept his eyes fixed on the younger detective. That is until the detective began to move, taking two very deliberate steps to the left. Brian made sure both eyes kept staring at the space he'd vacated.

"You're seeing things, Matt," said Bob, dismissing his

partner's concerns with a wave of a hand.

The young detective wasn't giving up.

"How come the perp slashed all the mattresses and cushions, but left the bears?"

Don't focus on the bears. Focus on the book. What you're after's in the book! Brian tried to nudge his suggestions into the young detective's head, aiming at a volume just below a soft whisper. Nothing schizophrenic, no commands from God, just a friendly suggestion. *This bear is not the bear you are looking for.*

It didn't work. Matt's interest was well and truly piqued and fixed on Brian.

"Have you got a knife?" he asked his partner.

Double Shit! Matt stepped closer. Brian increased the volume of his suggestions. *Forget the bear! Look at the book!*

"You really want to rip open the kid's toys?" asked Bob.

"There might be something inside."

No, there won't! Look at the book!

Matt didn't look at the book. Matt showed no interest or inclination to look at the book. He was only interested in the bear. He leaned forward, mere inches away now, and stared into Brian's eyes, stared at his nose, his stomach. Brian could hear his thoughts. He wanted to cut the bear open. He was becoming convinced there was something inside. A theory was forming in his head. Drugs. A gang had stashed a kilo of smack inside the bear. Somehow the bear had come into Chelsea's possession. A terrible mistake. The gang had to get it back. They sent someone to fetch it, but Kayla surprised them. She had to be killed. Now the gang was back, looking for the drugs.

"Get a knife," said Matt. "There's something in there, I'm sure."

No, no, no! Your logic's all wrong. If the gang hid the smack, they'd know where it was. Check the book!

What was wrong with this detective? Brian was pushing suggestions into his head, but he wasn't reacting. Why? He had to hear them. Okay, they weren't pitched above a whisper. But a whisper was still a whisper. Schizophrenics had been known to kill people with less encouragement.

"You're the boss," said a reluctant Bob, taking his time to

get up from the floor. Brian could hear the ow, ow, ow in his head as he struggled to straighten his complaining back.

Then Matt grabbed Brian by the arms and lifted him from the shelf.

"He feels kinda heavy, too. I'm sure something's inside."

He gave Brian a shake. And a squeeze. Neither was pleasant. It was difficult enough trying to contain a five foot nine shape in a two foot tall bear without being shaken and prodded. But Brian did take the opportunity to bring his eyes back facing front. After all, some cuddly toys had eyes that could move. Why not this bear?

And on the subject of things that cuddly toys could do...

"Read me a story," said Brian, attempting a Disneyesque bear's voice.

Matt almost dropped the bear.

"It can talk."

"Read me a story," Brian repeated, wondering if he could get away with pointing a stubby paw at the Chicken Little book.

The detective examined the bear closer, turning him over and around, looking for a seam or a zip – somewhere a battery might fit. He was thinking he might not need the knife – that maybe there was a flap, or an opening he could pry apart with his hands.

Brian smoothed out his seams. He couldn't give the detective any encouragement. And he had to divert him.

"Read me a story," he repeated, reinforcing the words with a mental shout – forgetting about whispers – trying to implant the thought directly into Matt's brain. *Read me a story. There's a book on the shelf.*

No reaction. Not even a puzzled thought. Was Brian losing his touch? Was the detective immune, unsusceptible?

Bob returned. He had the knife. "Here," he said, handing it over.

The situation was verging toward disaster. Brian had to do something, but what? If he knife-proofed his skin the detective would only get more suspicious. He'd call for help. Brian would become the center of attention and probably sent away for forensic analysis.

But if Brian allowed the knife to penetrate, God knows what would happen. He was having enough trouble maintaining the bear shape. It was too constricting. He was a five foot nine man stuffed inside a two-foot bearskin. If he tried to simulate a rip in the bear's fabric he might spill out. And that would – literally – open up an entirely different can of worms.

There was only one thing to do.

"I need go pee pee," said Brian.

The detective stopped and gave Brian a quizzical look.

And promptly got squirted in the face by a jet of liquid emanating from a swiftly fashioned nozzle in the bear's nether regions.

The detective dropped the bear and jumped back spluttering.

"My sister had a doll that did that," said his colleague. "Though not with such force."

Both peered down at the bear. Neither of them bent down for a closer look.

Brian switched his attention to the other detective. Surely one of them had to be susceptible? *Forget the bear. It's a stupid toy. Check the shelf again. Books make great hiding places.*

He aimed the suggestions at Bob's head, pitching them soft, barely a whisper, a series of thoughts sliding towards his subconscious mind.

But would he have enough time? The younger detective had reached down, grabbed Brian by the paw and lifted him up. The knife loomed closer. He was going to cut Brian open.

"Uh-oh," said Brian. "I need go number two."

Brian wasn't dropped this time. He was thrown down. And both detectives took two giant steps backwards.

"My sister's doll never did that," said Bob.

For one fleeting moment Brian contemplated dowsing both detectives with projectile slurry. But that would have stretched plausible deniability a tad too thin. And, besides, this wasn't the woods.

Instead he decided to take his battery driven bear act a step in a different direction. If he could talk and pee why couldn't he move as well?

He lifted a paw and pointed. "Read me a story."

"Is that bear pointing at the book shelf?" asked Bob, amazed.

Brian seized the opportunity, reinforcing his suggestion. *Books. People hide things in books. They slip notes between the pages.* Again, he fired the words at Bob's brain – no more than a whisper – but more insistent. Repeating them over and over again.

Bob's head was turning. He was looking towards the bookshelf.

Brian concentrated harder. *Books. Hiding places. Between the pages.* Bob was moving now, walking over to the shelf. But not Matt. His eyes hadn't left Brian, he was still obsessed with the bear and convinced there was something inside.

Brian tried to watch them both, sampling their thoughts in snatches, juggling his attention between the two. What was going to happen first? Bob reach for the book, or Matt for the bear. Brian prepared a bladder full of liquid just in case. But he didn't want to use it. He didn't want to do anything that might distract Bob from looking inside the book.

Matt stepped forward. He'd made up his mind. He was going to pick up the bear and open him up. Bob was still dawdling, his hand hovering between the Chicken Little book and its neighbor. Brian had to act. He locked his eyes on Matt, rolled back slightly, raised both legs, and spread them.

He added a wink – a Clint Eastwood *Dirty Harry* wink. Are you feeling lucky, punk? Do you think this bear contains one projectile bodily function, or two?

Matt froze, a drop of water hung from the tip of his nose from his last encounter with the bear. Did he feel lucky? No, he didn't. He stepped swiftly to the side.

"Have you searched these books?" asked Bob.

"What?" said Matt, distracted, still keeping both eyes on the bear in case it swiveled round to face him.

"These kid's books. Have you searched them?" He had one book in his hand. He was flicking through the pages. Brian couldn't see which one it was.

"No," said Matt.

Then the picture fell out, half spinning, half gliding to the floor. Bob bent down, picked it up and, from that moment, the Kayla Anderssen murder enquiry changed tack.

Brian watched from the sidelines as the picture was rushed to the lead investigator. Everyone became excited. It was their first lead. And such a good one. A few officers were detailed to stay behind and complete the search while the rest ferried the picture back to the station. Brian used the opportunity to de-bear and fabricate a new bear from carpet fibers and other toys, in case Matt or Bob came back for a bear count.

Brian's job now was to stay with the lead detective and wait. It might take a day or so, but Brian had to be on hand the moment anyone made a credible identification of Daddy.

Chapter Twenty-Seven

Brenda decided she was no longer any good at waiting. The old Brenda had excelled at waiting. No period of time was too long to fill. She'd switch on a soap, curl up with a book, or lie back and daydream. But the new Brenda was a crime-fighting action hero. She needed the rush of adventure. As long as it wasn't too adventurous and there were frequent comfort stops ... and protective shields ... and she could choose her wardrobe.

She sighed, wondering if the police had found the picture. Brian had been gone an hour. He'd have come back and told her if anything had gone wrong, wouldn't he?

She decided he wouldn't. He'd extemporize and dig himself into several holes until either he found a way out, or everyone else fell in.

She paced. She monitored the news broadcasts. She hovered by the phone.

Maybe she could do her own detecting? Summon up Kayla and find out who killed her. They'd need to do that to put things right once Daddy was caught.

Or...

She could use the time alone to investigate Brian. She could summon up his ex-partners!

She liked the idea, but ... what about Cynthia? Wouldn't she intercept any call Brenda made and sabotage it? She was just the kind of vindictive spirit who would.

Brenda paced some more. Maybe if she moved her summoning to a different room and opened a portal there. A kind of back portal that Cynthia wouldn't be watching.

Brenda had no idea if it would work – or even if it made sense – but she needed to know more about Brian, and that was something worth taking a risk over.

She moved through to the kitchen. It was the room Brian's

previous partner had chosen to materialize in. Maybe that would make it easier to contact her.

Brenda pulled the kitchen chair out from under the table and repositioned it so she was facing the fridge. That was the place the ghost had first appeared, so that was the place Brenda would focus on. She'd imagine the fridge door was a back portal to the astral plane and throw it open with her mind.

Brenda went through her pre-summoning ritual, then filled her mind with the image of the woman – her pinched features, the dressing gown – concentrating hard, trying to give her form and substance. She may not have known the woman's name but she could project a picture of her – like a giant Bat Signal – far out into the astral plane. She threw open the fridge door with her mind and shot the image through.

'Brian's partner. The medium working with the Vigilante Demon. I summon you. Here! Now! You know the way. You've been here before.'

Brenda waited, peering at the fridge door. Not a ripple. She tried again. And again. Then expanded her search. 'Anyone whoever's worked with Brian, the Vigilante Demon. I summon you! I need your help. I need information!'

Still nothing. Did it work better if she had a name to work with?

That's when she remembered Brian Trafford's wife. Annie? Julie? Her name was in the crime report Brenda had taken from the FBI files. She could have been one of Brian's partners – killed in a takedown gone wrong.

Brenda ran to the lounge to find the report. Where was it? So many stray pieces of paper lay scattered over surfaces. She chose the largest pile. There it was! Angela! Angela Trafford.

She took the page back to the kitchen and went through her routine again, this time using both name and picture. 'Angela Trafford, I summon thee!'

She pressed harder on the picture in her hand, squeezing the paper between finger and thumb. 'Angela Trafford! I need you! Here! It's about Brian!'

"What's happened to him?"

Angela Trafford exploded into the kitchen. No hesitant,

semi-see-through apparition, but a vibrant, flaring figure, looking like an oversaturated image with every dial turned to max – color, brightness, sound.

She was distraught, bloodstained, and panicking.

"Where's Brian? Did they kill him? Is he alive? Where's Julie? Julie!"

Brenda was taken aback. The woman was screaming, her bruised face contorted, her image darting around the kitchen, desperately searching for her daughter, for Brian – barely staying in one place long enough for Brenda to catch her eye.

"Angela, stop! Listen to me! Listen!"

The ghost stopped, hovering high above the kitchen table, her wild eyes staring down at Brenda.

"Who are you?"

Brenda wasn't sure what to say. One wrong word and anything could happen. Angela could disappear, or go berserk and be worse than a thousand Cynthias. She looked so volatile, looking every inch a distraught mother who didn't know if her daughter and husband were alive or dead.

And she had an English accent. Maybe she really was an innocent.

"Who are you!" Angela screamed.

"I'm Brenda. I have news about Brian. He's alive."

The ghost dropped like a stone, her legs falling through the table, her face now level with Brenda's. She was crying and smiling.

"And Julie?"

"She's ... fine."

Brenda felt terrible but ... what was the point in telling the truth if the truth was like a knife to the heart? Angela would be gone in a few minutes. She didn't need to know her child was dead. She'd been tortured enough without Brenda adding to her pain.

"Thank God!" She started sobbing, and laughing. Years of not knowing dissolving around her.

"Can I ask you a few questions," Brenda asked.

"Yes. Of course. Thank you." Angela wiped her eyes and sniffed back the tears.

"I know this is a painful but, can you tell me what happened in Florida when those men attacked?"

For a second, Brenda thought she'd lost her. The ghost recoiled, her image flaring ... then settling down.

Angela swallowed. "Why do you want to know?"

"I want to catch the men who ... attacked your family. It's what I do. I'm a medium. Has any other medium ever contacted you about this before?"

Brenda held her breath waiting for the reply.

"No. You're the first ... person I've seen since ... since the attack."

Strike one for Brian and his 'Angela Trafford came to one of my previous partners' story.

Brenda listened as Angela recounted the same story she'd read in the crime report. An unprovoked, violent attack on an innocent family who'd already handed over all the money they'd had. The husband had been attacked first. He was being beaten to death when his wife tried to drag the men off. She was elbowed hard in the face, knocked to the ground, and shot.

If Brian had had superpowers, he'd had the time to use them. So, either he made a monumental misjudgment, or he didn't get his powers until later – probably from the gene therapy.

Or Brian was messing with her mind. Creating a Brian Trafford conspiracy as a test of her investigatory ability.

"How are Brian and Julie?" asked Angela. "What are they doing? Is Julie still in school?"

Brenda lied, fabricating the kind of story that she would have liked had the roles been reversed. Brian and Julie were as close as any father and daughter could be. The early years had been difficult but, together, they'd got through them. Julie was doing well at school. Brian was doing well at work. Brenda kept the story light on detail and heavy on feelgood factor.

She kept that up for three minutes. Angela's face just eighteen inches away, her eyes full but sparkling, tears running down her cheeks, her smile ... her smile as wide and as happy as a smile with a busted lip and three broken teeth could ever be.

When Angela left, Brenda broke down.

After the tears, came the need to be busy. Anything to

take her mind off Angela and Julie. In the lounge, her eyes alighted on the parcel of incriminating evidence waiting to be sent to the FBI. That was something she could do.

It whiled away thirty minutes. She put on gloves and gave the box a thorough wipe. She found the address of the nearest FBI office to Stamford, printed it clearly, made up a credible sender's address – carefully avoiding the name of any fictional detectives and fighting the urge to use 221b Baker Street – and dropped it off at the Post Office.

Driving back she thought of one other productive task she could accomplish – returning the Jaguar.

Luckily her inner Brenda's inner Brenda – a devilishly devious woman of fox-like cunning – came up with several reasons why returning the Jaguar would be a bad idea. Top of the list being that Brenda was on crime-fighting stand-by and couldn't risk taking three hours out to drive to Wellesley and back. She had to be close to home, ready to answer Brian's call. Then there was the matter of her altered looks. Would the car dealer hand over fifty thousand dollars to a stranger? Or would he get suspicious and call the cops?

But the clincher was the simple fact that there wasn't an 'r' in the month and *everyone* knows you can only hand back expensive cars when there's an 'r' in the month.

The day dragged into evening with still no word from Brian. Kayla's murder was covered by a few of the news channels, but there was no mention of any new evidence. Brenda managed to pick her way through the opening chapters of *Strong Poison*, but even the imminent entanglement of Harriet Vane and Lord Peter failed to engage her as much as it usually did. Only a jaw-dropping installment of *The Rich, The Spoiled, and the Surgically Enhanced* managed to snap her out of her growing lethargy.

Celeste, the drama queen's drama queen, discovered she had a brain tumor. Apparently it was pressing on the part of her brain that controlled the buttoning and unbuttoning of her tops. Brenda marveled at the wealth of medical information one could pick up from quality TV. With Poor Celeste staring at a future of worsening décolletage, she was rushed to see the world's top neurosurgeon, Storm Canaveral, a former pro linebacker, who'd taken up medicine in an effort to cure his own football-related brain tumor. Storm took one look at Celeste's cleavage and whisked her away to his own private hospital yacht moored in the Mediterranean. But had he left it too late? The episode ended with Celeste flat on her back – a position not unknown to Celeste – but this time she was complaining of a headache. And that was a first.

The rest of the evening could never compete with that, and a scratchy-eyed Brenda retired to bed with her book.

The next morning brought better news. Daddy's picture had been released to the media. It wasn't being covered by all the television channels, and the item barely rated a forty-second segment on those that did, but it was a start, and the local media around Syracuse had to be covering the story in full.

Brenda's spirits rose for a heady ten minutes. Then her mother called.

"Have you given any more thought to where you're going to be this weekend?"

Crap. Brenda had forgotten what story she'd fed her mother the last time. Was Fabio pulling double shifts at the hospital, or the fire station? And where was Brenda supposed to be? On vacation? Horse riding across the Rockies?

"Only," continued her mother, using the warding form of the word which usually preceded an extremely hard sell. "I have this little dinner party...."

Alarm bells, augmented by the occasional siren, sounded in Brenda's head. Dinner party. She was going to be served up and grilled. All her mother's cronies would be there. All wanting to know every detail about Fabio. And they'd be relentless. They'd want to know where his hospital was. How many castles his family had and where exactly they were. They'd probably bring Atlases along, and books on Italian peerage. They'd fact-check her to death!

Brenda stalled as best she could, wondering if she could fall back on the 'r' in the month ploy, but wisely decided not to. She used the bad connection ploy instead.

"Hello? What did you say? I can't hear you. We're in the mountains and the signal's terrible. I'll call you when we get back."

She hung up, fighting the urge to run and hide behind the sofa. Her mother wouldn't give up. Brenda had bought a day at the most. Perhaps it was time to kill off Fabio? Say he'd been eaten by wolves during their trip into the mountains.

She was still working out the best way to ditch Fabio, when the phone rang again. This time it was her landline, not her cell. Her answering machine sprang into life.

"Pick up. I know you're there." It was Susan, her sister.

This time Brenda did hide behind the sofa.

"Brenda Steele! Pick up the phone."

Brenda crouched lower. She was not at home. She was on a riding vacation, fighting off wolves in the Rockies. And she was definitely not answering the phone while Susan was deploying surnames.

An exasperated sigh hissed from the answering machine.

"When are you going to come clean and tell Mom? You know the longer you wait, the harder it's going to hit her."

She did. And she also knew who was going to suffer most from the fallout. Brenda Steele, the one with the surname. First she'd be shouted at, then shunned, then, when they realized that she liked being shunned, they'd turn up at her doorstep with a team of crack deprogrammers.

Hiring a male escort was an obvious cry for help, Brenda. We're here to turn your life around.

And she'd never stop spinning.

About five minutes into the scenario, and just before they'd pinned her to the ground and injected her with industrial strength Prozac, Brenda had a minor epiphany.

What if she just said no? After all, she'd faced down street thugs. She'd smart-mouthed crime bosses. Why not stand up to her family?

If her inner Brenda could have taken physical form, she'd have bitch-slapped her host across the room. *Are you mad, girl? There isn't a protective shield strong enough that Susan and your mother couldn't find a way through. Family can hurt you in ways a mob boss can't imagine. And if you hurt them back, it'll be worse.*

Brenda's day went downhill from there. She couldn't go out in case Brian called, and if she stayed in, there was a good chance that in three hours' time Susan would be hammering on the door. And, knowing Susan, she wouldn't go away. She'd peer in every window and camp out on the lawn.

Brenda carried her TV and computer upstairs. She'd lock all the doors and hide in her bedroom. And draw her curtains in case Susan got hold of a ladder from somewhere.

By the afternoon she was just starting to calm down.

Then the rhino arrived.

Brenda was too shocked to scream. It was a small rhino – barely eighteen inches long – with white horns, jet-black eyebrows and furry grey skin. For one second she thought it was a ghost. Dead people were bad enough, but dead cuddly toys...

Did Chucky have a pet?

Then it spoke.

"Quick," said Brian. "Fetch me a map. They've found Daddy."

Chapter Twenty-Eight

Brenda logged into Google maps. Half of her was rushing to find Daddy's location. The other half wanted to know why Brian had appeared as a rhino.

"I was just showing off," said Brian, back in human form and stretching his shoulders. "And demonstrating the considerable lengths I had to go through to hide in the lead detective's office. I saw his Rochester Rhino mascot on his desk and it was either that or swap places with a picture on the wall."

Brenda brought up the map and centered it on Syracuse. "Are you sure it's really Daddy?"

Brian shrugged. "We'll only know when we get there. But the police are confident. They've got two independent witnesses – a postman and a storekeeper. Both describe him as polite and quiet. Someone who keeps to himself, never initiates conversation, and lives alone on the edge of the Adirondacks."

According to both witnesses his name was Andrius Luksa. He had no criminal record and, from what the police could find, no driving license, or employment record, either. At least under the name of Andrius Luksa. They were still checking.

"It's north east of Rome," said Brian, pointing at the screen. "Around Scratch Hollow ... at the end of Forester Road. There! Now zoom in."

She zoomed to the highest magnification possible. There was a single house at the end of long winding road. Isolated, surrounded by trees. The nearest neighbor was a half-mile away. Nothing but forest and what looked like brown scrub for miles in all other directions.

"What do we do next?" she asked.

"I'll send my inner eye off to have a look around. We'll

take it from there."

~

He took one last look at the map, then sent his eyes racing back to Syracuse. From there he took the I-90 east, slowing when he came to road signs, following the signs first for Rome, then heading north east and gaining height, rising to cloud level and looking down, trying to match the landscape below to the image he'd seen on the computer. Then dropping fast, aiming at what he was sure was Scratch Hollow, and veering north and east to the small road heading into the forest.

Now he was at head height, flying along the road, invisible and silent. Trees and scrub and rocky outcrops all around. A few houses. A few distant views of mountains and lakes. Almost there. The road bending and twisting, the trees encroaching closer and closer.

And then the road stopped. There was a small clapboard and shingle cabin in a clearing off to the right. Brian slowed, dropping to a few inches above ground height. He could see a garage and a shed, but no sign of Daddy. There was no car in the drive and the cabin door and windows were closed.

Was Daddy elsewhere? Were the girls in the cellar alone? And where would the cellar be? Under the house? The garage? Buried in the grounds?

He rose and circled the property, looking for signs of trap doors, wishing his inner eye could switch to infrared so he could pick up signs of life. Then he moved towards the house.

And hesitated. He wasn't sure what Daddy was. Or what powers he had. From the initial police inquiries, he didn't appear to be a plastic surgeon. Which meant either there was an incredibly large number of Mary Alice lookalikes on the planet ... or Andrius Luksa could shapeshift people.

And if he could do that, what else could he do? Would he be able to see Brian's inner eye?

Brian decided to play it cautiously. He knew Sacrifice had probably been kept underground so he'd check the buildings for cellars. He'd avoid the rooms above ground altogether and slip straight in through the base of the external walls.

He circled the cabin. There were no obvious signs of a

basement. No door, no window wells. The clapboard stopped a foot above ground level. Below that was what looked like a concrete footing.

Brian aimed at the footing, angled down and slipped through. Everything went black. He edged further forward, not sure if he was in a sealed light-free basement, or travelling through bedrock. He kept going – slowly – trying to suck in as much light as he could, straining to see ... something, anything, a shape, a variation in the all-encompassing blackness.

He bobbed upwards, hoping that he still had an idea where 'up' was. Light almost blinded him as his eye emerged from a carpet. He was in a sparsely furnished room, light streaming in through the windows. Simple wooden furniture, shabby carpet. No sign of Daddy. Not that he stayed long enough to look. He flew across the floor, keeping low, then ducked back down through the floorboards. This time he found something. It was dark, but not pitch black. There was a thin strip of light coming from what could be the base of a door away and down to his left. He moved towards it. Now he could make out steps running along a wall to his right. No light came from the top. Whatever door or opening led to the house above, it was well sealed.

Brian circled the cellar room. It was larger than he thought. There was some kind of cupboard against one wall. And just the one door. Unless it led to a warren of cells spreading out from under the cabin, it didn't look like Daddy had room to keep more than one girl.

Brian paused in front of the strip of light at the bottom of the door in the cellar. Who would be on the other side? A hostage on her own, or would Daddy be with her? He had no way of telling. He couldn't listen at the door. He couldn't knock. He couldn't whisper through the crack.

All he could do was pass through the door and look.

He floated towards the door, gently sliding into the wood, slowing as he did so, not wanting to protrude into the room a millimeter more than he had to. And getting ready to flee, to spiral up and into the clouds the moment anything untoward occurred.

Light. Bright and sharp. He could see the entire room. A ten-by-twelve carpeted cell with a bed, chair, small table, chest of drawers, sink, toilet and shower. And Sacrifice. She was standing by the table, looking like a teenager plucked straight out of the sixties - long flowing cheesecloth dress, hair cascading down to the small of her back. She could have been abducted from Woodstock. She had to be at least seventeen. Which was strange. Mary Alice Cassini, Ashley Peterson, Lauren Stone, all the Sacrifices Brenda had summoned - they'd all been much younger. Prepubescent most of them. Whereas this girl was a young woman. She might even be eighteen or nineteen.

Was he changing his MO?

And should Brian act now? He could materialize in a matter of seconds, open a path between here and Brenda's bedroom, grab Sacrifice and whisk her back to safety. It was the sensible thing to do. He could then assume Sacrifice's shape, teleport back and take her place. Maybe turn the tables on Daddy? See how powerful the man really was, and extract a little retribution before the police arrived.

That was what had Brian intended. But he never got the chance. The girl suddenly turned, looked towards him, and everything went pink.

He tried to pull back, but experienced no sense of moving. Everything around him was pink static - random patterns that made no sense. He thought *up*, he thought *down,* he thought *home*. Nothing happened. Nothing changed. He tried to snap back inside his head. He tried to propel himself forward, to pull away, to duck and dive. Nothing!

Was he trapped? Blind? Had his inner eye been destroyed?

~

Brian's head jerked suddenly. His eyes widened in panic. He started shaking his head wildly.

"What's happened?" asked Brenda. She'd been biting her tongue for the past two minutes, watching Brian sitting on her bed doing his spaced out Stevie Wonder impersonation.

"I can't see," he said, panic in his voice, waving his head around like a demented child. "I can't move my eyes. I'm ... I think I'm blind."

"How?"

"I don't know."

"Did Daddy do that to you?"

Brenda's eyes darted around the room, looking for Daddy. If he could blind Brian could he follow him home?

"No," said Brian. "It was Sacrifice."

"Sacrifice?"

"What do my eyes look like?" He turned his face towards her, leaned forward and opened both eyes wide. "Do they look normal?"

"They look fine."

"Are you sure? Look closer."

She looked closer. His eyes looked perfectly normal, perhaps a touch bloodshot.

"Can't you grow a new pair?" she asked.

His eyes morphed in front of her. She grimaced, fighting the urge to look away as his eyeballs turned bright white before growing a new pair of brilliant blue irises.

Brian's turn to grimace. "I still can't see. Shit!"

"You said Sacrifice did this?"

"What? Yes, she looked at me and – zap – everything went pink. And another thing. How old would Mary Alice be if she were alive today?"

Brenda did the math. The girl had been four when she'd been abducted thirteen years ago. "Seventeen. Why?"

"The Sacrifice in the cell is seventeen. And a dead ringer for Mary Alice."

Brenda's turn to invoke the expletive from Planet Brown.

"Did she ever strike you as odd when you talked to her?" asked Brian.

"She was a ghost," said Brenda. "They're all odd."

Brenda considered this. Were the Sacrifices odder than most? Besides having untamed hair like the girl from *The Ring*, Brenda didn't think so. The oldest Sacrifice had a strange calm about her, but at the time Brenda had put that down to brainwashing.

But If Mary Alice was still alive...

"How can Mary Alice be still alive? I talked to her ghost."

"Are you sure it was a ghost?"

Crap. Brenda was no longer sure about anything. She had no idea how or why she saw whatever it was she saw. Maybe none of them were ghosts. Maybe they were all delusions. Maybe she was being manipulated by demons.

"And maybe someone was setting a trap," said Brian. "Using you to get to me?"

"Who? Do you have any enemies?"

He gave her a look. "You've seen what I do. I create a new enemy every week."

"But how many can steal eyes?"

He put his head in his hands. Brenda had never seen him like this. Even when he'd been chargrilled black and shot through with holes, he'd still exuded a crazy optimism. But now...

His head suddenly shot up. "What if it wasn't a trap? If she wanted to blind me, there are a hundred and one easier ways to do it. She could have given you the cabin's location the first time she came to you. Why the wait? Why all the different Sacrifices with different ages? Why make it so hard to find her?"

"Could your blinding have been an accident?" suggested Brenda. "She panicked and lashed out? After all, how could she know it was you? Aren't you kind of invisible? She might have sensed someone watching her and thought it was Daddy."

He shrugged, eyes downcast, staring blindly at the bed. "I have no idea. I have no idea about any of this. None of it makes sense."

None of it had made sense to Brenda for quite a while. Was Sacrifice one person or several? Dead or alive? Was Daddy her abductor, or her accomplice? He might even be human. They'd only pegged him for a demon because he had to be a shapeshifter to make all the Sacrifices look the same. But if there was only one Sacrifice, then he didn't need to be a shapeshifter.

"He could even be one of the good guys," interjected Brian.

"What?"

"He could be Sacrifice's jailer. A government agent tasked to look after criminals with superpowers. People who can't be contained in ordinary prisons."

Brenda was incredulous. "He's a killer, Brian. It wasn't only Sacrifice who identified him. Lauren did, too. He killed two little girls thirteen years ago."

"If you can trust what Lauren said. What if she were

Sacrifice too? What if Sacrifice is a shapeshifting ghost?"

Brenda threw her hands in the air. "Next you'll be saying that I'm in it with Sacrifice, too. The whole world's conspiring against you."

Brian smiled sheepishly. "It might be."

Brenda rolled her eyes. "And even if Sacrifice is the prisoner of some super secret government agency, it doesn't mean she's bad. She could be like you. Someone with superpowers, except she got caught. Then, somehow, she found out about us and managed to send some kind of spirit message to us-"

Brian interrupted. "Why the different ages? Why not come right out with it and ask for help?"

"I don't know! Maybe she wasn't sure if we'd help? But it explains everything else. She doesn't know where she is, so she can't tell us. And the reason you lost your eye wasn't because of Sacrifice, but because you triggered some magical ward the government threw around the cell to keep her in and people like you out."

"So how come I wasn't zapped until she noticed me?"

"Because," said Brenda, pausing while she struggled to find something cogent to say next. "Because she heard the alarm as the mechanism was triggered and turned towards the door to see what was happening."

Brenda smiled smugly. Not bad for a speculative punt.

Brian appeared to agree, his head nodding slowly. "And my ears were here. The only sense I had in that cell was sight."

Then he shook his head and sprang to his feet. "This is getting us nowhere. The only thing we know for certain is that in less than an hour the police are going to storm that cabin and we haven't a clue who the bad guys are, or how dangerous they might be. There might be a blood bath. We might be the cause of a dangerous supervillain being freed."

Brenda was sure she knew what he was going to say next. That the pair of them had to rush off to the cabin and save the world.

She was wrong.

Chapter Twenty-Nine

"What are you doing?" she asked.

He was changing in front of her eyes. His ears growing tall and pointy, flaps appearing on his cheeks, his nose pushing out like a dog's, his neck thickening.

"There's more than one way to see." His voice had changed. It was higher and distorted. "Bats can see by sonar. Dogs by smell. If I can see again we'll have a chance."

Brenda watched, stunned. He'd parted his lips. Maybe he was emitting high frequency sounds. His head tracked jerkily from left to right and then up and back. He sniffed the air.

"It's just a matter of getting the frequency right and training my brain."

"Are you ... getting anything?" Brenda asked.

"Only this strange desire to find a lamp-post and catch flies."

There was silence for a while, then the corners of Brian's mouth began to rise and Brenda lost it – laughing uncontrollably. Brian joined in. It was the first time she'd seen him so much as smile since losing his sight.

"Seriously," she said, wiping her eyes. "Is it any good?"

He didn't answer. He held both hands out in front of him and started to walk. His head jerking in what appeared to be a random mechanical fashion.

"The door's over there," he said, pointing – correctly – towards the bedroom door. He spun on his heel, made a few tentative steps towards the window. "I can sense where the furniture is, but ... I have no fine tuning. I can't discriminate between a chest of drawers and a dresser. Or a box for that matter. They're all meaningless shapes. I can smell you, though."

Thank you very much, thought Brenda. Just the kind of thing a girl not wearing perfume appreciates.

"It's no good," he said, ditching his black nose and bat ears and morphing back to Brian. "You're going to have to be my eyes. Take my hand. You're going to fly us to the Adirondacks."

Brenda was hit by two competing waves of emotion. Excitement from the right. She was going to fly! Be in charge of a real life teleportation! And trepidation from the left. She was going to fly? How?

"We'll take it slow to start." He beckoned her with his hand. "Come on. Do you see a spare Labrador in the bedroom? I need my seeing eye Brenda."

The first wave of trepidation may have broken, but two others were gathering on the horizon. Brenda wasn't going anywhere without a plan or a map.

"I can't memorize the way there. It's over 500 miles across country."

"We can follow the roads. Log on to your computer and print off an itinerary."

That solved one problem, but not the other. What were they going to do when they got there? Being a seeing eye Brenda was fine in a teleportation bubble. Fun even. But, once they materialized, how would it work?

"You're *not* turning me into a dog!"

"Brenda, we don't have time for this. The police are probably half way there by now and they have a 450-mile head start."

He was *so* annoying when he was right. But he was also wrong, too. Stumbling into a dangerous situation without a plan was crazy. Lives were at stake.

"We'll think one up on the way down. Now, come on!"

He grabbed her. One of the plaster cornices on her bedroom ceiling warped and buckled alarmingly before sucking her up from the floor. They were teleporting blind.

And stopping almost immediately, the two of them hovering above the rooftops. He stood behind her in the invisible bubble, his left arm wrapped around her waist, his right arm held out in front of her.

"Now use my right hand to steer. Point my index finger in the direction you want to go and say faster, slower or stop."

Brenda soon got the hang of it. It was simple. It was fun. But was it fast enough? She was having to slow down so often to make sure she didn't miss a turn, she doubted if they were averaging more than seventy miles per hour. The first part of her itinerary was full of 0.5 miles along this road, and 0.3 miles along that. It wasn't until the other side of Cleveland that they'd have a long stretch of interstate.

"Try gaining height," said Brian. "You can see farther."

Brenda raised Brian's finger and leaned back. They rose above the countryside. It was just like flying a small, silent plane. She could bank and dive and accelerate ... and lose sight of the road she was supposed to be following. Shit! She'd looked away for a second to admire the view and now all the threadlike roads below looked the same. She slowed and angled the bubble down, one eye on the roads below, one on her itinerary, trying to make sense of them both.

She dived down faster, leveled out, slowed. Where was a road name? There had to be a sign somewhere?

She found one. Webster Road. Where was that? It wasn't on her itinerary.

"We'll have to materialize and ask directions."

"No!" said Brian, which, seeing he was a man and in possession of the 'never ask directions' gene (a recessive gene if there was one), was hardly surprising. "It'll take too much time. Gain height. Find the biggest road and follow it until you see a road sign. There's got to be one heading for Cleveland. We'll pick up the I-90 there."

Brenda took them higher, wondering how good her geography was. The sky was cloud-free. If she gained enough height, she should be able to see the Great Lakes. If she used them to navigate by, it would cut their journey time down dramatically. They could fly at hundreds of miles per hour. As long as she picked the right lake and didn't take them to Canada.

"Stay south of the lakes and you should be fine," said Brian.

She rose higher. She could make out a dark line on the horizon to the north. She rose higher still. The dark line widened and took form. It was either a coastline or a black forest. And the shape looked right.

She went for it. Faster and faster, the ground too far away to blur. She swung to the right in a long arcing curve. It was definitely a lake. She could see a huge sand bar poking out from the northern shore. She followed the lake northeast. There was another lake beyond. Ontario? She wasn't sure if I-90 continued along that lake's shoreline as well or cut inland.

She dropped down, the ground coming up fast and starting to blur. She slowed, aiming Brian's finger at Lake Erie's shoreline, looking for the widest, straightest road. One stood out. It was a little distance inland and it seemed composed of two strands that kept splitting apart and re-joining. It had to be the I-90. Or a train line.

She swung down lower, slowed some more. It wasn't a train line. It was definitely a road. Lower still, the road snaking and blurring. There was something up ahead. She slowed some more, easing right back until she was matching speed with the traffic below. It was a service area. She could see a sign. Angola Service Area.

For one second her jaw dropped. Angola? They were in Africa? Then she saw the sign with I-90 on it and sped up.

Miles flew by. They had to be touching two, three hundred miles per hour, but was it fast enough?

"Wouldn't Syracuse have called the local police and asked them to surround the cabin?" she asked.

"No police force is going to let someone else take over – or mess up – one of their cases. Especially one as high profile as this. They'll give the locals a courtesy call and ask them to stand by, but they won't want them within half a mile of the cabin."

It sounded logical. But real life had a habit of ditching the logical at the first opportunity. "Faster," she said, and took the bubble to the limit of her ability.

Time passed in a blur. She didn't dare take her eyes from the road. She wanted to check her watch, but couldn't. She wanted to formulate some kind of plan for what to do at the cabin, but couldn't. Staying on the road took all her concentration.

Then she was slowing, monitoring the road signs, looking for the turn-off, back on the smaller roads, slower still, time pouring through her fingers. How much longer? Were they too late? She hadn't seen a police convoy anywhere below.

She saw her first police car just past the tiny settlement of Scratchy Hollow. It was parked next to an ambulance a hundred yards back from the turn off into Forrester Road. She sped up, leaning into the right turn and accelerating. Everything was so silent. There could be a gun battle going on at the cabin and they'd have no idea. The air could be full of sirens and explosions.

Another car up ahead. She slowed. It was parked on the verge a few hundred yards back from where the road petered out into a track. An unmarked police car? It looked like it, there were two men sitting inside.

She sped past, slowing again as the clearing approached, then stopped. "Now what?" she whispered. She could just make out the cabin through the trees. She couldn't see any other cars. Or SWAT teams or helicopters. But it couldn't be long.

"We haven't time to be cautious," said Brian. "Aim for the front door and set us down in front of it."

"Are we just going to materialize?"

"Is anyone watching?"

Not that she could see. But anyone could be hidden in the trees.

"Just go," said Brian. "Get us in position, then have another look from there."

She grabbed Brian's finger and sent them arcing into the clearing. She did a quick circuit of the grounds, keeping her eyes on the edge of the woods. It looked clear. Then she headed for the front door, setting them down on the porch. She couldn't see anyone at the windows.

"We're here," she said. "What's the plan?"

"I need to see if I can read Daddy. Here." He handed her a plastic ID card. Stephanie Plum, Help the Blind.

Stephanie Plum! She gave him a full second blast of the Medusa. He might be blind, but he still deserved to be turned to stone. Why couldn't she ever be Miss Smith!

"It'll work," he said. "Knock on the door, ask for a donation and leave. All I need is an opportunity to read his thoughts. I'll be your dog."

"My dog?"

He morphed into a dog – a strange looking Chinese type of dog with bat-shaped ears and a wrinkled face – and as he did so the silent bubble around them burst. Suddenly, birds were calling in the woods and a light breeze blew against her face.

She took a deep breath and knocked on the door.

No answer.

She looked down at Brian. He had his head turned to one side and was sniffing the air – hopefully for Daddy or she'd get a complex.

She knocked again, silently rehearsing what she'd say when he opened the door, getting ready to step back if he came at her with a syringe full of a poison. She shuffled her feet, took another deep breath, adjusted her clothes. Wasn't he in? Should they move on to Plan B? Did they have a Plan B?

The door opened. Daddy was standing there – a spitting image of his picture – six four, six five. And well built. He filled out every inch of his jeans and check shirt.

"What you want?" he barked.

She held up her ID and hoped he didn't read too many mystery novels. "I'm collecting for the blind," she said, her mouth so dry every word was punctuated with a click.

He looked at the card, then at her, then Brian. He looked like the kind of man who rarely smiled. Unlike Brenda, who was smiling with the tenacity of a crazed beauty contestant.

'Well?' she screamed at Brian through the ether. 'Can you read him? Is he a super secret government jailer, or a child-killing maniac?'

'He's like Abbiati. Completely blank to me.'

Shit! She swore silently through clenched teeth, wondering if Daddy could read minds too.

One way to find out. She imagined she could see Sacrifice creeping furtively behind Daddy. She gave the thought as much power and belief as she could and screamed it at the man in the doorway.

Daddy didn't stir. He was still looking at her ID. Either he was an extraordinarily good actor, or he couldn't read minds.

Unlike Brian, who pulled on his lead.

'You can see Sacrifice!' he screamed. "Where? I can't sense her at all!'

'Relax,' replied Brenda. 'I was testing Daddy to see if he could read minds. He can't.'

"Where's your car?" asked Daddy.

"My car?" said Brenda, suddenly brought down to earth

and having to stall while her brain searched for something plausible to say. "It's ... back there." She waved a hand towards the general direction of the unmarked police car. An extravagant wave. There was something about lying that brought the arm waver out in Brenda – and the overpowering desire to behave like a ham actress from the silent film era.

And babble.

"It was such a lovely day I thought I'd take Stinky for a walk."

She patted Brian on the head and was about to launch into a long roundabout story explaining why that necessitated parking a long way back from the house, Stinky's lifelong battle with incontinence, and the difficulty of taking him for walks in the town because of his antisocial behavior ... when she remembered that the worst lie was a long rambling one, and fell back on the ditzy laugh and the crazed beauty contestant smile. "It is a lovely day, isn't it?"

Daddy grunted and handed back her ID. Then he dug one of his giant hands into a pocket, came up with some change and handed it to her without a word, closing the door on her before she had time to say anything more.

Not that she wanted to say anything more. She was more than pleased to exit the conversation and step away from the porch.

'Now what?' she asked. 'Are we any wiser? He could still be a killer or a super-secret jailer.'

'Walk towards the road. I'll slip the lead before you get there and run off into the trees. Run after me. Put on an act in case anyone's watching.'

Put on an act? From deep within came a welling desire to extend her left arm to the heavens, place the back of her right hand against her forehead and swoon at the sudden departure of her beloved Stinky into the bear-infested woods. But she wisely suppressed the desire and ran after him instead, wondering how long it would be before his bat sense deserted him and he ran smack into a tree.

He stopped after thirty yards or so and turned.

'Hurry up! I can hear sirens in the distance. Grab hold!'

Brenda ran harder. She couldn't hear any sirens, but then she didn't have bat ears.

They teleported immediately. Brian morphing in her grasp,

rippling and growing from dog to human.

"Swing round to the other side of the house. That's where the cellar is."

She followed his instructions, stopping the bubble midway along the sidewall.

"Now angle my finger down about forty-five degrees and point it at the base of the wall."

"Done."

They shot inside. The light vanished. She strained to make out her surroundings. It wasn't pitch black, but it was close.

"Can you see the light under the door?"

She couldn't. Her eyes were slowly becoming accustomed to the gloom. She could make out steps. They followed the wall down, then turned at right angles along another wall. Perhaps the cell door was around a corner?

She took the bubble into the center of the room, dropping slowly towards the floor. The thin line of light came into view. It had been hidden by the wall.

"Now think of Daddy and hold the image of him in your head," said Brian. "I'm going to morph into him, and I need to know what he's wearing and how big he is."

He changed, growing and filling out.

"Now set us down on the floor and find a light switch. Here." He pulled on the front of his shirt and teased the fabric into a pair of gloves and handed them to her. "Don't want to leave any fingerprints to confuse the police."

They dematerialized. The room smelt dank. It had a cold, airless, moldy feel. And it was quiet. No sound from upstairs, not even a footstep. And no sirens from outside either.

Brenda searched along the wall for a light switch. Logically there'd be one by the stairs. She climbed the stone steps, treading softly, brushing her hand lightly along the wall until she found it.

She paused, taking a closer look at the ceiling above. She couldn't see any light seeping through so no light should seep out either. It should be safe. Unless the switch opened a trap door in the ceiling...

'Switch it on,' insisted Brian. 'I don't do flashlights and there's a cupboard down here I need you to search.'

She flicked the switch, wincing as she did so.

Light filled the cellar room.

'Quick. Find the cupboard and look inside.'

She moved swiftly down the steps. The cupboard was a large grey metal cabinet – five foot tall and three foot wide with two doors. She eased the right hand door open, then the left.

'It's full of medical stuff.'

'What kind of medical stuff?'

All kinds of medical stuff. There were shelves full of syringes and needles and little boxes. She took one of the boxes out. It contained some kind of drug. Adenosine. There was a bottle inside. With a rubber top so you could fill up a syringe.

She checked further. There were three different drugs – Adenosine, Lignocaine and Trimazepine – there had to be two dozen bottles of each. And there was surgical spirit and cotton wool. Everything you'd need to inject someone. Just as the older Sacrifice had said. Daddy killed her by injection. But why so many bottles? Why so many needles?

'Maybe she's not that easy to kill,' said Brian. 'Take one of each. We'll find out what they do later.'

She grabbed three and stuffed them inside her jeans, filling three pockets. And she kept looking towards the cell door. What kind of being was Sacrifice? Was she really being killed? Were the ghosts real but, somehow, she kept on coming back? Was that her superpower – the ability to return from the dead?

And why keep her here? It didn't look like a government facility. If the government were holding her, wouldn't they have her in a state-of-the-art prison with extensive testing facilities and teams watching over her?

Or was Sacrifice so powerful that something went wrong? They had to dispose of her, kill her in a way she'd never be able to return, but her minder – Daddy – wouldn't comply. He brought her here instead. Having to inject her every year, every month, every week, however long it took to reduce her powers and keep her contained.

'Maybe we should leave her here,' she said.

'And risk her being discovered when the police smash their way into the cabin.'

She looked up at the ceiling. She still couldn't hear

anything, but that could be because the cellar was soundproofed. Anything could be happening up there. Any second the trap door might be found.

'Anything else in the room?' he asked.

She looked around, scanning the walls, There was a key on a nail by the cell door.

He held out his hand. 'Give it to me.'

'Are you sure?' she asked.

'What choice do I have? If I teleport through the door I might get fried like my eyeball. Someone's got to open this door. It's either me or the police.'

She handed him the key.

'Now point my left hand at the lock and stand well back.'

Chapter Thirty

The door was a rectangle of slightly less blurred static in a room full of barely recognizable shapes shot through with random dots and flashes. Brian had kept as much of the inner workings of his bat sonar as he could without compromising his appearance. It gave him enough vision to notice movement and large shapes, but that was all. Hopefully that would be all he'd need. There was no time to take things slow.

He turned the key in the lock and stood back, pushing the door open with the tips of his fingers. A quick glance towards the top of the doorframe. No alarm. No booby-trap. No bright flash of energy.

A shape that had to be Sacrifice rose from the bed. Brian flexed his knees, moved his weight onto his toes, ready to spring to the side, or grab for the door the moment she did anything untoward.

Could he read her thoughts? He felt there was something there. A presence, not the blankness he experienced with Daddy and Abbiati. Yes! There it was.

I have to do this. It's who I am. But it hurts!

What did she mean? Her thoughts had no context. She was conflicted, but about what? Killing Brian? Zapping him as he stood in the doorway?

"Is it time?" she asked.

"Not yet," he replied, trying to mimic Daddy's voice as best as he could. As best he could in between emitting high frequency sounds from his mouth to refresh his rudimentary vision. She didn't appear to hear them.

He dwelt in the doorway. He'd teased information from countless people before, but never felt pressure like this. He wasn't sure what she was, or what she could do. She could be an innocent. She could be like him. She could be brainwashed, damaged, twisted by years of incarceration.

And even if she *was* harmless the cell might not be. The door could be booby-trapped. One step towards her could lead to his death.

Why are you here? What do you want?

More thoughts from Sacrifice, but was she referring to Daddy or Brian? Had she made him? Could she read his mind too?

He had to press on. No time to be cautious. He tried his best to mimic Daddy's speech patterns.

"Something happen here one hour ago. You see anything unusual?"

"I heard a bell ringing."

"You know why?"

She moved slightly – maybe a shrug. It fitted with the thoughts he was picking up. Confusion and conjecture. She wanted to ask Daddy what the bell was for, but was fearful how he'd react.

If only he could see her face. He wasn't sure if he was being played. She sounded sincere, but so much was riding on his interpretation. If he got it wrong...

He tried another tack.

"Do you remember a time when you didn't live in this room?"

"I've always lived here. You know that. This is my home."

There was pride in her voice. *This is my home.*

"Not a prison?"

Now came anger and surprise. *Why are you speaking like this? This has never been a prison. This is my home!*

"I'm Sacrifice. This is where I have to be."

"Maybe it's time for you to go outside."

"No!" The shape moved, growing. Or was it coming closer? He had no confidence in his depth perception. He couldn't hear her feet on the floor. Her thoughts were becoming garbled and confused.

He transmuted his flesh, hopefully invisibly, meshing his skin with an impenetrable heat-resistant barrier.

The Sacrifice shape stopped four, five feet from the doorway. He could smell her now, sense her. "You can't send me out there," she pleaded. "I'm needed here. I'm Sacrifice. You told me!"

Everything about her screamed brainwashed victim. She didn't want to leave. She hadn't tried to harm him. He could read her mind. She'd even confirmed hearing an alarm bell an hour earlier when he'd lost his eye.

But was she playing him, feeding him all the things he wanted to hear? *Look at me. Look how innocent I am. I don't want to leave. It wasn't me who robbed you of your sight.* What would be next? *Okay, I'll come with you. Take me to your home. Hide me. Give me a new face.*

'Behind you!'

Brenda's voice screamed a warning inside his head. If it *was* Brenda. Sacrifice could be trying to get him to turn his back.

The cell door slammed shut in front of his face. Then he was moving towards it, face first and fast. A blast of air had lifted him off his feet and was propelling him forward.

Smack! He hit the door with his forehead and hastily thrown forward hands, then he was moving again, backwards this time, picked up by some unseen force and tossed towards the far wall.

He teleported, stepping into the ether and killing his momentum. Now he was really blind. No bat sonar to ping off walls or objects. No sound, no smell, no feelings at all. Just a fuzzy pink static in a sea of sensory deprivation.

He had to return. Brenda was in there alone. With Daddy or Sacrifice or God knows what. He grew his ears and nose, then materialized, crouching and dropping as he did so, filling the air with hundreds of high frequency shrieks. There was a large shape in the center of the room. It smelled like Daddy. Another shape crouched by the foot of the steps.

'Brenda? Is that you? Show me what you see!'

He rolled as he landed, keeping moving, trying to get a sense of the room around him. Was Sacrifice still in her cell? And was that Daddy who'd attacked him?

'He can teleport!' screamed Brenda. 'He came out of nowhere.'

He could do a lot more than teleport. A blast of air caught Brian, picked him up as though he was no weight at all, and smashed him into the wall. Brian rolled with it as best he could, healing his cracked and broken ribs as he did so.

'Think harder,' he called to Brenda. 'Keep your eyes on

Daddy and show me what you see. I need your eyes.'

Daddy was still a shape to Brian. He knew where he was, but not what he was doing with his hands, or where he was looking.

Stroboscopic images flashed into Brian's head. Stop start pictures of Daddy as glimpsed from the foot of the steps. Daddy had his back to Brenda. He was looking at the other Daddy – the bat-eared, serpentining Daddy. He made a sweeping motion with his right hand and...

Brian was lifted off his feet again and smashed into a wall. How was he supposed to get close to Daddy?

And when would Daddy turn his attention to Brenda?

Brian picked himself up, waited for an image from Brenda, then memorized it. He teleported, nudged himself what he hoped was a few yards forward and a few to the right, then re-materialized. Crouching, he fired off another series of bat sonar squeaks, worked out his bearings, then teleported again, aiming this time for a place a yard or so behind Daddy and to his right.

He materialized. Not exactly where he'd expected, but close enough. He charged, head down and arms ready to grab and slice. He extended his fingers, changing them to talons, razor sharp and strong.

He smashed into Daddy's back, lifting him off his feet, grabbed him with his left hand and slashed at his legs with his right. His talons bounced off. He'd expected to have opened up a sizeable gash in the man's thighs, but Daddy's skin was somehow impervious.

Something incredibly powerful grabbed Brian's left forearm. A hand like a vice. He could feel his bones cracking and grinding to powder beneath the grip. And suddenly he was swinging through the air again, even faster than before and – smack – he found the wall.

This time he took longer to get up. More bones needed to be set and – smack – there he went again, into the wall, then out, spinning this time, impossibly fast, like a spin drier out of control.

He teleported. The spinning didn't stop. Physically it might have, but his brain felt like mush – terminally disorientated mush that had lost the ability to know or care what was up, down, back or forth. He was going to be sick. He was going to fall over. He was going to do both at the same time.

But he had to get back. Brenda wouldn't stand a chance.

He materialized, collapsing as he did so, trying to clear his mind, trying to roll, trying to pick up an image of his surroundings from Brenda. And then he was picked up and moving again. Up this time – against the ceiling – then down much faster, smashing into the rough concrete floor. He could barely move.

'I've switched off the light,' screamed Brenda in his head. 'Use your sonar!'

He rolled. He teleported. He changed position, materialized, fired up his bat sonar, worked out where Daddy was and repeated the process, stepping in and out of the real world. Twice a blast of air almost caught him, but Daddy was firing blind, turning this way and that, and Brian was working his way in closer.

Brian morphed both hands into cone shaped daggers. He'd punch through Daddy's skin somehow and rearrange the guy's atoms.

He materialized above Daddy's head and fell on him, punching down at the man's neck with all the power he had. His dagger hand bounced off, sliding ineffectually to the side.

He dematerialized, thinking fast. If he couldn't penetrate the man's skin by force he'd try by stealth. He thrust his right hand out to where Daddy's body had been and tried to materialize. Nothing happened. His right arm started to tingle, but he couldn't force himself into the physical world. Something was preventing him. Then he was falling. He'd materialized, but Daddy must have moved. He hit the ground hard.

Daddy fell on him. A giant hand closing around Brian's left wrist. Brian tried to teleport, but couldn't. Daddy had to be blocking him somehow. The giant hand closed tighter. Bones cracked. Concentrate! He focussed on his skin in contact with Daddy's, imagined it growing microscopic filaments, each of the filaments pushing out, looking for an opening, a pore, some way of pushing inside Daddy's skin.

Nothing. No pores, no microscopic cracks. He tried to make a microscopic crack, brought the full force of his attention onto Daddy's hand and tried to transmute it to paper, to jelly, to something he could work with!

Nothing. And Daddy's other hand had closed around Brian's neck.

Blind limb-thrashing panic. He couldn't teleport. He couldn't penetrate Daddy's skin. He hadn't a fraction of Daddy's strength. And any second now his magic would be used up and he'd no longer be able to regenerate his broken body.

~

Brenda was halfway up the steps wedged against the wall. Her eyes were gradually becoming accustomed to the dark again. She could make out the two figures fighting but, worse, she could hear the bones cracking. And there was nothing she could do!

There were no weapons to hand. There were no...

That's when she remembered the drugs cabinet and the needles. She didn't know what the drugs did, but a cocktail of all three couldn't be good. Especially when injected with force into the eye or somewhere vulnerable.

She crept down the steps, cringing at the noise from the center of the room. She skirted around them, following the wall to the cabinet, hoping that Daddy would be too preoccupied to notice her. She eased the cabinet door open, felt for the biggest, meanest looking needle she could find. Then moved to the drugs, opening one box after another, filling the syringe, her hands shaking, adding a good measure of air, even if the drugs weren't lethal an air bubble might be.

Then she was moving across the floor.

'Brian? Can you hear me? I've got a syringe full of drugs. Can you make your skin fluoresce so I don't inject you by mistake?'

He didn't answer. He didn't fluoresce.

'Brian!'

A scuffling, creaking noise sounded from above. It was coming from the trap door! Light began to bleed in from the room above. And flashlights, their narrow beams criss-crossing through the murk.

The fighting stopped immediately. Daddy teleported out, leaving Brian lifeless on the floor. She dropped the syringe and threw herself on top of Brian.

'Teleport now!' she shouted, gripping him tightly. 'I don't think they've seen us.'

"Police! Freeze!"

Shit! They weren't teleporting and light was streaming in from above. The police had thrown the trap door open. Someone was running down the steps. Cones of light cut through the air. And Brian felt strange – not like a human so much as a badly stuffed dummy – lumpy and lifeless.

'Brian! Are you all right?'

'No,' he said. 'I'm hurt and running out of magic. It's up to you. Be a hostage. Talk your way out. Daddy's the demon. Sacrifice is innocent. I'll find you as soon as I can.'

He rolled on top of her. His body felt weird, lumps were moving and growing together. Was he shapeshifting on top of her?

Suddenly her face started tingling.

'You're changing my face!'

'I have to.'

His hands had moved to her neck. He was strangling her!

"Step away, or I'll shoot!"

Light stung her eyes. She was blinded. People were shouting. Boots clattered on the steps.

Then gunfire. Two shots and she felt Brian relax his grip and fall away.

She lay there, eyes screwed up against the dazzling light, breathing hard. Was Brian all right? He could take two bullets, couldn't he? 'Brian? Are you there?' He didn't answer.

Someone must have found the light switch at the top of the steps because the quality of the light suddenly changed dramatically. Flashlights no longer shone in her face. She could see again. There were half a dozen men crowding around, some head to toe in SWAT black, some in vests...

Why's everyone looking at me like that? That's the second man to grimace and turn away the moment they saw my face.

Oh, crap. I let a blind man mould my face! I've probably got a nose on my forehead and three ears!

Her hands flew to her face. Her skin felt rough. *He's given me scales!* At least the nose was in the right place. A bit on the large side and ... squashed? *And what's that huge lump on my cheek!*

"Medic!" shouted one of the officers. "I wouldn't touch it if I were you."

Oh God was it that bad? Everyone's grimacing!

She looked at her hands. Was that blood on her gloves? It looked like blood. Was she bleeding? Had he opened up an artery by mistake? Turned her face inside out?

"Don't worry, lady." Another officer was kneeling beside her now. He turned his head and shouted towards the steps. "We need that bus now! Two down!" He turned back to Brenda. "Look at me. What's your name?"

What's my name? Does the Elephant Man have an ugly sister? Slap! That was the inner Brenda giving her host a mental slap across her hideously deformed face. *Snap out of it, Brenda, and concentrate! Everything hinges on you now. You can either rescue the situation, or turn it into a farce.*

Farce sounded a good bet.

Slap!

"Jane Smith," said Brenda. "I'm Jane Smith and ... he abducted me!"

She stabbed a finger at the motionless body beside her and screwed up her face, feigning pain while she thought of what to say next. Jane Smith had been a good sensible start. A nice common name at last. Jane Smith from New York. That ought to buy her some time.

"This door's locked," said a voice behind her. "The key's in the lock, but it's not working."

It was the door to Sacrifice's cell. Daddy must have sealed the door somehow when he slammed it shut.

"There's another girl in there," said Brenda. "Mary Alice something. He told me he took her from a park in Stamford when she was only four. He's sick. He said he was going to build me a home here in the cellar where we'd live like a family."

'Brilliant,' said Brian's voice in her head. He sounded exhausted. 'And don't worry about your face. I ... I had to give you cuts and bruises to ... to reinforce your story that ... you're a victim not an accomplice.'

"Break the door down!"

"Be careful," said Brenda. "She's been in there for

thirteen years. She's brainwashed."

They smashed the door off the lock. Sacrifice was terrified. She stood at the back of the room, pressed up against the wall.

"Mary Alice? It's all right. We're here to help you." said one of the officers.

"Don't call me that! I'm Sacrifice. Where's Daddy?"

"That's what he forced her to call him," said Brenda. "He's Daddy and she's his Sacrifice."

"Do you know what these drugs are?"

Brenda swung her head round. Another of the detectives was standing by the open drugs cupboard. "No idea," she said. Then she remembered the syringe on the floor. "He was trying to inject me with something and I managed to grab it off him."

Another box ticked. She'd explained the syringe. She'd named Mary Alice. What was left?

An alibi for Daddy. She had to make sure Kayla's murderer wasn't given a free pass. When was Kayla murdered? Sunday morning around breakfast time?

"He took me Sunday morning. I was jogging in Central Park. Are you writing this down? It was just after eight. In the middle of New York. He's had me for three days!"

She turned away, feigning tears. She'd given them enough – any more and she was bound to contradict herself.

Sacrifice started screaming.

"No! You can't take me away! Where's Daddy? Daddy!"

There had to be half a dozen officers in the cell with her. All male, all armed, all wearing vests or full combat gear. It had to be intimidating, even for someone who hadn't been locked up and brainwashed for thirteen years.

"It's all right, Mary Alice."

"My name's Sacrifice! What have you done with Daddy? Take your hands off me! I'm not leaving. I'm Sacrifice. I have to stay here or people will die. I'm the only one who can save them."

She was becoming hysterical.

A clattering from above heralded the arrival of a doctor and a couple of paramedics.

"Gunshot wound over here," said one of the detectives. "Looks bad. The woman need attention and there's a girl in there."

The medical staff dispersed. Brian was pronounced alive but critical; Brenda had her face prodded and a pen light shone in her eyes; and a paramedic was sent to see if he could quieten Sacrifice.

"What are you doing with that needle?" she screamed. "Are you going to kill me? He said it wasn't time?"

"Time for what?"

"To save the world. I'm Sacrifice. You *must* know that! Without me the devil wins. I have to die so the world can be reborn."

She sounded crazy. The whole story sounded crazy but... there *were* all those Sacrifice ghosts. Something was going on. Brenda didn't have a clue what, but he hadn't held her prisoner for thirteen years for nothing.

.

Chapter Thirty-One

Brenda was helped to a waiting ambulance. Now what? She'd done all she could to manipulate the police. If she stayed any longer, things could only go pear-shaped. The three bottles of drugs in her pockets for instance. No one had thought to search her, but very soon they would. And they'd want to know her address and phone number, where she worked, where exactly in Central Park she'd been abducted from.

Should she try and escape, or would that throw into question everything she'd told the police?

And where was Brian? He'd been stretchered out earlier, but she couldn't see him anywhere outside.

~

Brian was strapped down on a stretcher in the back of an ambulance. He'd heard there were two ambulances at the cabin, so Brenda had to be in the second. Which wasn't ideal. His reserves were already far too low. He wasn't sure how much magic he had left. Enough for a single teleport. Maybe a trick or two. If his head didn't explode first. Already the migraine flashes were illuminating his vista of Barbie pink static.

And whatever he was going to do, he had to do it quick. The ambulance was already moving. Any surgeon who tried to open him up was going to find a hell of a lot more than two bullets.

Teleporting was out of the question. He had a paramedic and a detective in the back with him and both were watching him intently.

So he extended a finger, driving it down and through the bed, transmuting on contact any metal or fabric that blocked its way. He had to find the petrol tank and ensure neither of

276

his watchers noticed a thing. He found the tank, rooted around until he found the fuel line, snapped it, retracted his finger and waited.

The engine began to splutter.

"What's happening?" asked the detective.

"Don't know," said the driver. "It was fine driving down."

The engine died and the ambulance slowed to a stop.

Brian waited. The success of his plan depended on what happened next. The second ambulance had to stop and pick him up. He was critically wounded, they couldn't drive past. And Brenda had to be in that second ambulance. If not...

He didn't want to consider the 'if not' scenario. He didn't have enough magic for a plan B.

The second ambulance stopped. He could hear people talking outside through the open door at the back of the bus. The detective who'd been watching him was outside now talking to a colleague and the paramedic from the second ambulance. They wanted to move Brian to the other bus, but were concerned about Brenda.

"She can't stay in the back with her attacker. It wouldn't be right. Every time I try to question her about what happened, she starts to cry."

"She's walking wounded. She can sit up front."

Not ideal, but at least Brenda was there. He felt her mind as they wheeled him from one bus to the other. 'I'm ready, Brian, but make it quick. I don't know how much longer I can string them along.'

They strapped him in the back of the second ambulance and prepared to set off. Brenda was in the front with the driver. Two paramedics and a single detective were in the back with Brian. The other detective had cadged a lift to the hospital with the escort car.

Now was the time to show his hand – or, more accurately, what he was holding in his hand. A grenade. Not a real grenade, but one he'd teased into shape from the sheets and material his hand had been resting upon. He slipped his restraints and held the grenade aloft, holding his finger where the pin should have been.

"Everybody out," he said. "My finger could slip any time."

He gripped the grenade tighter, not sure if the sole detective would try and grapple for it.

Both paramedics wanted to leave, but the detective wasn't moving. And he was between them and the door.

"Come on," they urged. "We've got to get out."

Brian scanned for the detective's mind, picking up a rush of thoughts, most were garbled, but some were crystal clear. *Where'd he get the grenade? Didn't anyone search him? What am I going to do?*

"Do what I say and no one gets hurt," said Brian. Every word was a strain, but he had to get his message across. "I just want to talk to Jane. In private. That's all. I know I might die. I need to make my peace with her in case I don't make it."

The detective wasn't buying it. He didn't trust Brian and he didn't want to leave Brenda alone with him. But there was something else, a series of thoughts bubbling up behind the others, tantalizingly close, but every time Brian thought he had them his concentration was rent by zigzagging flashes and pain. Such pain. It was like having all his teeth struck by lightning one after the other and then plunged into ice.

He clung on, fighting through the pain. There! He had an image now. A woman and two children. In a picture frame. On a video. In the flesh.

"Do you want to see your children again!" Brian shouted, shaking his fist. He could barely focus. "My finger's slipping. I can feel it!"

The driver was the first to run. Then the rear doors were wrestled open and soon everyone had piled out.

'Brenda, come into the back and close the doors,' said Brian. 'We're going.'

As soon as Brenda closed the rear doors he rolled over and thrust his right hand through the body of the ambulance into the petrol tank. The pain was constant now. He gritted his teeth, made a hole in the top, then fashioned a fuse from the bed material, plunging it deep into the tank, soaking it thoroughly, then pulling enough free to give them enough of a delay.

"You're going to blow it up?" asked Brenda.

"Can't have them looking for us. They've got to think we're dead."

"But they won't find our bodies inside. Will they?"

"Tomorrow's problem. Stand behind me and grab hold."

He reached into his shirt pocket and pulled out a book of matches. An essential part of his crime fighter's wardrobe.

He lit the fuse, waited just long enough to feel it catch, then pushed all his remaining power into one final teleport.

~

Brenda looked down at the scene below. They were hovering at tree height above Forester Road. The escort car had pulled over fifty yards down the road and one of the officers was running back towards the ambulances. The other officer was standing twenty yards back from the rear of the second vehicle. The paramedics had scattered. There was no one else for miles. Then came the explosion. A roiling ball of flame and silent black smoke rising towards them.

"It's blown. Now go!" shouted Brenda, clutching Brian's hand and pointing it at the sky.

They rose, streaking into the cloudless blue sky. "Make this quick," said Brian. "I don't know how long I can keep this up."

He looked terrible. The gunshot wounds were bad enough, but his face had a pale sickly pallor. His hands were cold and he was sweating.

"Faster," said Brenda. "As fast as you can." She'd fly high enough to see the Great Lakes this time, and cut out as many roads as she could.

"Stop!" She could see them now away to the left and behind. She adjusted position, aligning herself with north. Now, whereabouts would Richwood be on a map?

"Hurry," he said.

She hurried, pointing his finger where she hoped her house was and telling him to go for it as fast as he could.

"When you say you'll not sure how long you can keep this up. Do you mean literally? We might materialize any second?"

"Yes."

Crap! She urged him to go faster. The ground moved beneath her, sliding past so fast they had to be travelling at tens of thousands of miles per hour. Spaceship fast. Would he be able to stop?

"Slower," she said. "Slower. Brian, you're not slowing. Brian!"

His eyes were closed and he was starting to slump in her arms. She shook him. "Brian!"

"What?"

"Slow down."

They slowed. Brenda tried to get her bearings. Everything was passing by so fast. Why weren't all towns placed next to distinctively shaped lakes?

She made a guess and adjusted Brian's steering finger.

That's when they materialized.

Crap. Brenda was in free fall, twenty thousand feet above something very, very hard. Wind whistled past her ears. She couldn't breathe. It was freezing and ... she'd let go of Brian.

Did she mention the spinning?

Sky, ground, sky, ground, there went lunch.

She punched her hands and feet out. Isn't that what skydivers do? The world stopped spinning. And started coming up at her very, very fast.

Shit! Shit! Shit!

She saw Brian. He was a plummeting rag doll hundreds of feet below her and over to her left. Think, Brenda! You can do this. You saw that documentary on skydiving. How did they steer?

Hello? Paging inner Brenda.

Not a squeak. Inner Brenda was probably pinned against an intra-cranial ceiling.

Brenda experimented. It had to be something to do with moving your arms and legs. That was it! And if you tucked your hands and legs in and pointed down you sped up. She aimed at Brian, streamlined her body and accelerated. She overshot, she threw her limbs out and slowed herself, she banked left, she banked right, she spun uncontrollably. But little by little she was getting closer to Brian until...

She grabbed him by the arm.

"Teleport! Brian! Teleport now!"

Not a word. Maybe he couldn't hear. The wind noise was overpowering. She pulled him closer, grabbing his other arm as well. She shouted with her mind this time, screaming his name and aiming it at his head. 'Brian! Wake up! If you don't wake up we're going to die!'

'What?'

'Teleport! Teleport now! It's our only chance!'

The ground was coming up so fast now. She could see individual houses and cars. Come on Brian!

They dematerialized. Away went the roar of the wind and the heavy tug of gravity. They hung there, in a silent bubble a thousand feet in the air. He looked like a zombie – white face, bloody wounds, and empty half-lidded eyes. She grabbed his index finger and stabbed it at the ground. "Down. Fast. And stay with me this time. Keep talking."

They reached the ground. Brenda headed for the nearest road, making sure they never rose more than ten feet off the ground. And she kept him talking, even though his conversation was limited to grunts and mumbles. At least they didn't have far to go. The road led them to a small town she recognized. Ten miles to go at most. 'We can do this, Brian. *You* can do this.'

Brenda wasn't sure how many times she breathed during those last ten miles, but it felt like the entire journey was accomplished in one long bated breath. As soon as they reached Brenda's living room, they both collapsed.

She lay there, counting her blessings. One, she was alive and, two, she didn't have to feel guilty about the extra calories she'd consumed at lunch – they were now fertilizing someone's cornfield.

She rolled over and looked at Brian. He was shivering now, a feverish white-faced zombie. She dragged him across the floor and onto the sofa, then ran upstairs and grabbed a handful of blankets.

"Is there anything else I can do?" she asked, enunciating each word and giving his shoulder a shake to make sure he was listening. "Do you want sugary food?"

He made a grunt that sounded like a 'yes' so she rustled together an assortment of cookies and chocolate and put the kettle on for a mug of hot sugary tea.

Then she rushed upstairs. After that free fall she so needed to visit the bathroom.

An hour later Brian was still out of it, but at least he'd stopped shivering and his color was coming back. Brenda went upstairs to Google her three mysterious boxes of drugs.

Adenosine appeared to be primarily an antiarrhythmic

drug used to treat heart conditions. It seemed to have other uses too. Pages of them – all written in obscure medical-speak. The one common thread was that Adenosine worked on the heart.

Lignocaine was an antiarrhythmic drug too, but primary it was a local anaesthetic.

Trimazepine was used to treat cardiac arrest. It was an enhanced version of Epinephrine.

So, three heart drugs – what did it mean?

She tried searching on all three to see if they were used in combination and found a hundred thousand hits. She picked through pages and pages of abstruse medical texts before finding what she was looking for.

Administering Adenosine and Lignocaine together stopped the heart. The other shoe dropped immediately. Trimazepine was used to start the heart.

She sat up and blinked. Was Daddy deliberately killing and reviving Sacrifice? It might explain the ghosts. If ghosts were a snapshot of personality, something ejected into the ether at death, rather than, for want of a better word, a soul.

She shook her head. It still didn't explain why he was doing it. Was he feeding on her death? If so, wouldn't it be easier to hang around hospitals? There'd be a continuous supply there, and far less hassle.

She switched on her TV and made another sweep of the news channels. Still no word on the raid on the cabin or the exploding ambulance.

Time to check on Brian again. As she trotted downstairs, she was surprised to see him up and walking. He'd even healed his wounds. His red check shirt was unmarked. Then she saw the other 'Daddy' still asleep on the sofa, and realized.

Daddy had found them.

Chapter Thirty-Two

Brenda froze. Her brain trying to catch up with her fear. How had he found them?

"Move and I squash you like bug." Daddy was glaring at her, his right hand raised, fingers spread, ready to send her crashing against the wall. She'd seen what he'd done to Brian. Her bones wouldn't regenerate if smashed.

"What do you want?" she asked.

"You come down. Go stand in corner by TV."

She obeyed, firing a thought towards Brian as she descended the stairs. 'Brian? Are you okay. Has he hurt you?'

'I'm pretending to be unconscious. Do as he says.'

"No touch him," commanded Daddy as she approached the sofa. "Keep hands in air, walk past, be quiet."

'Can you teleport?' she asked Brian. 'I might be able to grab you before he can react.'

'Too weak,' he said. 'I need more time to recover.'

She reached the TV and turned. Daddy had pulled out a small black box the size of a cigarette packet from his shirt pocket. He was standing over Brian, sliding back the lid.

'He's taking something out of a small box,' said Brenda. 'It's...' She strained to make it out. It looked revolting. 'It's like a large, green slug flecked with yellow.'

He had it in his hand now. Was he going to put it on Brian? Make him eat it? Let it crawl inside his ear?

What happened next was so fast Brenda didn't have time to fire off a warning. Daddy fell on Brian, pinning him with his left arm and body while his right hand placed the slug on Brian's forehead.

Brian's eyes opened wide. He struggled ineffectually.

"You no teleport now," said Daddy, his face inches away from Brian's. "Leech stick like glue. I bet you think, 'no problem. I shapeshift leech off when he not look.' I say, 'go ahead. Many shapeshifter try. No one ever succeed.' You mine."

Brenda couldn't keep her eyes off the leech. It was moving, flattening itself against Brian's forehead. Was it feeding on him? Leeching the magic out of him?

'Do you know what it is?' she asked. 'Will it kill you?'

'No idea.'

Daddy was still on top of Brian, studying his face, sniffing at him. "What are you?" he asked. "You smell human, but ... you not."

Brian didn't answer.

"And why you mess with me? Why you come my house and poke nose in business that no concern you?"

"I was looking for the girl," said Brian. "You abducted her."

"So? I break no rule. I do everything Synod tell me. Be discreet, they say. I be discreet. No one see me take her, and no one know I have her."

"The Synod have to check up now and then."

Daddy lifted his head slightly. His eyes narrowed. "You no work for Synod. If Synod want know what I do, they come see me. They no sneak in basement."

"They do now."

"You lie! You smell like liar. I give you to Inquisitors. They soon find out what you are."

This was going from bad to worse. Brian didn't have the magic to get out of the situation, now it looked like he couldn't talk himself out either.

"We're private investigators," said Brenda, so desperate she was about to fall back on the truth. Well, a near neighbor. "We're contacted by spirits of people who die. Sacrifice kept coming to us and that's how we tracked you down. She was the one we were looking for. Not you."

Daddy pushed himself off Brian and stood up. He narrowed his eyes at Brenda.

"You see dead?"

"Yes. I don't want to, but ... they keep coming to me."

"Why my Sacrifice come to you?"

Good question. Now she needed to keep him talking. The longer she delayed him, the more time Brian had to recover.

And knowledge was power – if they were to stand a chance of outwitting Daddy, they had to know more about him.

"She wanted to know why you, um, feed off her. She couldn't–"

"You lie! She would never say that. She think she die to save world."

"Not the young Sacrifice. Not Mary Alice. The girl that came to me was only five or six years old."

His anger died down. He looked surprised.

Brenda pressed on. "She kept asking why you didn't go to the hospitals."

"What hospitals? What you talking about?"

He was getting angry again.

"To feed," she said. "She couldn't understand why you fed on her, when there were thousands of people dying in hospitals."

He looked at her as though she were crazy. "You eat rotten food? Sick people taste bad. Everyone know that. Disease. Bruising. What you think I am? Ghoul? I dzindi."

"Dzindi?"

"Yes, dzindi. How you say? Addict? Not my fault. Human life essence very addictive. And children...." He licked his lips as if recalling a fine wine. "Essence of human children very pure, very strong."

"Is one child enough?" asked Brian. "Do you have other girls besides Sacrifice?"

Daddy turned on him. "Why you ask all these questions?" He thumped his chest. "*I* in charge here."

"Sorry," said Brian. "We're curious that's all."

Daddy ignored him. He beckoned to Brenda. "You. Come here."

Brenda stayed where she was, contemplating whether this was the moment she should run for it. She might be able to dive behind the sofa, roll and come up running. If Brian could distract him she might be able to reach the back door without being blasted by magic.

'No!' That was Brian in her head. 'I can't do anything yet. Try to keep him talking.'

"Come here!" said Daddy.

Brenda walked towards him, taking slow deliberate steps. She felt like she was walking meekly to her death when she should be running or fighting. But what could she do? Except play for time and hope.

He sniffed at her face. Brenda closed her eyes. Her body began to shake.

"You no bruised," he said. "Your face shapeshifted. Why? So I not feed on you? You think I no smell fake broken nose?"

Brenda swallowed hard. "No, it's a disguise. How do you-"

"Bad disguise. Come. Over there by table."

He pulled her towards the dining table. Her brain cycling wildly. What was he going to do? And where had that black leather bag on the table come from? It wasn't hers.

He lifted the bag with his free hand and placed it on one of the dining room chairs. "You lie on table. Now!"

"Why do you want me to lie on the table?"

"Move!" He lifted her off the ground, swinging her by the shoulders up and onto the table. She slid on the highly polished surface.

'Brian! How much longer do you need? This is looking bad.' More than bad. What was he going to do? Why the table?

'Delay him,' said Brian. 'Play along, get him talking, be nice, anything!'

Anything? Be nice? Did that include taking one for the team? She was either going to be eaten or ravished. She'd seen *Rosemary's Baby*. She hated raw liver.

Daddy reached down into the black bag and brought out four webbing straps. He was going to tie her up!

"Stay still and I no hurt you."

'Ask questions,' shouted Brian.

Ask questions! Like what? Like how come Brian gets a leech and I get... She didn't want to put into words what she might get, in case it encouraged Fate to make it happen.

'Calm down. We need to know more about him.'

Daddy grabbed her right wrist and began to wrap one end of the webbing around it. Her body wouldn't stop shaking.

"How did you find us?" she asked, her voice quivering. "We thought we'd lost you."

"I have his eyes. I find him any time I want."

'Good,' said Brian. 'Keep probing. Ask him about the drugs we found in his cellar.'

'I already know that. He uses two of them to stop the heart and Trimazepine to restart it.'

Daddy left the other end of the webbing strap dangling free before asking for her other hand.

'Ask him how he feeds.'

He tied the second strap around her left wrist.

She swallowed. "How do you feed?" she asked.

"Feed on humans you mean?"

"Yes."

He took the two remaining webbing straps and tied them to her ankles.

"I smell life essence moment it start leave body. It come from here." He tapped her on the nose. "Then I breathe in." He demonstrated that too, pushing his arms back and swelling his chest. "Trick is to take only what you need. Take too much, girl die."

"Doesn't it harm the girl? Cause her to age?"

He shook his head. "Not if girl young and strong. Sacrifice feed me twelve time per year. You," he looked at her disparagingly, "maybe four. Trick is to leave just enough for girl recover. Like your blood donors."

Brenda watched him return to his black bag. What was it going to be now? A syringe and two bottles of drugs?

It wasn't. He brought out a mallet.

Aaaarrrgghh! I'm not just going to be eaten. I'm going to be tenderized first!

He reached into the bag again and brought out four pieces of metal that looked like gothic tent pegs. Large, substantial tent pegs with serrated shafts.

"What are you doing?" she asked, starting to rise from the table.

"Down!" He threatened her with the mallet. "Lie still and you no get hurt. Move and I smash you."

She lay back down, firing a thought at Brian. 'Are you ready yet. Do you have a plan?'

'I do, but .. you won't like it.'

She didn't. It was the worst plan he'd ever had. It was the worst plan *anyone* had ever had!

And, while she argued, Daddy walked around the table hammering tent pegs into her oak floorboards, pulling each strap tight, tying them off and stretching her limbs to the limit.

'Ok, Brian, you want a running commentary? Well, I'm spread-eagled on the table and my oak floor's ruined!'

And now she could hear Daddy rummaging in the black bag again. She lifted her head to look. He took out a syringe and two bottles of drugs.

She was breathing hard, her mouth dry. "Why are you doing this? You said I was too old."

"I have do this. You loose end. You know too much."

What? This didn't sound like a feeding any more. "You *are* going to revive me, aren't you?"

"Risk too big. You will feel no pain."

She struggled against the ties, but they were so tight and the more she struggled, the deeper they cut into her wrists.

'Brian, forget the plan. Do something now!'

Brian spoke. "Does the Synod know about Lauren Stone and Ashley Peterson?"

Daddy held the syringe up to the light and pushed the needle onto the end. "Who?"

"The two girls you murdered thirteen years ago."

Daddy swung round to face Brian. "I pay for that! I do everything Inquisitor say. He show me how follow rules."

"Isn't killing me against the rules?" said Brenda.

"I have blood right. You take my Sacrifice, I take you."

Now he was opening one of the boxes, pulling out the bottle.

"Who are the Inquisitors?" asked Brian. "I've never heard of them."

"You will soon."

"Will they kill me?"

"Maybe. They hurt you for sure. But if you tell truth, they can help you, too. They show me how to manage my dzindi. 'Never draw attention to yourself,' they say. 'Be smart. You batter girl, she taste bad and humans make big fuss. Even bigger fuss if you kill new girl every month. But if you take one girl, keep her and brainwash her – everybody happy.'"

He inverted the bottle and held it up to the light, pushing in the syringe needle and slowly pulling the plunger back.

"They even help me brainwash girl. 'First give her faith,' they say. 'Plenty books, plenty TV evangelist person. Then show her how bad world is, and how only she can save it.

Then after she sacrificed, news all good. Many happy stories. That way she believe. Same happen next month. You make good news tape, bad news tape. Girl get brainwashed, and don't bruise when you kill her.' Clever, no?"

He tapped at the syringe with his finger to remove any air bubbles.

"They'll make a big fuss when they find me," said Brenda.

"No. You die heart failure. Humans die heart failure every day. No investigation. No fuss. And no repercussion for Andrius. Which is good, no?"

No. And what was that smell? A musty...

Ghosts. Two of them – an overweight middle-aged man in a badly fitting suit, and an emaciated skeleton of a woman in what looked like a Victorian night dress. They were over by the kitchen door watching.

And there was another – over by the front door. And – she craned her neck to be certain – another two by the TV.

What was this? Her home had been a virtual ghost-free zone for the past two weeks. And why the silence? They were all watching her, but no one was saying a word. Were they here to save her? It was about time someone was. Or were they here to take her to the other side? Were these the five people she was supposed to meet when she died? All of them strangers! All of them in need of a good deodorant!

Ask them for help. That was the inner Brenda, who'd at last deigned to put in an appearance, with the least likely suggestion she'd ever made. *We've never been strapped to the dining room table before! Well, only the once. And he wasn't standing over us with a syringe full of poison!*

Maybe she *could* ask them for help. It made more sense than Brian's plan. His plan was to attack Daddy when he was feeding. A blind hope that he'd be more vulnerable, and have to lower his magical shields. How Brian would know the exact moment when Daddy was feeding was glossed over. *He might make a noise.* What kind of noise? *A deep breathing, sucking noise.*

Very convincing. Any plan that began – first, stop Brenda's heart – could not be considered a plan. And one that regarded, as a good thing, the possibility that Brenda might still be conscious and watching while her life essence was sucked out through her nose – and therefore able to give Brian the all-important, 'go ahead, he's eating my brain' signal – was so far removed from being a plan that it was a veritable anti-plan.

'It might work,' said Brian.

And a passing pig might crash through the window, sing *Blue Moon,* and knock Daddy over with a feather.

She felt Daddy take her arm and roll up her sleeve. It was now or never. She started to summon, imagining her living room riddled with rents and rips through to the astral plane.

'Lauren Stone and Ashley Peterson, I summon thee! Take revenge. The man who killed you is here. Together we can kill him.'

She yelled her summoning into the ether, felt the prick as the needle entered her body, the burn as the contents were pushed inside.

'Mary Alice Cassini. I summon thee. Daddy's here. We can fight him together.'

The burning sensation spread up her arm. She used it to redouble her efforts, taking the fear and panic and using it to fuel her desperate calls.

'I summon you all. Any victim, any spirit who's ever been murdered, heed my voice and come. All of you! Any angry son-of-a-bitch spirit looking for vengeance. I summon you in spades.'

She was feeling light-headed. Maybe it was the drugs, maybe the exhilaration.

'I have a raping, murdering kiddie killer here. Let's give him a taste of something he'll never forget.'

She opened her eyes. She had to look. The room was darker than before and distorted. But she was sure she saw something. They must have come. They had to have!

Chapter Thirty-Three

Brenda looked down at the body lying spread-eagled on the table. It didn't look like her. The broken nose, the swollen face. But it was.

"Whoa," said the ghost next to her. "What you been doin', girl. That looks nasty."

Stop looking at yourself and do what we're supposed to do!

Ghost Brenda blinked. She had an inner Ghost Brenda? Damn right! said the inner Ghost Brenda. Now get that son-of-a-bitch.

All the ghosts were looking at her. Dozens of them. Mary Alice, Ashley, Gabriella Czerna, Angela Trafford. Most of them women, most blood spattered or bruised, their clothes ripped or stained.

And there was Daddy. His nose twitching as he sniffed at the air above dead Brenda's body. And there was her life essence! A sparkly stream rising up from her nose. Daddy must have smelled it. He puffed out his chest, closed his eyes and began to straighten up, throwing back his shoulders as he inhaled.

"Now!" cried Ghost Brenda, stabbing an ethereal finger towards Daddy's face. "That's him! He's a raping, murdering kiddie killer. Follow me! Aim for his nose and fly inside. We're going to possess his ass!"

~

Brian lay there, listening and waiting. He hadn't felt this powerless since the day he'd lost his wife and child. He'd been unable to move that day, too – lying on the ground, racked with pain, his vision a bloody blur. Angela screaming. Julie screaming. The gunshots. The looks on their faces, the shock, the despair.

That wasn't happening again. Not today.

As long as he could get his timing right. Why hadn't he asked Daddy how long it took him to feed? He might have seconds. He might have fractions of a second.

He didn't even know if he had enough magic. But he did know one thing. He wasn't just a shapeshifter; he was a shapeshifter who could detach his head. And if he could detach his head, why not the tissue the leech had fastened itself onto?

The only problem was when to slough off the leech. Too soon and Daddy might notice. Too late and Daddy might have stopped feeding.

He couldn't wait any longer. He felt with his mind, sensing the area around the leech. In places, its jaws had fused with his skin. And there was something else. Filaments of foreign matter spreading out from its mouth. He drew back from them, mapping out an area, separating the untouched part of him from the compromised. It was a sizeable chunk – about five inches in diameter and, in places, approaching an inch in depth. He isolated the area, grew fresh skin around the boundary and ... pushed with his mind, turning his head as he did so, sloughing the lump of flesh from his face and letting it slip noiselessly onto the carpet.

More waiting, unable to see, barely daring to move. He'd never faced a situation remotely like this. He'd always been the one with the power – ever since the gene therapy – the invulnerable Brian Trafford, Vigilante Demon, who could walk into any room, face any number of foes, confident in the knowledge he could magic his way out of anything.

Until this case. What the hell *was* Daddy? If he started feeding off Mary Alice thirteen years ago, that pre-dated gene therapy. And what was the Synod? The Inquisitors? Were there real demons out there?

Time crawled. The silence was unbearable. He'd hoped he'd be able to sense Brenda's thoughts right up to the second Daddy began to feed, but she'd been silent for close on a minute, and her thoughts before that had been all over the place. He hadn't had the heart to tell her that summoning an army of ghosts was a waste of a time. The dead can't attack the living.

There was a clunk from over by the table. Brian couldn't

work out what it was. Then there was another. He focussed every sense he had on that area of the room.

Then something strange happened. Daddy's mind was no longer blank. There was something there. Brian zeroed in on it. Did Daddy's mind open up when he started to feed? And was that a voice? A thought? He concentrated harder, sucking the sound closer and closer, louder and louder until...

It was Brenda. 'Get your ass over here and blow this bastard up!'

He teleported immediately, spread-eagling his body and stretching. He had no margin for error and no magic for a second attempt. He had to materialize with one part of his body inside Daddy's.

He materialized, spread-eagled horizontally maybe a few feet off the ground. His left arm was inside something warm, wet and flesh-like. Daddy or Brenda? He twisted his body, reaching up blind with his right hand as he fell, grabbing and feeling for a face.

It was Daddy.

Daddy swung violently around. Brian was sent crashing into the table, but he held on, pushing all his magic into his left hand. Shapeshift! Shapeshift him to dust!

Daddy disintegrated. No explosion. No screams. Just a fine mist spreading out in all directions.

A fine mist that Brian could see.

He had his eyes back! Daddy's death had restored his sight. Now he had to bring Brenda back before her life essence drained away.

Where was the Trimazepine?

Flash! There was the first of his magic-fatigue migraine explosions. Followed by the nausea, the brain-splitting pain.

He staggered to his feet, the room spinning, stopping, spinning, stopping. He searched Daddy's black bag in between the spins. Nothing. Just more of the other two drugs. Daddy'd never intended to bring Brenda back to life.

He searched Brenda pockets. Nothing. Where had she put the drugs she'd taken? He circled the room. The room circled him. He fell down, got up. Keep going! He checked surfaces, shelves – feeling, patting his way when he couldn't see. Then ran upstairs, pumping rubber legs, staggering against the banisters, grabbing hold, hauling himself up and onto the landing. The drugs had to be in her bedroom. She'd have been in there doing a computer search.

He found them. Wrong bottle, wrong bottle, right!

He descended the stairs, grabbing for the banisters, missing, tumbling from halfway down.

He crawled across the living room floor. Where was Daddy's syringe? He looked for it, he felt for it, he found it. No time to worry about shared needles or the exact dose. He half-filled the syringe, staggered to his feet, leant heavily against the table and searched for an arm, a vein, feeling with his fingers when he couldn't see, using his internal powers of visualization, in and push!

And wait ... and hope.

Should he give her another dose? Administer CPR? Call for an ambulance?

He checked for a pulse. There it was! She was alive!

Chapter Thirty-Four

"Are you always going to have that lump of flesh missing?" asked Brenda.

He looked like an extra from a CSI post mortem scene, lying on the sofa, eyes closed, a raw gash the size of a large cookie spreading up from the bridge of his nose.

"Only until I work out how to remove the leech."

Seeing as Brenda was the official custodian of the leech – Brian being too wary to risk handling it – that moment could not come quick enough. She'd had to pick it up with a pair of tongs and put both leech and icky flesh into a plastic container – thank God for Tupperware – and stored it in her fridge.

"When I'm strong enough, I'll shapeshift the gash to somewhere it can't be seen."

Brenda slumped further back in her armchair. She still felt exhausted. Three hours had passed since she'd come round. God knows how much life energy she'd lost. And how much of it was currently stuck to her wallpaper.

"I'll have to have this room professionally cleaned," she said. "The furniture too. I might be sitting on bits of him now."

She was too tired to check, and too tired to sit anywhere else. Stairs were something she'd contemplate tomorrow. Tonight she'd sleep where she was.

Tomorrow. So much they'd have to do tomorrow.

"Is it always like this?" she asked.

"Like what?"

"That you end up spending more time sorting out loose ends after the case than you did during the initial investigation."

"Depends. I've never had a partner who went shopping for Jaguars before."

"Hah. Talking of partners, isn't it time you told me what happened to your last one?"

"If I told you, I'd have to eat you. We have strict secrecy rules in Hell."

"Come on, Brian. I really need to know."

"I'll tell you tomorrow."

"Why not now?"

He opened his eyes for the first time and glanced her way. "You're not going to give up on this, are you?"

"No."

"Okay, let's just say Tonya was a mistake. Excellent medium, but ... unbalanced. She was becoming difficult to work with, so I started looking for a replacement. Tonya took exception, and ... branched out on her own. It didn't end well."

"She died?"

"You know she died. I've read your thoughts, Brenda. She blames me for what happened to her, and she probably has a point. But I wasn't there *when* she died. I didn't even know she was carrying out her own investigations. I hadn't seen her for weeks."

"Is that true?"

"I'm too tired to lie."

She stared at his face for a good two seconds, while trying to make up her mind. He didn't look like he'd been lying, but then he never did. And he did look shattered. His eyes had closed again and his skin was ashen.

Her thoughts returned to all the loose ends they'd have to tie up – Kayla's murder, the exploding ambulance. What if that became big news? Ambulance explodes and no body parts found inside. It was tailor-made for UFO nuts and conspiracy theorists. It could be talked about for years.

"We'll sort it out tomorrow," said Brian. "I'll beam body parts in or doctor the findings somehow."

Then there was the money. How were they going to spend it? On spare body parts?

"And what about the Inquisitors and the Synod?" she asked.

"Tomorrow," said Brian. He sounded exhausted, but then he usually did when he didn't want to talk about something.

And there was still that little matter of whether Brian was

a demon or not.

A musty smell wafted under Brenda's nose. Had those ghosts come back?

One had. A woman with a broken nose, a badly bruised face and ... she was wearing Brenda's clothes.

"We did it," said a jubilant Ghost Brenda, her smile undiminished by the lack of several teeth. "I knew we'd make a great team."

Brenda just stared. *Oh. My. God. I haz ghost. With a giant red broken nose! And I smell already!*

~

Carl Briant – aka Septimus Holroyd, aka Louis de Mazarin, aka Diego de Aguilar, aka Yussuf ibn Tashfin, aka Hreidar Bloodaxe, aka Marcus Valerius Sabinus, aka Leonidas of Sparta, aka Rahotep, aka countless names stretching far back into pre-history – was having a quiet drink with a colleague when he noticed a familiar face on the television screen.

"Hey, turn that up!"

His colleague, Hiro Tanaka, a mere youngster of two thousand summers, punched at the remote, turning up the volume on the television set.

A picture of Andrius Luksa, aka Daddy, filled the screen.

"...when the ambulance he was travelling in exploded. A woman was also killed. Police have yet to release her name, but sources close to the investigation say that she was another of Andrius Luksa's hostages. The parents of Mary Alice Cassini have flown to Syracuse to meet their daughter."

Tanaka killed the sound. He was angry. "What does Andrius think he's doing, drawing attention to himself like that? We told him one human at a time and *don't* get your face on the news."

"I think we have a bigger problem. Didn't Abbiati say that boy and his mother kept mentioning Mary Alice Cassini?"

"That's right." He paused, turning his head back to the screen. "You think they're connected?"

"I think we better find out."

~

It was a new day and, for Brenda, a new face. Well, it was

the old one, but after spending the best part of a day with a large red nose staring back at her from the mirror, it felt new.

And Brian had changed too - at last - shapeshifting that missing cookie of flesh somewhere else on his body. Brenda didn't want to even think where.

"Anything more I can do before we get back to work?" he asked. "New dress? New hair?"

"Well...." She twirled a stray strand of hair. "Is Count Fabio busy this evening?"

Acknowledgements

A big thank you to my editors, Jennifer Stevenson and Sherwood Smith.

About Chris Dolley

Chris Dolley is a *New York Times* bestselling author. He now lives in rural France with his wife and a frightening number of animals. They grow their own food and solve their own crimes. The latter out of necessity when Chris's identity was stolen along with their life savings. Abandoned by the police forces of four countries, who all insisted the crime originated in someone else's jurisdiction, he had to solve the crime himself. Which he did, and got a book out of it – the international bestseller, *French Fried: one man's move to France with too many animals and an identity thief*.

His SF novel *Resonance* was the first book to be plucked out of Baen's electronic slushpile. And his first Reeves and Worcester Steampunk Mystery – *What Ho, Automaton!* – was a WSFA Award finalist in 2012.

About Book View Cafe

Book View Café (BVC) is an author-owned cooperative of over forty professional writers, publishing in a variety of genres including fantasy, romance, mystery, and science fiction.

Our authors include *New York Times* and *USA Today* best-sellers; Nebula, Hugo, and Philip K. Dick Award winners; World Fantasy and Rita Award nominees; and winners and nominees of many other publishing awards.

BVC returns 95% of the profit on each book directly to the author.